ORCHID HOUSE

CINDY MARTINUSEN

NASHVILLE   DALLAS   MEXICO CITY   RIO DE JANEIRO   BEIJING

Published in Nashville, Tennessee, by Thomas Nelson. Thomas Nelson is a registered trademark of Thomas Nelson, Inc.

Thomas Nelson, Inc., titles may be purchased in bulk for educational, business, fund-raising, or sales promotional use. For information, please e-mail SpecialMarkets@ThomasNelson.com.

Publisher's Note: This novel is a work of fiction. Names, characters, places, and incidents are either products of the author's imagination or used fictitiously. All characters are fictional, and any similarity to people living or dead is purely coincidental.

Page Design by Casey Hooper

Library of Congress Cataloging-in-Publication Data

Martinusen, Cindy McCormick, 1970-
  Orchid house / Cindy Martinusen.
    p. cm.
  ISBN: 978-1-59554-151-2 (softcover)
  1. Americans—Philippines—Fiction. 2. Philippines—Fiction. I. Title.
  PS3563.A737O73 2008
  813'.54--dc22

                    2007050975

Printed in the United States of America
08 09 10 11 12 RRD 6 5 4 3 2 1

THIS IS FOR AND WITH
NIELDON AUSTIN B. COLOMA

Other novels by Cindy Martinusen include

EVENTIDE

THE SALT GARDEN

NORTH OF TOMORROW

WINTER PASSING

BLUE NIGHT

PROLOGUE

June 1840
Hacienda Esperanza
Province of Batangas, Philippines

They would never tell a soul.

For how could they explain what drew them out the grand hacienda doors and into the depths of that summer night?

He released her hand and pulled her closer. The house stood silhouetted against the night sky.

"It is finally quiet," he said with a chuckle. Their adult children and young grandchildren kept the many rooms and corridors filled with life-giving noise and activity. The image of them sleeping brought tears to his eyes.

"We are no longer young," she whispered, but neither regretted it. The years of love and memories were there between them. And beneath a tropical moon with the earth cool beneath their bare feet, they felt nearly as youthful as the night they found each other during that great Philippine storm.

He took the basket of orchids from her arm, and they walked along the dirt path away from the house. The imposing gates didn't take long to reach, and then they found the property's cornerstone in the moonlight. It was a metal spike, hammered into the earth decades earlier by her ancestor, the One-Armed Spaniard, who first built upon this land.

"You do the first one," he said, extending the basket. The light pink petals of the orchid seemed to glow in the moonlight.

She took a blossom in her hand and remembered the day she'd found the orchid. She had been at her lowest, but that day turned into the beginning of a life that was more than she had hoped for or imagined.

These orchids were different from all the other ones she'd ever seen, not at all like those that grew in the fields near the hacienda house. Once she'd found a book of varieties, and even there she could not find the orchid now called by her name, in her honor.

"Do you remember?" he said, knowing that she did.

"Do you?" she said coyly.

"I have remembered every day of my life since then," he said, touching her cheek. "Now go ahead, my beloved."

With a nod, she bent down and dug at the fertile soil, placing the orchid blossom inside. Her husband bent beside her and covered the flower.

She closed her eyes and made the sign of the cross at her breast and spoke aloud.

"My ancestors built something here, and it has been blessed with growth and prosperity. My husband and our children and I have continued to prosper with many harvests and, more important, with great love and joy even in the years of hardship.

"Now, together we will go to the corners of our land and bury a blossom of this orchid—the flower that bonded us together. They will not sprout in these places. No one will know what we have done, except You, God Almighty, who sees all things. We do this as a symbol of Your presence upon this land and our request for Your continued protection and blessing in the ages to come."

She opened her eyes and gazed into the starry sky. Then she grasped his arm with worry in her expression. "There will be times of much adversity. Blood and tears I can nearly smell upon the future." A wave of panic washed over her.

"Do not fear, my love. We can do nothing but one thing. It is all the more reason for us to ask for divine protection and guidance."

She knew he was right, and yet how she grieved to sense that pain was creeping along the fringes of future decades or more away.

He took her hands, and they stood. With his strong grasp and steady gaze, she felt her fear and grief diminish.

Then he spoke with the gentle strength he'd shown all his days. "Father God in Heaven. Creator of life, love, mercy, and grace. Bless our children, grandchildren, and our descendents to come. Draw them to know this place on earth and to discover Your will and Your ways. And through the years of hardship to come, sustain them, protect them, and restore again and again."

Their prayers continued, and peace came as the blessing was complete.

He took her hand. "Let us walk the border and ask God's feet to follow."

And as they walked, she wondered about all their descendents to come. It amazed her to think of the lives already born from the love they shared. Though some might travel far away and times of adversity would come and go, this land would be their refuge.

This she did not doubt.

ONE

June 1991
North Beach, San Francisco
A death and a foreign land.

B etween the one and the other, Julia moved through the days.
Her grandfather was gone; she'd witnessed the months until
his final breath. And in two days she'd hop an airplane for
Manila—to a land more alien, though closer to her own heritage,
than any she'd yet experienced. No wonder the disjointed feeling
persisted.

And on that morning between a death and a foreign land, as an
unusually cold wind howled deep and hollow beneath a clear
San Francisco day, Julia saw Nathan for the first time in six months.
She was hurrying down the street, arms crossed tightly at her chest,
holding her thin jacket closed against the wind. As she reached for
the door of the Blue Mill Bakery, he pushed it open from the inside.

"Julia," Nathan said, holding the door with his foot. The wind whipped around them.

They had loved this place once. They had loved each other once as well. Now they were nearly strangers, and yet not strangers at all.

"Hi," came from her lips, then a moment without words. Finally she said, "Still drinking cappuccino, I see." She looked at the two cups he held. She had not heard if he and his girlfriend were still together. Maybe he was married, for all she knew. Their common friends were few now, and even fewer the ones who spilled details whether she wanted to hear them or not.

"It's black coffee. I ended up lactose intolerant."

She used to find his sheepish grin so endearing. He was as handsome as ever.

"Too bad," she said, thinking about the cappuccinos they'd learned to love in the coffeehouses of Vienna. The wheels of change gave such things and took them as quickly. "Does that mean no almond fudge ice cream either?"

He grinned again. "Well, sometimes I can't resist."

He must have suddenly grown aware that she was shivering and motioned her inside. The scent of yeast, cinnamon, and baking bread surrounded her as the door closed, shutting out the wind but not the chill creeping deep into her bones.

He held the cups awkwardly. "This weather is stunning. What happened to spring?"

Julia glanced through the window to the tree-lined streets that sloped down toward the bay, where sailboats would be skimming happily through the whitecaps. Their old table by the window was empty, she realized. She hoped he hadn't noticed her glance that way.

"I wasn't here for spring," she said quickly. "Hopefully we'll get warmed up soon." Then she realized she wouldn't be here for that either.

He set the cups on a table behind them. "I heard about your grandfather. Did you get my message?"

"Yes, Lisa told me you called." She'd seen his name on a list titled "Sympathy Calls" that her roommate had compiled until Julia returned to her condo. "Thank you for that."

"Jules," he said softly in the voice that tugged at memories resting long and buried deep within her. She realized she'd been trying to look everywhere but directly at him.

"I can't imagine how hard it was. Were you with him when he died?"

A woman came toward them laden with a purse, several books, and a large cup of hot chocolate. As she opened the door, the wind sent a dollop of whipped cream right across Julia's jacket. The woman went on her way without seeing the mishap; Julia stood with her arms hovering at her sides, staring as the stain soaked into the material.

Nathan muttered apologies as if he were at fault and grabbed some napkins from the condiment counter. He came toward her, and without thinking Julia stepped backward.

"I'm sorry. Just trying to help." He handed her the napkins instead.

"It's okay, I didn't mean anything." She dabbed at the stain and watched it spread wider. "It's just . . . I'm not used to you being close. I'm . . . not used to you at all."

A pained expression came and went across his face in an instant. "I guess that's what I get," he said.

He handed her another napkin, and Julia wondered what he expected after all this time, after all the hurt and loss.

She sought a way to leave him now, glancing toward the display case of freshly baked goods.

He held her with more conversation. "Lisa told me you were coming home, but not for long."

"Yes, I leave for Manila on Wednesday. My grandfather will be buried there, and I'm the family representative for the land—whatever that means. I'll contact the lawyer as soon as I get there."

"The political climate isn't good in the Philippines. Assassinations, government coups, Communist rebels, Muslim and Christian conflict in the southern provinces. Though they do have the first female president in Asian history."

"You been doing research?"

He smiled, and she tried to decide if she liked his smile. Once it had been nearly everything to her.

"Actually, I have. Did you know it's the most Christian and Westernized nation in Asia? It can feel more Spanish in heritage than Oriental—the islands were occupied by Spain for three hundred years."

"You have been reading. So are you going to try to talk me out of it too?"

"Oh no. Have others?"

"Most of my family believe it's too dangerous for a single woman to visit. My stepdad did research as well. And as you may recall, anything regarding my grandfather, my mother is never overly supportive of. My uncle was supposed to come, but he's having surgery. No one else could get away, and my grandfather wanted me to do this."

Julia paused and then spoke with a confidence that surprised even herself. "And I need to do it. I'm off to go 'find myself,' as someone I know often told me to do."

Nathan nodded and rested his elbow on the railing, leaning ever so slightly toward her. "Well, I'm proud of you."

"You are? Why?"

"Well, going to find yourself is something many people run from their whole lives. This is a pretty big thing to do alone. Third-world country, burying your grandfather with people you don't know, facing who knows what kind of adventure across the sea."

She thought of casually brushing off his remarks, but then she felt the weight of all that he'd said. "Yeah, I guess it is a big deal. I've been so tired, with so many details to tend to, part of me hasn't really thought it through. Perhaps I will find some adventure."

There was a look in his eyes she knew well, and she wondered if Nathan was thinking the same thing she was—that if they'd remained together, he'd have been part of these past four months with her grandfather. He would be going to Southeast Asia with her now.

They were silent until it turned awkward.

"It was good seeing you," she said, sounding as if they were old friends, not former lovers.

He was the one who had ended what they had, though they'd both struggled for a year. Still, she wondered if he ever missed her. He'd had several girlfriends, while Julia's dating life was sporadic. Nathan said once that he'd moved on and so should she. He said she had lost herself along the way. He said that she stayed with him because their relationship was safe for her.

"Did you hear that I'm doing freelance marketing now?"

"No, I didn't hear." She felt a wave of anxiety with all these memories flooding through her. "Congratulations. Is it going well?"

"Too well. I need some employees or other freelancers to share the accounts I'm getting. You interested?"

"Uh . . ." Unbidden, something her grandfather had said before his death came into Julia's mind.

During the last two weeks of his life, Julia spent Grandpa Morrison's wakeful hours at his bedside. They no longer worked on puzzles of covered bridges on the card table or watched *Jeopardy!* or talked about his garden or shared the latest gossip—about movie stars or their own family. Instead, for fourteen days, Julia sat with her bedridden grandfather as other family members, including her mother, came and went. Grandpa asked Julia to remain.

Sometimes he called the name of Julianna, and though Julia came and held his hand, she knew he longed for another. His heart and mind could not forget his Julianna, long dead and buried far away. He talked about sugarcane fields that needed to be burned and projected yields. He promised his Julianna they'd take the Cadillac to the bamboo grove on the next Sunday whether it rained again or not.

In his lucid moments, Grandpa Morrison was no longer the quirky, endearing man she'd always known. He asked her to bring his logbooks, and he'd scribble down instructions to be faxed to a man named Raul, the hacienda foreman, and to Markus, the hacienda lawyer. He'd said, "Markus Santos sounds like a great young man on the telephone—sharp as a whip—and he loves the hacienda as well."

The papers she faxed made little sense to her, and she didn't try deciphering them, with the worry over his sudden decline. An urgent intensity encased him.

"When in your life were you the most at peace?" he had asked one night, staring at her with probing blue eyes.

"I don't know. I guess when Nathan and I were together."

He'd shaken his head. "No, dear girl, that's not it. He was a nice young man, but you weren't yourself during that time. But perhaps you've never been truly at peace."

Julia had not responded, but asked instead, "What about you, Grandpa? When were you most at peace?"

The answer, long in coming, surprised her. "There was a night during the war."

Grandfather spoke often of the years when they feared America had forgotten its men in the Pacific theater while it chased Hitler around Europe.

"There was this night . . . ," he said again. "I cannot forget it. The war in the Philippines had destroyed the land. Chaos and death were everywhere. People did whatever they could to survive. My men and I had seen so much fighting, such terrible scenes of slaughter, and still we were forced to continue on. On this night, we were hungry. We'd been hungry before, but not this much—and so tired I think even the hairs on my arms ached."

He sighed as he remembered. "And then we reached Hacienda Esperanza, where your grandmother's family hid our small band of soldiers. It was then I knew a trust and faith among the men and that family so strong you could nearly touch it. I found peace in the courage of a family who'd already experienced the ravages of war but continued to do what was right. The family that would become my very own. Your family."

Julia had memorized the map of lines in her Grandfather Morrison's face; they grew deeper nearly every day from the loss of weight. She wished to kiss his forehead and bring such peace to him again. She settled in for a story that would last until he fell asleep.

"We were a mixed bunch, separated from our original units. Americans, Filipino guerrillas, an Australian soldier who was killed by a sniper days later. But that night we slept in a small shanty within the safe boundaries of the plantation with bowls of rice and bits of the lone chicken the family sacrificed for us to share. And you know, my dear, I was amazed by the peace that was felt throughout the room.

"*Esperanza* means hope, my dear Julia. When you have your most peaceful times, they will also bring you hope. You must remember such times—though I think they are impossible to forget."

Ironically, she knew that night how the simplicity of the past months with her dying grandfather could be numbered among her most happy times. There was peace with him.

On another day Grandpa Morrison advised, "Listen, dear girl. You must return to certain pasts. But only those you have not finished building. Some things we are made to walk away from. Others are for returning and completing."

Standing now with Nathan in the Blue Mill Bakery, where they'd sat for hours with hands entwined, talking of the future, Julia wondered if he was something unfinished in her life, something to return to and complete. Or was that relationship forever past, something meant to "walk away from"?

Nathan shuffled his feet restlessly, and Julia realized she'd been staring out the window again. "Sorry I'm so distracted," she murmured.

"It's okay. A lot has happened to you lately. Anyway, think about it—the job, I mean." He picked up his coffee cups. "I'm moving fast with all this, I know. But, confession . . . I've been coming here for breakfast and lunch for the past week, ever since Lisa said you were back. It's actually out of my way."

"You could have just called."

He nodded. "When you get back, I will call. We'll have dinner. Or even before you leave?"

She glanced at the two cups in his hand. "I'm not sure that's the best idea."

He chuckled. "Oh no. I buy two so I can work at home without drinking my own terrible brew. Jules, I'm not seeing anyone. Shelly and I broke up two months ago. I haven't been seeing anyone in all that time."

She wanted to laugh. *All that time.* Nathan could never be alone for long.

"Well, maybe I'm seeing someone." She smiled at the way his eyes darted away and his composure failed.

"I didn't mean to presume."

She did laugh then. "It's okay. I'm not."

"Well, good then. So, dinner?"

"And we'd go as what . . . old friends?"

He shrugged and smiled. "Old friends . . . new friends. Two people who were once engaged to spend their lives together and then . . ."

"And then didn't."

"But maybe needed some time apart to see if it was meant to be. What do you think?"

The cold crept deep, and her stomach growled. "I think for the past four months I've been living with the end of a life, and now I'm traveling far to put what remains into the ground. Other than that, I haven't thought of much. Except that I really need some coffee."

"Ah, why didn't I think of that? I shouldn't propose such things before you've had your coffee. Not wise at all. Let me buy you one."

"How about when I come back?"

He nodded with disappointment in his smile. "And dinner, remember. Just make sure you don't fall in love with a Filipino rice farmer while you're there."

They both laughed at that.

Seven years they'd been together. For two years they'd been apart. What had happened to them? And yet, to think of them together again, to look at them now . . . the whole thing felt disjointed and surreal.

A death, a lost love, and a foreign land. Julia wondered what was coming next.

Jungles of northern Luzon, Philippines

IT WAS AN ETHEREAL LIGHT THAT CAME THROUGH THE TREES. Originating from the sun, now unseen at this time of night, the light reflected off the moon and onward toward an archipelago of seven thousand islands called the Philippines and then to one island and one mountain where it broke into a thousand pieces through cracks of leaves and branches where one man stood in the shadows.

Manalo stared upward and enjoyed a moment alone. He could hear the voices of his men through the jungle thicket. He'd need to remind them to keep to muffled tones. They were getting soft at the edges, letting down their guard, growing restless for home. He felt it as well, perhaps more than they.

He walked farther from their camp, his footsteps silent in woods where the sounds of the night creatures surrounded him. Crickets and frogs and large lizards called *toko* joined in a nocturnal song.

A portion of moonlight came to him, and a portion went to her. He wondered if Malaya was even now looking upward and thinking of him. Did the moonlight caress her smooth complexion and strands of black silk hair as his hands would if he were with her now? Did she sleep at night with their son resting against her breast? Did their daughters play in open fields by day, singing and putting flowers in each other's hair? How quickly the years had passed. His older sons now walked the hills of his own youth and fished the jungle streams. Did they think of him as often as he thought of them?

He had called Malaya a month ago from a pay phone in a mountain village. It was planned that way, on a date that changed each month. He would not endanger her or the children. If someone discovered they were the wife and children of Manalo, head of the notorious Red Bolo Communist guerrillas, then they could get to him. And though his men might not believe it, and he would never let them know the truth, Manalo knew he might betray even his most trusted comrades for the lives of Malaya and their children.

The call of home grew louder by both night and day. By kilometers, it wasn't far. He could reach her in four days of walking, one day if he hitched a ride. And yet by duty and expectation, the calls were unknown months apart.

He took a breath of crisp night air. Time to return to camp. To his calling. His men needed him, depended and lived by his guidance. It was a role he had never desired, but with the death of his brother, a destiny he could not deny.

A final glance toward the sky before returning to the men where dinner might be ready . . . then something stirred in the thicket on the opposite end of the meadow. With ginger steps, a deer walked into the open field where moonlight stroked its hair and horns. The deer wasn't large, but there was dignity in its careful walk.

Manalo recalled the last deer he had seen—a gutted beast from two seasons past. The Philippine sambar was rare and near extinction, and Rigo had chastised Emil for shooting the animal. Rigo wouldn't eat the first red meat they'd had in many days, out of conviction and sorrow for the fallen creature.

The moonlight cast an eerie glow over the stag. It stopped, one foot held midstep. It had seen Manalo and sniffed the air to catch his scent. He didn't move. Was it a sign of another destiny? Or further confirmation to go home?

The deer's attention shifted toward a thicket where his men resided. Then the creature turned and walked to the far end of the meadow and began grazing.

Manalo realized there was an unnatural quiet coming from the direction of the camp. He knew his men, and silence meant nothing good. He headed back without hesitation, wondering if he had startled the sambar by his abrupt departure.

He emerged from the darkness of the jungle into the circle of light by the two small fires. His men, about thirty in number, were huddled close together. He saw at once an extra man among them. He knew this man, or rather, boy. He was a courier.

It had been three months since any courier had contacted them. The guerrilla groups disappeared even from each other at times.

The courier and the men had waited his arrival, anxious for the news to be told.

"*Magandang gabi*, comrade," the boy said.

Edo was his name, Manalo recalled. He'd worked hard to learn the names of the men in even the splinter groups.

"What word do you have from outside?" Manalo stepped away from the fire and toward his tent with the boy walking beside him. They spoke in low tones.

"There is important news. We wish for your direction."

Manalo sat on a chair outside his canvas tent. He felt unusually weary tonight. "Proceed."

"There is a hacienda that was very powerful before the Marcos regime, but it fell into foreign ownership. The owner is now deceased, and the land's future is in question."

"Where is this hacienda?"

"Batangas."

"Hacienda Esperanza?" It had been many years since he'd spoken the name.

"Yes, sir." The boy looked surprised.

"I know the land. A very important place for a time. My grandfather grew up there. He fought the Japanese with Captain Morrison for a time."

"Captain Morrison . . . that was the news. The American. He is dead."

Manalo gazed up at the stars. "He joins my father and many others. May he rest in peace."

"Ka Manalo, this is the message. The American captain had legal ownership of the hacienda because of his marriage to Julianna Guerrero and the death of Don Miguel, Julianna's brother. It is unknown what will happen now that the captain is dead. But they will return him here for burial, and his family representatives will decide the fate of the land. I am to find out what you want to do."

Manalo's mind gathered and sorted as he spoke. "First, we must make sure this information is correct. Reach our officials for legal documentation."

"Timeteo," he called to his closest adviser. "Gather the men."

Even as he spoke with the courier about sources and possibilities, Manalo was thinking of Malaya and the children. What future would they have in their homeland?—that was the question that kept him in the jungle. While the world modernized and grew strong, his nation continued under the tyranny of one regime or another. Manalo had read about developing technology, that someday soon everyone would have a telephone in his car, that already many people in Manila and most in the States had their own computers. The entire world was changing.

And here they lived in the jungle, hiding from the government, rallying troops for the people, seeking a way to be a strong nation. The Communist way would change everything. It would give the people power without the class distinctions that kept so many locked in poverty. Manalo wanted his heirs to know equality, unlike the life he had experienced.

He sighed long to expel the dream of going home and to gather himself for what awaited. Sometimes, he admitted more and more, it felt a futile and worthless cause for all that he sacrificed.

The men came together, holding their AK-47s. Some rested on one knee; all waited for his direction. The news of the American's death had already spread. Many had heard of Captain Morrison from war stories the older men told. Rumors would undoubtedly exaggerate, and he always tried to squelch gossip that might divide or cause dissension.

Manalo repeated the courier's message. And then he spoke the words that would rouse them to action. "That land should not belong to foreigners. That is what we fight for. Our land and our country must be for the people. No more wealthy leaders stealing from the poor. No other nation conquering our land. No more puppet governments serving the interests of foreign corporations and administrations. That is what our fathers fought for. That is why we live in the jungle instead of with our wives—for some of you, your wives and mistresses."

A few chuckled at that. He allowed it, then waited for them to hear his final point. "That is why we fight." He saw it in their eyes and the set of their jaws. His men would follow him down any path, even one that led to death.

Hours later, when all but the watch slept, Manalo returned to the meadow. The stag had moved on, as had the moonlight that now fell low through the jungle thickets.

Why would not Captain Morrison return the land to its people, Manalo thought with anger, but also with despair. He was weary of strategies.

In truth, that men would give up their lives for his words, that governments might pillage his country, or that he swore to his brother of duty . . . all this mattered less and less to him.

All that the revered leader of the Red Bolos wanted was home.

Barangay Mahinahon
Province of Batangas, Philippines

FROM OUTSIDE, EMMAN LEANED ON THE OPEN WINDOW FRAME with the other boys. The small television screen on the far side of the room was visible for all unless someone else tried to squeeze in. His feet scuffed the dirt outside the window. When Mrs. Jiminez was alive she had kept a row of flowers here. Now the years and the practice of viewing from outside looking in had packed down the earth outside the small one-bedroom house.

If the kids were quiet, Mr. Jiminez would let them to stay till the end of whatever show was on. And once in a while, if the old man fell asleep in his chair, they might get past the news where they'd hear about events in Manila or China or even the United States of America. When the signal blinked off in the lateness of the hour or Mr. Jiminez woke as if from some hypnotic dream and shooed them all away, a cloak of disappointment came over Emman. He'd walked the dirt pathway home and wondered if he'd ever truly leave the Philippines.

Tonight one of his favorite shows was on, and the old man had fallen asleep. The boys silently smirked and pointed. They would see all of *Magnum, P. I.* tonight.

The P. I. stood for "private investigator." Emman thought that would be the best job in the world, especially on the island of Oahu in Hawaii. He shifted the wooden gun that leaned on the outside of the house beside him and watched as Thomas Magnum hopped into his bright red Ferrari to chase a criminal who was trying to escape.

Hawaii looked a lot like the Philippines at times. Their President Marcos had died in Hawaii only a few years earlier. Emman wondered if President Marcos ever met the actor named Tom Selleck.

America.

Red Ferraris. Helicopters. Beautiful women in bikinis. Private investigators.

Everything was better in America.

His friends teased him about his obsession. Emman saved his small earnings for the movie house in San Juan. One of his most prized possessions was a poster of *Indiana Jones and the Temple of Doom*.

As Magnum followed the clues of his latest case, Emman recalled how Emman, P. I., had been on his own case today.

He already knew that the great Captain Morrison was dead in America. But something more was happening at Hacienda Esperanza. There were meetings with Mr. Raul and Amang Tenio. The lawyer, Markus Santos, had spent several days with Mr. Raul in his office. Everyone Emman talked to was abuzz with guesses, but no one knew for sure what it meant for them that the old war hero had died in the States.

Emman was most interested in the lawyer from Manila. He knew Markus Santos had ties with the hacienda, that is, with the family who lived there before Emman was born. So how had the man, who appeared to be in his thirties, gone from there to a life in the city?

Though their capital city wasn't America, it had culture like the megamalls and wealthy Filipinos. Emman had never been to Manila, but he'd once seen a rich kinsman from there. Surely Manila had private investigators as well. These were just some of the things he wished to ask this Markus Santos.

Emman felt a nudge at his back. It was young Bok, who followed Emman like a stray puppy. He motioned for Emman to come away from the open window.

"I'm watching *Magnum*." Emman saw Magnum and T. C. chasing a Hawaiian man through burning sugarcane fields.

Bok squeezed in next to him, bringing a round of complaints from the other boys. He whispered out the side of his mouth, "I just heard important news."

"What is it?"

Bok wouldn't respond. A commercial came on for Mr. Clean laundry detergent, so Emman left his coveted spot at the window and watched the other boys merge into it. Bok knew well enough not to interrupt *Magnum* with trivial happenings. He was like Magnum's friends Rick or T. C.—willing to join in the investigation. This surely must be important.

"The meetings at the hacienda—I know what they're about. Raul said for no one to tell yet."

"So how did you find out?" Emman was annoyed that he had not tracked down whatever it was Bok was about to reveal. But even Magnum needed his sidekicks.

"You know that Captain Morrison is dead," whispered Bok.

"Everyone knows that."

Bok leaned in closer. "Well, he asked to be buried at the hacienda, and the government gave permission. They are bringing his body back, and his American family is coming as well."

Emman felt a shudder pass through him. "I gotta go. Come on," he said and was already running.

As his bare feet pounded the dirt path, Emman felt a surge of joy. Even though it was in death, the American, Captain Morrison, was finally returning home.

TWO

As the plane flew through the darkness over the Pacific Ocean, Julia realized that her grandfather had chosen this role for her. He'd been motivated by more than a desire to be buried in the earth of the country he loved. He'd not only wanted the grand-daughter he loved to see the land that he loved, but Grandpa Morrison had known that she needed to change the languished path of the previous years. This was a plot.

She smiled at the logbook on her lap. *I know what you're up to*, she wanted to say.

As the drink cart came along the aisle, Julia returned to perus-ing her grandfather's book. The pages were packed with his writ-ings, notes and reminders, sketches, and clips from newspapers and magazines. One article explained a new irrigation system; another described how a couple remodeled a castle in Scotland.

She pictured him cutting out the articles with his thick fingers and placing them in this book with expectations and dreams. He'd have his glasses perched on his big nose, and when they slipped down he'd squint and then smile at her as she entered the room. Julia ached with longing, wishing she'd spent more time with her grandfather before his illness.

Along the bottom of one page she had found a note: *As King David didn't finish all that he wished, there are times it is our children or our grandchildren who complete what we begin.*

Julia wished she could tell him, *I'm on my way, Grandpa Morrison. I'll do everything I can for your beloved hacienda, and then I'll come home and somehow make you proud.*

"Would you like something to drink?" asked the flight attendant.

On impulse she said, "Could I have a Shirley Temple?"

The woman chuckled. "Why, yes, you can."

Julia's first sip was like tasting childhood. When her parents had dinner parties, she'd proudly carry her Shirley Temple with a cherry bobbing in the glass while the grown-ups drank their wine and mixed drinks. At slumber parties, holidays, or just at home on a special night when her father rented a VCR and movies, they would make the lemon-lime and grenadine brew, sometimes with a skewer full of maraschino cherries.

There was a girl she had been once, long ago. That girl's favorite color was purple; her favorite shows were *Scooby-Doo* and *The Wizard of Oz*. Every fall Julia and her mother planted tulips along the driveway and watched expectantly every spring for their waxy petals to open for the day and close for the night.

That Julia had dared to eat Pop Rocks and drink a swig of Coca-Cola even though her classmates said her stomach would explode and that a kid in Kentucky had died that way. She survived and gained notoriety among the other third graders. She'd been a brave girl of dreams and stories and creativity.

Where had that girl gone? Not so far away after all.

There is still time, Julia thought her grandfather would say. God redeems lives and dreams again and again.

Julia could look at who she had been and what she'd become. And flying to a land her grandfather had loved and where her grandmother lived her entire life, Julia knew she was still that girl and could be so much more. She needed help, and so she sought guidance where she hadn't gone in years.

God . . . mainly, I just need help. I'm not even sure what for, or what kind of help. So . . . help me, please.

Julia knew if God was still the God of her childhood, then He'd know exactly what she prayed in those words and what more she should pray if only the future were before her eyes.

After the flight attendant took her empty plastic cup and before dozing off, Julia felt a surprising peace encompass her. She was about to face a land and circumstances she couldn't begin to fathom, this she knew. And yet peace enfolded her, and it was a peace to remember.

HE WAS NO FUN ANYMORE, OR SO EMMAN'S FRIENDS SAID. THEY whispered this behind his back, not directly to him. If they did, he'd call them *bakla*, which would shame them, and someone would end up in a fight, most certainly himself.

Emman grinned at the thought, at how such escalations were normal occurrences among his friends. They were barbarians, he supposed, and he enjoyed the image.

The wide arms of an acacia tree cradled him high above the ground and within view of the grand hacienda mansion and back courtyard. Deep twilight feathered itself down to mesmerize the day-walkers and rouse the nocturnal.

An unlit cigarette butt dangled from his mouth. It had already been burned nearly to the end, but enough remained for a few inhales. He struck a match knowing his shirt pocket was full of cigarette butts. A few even had more than half the stick unsmoked.

As he inhaled and savored the taste, Emman watched some hacienda children play on the vast lawn while a woman pulled white sheets from the clothesline and scolded the children as they tried to hide in the folds. How different it was for the children of the hacienda compared to those of his village of Barangay Mahinahon—though they were only kilometers apart.

These children lived on the hacienda grounds. Their parents were field-workers, maintenance staff, or housekeepers, or they worked in town but had a relative with a hacienda connection who had taken them in. They lived in the cluster of staff houses beyond the trees, a short walk from the main house. After attending school all day, these children might help their parents at their jobs or in their own humble houses or gardens. Then they watched television, for nearly all the little homes had TV sets, talked on the phone, played their games. They acted their ages. They would grow up into the same positions as their parents, except for the very few who left for universities or whose relatives sponsored them to Canada or the United States or some other nation that offered a better life.

A lonesome feeling came over him. He strained to hear any sound from the jungle and wondered where Bok was. The boy asked to come, and Emman had discouraged him before finally relenting. Bok followed him so often Emman grew annoyed at times—but tonight he would appreciate the younger boy's carefree presence.

"*Umuwi na kayo, dali,*" the woman called to the children. She carried the folded linens to the back entrance as the children grabbed up their toys from the lawn and headed down the path toward the staff houses. One boy tagged a girl on the arm and ran off ahead, ignoring her cry of displeasure.

The children of the Barangay Mahinahon didn't live this way. They weren't typical of any children of the world, at least Emman didn't think so from the movies and shows he'd seen. They were a community of history and purpose. They were trained and disciplined to fight if needed and always to be prepared.

History, storytelling, war strategy, and the use and maintenance of a variety of weapons, mainly guns and knives, were included in their education. Their training was focused, disciplined, and regimented. Every day they woke in the early morning and aligned themselves in neat little rows as their instructors shouted out the exercises for the day. Little of their schooling was indoors or with books and chalkboards.

When the children of Barangay Mahinahon grew up, most remained or were hired out for specific short-term jobs. A few had left for Manila or overseas, but all had returned. No other place offered such community, they said, and they missed their simple yet honorable ways. The world changed around them, but except for some modern conveniences like vehicles and televisions and CD players, the Barangay Mahinahon remained as it had for half a century since the end of the last World War.

But as much as he loved his village and believed in its continued heritage, Emman thought he'd be the first to leave if the opportunity arose. There was something different in him. He couldn't find satisfaction in what the other children enjoyed. The restlessness to go beyond the mountains would not be quenched.

He squished out the red cherry of the cigarette against the tree bark and saw the lights come on in several of the upstairs rooms. The doors of a second-story balcony were pushed open, and an older woman carried out rugs and then a broom made of twigs. The household staff was preparing the mansion for its first guests in many years.

While the great lands of the hacienda still bustled with activity, no one had lived in the mansion for more years than Emman's twelve—ever since Captain Morrison was forced into exile. The head foreman over the entire plantation, Raul Sarmiento, occupied the downstairs office for business use, and the staff cooked in the kitchen, but the bedrooms upstairs and grand rooms were like a dusty museum. At least that's what Emman had heard. He'd never been inside.

Emman caught another scent of burning tobacco. This was sweet and woodsy—Mr. Raul smoking a pipe in the back courtyard, he guessed. The crickets had awoken to sing their evening song, joined by the bullfrogs in the streams and ponds.

Most of the kids spoke of specters and ghosts wandering the rooms at night, but Emman didn't believe in such things—even though somebody knew somebody who had seen a ghost in the windows, and laughter could be heard on some nights from inside the house.

Within the vast hectares of land that composed Hacienda Esperanza, there rested places worthy of true ghost stories. One was the stone remains of the old storehouse where the Japanese had massacred the men and boys during World War II. No one joked of that as a haunted area. It was inhabited by sorrow and was holy ground for the people of the hacienda, Barangay Mahinahon, and the town of San Juan.

Emman leaned his head against the tree branch and reached into his pocket for one of the longer cigarette butts. He'd gathered them from his cousin's porch steps, sifting through the ones with lipstick and those smoked to the filter. He'd learned this trick by watching the older boys. He knew it would be best to quit the habit. The women frowned upon it, and the other men teased him, saying his growth would be stunted or he'd never get his manly hair. But all the tough men smoked.

A forlorn chirping echoed through the jungle. Emman saw

Mr. Raul take a few steps from the courtyard to the edge of the wide lawn. The man had heard the call and would know what it meant. Emman continued to take drags on his cigarette, and hung the strap of his wooden gun to dangle on a tree branch.

Emman heard the snap of a twig and turned to see Bok surprisingly close.

"You didn't hear me coming through the jungle till that one twig, right?"

"No, you did very well." Emman smiled at his young disciple. The boy learned quickly.

"I have more news," Bok said, scrambling to reach the high branches where Emman waited.

Another bird's call sounded from the mansion.

"Who was that? It sounded different. Was it a real bird?" Bok appeared nervous.

"It was Raul," Emman said with a smile, watching the foreman rise from a chair with pipe in hand and return to the house. "I wouldn't have guessed it from him, he's so grouchy and serious all the time. As a kid, he played with my uncles and dad. But what is your news?"

"It's about the Americans," Bok said, settling his small frame into the crook of the branch that cupped him like a hammock. "Captain Morrison's granddaughter and her escort—an uncle— are arriving tomorrow in Manila."

"Where are you getting this information?"

"My sister's boyfriend, Artur, is a hacienda driver. If I do her chores, she bribes her boyfriend into answering my questions."

Emman thought on this a moment. "So what does Artur get in return?"

"Ugh, it's gross." Bok made a gagging sound. "It's kissing. A kiss for every question answered."

Emman chuckled at the image of lean and tough-looking Artur

begging for a few kisses from his skinny girlfriend who wore too much makeup. Emman wouldn't kiss Bok's sister if she gave him a whole pack of unsmoked cigarettes. "And you have to do her chores?"

"I'll be feeding the chickens and gathering eggs for the next month. I refuse to wear her gathering apron, though."

Emman laughed until he nearly fell from the tree. But Bok's cunning certainly impressed him. "You'll make a good spy someday, Bok."

"I know," the younger boy said with a proud grin that shone in the last light of evening. "That's why I'm following you around at night instead of playing *pusoy* with Bubot."

Emman knew he had not been much fun lately, but he didn't regret it. His determined agenda was directed at one goal—to be ready for the arrival of the Americans. And now he knew it was Captain Morrison's very granddaughter who would be coming.

Since hearing of their imminent arrival he'd increased his disciplines threefold. Today he had practiced the nunchakus with images of Bruce Lee in his head; then he sparred with Bok and accidentally gave him a bloody nose.

"I'm glad it didn't break," Emman said, motioning toward the scab along the bridge of the boy's nose.

Bok touched his face. "It hurt so badly, I wish it had broken. Then at least I'd have a battle wound for all the pain."

Emman preferred to work alone, but he'd let the kid tag along for now, as long as Bok didn't distract or disrupt his plan. Emman daydreamed scenarios for which to push his twelve-year-old body harder, faster, longer.

He imagined modern-day versions of Japanese troops invading the country like the one led by the infamous and ruthless Colonel Saeta Takada. Another surprise attack like the one the day after Pearl Harbor was attacked. Or like the followers of Marcos, or

Muslim insurgents, or Communist rebels overthrowing the government and infiltrating the hacienda boundaries. Always danger came; women screamed; men cowered in fear. But not Emman.

Sometimes in these visions Emman gave his life, dying slowly as a beautiful American woman and her sisters wept and said he was their hero. As he sat smoking in the tree now, he thought of Captain Morrison's granddaughter. What would the woman be wearing in such a scene? The first image came of one of the bikini-clad women of *Magnum, P. I.* or the show his mother would never have allowed him to see—*Baywatch*. He felt his face flush, and he made the sign of the cross over his chest as he'd seen others do at such images mixed with the thought of one's mother, God rest her soul.

If he served well, if he proved his ability or saved someone's life, maybe they'd take him back to America. He could guard their fancy house, be their bodyguard, or do whatever they wished as long as he could be in the United States of America.

"So, do you think I'm not fun anymore?" he asked Bok.

But the boy was asleep, his head resting against the groove in the tree branch. He looked so young in the moonlight, and Emman remembered he was only eight. In their sleep, perhaps all the children of the Barangay Mahinahon looked like cherubs— even though in daylight they trained as future soldiers.

An American woman is coming, he thought. *And I will protect her.*

THREE

The vibration that started in the huge engine was multiplied like a rock tossed into calm water to reverberate through Manalo and his men as they tried to rest in the bed of the truck. The highway didn't add any comfort to what might have been a soothing lullaby, with the jarring of potholes and stop-and-go of traffic.

Manalo heard the radio from inside the cab. There was a report about Mount Pinatubo showing increasing volcanic activity. Further evacuations had begun. He was relieved that Malaya hadn't gone to her family in San Fernando near the mountain, but instead moved to a location near the Philippine Sea.

Manalo and his men had been riding for the past five hours. The truck continued its forward, slow, stop, forward pace through the traffic as they approached Manila.

A knock came from inside the cab, and the head of the driver's teenaged son peered through the back window. "Comrade, sir, my father received a radio message."

Manalo strained to hear the boy over the noise of the engine and tires on the road.

"There is a situation."

"Where?"

"Quiapo."

"Quiapo? They expect us to stop in Manila for this?" Manalo glanced at his men, who feigned rest in the back of the truck with heads leaned back or with arms on bent knees. He knew they were anything but relaxed.

Manalo sighed. He had wished to go around Manila all together, and now they'd go straight into its heart to the old district of Quiapo. They were all in one vehicle, which was against his usual protocol, but time restraints forced such decisions. "Okay," he said to the boy, who nodded back.

Through the gaps in the canvas slivers of late-afternoon light, other vehicles, roadside markets, and tall factories made brief appearances. His men returned to dozing despite the rattles and bumps.

Timeteo dozed beside him, his right-hand man—though sitting on his left at the moment. His dark face was crevassed with lines though he'd yet to turn forty-five.

The childlike Luis was next, leaning against Timeteo. He was the first to jump in a river with a whoop, the one who couldn't stop from whistling or singing a tune—which had both helped and harmed them in times of danger.

Donny rarely spoke. He took everything in and could be counted on to follow through with one word of instruction. In his inside pocket he had a photograph of a palm tree with a boy leaning his hand against it, but no one knew why. He was twenty years old, had never spoken of his family. Questions always fell to his feet with a shrug of his shoulders.

Leo and Ton were twins and as alike as they looked. Manalo's twin daughters had distinct personalities from each other, but Leo and Ton—both called Lon by the men—seemed alike in every way, as though they shared one identity. Thankfully they were most always together, so any conversation a man had with one was with the other. Manalo teased that they were twice the man.

Before dawn, the truck had stopped briefly in a small village and a six-year-old boy was loaded into Luis's arms through the canvas. It had been a year since Luis had seen his son. His wife had died in childbirth, along with a second son, and after their burial, the older boy stayed behind with another family while Manalo and his men were sent away. The family could no longer provide for the boy, and Luis needed a way to get the child to his grandparents in the southern provinces. Now Manalo watched the boy sleep with his head against his father's shoulder, one small hand holding Luis's dark tattooed arm.

Manalo closed his eyes but kept his ears attentive as they continued. The highway was busy; they were coming into Manila and now would take the traffic-laden streets into Quiapo, where drugs and foreign mafias mixed with religious fanatics and open street markets. A truck backfired, but the eyes of his men barely opened. They knew real danger from counterfeit.

Luis's son, however, woke with fear in his eyes. A tear trailed dirt down his cheek, though he didn't cry out. His father slept on. The boy noticed Manalo, who motioned him to come. The child hesitated, then crawled over legs and sleeping men to a small space Manalo patted beside him.

Small black eyes stared up at him, above cheeks that were smooth and round. Manalo felt a pang of longing.

"I have a son as well," he said. He hadn't meant to speak aloud, for the boy did not understand anyway. He had been taught Ilocano, not the usual Tagalog or English. When he went to his family in the south, it would be some time before they could communicate in the same language. The sadness in the boy's eyes stung Manalo's heart. If his own children suffered such longing, it would be more than he could bear. Manalo wanted to turn from the child, and at the same time wanted to hold him tightly and make his life safe and happy.

From his pocket he pulled out a piece of string. The black eyes studied him with interest as Manalo demonstrated how to tie a slipknot, winding the string around and pulling the ends for the knot to disappear. The boy learned quickly, after only several tries, and smiled proudly when his knot pulled through into a straight piece of string again.

Manalo winked at the boy, then nodded for him to return to his place. Hesitation . . . a gaze of longing . . . ah. Manalo handed him the string. The child clutched it as though it were a costly treasure.

The traffic grew thicker, and Manalo felt the pressing in of civilization. Exhaust and humidity stung his lungs, and beads of sweat rolled down his back. He missed the mountain air. The city felt like a death trap pressing closer around them. And he couldn't stop watching as Luis's son shook his father awake and demonstrated his new skill. Manalo hadn't seen his own son since his third year. He was six now.

Soon they'd pass Luneta Park where the statue of José Rizal stood holding his books in his hand. Though Manalo resented that it was the Americans who had pushed for Rizal to be the national hero—someone for the people to admire and see how change could come in peace—still he respected the man whose two novels sparked a revolution and cost him his life. His nation again needed words that stirred change and brought a better life for all Filipinos. Such drive and fire were too far from him now.

"What is it, Manoy?" Timeteo asked in a low voice beside him as the truck lurched forward again. The loud rumble of a bus passed by.

Few people called him by his nickname. His childhood friend knew Manalo as no one else did, except for his brother and Malaya. Timeteo had killed the man who murdered his brother, and he would give his life to protect Manalo. Of the few men he might uphold as trustworthy, Timeteo was undoubtedly the greatest—he'd entrust his family to Timeteo's care.

Manalo sighed and dabbed his forehead with an already damp handkerchief. "I grow weary of this."

Timeteo knew he referred to more than a need for sleep; the exhaustion ran to his bones as well. He nodded. "It is time to retire, you and I. There are younger men for such work."

"Forty-two and ready for retirement? I do not see that as an acceptable age."

"We have lived much more than most men of forty-two."

Manalo thought how true these words were. "And what would you do in retirement?"

Timeteo coughed and rubbed his eyes. "This blasted smog." He leaned back his head. "Hmm, what would I do? I will tell you a story. Many years ago, when we were still children, your brother traded me a pig for my broken bicycle. He said it was a very intelligent pig that could learn tricks and put on shows. Since my bicycle was broken anyway, I thought I had the better end of the deal. I worked and worked with that pig . . . while Ricky traded some bottle caps for a new chain and very quickly was riding the bike."

"Oh, I remember," Manalo chuckled. "Ricky gave me rides on the handlebars, and once we watched you trying to train that pig. I was crying with laughter, it was so funny! But my brother kept his hand over my mouth. He said you'd hurt us if you spotted us laughing."

Timeteo nodded grimly. "And I would have, most certainly. That pig did nothing but destroy my mother's garden."

They laughed at the memory.

"But, though that pig never did any tricks, she grew into an incredible birthing sow. Some say she was magic after all. I have sold many piglets over the years, and her piglets gave me more."

"How did I not know of this?"

"Because for, how many years now . . . seventeen, I have been with you in the jungle more than with my family and pigs. My mother puts one-fourth of the sale of each pig into a jar for when I come home."

"How capitalistic of you all!" Manalo said, teasing.

"Ah, yes. When we have a Communist nation, *then* I will share all in equal measure with my countrymen. Until then, I put away for myself, or perhaps for your children since I have none myself. When I retire, I will be a lazy old man with a boat to fish on Laguna Lake and a pipe to smoke day and night."

"And you will deserve it, my oldest friend." Manalo patted his shoulder gruffly; then he felt the weariness return. "Until then, we continue to follow orders from men we do not know. And today that will take us into Quiapo."

"Then rest, will you? You have not slept this entire journey. With this traffic, it will take us hours to get through the city."

Manalo heard the concern in Timeteo's advice. So others, or at least Timeteo, had noticed his restless nights, how his subconscious betrayed him. Lately the nightmares had expanded beyond the borders of the subconscious. Images came throughout the day as well, at times with his eyes wide open. The day before he had heard the voice of an old rival calling to him—a rival he had killed fifteen years earlier. And in his eyes flashed bodies of the dead, many he'd forgotten, as if specters who'd gained access to haunt the corridors of his thoughts. Did insanity grow from the sleep world to overtake the daylight hours?

In childhood, Manalo's parents had taken him on a final visit to his grandfather, who raved like a madman in the asylum they'd been forced to put him. The horrors of war had taken his mind. Manalo realized in the years that followed that there was a history of weakness in the minds of his ancestors. His mother suffered enormous mood swings until she found that alcohol soothed her to an oblivious state. His father was consumed with a rage that hurt them all, and which Manalo later confronted. An aunt and a great-great-uncle had committed suicide. Manalo and Ricky kept such facts secret, as their father had instructed them. Yet even with such a history, Manalo didn't fear his own mind to that extent—at least not yet.

Timeteo stared at him. "Get some sleep. I will protect the men and wake you if trouble comes. From now on, let us take turns."

Manalo nodded and leaned his head back. He stared at the boy still playing with the string, trying to undo a knot that had formed. Soon they would arrive in Quiapo, to some kind of evil in need of rectifying. Manalo's word would be law. His men's lives would rest on his shoulders. For now, he must sleep and hope he could win the battles within his own mind.

Organized mayhem.

Or perhaps simple mayhem best described the streets and intersections of Manila.

Julia stared in fascination out the taxi's side window while clutching the seat in front of her. She'd ridden with other crazy taxi drivers in her life, but this one kept her hanging on to keep from being bounced around the backseat as he sporadically hit the brakes and honked with enthusiasm. At another abrupt lane change, her grandfather's logbooks scattered.

In grasping for the seat in front of her, Julia grabbed part of Raul Sarmiento's shirt.

"Oops, sorry," she said, grabbing up the books and trying to balance herself by holding onto the door.

Raul grunted a reply. But the grouchy and closemouthed fore-man of her grandfather's plantation couldn't suppress the wonder surrounding her. She was really here . . . in the country she'd heard so much about. It felt surreal—like coming to a land of sto-ries and dreams—and yet it was as real as home.

Manila was a mosaic of contrasts at every turn of street: impres-sive financial buildings, primitive enclaves, banks and elegant cafés, statues and monuments, an entire street of outdoor markets, dank alleyways, and residential homes from the most affluent to shanty-type neighborhoods. And all within blocks of each another. They passed several open stores where all kinds of goods were sold on the streets. Children barely dressed sat on store steps while young students in pressed school uniforms walked past them. She noticed that Raul paid little notice to a blockade down a major side street where gun-clad soldiers stood as solemn as statues.

The foreman had arrived nearly an hour late that morning without excuse or apology. She'd waited in the lobby of the Hotel Manila, admiring the massive chandeliers, wood carvings, and marble floors while trying to relax to the cheerful chords of the piano played at the other end of the grand ballroom-style room. Nervousness and excitement battled within her. Perhaps all great journeys included both.

When Raul had opened the glass doors, Julia knew at once that the tall and fit-looking man in worn boots and starched work shirt must be the head of the plantation. Observing the stiff confidence in his movements, she wondered if he had a military background. He had given her a small bow and, "It is an honor to meet the granddaughter of Captain Morrison."

The somber expression had not left the foreman's face from the moment she met him.

"Perhaps a rented car," he said now, turning in the front seat. Julia moved to the center of the seat to hear him. "But we would need a driver . . ."

"No, really, the bus is okay," Julia said for the second time.

Evidently the hacienda car had broken down on the road to Manila. The driver stayed behind while Raul came for her. He had wanted her to remain in Manila while the car was being repaired.

"I'd really like to get to the plantation today. I can't wait to see it. I'll go by bus, taxi, or one of those funny-looking vehicles that looks like a giant jeep." The elongated jeeplike vehicles littered the road, mixed with motorcycles with sidecars and then cars and trucks of every variety.

Raul didn't respond. Apparently another day's delay wasn't a problem, but going by bus was going to be a huge predicament.

"What are those called?" Julia leaned forward to hear his answer.

"That is a jeepney. The King of the Road, a major transportation in the Philippines."

At stops along the street, passengers jumped in and out of the open backs of the long vehicles and sat on benches along the sides.

"I've never seen anything like it."

"You don't have them in the United States? They came from the U.S. military jeeps after the war."

A jeepney completely covered in chrome came into view just then with various neon-colored messages on its sides: Made in Philippines, Thank You, Lord, and Praise to Jesus. She smiled at the thought of a California highway populated with the vibrant and gaudy vehicles. "No, there are no jeepneys in the States."

Another grunt response came from the front seat.

"Oh, Raul, I was supposed to see Mr. Santos before going to the plantation."

"Yes, that was the plan. And Markus apologizes greatly to you.

He was called into court today. He will come to the hacienda in a few days."

"Ah, okay," Julia said, trying to hide her disappointment. If she remembered correctly, Markus was a major advocate for the plantation, and beyond his law practice, he desired the Philippines to be a strong and successful nation. He might have been the one who spoke a phrase her grandfather used to say about the Philippines—"a land to redeem."

The taxi braked again suddenly, and several pedestrians took the chance to cross in front of them. The video game of Frogger came to Julia's mind, where a player moved the frog in and out of traffic trying not to get squashed. The pedestrians were the bravest souls on the chaotic streets, dodging cars, jeepneys, motorcycles with sidecars, and even horse-driven carriages and bicycle-driven carts as they crossed and waited in the middle of the divider lines, even on the busiest thoroughfares.

She noticed Raul, too, had a hand of support on the dashboard. Taped to the dashboard were various religious pictures, while a crucifix dangled from the rearview mirror.

"How far is the plantation from Manila?"

"Five hours perhaps. Depends upon traffic. I apologize that we must take the bus."

"Oh, that's all right," she said with a laugh. "It's more of an adventure for me this way."

His lack of personality could dampen any mood, she thought. As the car idled in traffic, the driver honked several times, then suddenly turned up the radio and sang along, "You're the inspiration. You bring meaning to my life. . . ." He hummed when he didn't know the words.

Julia suppressed her smile and saw no reaction from Raul, though the driver continued to honk his horn and sing with the radio as if both were customary.

At the next intersection, a horse-drawn carriage came up beside them with a businessman sitting in the passenger seat.

"Miss, Miss!" A young boy slapped at her window and held up cigarettes and silk flowers.

"What does he want?" she said.

"He's selling those items, but do not open the window." Raul's voice was firm.

"Miss, Miss, please." His small hands continued patting the window, and a few older children appeared to join him.

The taxi quickly left them behind, but Julia noticed how vendors moved through the traffic with trinkets, water bottles, and snacks.

The longing in the boy's face remained with her, and Julia thought of the decades of struggle this nation had endured. She leaned toward the front again. "My grandfather said that Manila was mostly destroyed during the war."

Raul grunted an incoherent response, and Julia decided that was the end of her questions for now.

She watched out the window, absorbing the sights and wondering how to describe this to friends and family back home. Her mother might want to know more about the country she was born in. She was just a young girl when her own mother died, and Grandpa Morrison had sent her to relatives in the States for her safety and education. It seemed to Julia that her mother had never forgiven him for it.

This humid and congested metropolis was nothing like the small coastal town of Harper's Bay on the rocky and cold northern California coast where Julia had grown up. After graduating from college in San Francisco, she'd remained in the Bay Area. She loved life in the city and all it offered, though she went home often to visit her mother and stepfather as well as old friends. With Nathan she'd fulfilled her dream of seeing Europe, touring Germany,

France, and Austria. He was a lover of historical war sites and she a lover of art. They both loved the lavender fields of France, the vast green hills and sharp peaks of the Alps, and the culinary delights.

But the Philippines were so far like nothing she'd experienced before, with a mix of tropics, chaos, messy streets, brown faces, and beautiful scenery. And on the tinge of her desire to take it all in, Julia wondered at the dangers that might lurk in the hovels and alleyways of a country ever on the brink of upheaval.

The driver suddenly crammed his taxi between two parked cars, resulting in fierce honks and swerving vehicles around them. Raul hopped out and opened her door as the driver moved quickly to get her luggage.

"Remain here, please," Raul said and rushed off before she could respond.

The heat beat down on her, and Julia wished for one of the umbrellas she'd seen other women carrying. Her face was damp, and she could feel the small hairs curling around her face. The taxi disappeared into the veins of the city as she stood with her pile of luggage. Streams of pedestrians moved around her, and cars sped by only feet away. The eyes of nearly every passerby stared with great interest, surprise, or friendly curiosity.

Never had she felt so utterly, well . . . foreign.

I can't imagine living in such a place, she thought, but determined to make this the first adventure of the new Julia. She'd let nothing discourage her.

And then she saw the buses.

MANALO WANTED THEM OUT OF THE TRUCK AS SOON AS POSSIBLE. It was ridiculous to be in such a situation. A band of fugitive guerrillas traveling through the heart of Manila. They'd passed within feet of a military blockade of soldiers whom he knew had memorized the photographs of both him and Timeteo. They passed a bus station where two city policemen talked to a driver.

Taxis, jeepneys, tricycles, and pedestrians surrounded them; he recognized growing claustrophobia in his men's faces, in their bloodshot eyes and the stiffness of their backs. If they were glimpsed between the canvas flaps or stopped at a checkpoint, each man had his falsified papers, work permit, and individual story of the field work they performed. But a close inspection would reveal the shipment of guns beneath them and the suspicious myriad of documentation papers.

Most of their weapons were packed with their gear in the crate boxes, but their knives and pistols were within easy reach, hidden in waist belts and beneath pant legs. His men were guerrilla fighters through and through. They could survive in the jungle, but the city was a foreign landscape.

Finally the truck turned into an alley. Manalo peered through a crack in the canvas and saw a teenaged boy opening a narrow gate just wider than the truck.

Manalo motioned for the men to lean in close. "Donny, Leo, Ton, and Luis will go with the driver. Timeteo, Frank, and Paco, come with me. In the event of separation, meet at the safe house in Batangas or return to the bar in Gapo and find Boy. Questions?"

Heads shook and jaws were set. The truck continued through the gate and stopped, and the driver shut off the engine. Someone pulled back the canvas.

Luis climbed out of the truck and took his son in his arms, whistling a tune as if he were a laborer back from a day in the fields. The whistle turned to a Beach Boys song as brothers Leo and Ton joined in a duet with Luis's whistling. What band of hardened guerrilla fighters would include a whistle and song in their covert operation?

Manalo watched his men follow the driver to a gated doorway

that led to the city. By the time the men reached the chorus of "Don't Worry, Baby," the singing was lost in the sounds of Quiapo. Luis's son, high on his father's shoulders, stared at Manalo and lifted a hand to wave good-bye.

Manalo, Paco, Timeteo, and Frank watched them go, then entered the house within the small walled-off courtyard.

The shower was outside on a fourth-story terrace surrounded by potted plants, drying laundry, and three dogs that barely raised their heads at their arrival. An old woman led them up the flights of stairs; the elevator hadn't worked in ten years, she said. Piles of fresh, folded clothing of the civilized world awaited them.

The men took turns with a bar of soap beneath a heavy spray of cold water while the rest ate rice and adobo, drinking beer as if it were the finest wine from France. Manalo scrubbed his hair with the bar of soap and then his pants and shirt before peeling them off and letting the pounding water massage the muscles in his back. They'd been so long in the jungles that a shower, clean clothes, beer, and homemade Filipino food felt like pampering for a king.

Soon he sat before a plate of food and again thought of Malaya, as he continually did at odd moments throughout his days and nights. If only he could see her, just for a moment, like a ghost view's beside her. He'd do that next time they were together; he'd sneak around and watch her when she didn't know it. He wanted to see how she moved, read the different expressions on her face, hear her talk to the children or a neighbor or read her little list of errands and plans for the day.

"What's that smell?" Paco said, stopping with fork and spoon held dramatically midair.

"The question isn't what's that smell, but what is *not* that smell." Frank flexed his arms and sniffed the air; his bare chest rippled with muscles on his very small frame. Frank notoriously carried a scent that, as Paco said, would change even a lion's mind if lions resided in the Philippine islands.

With the teasing that began between his men, the tension and discomfort eased. Manalo returned Malaya to the folds of his mind and heart. He'd bring her back out when he couldn't sleep tonight.

He thought tomorrow he'd take the men to McDonald's, even if it was redolent of the disease of American capitalism. A Big Mac, fries with banana ketchup, and a bottomless iced tea or Coca-Cola. Perhaps coming to Manila was exactly what they needed before they faced what might be quite an assignment at Hacienda Esperanza.

Showers, food, and beer changed their dispositions considerably. Frank and Paco kept hinting about seeing *Die Hard 2* with Bruce Willis—after their assignment was completed, of course.

"Our destination is on the other side of Quiapo. I don't know why we are going." The shoddy data frustrated Manalo; he'd insist on better communication when he met his contact.

"I know it's an American movie, but it's Bruce Willis," Paco continued as they walked down the flights of stairs. He admired Bruce Willis as though the man were a true Filipino warrior, not just an American actor.

They'd first seen *Die Hard* on a small color TV and VCR in a shanty in a village in the provinces where they'd stayed two weeks of a rainy season. The men played the tape until it broke, and still quoted their favorite lines.

"Paco, give it a rest. We don't even know if there's a theater nearby," Timeteo said as they stepped into the courtyard.

"Two blocks away. I spotted it already," Paco said with a wide smile.

"I say, let's get this business over, and then I'm skipping Bruce Willis for the ago-go bars," Frank said.

They stepped out to the street below and, as if to punctuate his words, flashing lights and enticing images greeted them.

Frank grinned. "Look, it's a sign!"

Manalo shook his head as they walked onward. "Let's just get through this meeting first."

"THIS BUS HAS NO AIR-CONDITIONING. DO YOU HAVE A HANDKER-chief?" Raul asked as he sat down stiffly beside Julia.

Her luggage was piled high in the seat behind them, and she realized his shamed embarrassment that she was on a run-down bus and not in the hacienda car.

"A handkerchief?" she asked, shifting to the right of a sharp tear in the seat.

"Here." He pulled a white square of cloth from his pocket and pantomimed patting his forehead with the fabric before giving it to her. He took out a flowered handkerchief from his back pocket and dabbed his own neck and face.

"Thank you. You said it's five hours to the hacienda?" Sweat ran down the curve of her back and between her breasts, and she wondered if a bus this decrepit-looking could actually make such a journey. She noticed two red chickens in a pen several seats ahead.

"Unless traffic is lessened, but probably five, yes."

The bus rumbled to life, emitting a huge puff of black smoke. Passengers continued to glance back at her. A couple of children even sat turned with their hands on the back of the cracked vinyl seat three rows up, watching Julia's every move. She hadn't antici-pated that her skin would be such an anomaly in the Philippines. Celebrity or circus freak—she wasn't sure which they saw her as.

The bus took off with a start, lunging into traffic and making Julia wonder if their pilot was a former taxi driver who didn't real-ize he was now driving a bus.

Julia had the sense that she was truly on her way now. Part of her wanted to put out her hands and say, *Slow down, let me take this in, let me adjust to one thing and then the next.*

In the past two years, she'd lost the man who had been her entire life, left her company job for freelance work that she cared little to build, and faced her grandfather's diagnosis. Time had passed in a kind of dull resonance until the final months of being with Grandpa Morrison. Now she faced instant change—seeing Nathan again, flying to Manila, heading toward the plantation—it felt fast, too fast.

The highway passed towering malls and cinemas and colossal billboards displaying brands like Calvin Klein and Guess jeans. It crossed a sludgy brown river filled with garbage and lined with shanty houses stacked and staggered upon each other. Julia saw a television flashing through an open doorway and half-clothed children playing outside on the sidewalk with a scrawny dog. Poverty existed just blocks from tall professional buildings with restaurants and clubs. They drove along shops like strip malls without sidewalks, crowded with every class level of Filipino walking and shopping together. In a strange way, the juxtapositions mirrored herself—the woman she was, the girl she'd been, and the fight between them to be something new and more and better.

She was so lost in thought that she jumped when Raul asked, "Would you like a Coke, miss?"

The bus wasn't fully stopped when vendors came aboard.

"A Coke would be nice, thank you."

Raul waved a woman over, bought two Cokes, and popped the top off hers.

The cool liquid tasted much sweeter than at home, but it was a welcome relief down her dry throat. Julia's skin already felt sticky and ready for a shower.

Other vendors boarded the bus, offering chewing gum, drinks, paper-wrapped candies, boiled bananas, and other foods she didn't recognize.

As they drove from the city into the province lands, Raul leaned back slightly and slept with his hat perched over his eyes. The city and industrial areas turned to rice fields and rolling countryside pocked with gangly palms of various types and sizes.

An older jeepney of unpainted wood and metal stayed in line with the bus for a time, but instead of passengers peering out the windows, it was filled with large pink pigs. A few had fallen asleep, and their forked feet stuck out the back.

They passed a gated housing development with homes she might see in the Bay Area bluffs, and then a village with houses the size of large sheds where laundry dried on lines and men chatted outside on wooden chairs or worked on wood projects in dirt yards. At times, tin-roofed stands lined the narrow streets with overflowing shelves of fruit and flowers.

The bus stopped at intervals, taking on and letting off passengers as well as more vendors who came up and down the aisles offering homemade baked goods, foods, snack items, and even hot corn on the cob.

Julia tried to take in every detail of the tropical scene, the brown faces and the vibrant greens and multicolored signs and vehicles. She wanted something of this place to embed itself within her, just as a portion of her blood was born of this land.

Brightly colored signs and banners attracted her attention to some kind of a demonstration as they passed through another village. People were cheering and a man stood on a bench shouting to the crowd. A tank was tipped sideways, off to the side of the road. This complex nation would take more than a day to adapt to, she realized; she actually knew nothing of what she was getting into.

Raul woke and patted his forehead and neck again.

"Mr. Santos wrote that my grandfather's remains will arrive in five days' time."

Raul nodded. "Mr. Santos will come to the hacienda to discuss all matters. There was much paperwork, and Markus used his contacts for approval. It is not customary for an American to be buried here. We are honored by it. And there are other legal matters to discuss."

Julia nodded. The lawyers were taking care of it. With their help, she'd decide what to do about the future of the land her grandfather loved.

After a while, her bloodshot eyes stung with weariness and travel. The sound of the chickens and rumble of the bus were no longer foreign sounds, but grew soothing as the hours passed. With a dab to her forehead with her handkerchief, she leaned her head against the glass as the flash of green landscape eased her eyes toward rest. Oddly, it was California that was beginning to feel like a dream.

FOUR

❧✦❧

Quiapo was the home of religious fanatics, the poverty-stricken, and mobsters, with the wealthy and tourists mingling within as they searched for some of the best bargains in the city.

Manalo's men separated at a street corner. Manalo hung back at a newsstand while the others went ahead at differing paces and directions. Best to arrive separately and inconspicuously.

They came to the open square surrounding Quiapo Church. The revered "Black Nazarene" waited behind lock and key for his bi-annual parade to greet the thousands upon thousands of hands seeking healing and blessings with a touch on the dark-wood sculpture.

Two small barefooted girls ran toward Manalo with crucifix necklaces and rosaries outstretched in their hands. Their faces and dresses were smudged and black eyes pleaded more than words. He bent at the knees to feign interest in their wares and received a shy smile from the younger, who hid behind her sister's faded skirt. As he made the exchange of coins to rosaries, he heard the footsteps for a dozen more children come quickly to surround him.

"*Palimos po. Pangkain lang,*" said the children, asking for a few coins to buy some food.

Yes, it had been a long while since he'd been in Manila; he'd forgotten the ramifications of charity. This was the world of democracy, he thought, as he tossed a handful into the air and left behind soft-cheeked children to scramble like dogs for the scraps. A Communist state would eliminate such oppression. It had worked in other countries for a time—and how desperately his people needed some leveling force among the classes.

He decided to take a longer route to the Korean restaurant that was their destination, and turned down an alley. It amazed him still how Manila could have such streets of poverty just blocks from cinemas and shopping malls.

Outside a run-down ago-go bar, women, used up from a depraved life, stood and waited for business. They smiled and called to him as he went by.

"Two hundred pesos," an older woman said as she stepped in front of him. The makeup on her face did nothing to hide the hardness of her years.

"You sell your dignity for so little a price?" he said, smelling the stale cigarettes on her breath. "I'm sure men get what they pay for."

She might have struck him, but her frame was light from malnutrition, and he pushed her back, moving around her and some emaciated dogs that rummaged through garbage on the street.

Across the way two young boys played naked in a puddle of

water. They were near his twin daughters' age. He wished to scoop them up from the squalor. Water on a street such as this could be infested with germs.

He shouldn't have come this way. Once such sights might have incited him to the cause, the belief in a better world. Why couldn't the people see that this was the result of "freedom"? No one cared for the poorest children or that the innocents paid the highest price so the wealthy could live in luxury.

Yet they were losing the battle. Nothing had changed for all the sacrifice of years. For his brother's life. For his separation from Malaya and the children. For a thousand days of being alone. Worse, now the party had decided to collaborate with less than idealistic people. They called them "friends of the Communist brotherhood." *Friends* simply meaning the country's criminal elements. Was the enemy of your enemy really your friend?

Manalo had always despised working with these people, who were polar opposites of what their own purpose fought for. While the New People's Army fought for justice and equality for the masses, these men were motivated by nothing other than their own greed. But working with them had been beneficial, Manalo had to admit.

For a moment, he couldn't breathe—the air was thick with vehicle exhaust and thousands of carbon dioxide exhalations. His lungs burned, and he longed for the crisp air of the jungle.

After walking a few more streets, all crowded and bustling with people, Manalo began to feel confident that they weren't being followed. No one knew they'd come to the city. He again stopped at a newsstand, this one at a street corner, and perused the papers above a tray of X-rated videos. Timeteo walked by without a glance or comment, sauntering down the alley to knock on a back door. By the time Manalo had paid for a newspaper, Timeteo had disappeared inside.

Manalo entered the Korean restaurant by the front door and found a small table in a corner. The menu perused, a San Mig ordered, he asked the young waitress, "Where is the CR?"

He left the newspaper and a few coins for the beer that had not yet arrived and pushed out his chair as if he'd be back soon. Then he headed through the kitchen toward the comfort room. Two young men glanced up from their work over steaming pots and a sizzling grill, while a girl chopping vegetables never looked his way. He moved beyond the bathroom to a door with bold words in Korean that he understood without translation to mean *keep out*. In the corner of a storage area, a large man whittled on a stick and didn't meet his eye.

Manalo hesitated, put a hand to the door, and turned the knob. As the door opened, he knew instinctively he was entering an environment different from what the information relayed to him during transport had led him to expect. It was the vibrations he felt as the door opened, like a putrid smell coming from a crypt. His men marveled at Manalo's foresight into a situation, not realizing it had been perfected by the need for survival—a defensive mechanism from early childhood. He could pick up his father's joy or rage before he walked into the shack they called a home. His brother never did learn this art, and unless Manalo could warn him, Ricky often became a victim.

A slight hesitation with the door half-opened overwhelmed him. With fixed jaw, Manalo brought his hand to his waist where his .38 had become like another purposeful limb. He strode in with confidence and assessed that it was not danger that brewed in that dark back room, but fear.

In one dark corner he saw a bound figure, its hands and feet tied behind the back—clearly dead. The mouth was probably taped closed to keep screams from reaching the diners enjoying their Korean barbecue, but Manalo couldn't be sure without showing that he'd noticed the body. The face was turned toward the dark corner anyway.

"What went wrong?" he asked.

A tall figure moved from the circle of men who'd been conversing in muffled tones when Manalo entered. To his right, Timeteo, Paco, and Frank leaned against the opposite wall with the look of hardened killers ready to do his bidding.

The tall guy was obviously the leader, though he crooked his neck down as though ashamed of his height. Manalo didn't understand that. If he had height, he'd stretch up even taller, chin up, so that others would marvel at the view he must have of the world.

Tall Man cleared his throat. "We encountered a little problem. *May bata kami*, youthful and foolish. He's new and too zealous to impress, especially when he heard our red friends were coming. You know the type. He got a little too excited in getting information. That's him over there."

Manalo took a few steps around a chair turned on its side, stepped over the blood streak that extended from the chair to the body, and motioned the kid toward him. He positioned himself so the young man had to stand in the dead man's blood. *Ah, no pompous gaze now*, he thought. The boy's face was as white as a white man now, and Manalo thought how he and his men would laugh about it after this was over. But for now, none of it was humorous.

"What do you have for me?" Manalo demanded.

"*Wala*, nothing really."

Manalo turned back to the tall man in charge of this band of wannabe rebels. "Is it recorded?" He had already noted the tape recorder on a table beneath the dangling lightbulb.

"Yes," Tall Man said. "But we learned nothing of value."

"And what is the chance we are compromised being here?"

"None."

"None?" He stared hard at the man. "It is ignorance to believe there is a moment of time without danger. So what is the chance we are compromised?"

"Extremely low."

"That is acceptable then. But you have nothing for me?" Manalo moved his eyes between the two of them.

"A lesson will be thought of," the tall man said, glancing at the boy.

"Yes. Indeed it will." Manalo felt their shudder and that of his comrades behind them. "You have placed my men in grave danger. There is a nationwide government manhunt on each of us. Outstanding warrants and rewards that have kept us from Manila for three years. And yet here we are, put into this position, because of what?"

No one answered.

"Because one of the friends of the brotherhood had important information for us. We were already en route to a mission when we were diverted to Manila to recover this important information. So. All of this, and you have nothing from this interrogation except a corpse that must be disposed of."

The boy paled further than seemed possible as the gravity of his deeds set in. The leader nodded.

Addressing the tall man, Manalo said, "You will send the body to his family. Make it appear that this provincial boy just got mugged in the tough streets of Manila. Our brotherhood cannot be linked to this in any way. If your group is implicated, you cannot involve us."

He paced a few steps in thought, moving toward the body. "On the second day of the wake, send an *abuloy* to the family—six months wages from the Red Bolos with our condolences and the promise to bring the killers to justice."

The leader gave a short nod. The tension settled now, the

young man stepped back and made an inconspicuous attempt to wipe the blood from the soles of his shoes.

"Let us listen to the tape."

The quick glance between them did not go unnoticed by Manalo as the three of them went to the table. His intention was to shame this young man from ever displaying such a rash burst of pride again. Only a few bloodthirsty men were needed for their group, to do the jobs that Manalo didn't want to infect others with. But it was his own stomach that churned in displeasure as the tape played, at the sounds of the young man shouting threats and torturing the prisoner.

"I'm only a driver," the dead man said repeatedly, and nothing more.

When the tape ended, Manalo felt his head spin with weariness, though he clenched his jaw and kept his eyes steady and hard.

The leader defended the young man, for he was ultimately responsible. "The man was a drug dealer and an addict."

"Will not his family look for him still, and cause us trouble? He was also a son and perhaps a brother." Manalo felt his eyes drawn unwillingly to the corpse. The streak of blood was drying in a few places while the pool around the body inched wider like a thick crimson blanket growing around him.

He needed out of this room of death, a feeling that surprised him. He'd been in many such rooms; sometimes it was by his own hand that a body lay crumpled on the floor or dangled from a rope or stared with open eyes with a throat slashed wide like a scream from the neck. Nothing of joy came from such vile tasks, only abject necessity for something greater, a higher cause. The lines of good and evil, right and wrong, integrity and depravity were often smudged. He hoped that by his necessary sins, his sons might one day walk a path of clear integrity without constant questioning and regret.

"If he was only a dealer, only an addict, why was he questioned? And why bring me here?"

The leader and Manalo stared at one another. They were equals as leaders of their respective men, but Manalo was the superior man. A flicker in the eyes, and the leader was caught in the lie.

His words fumbled out in obvious fear. "This was the consensus from evidence we obtained."

"Tell me the truth, or I will kill you." Manalo spoke softly, enunciating carefully. Inwardly he seethed with anger that this low-level man, who wasn't even a Communist but wished to partner with them, would dare to conspire with his men to cover up their mistake. "Who was the boy?"

"He's not from here; he's from Batangas."

A vibration rose within Manalo, a foreboding . . . what was it? *Batangas. It couldn't be.* "You picked him up down there?"

"No, we got him here, in Manila. He said he was searching for parts for a vehicle. They'd been following the car since—"

"What was his name?"

"Artur Tenio."

A coldness swept through the room; Timeteo pulled away from the wall in surprise as if struck by it.

Timeteo walked forward. "Where was Artur Tenio from in the Batangas? Where was he from, exactly?"

The leader went to the table for the boy's ID card. "Barangay Mahinahon."

Timeteo and Manalo stared at each other. Timeteo looked ready to lunge. "Do you not know the men of Barangay Mahinahon?"

"We are recently from Mindanao, one year."

Manalo turned from the others to the body and closed his eyes. There were definable turning-point moments in his life, four he could recall with clarity: his sixteenth birthday, when he had stepped over his unconscious mother and brother to put a pillow over the face of his sleeping father, ending a childhood of fear and making him a man; his brother's death years later, which left him in mourning and with a leadership role to fill; the first time he made love to Malaya; and the birth of his first son—the only birth he was present for.

Perhaps this began several nights earlier when he'd seen the stag in the forest, but just as those past moments were known to him, Manalo knew this event meant something great. He'd not be going back to what had been before.

The leader had lost all composure now. "Boss, he is impetuous, a boy only."

Manalo found himself standing above the face of the dead man. But he wasn't a man at all. "He couldn't be more than twenty. And he is related to Amang Tenio, either grandson, nephew, or cousin. Amang Tenio is more than a respected leader; he is a legend. You have endangered more than you know with your actions. Remain here."

He turned and went for the door in the back of the room. Neon lights blinded him until his eyes adjusted. The metal door slammed shut; the men would be stunned by his abrupt departure. But that face of the dead boy, nose and jaw broken, blood covered . . . *Barangay Mahinahon*. His men were going to the mountains above the infamous "village of calmness" on the outskirts of Hacienda Esperanza. The boy was a driver, coming to Manila, looking for car parts. What did this all mean?

Superstitious by heritage and nature, Manalo fought to reject its grip on him. He believed in the Communist Party of the Philippines, not in signs and wonders and foreboding feelings. He believed in the people, in a cause, in a better tomorrow for future generations. God did not exist to him. God was as fanciful as his childhood dreams.

The bile rose to his throat. He leaned against a dumpster, sweat beading along his forehead. There was a dead dog in the corner;

flies buzzed around it, and he held his breath to keep from catching the scent. Then he vomited beside the dumpster, emptying his stomach until there was nothing left.

"*Kamusta?*" Timeteo had followed him out.

Manalo rose slowly and wiped his mouth. "Must be something I ate."

Timeteo laughed awkwardly and slapped him on the back, taking any shame from him. "Something finally cracked the stomach of steel, eh?"

"Yes, I think your wife's dinner last night."

Timeteo laughed harder. "If we had eaten my wife's dinner last night, then that would do it."

They both chuckled at that. Timeteo often jokingly referred to his favorite prostitute as his "wife," though he hadn't seen her in longer than Manalo could remember.

Their laughter died quickly, and Timeteo said, "We might have made war with a very unpleasant enemy. They will blame us even if the act came from the 'friends' of the Communists."

"Yes." Manalo's mind was busy considering possible solutions. "We must proceed warily."

He strode back to the building to knock, but noticed the door had caught on the latch. He swung it open to see the tall leader and another man huddled at the table, and several others gathered around the body in the corner. One spat and laughed, then turned with a grin that froze upon seeing Manalo in the doorway. It was the young man—a boy himself, really—who had killed the boy from Barangay Mahinahon.

Manalo strode the steps between them and smoothly pulled the knife from his belt. "We do not disrespect our dead," he said as the blade entered the young man's stomach, slicing through his liver and back out with such ease that Manalo was reminded how without even a thought, a man was so easily dead.

The other men jumped back as blood spurted from what looked like the splitting of an abdomen, they'd been so close.

The boy held his stomach, blood spilling between fingers, then went to his knees. His mouth gasped like a fish pulled from the water. Manalo thought of Timeteo's desire to fish more in retirement. They would never get to retire.

The young man fell beside the corpse. Turning his head, he stared into the empty expression of his victim. It could take time, this young man's death. Manalo thought to finish him, a cut to the heart or neck, but now it was too late. The brutality would turn the other men's shocked fear to terror if he jumped on the kid for another blow, however merciful his intention.

The suffering was excruciating. The others stood staring at the young man dying on the ground. None moved to help him. The boy cried tears but not words.

Manalo knelt down and took off his jacket, pressing it into the boy's wound. The boy gasped, and his body shook beneath Manalo's hand. Warm blood quickly soaked through the material. And then the boy was dead.

Manalo stood in the silent room. He knew all eyes were staring at him, but he didn't look toward any of them. "Do not let anything like this happen again. Discipline your men."

"Yes, Comrade Manalo."

"Take a photograph of your man there, and in two months' time send it to the family of the boy at Barangay Mahinahon. Do not sign it from us, but make it evident without confession that we have done this for the innocent slaughter of their kin. It will not help, not really. A terrible mistake was made here today, and we may all pay for it. But do what I say nonetheless."

Everything in its box, he thought. Organized mayhem.

Or perhaps nothing was organized at all, but all a form of mayhem.

Manalo and his men walked for a long while without speaking; then their spirits slowly roused and the mood eventually changed. They had participated in and seen too much death for it to cast lasting clouds over them.

They stopped for a Coke, and Manalo used the comfort room to wash his hands. He returned to hear Frank telling some animated story.

"Let's go," Manalo said.

"Back to the safe house?" Paco asked.

Manalo shook his head and slapped Paco's back. "No, to see Bruce Willis and *Die Hard 2*."

FIVE

They stood beside a rural highway with Julia's luggage stacked in the tall grass as the bus spewed out a hefty burst of exhaust before deserting them there. From the windows, dark eyes stared and an old woman waved good-bye.

"Where are we?" Julia looked from one end to the other of the long stretch of asphalt road. The dark gray highway cut through a path of lush vegetation that crept along both shoulders. Behind the shrubs, rows and endless rows of tall coconut trees dwarfed the foliage that grew taller than her own height.

"We are at the outskirts of the hacienda," Raul said.

Julia felt a flutter through her stomach. That close.

Raul carried the heavy pieces of luggage, struggling with their weight across the street toward a small wooden structure nearly overgrown by the encroaching jungle. Julia followed with her own purse and satchel, feeling the ache in her shoulder of two long days of travel since she left San Francisco International Airport.

Inside the shed, Raul picked up a walkie-talkie from a slot beneath a lone bench and talked into it, then got a static-laden response.

"Our ride will be here shortly. It is unfortunate, your entrance to Hacienda Esperanza. Your grandfather would be most disappointed, and I do make my apologies. I could leave you here with Abner and fetch one of the cars, but then you would be waiting longer. And evening comes soon enough."

At that very moment the bushes across the highway shook violently, and a creature materialized onto the road. It was a man, primitive or poor or both, with a long wooden pole on his shoulders that supported a bundle of about ten green coconuts on each end. When he spotted Raul, he smiled widely, revealing several missing teeth, and nodded his head in greeting.

Raul waved him over. His deliberate steps reminded her of a llama or camel crossing the road with a slow glance in both directions. He wore a thin white shirt with half the buttons missing, revealing a brown chest of skin-covered bones. His trousers were folded to his knees, and his barefoot heels looked as tough as the paved highway. But it was the wide jungle knife dangling from his waist to his ankle and swaying as he walked that kept Julia's attention.

"*Magandang hapon.*" He spoke to Raul and offered the head-nod greeting to Julia, which she returned with a smile.

He then put his bag down and selected two coconuts. Setting one on the ground, he opened its thick shell with deliberate slashes of his long jungle knife. He cut off the hairy outer shell and created a good container to hold while drinking the coconut juice inside. He then cut a small utilitarian spoon from the husk itself and handed it to Julia, motioning that she could scrape off the white meat inside if she desired. He smiled proudly through the entire process.

"Thank you," said Julia, amazed at his expert handling and admiring the cute little spoon he had made so easily. To Raul she asked, "How do you say thank you in Tagalog?"

"You can say *salamat*, and that will be enough for him to understand. Every region of the Philippines has a different language, and many dialects within that language. Although most people speak Tagalog or English, some from certain villages do not."

"Salamat?" she asked, and at his nod, Julia repeated it to the man, receiving his smile and nod. He reminded her of a figure only Walt Disney could create, and she wished to ask if he was part of the hacienda or he lived in the jungle. . . . What was the story of a man like that?

Raul's coconut was as easily opened as the two men talked. Julia tasted the watery milk, which wasn't as sweet as she expected, but it quenched her thirst. She gazed at the overgrown fields and trees.

The men's conversation was interrupted by the explosive whine of a two-stroke engine that grew louder as it came down the road that connected with the highway. The small vehicle with its chrome and angular features reminded her of a vehicle from Star Wars as it came zipping toward them.

These odd vehicles had jammed the streets in Manila and the road to Batangas. It was a motorcycle with a two-person aluminum sidecar attached to its flank.

The driver, a middle-aged man in shorts and a faded purple T-shirt, waved at Raul and gave her a curious look with his nod and smile. A young man hopped from the sidecar and motioned them inside with a "*Mabuhay*, welcome to the Philippines."

"Thank you," she said, hesitating to get inside the metal contraption. "Salamat."

"This is a tricycle," Raul said, catching her questioning gaze. "They will bring your luggage next. Abner will remain here to keep your belongings secure. Again, Miss Julia, I apologize for such an arrival to the hacienda."

"It's okay, really. An adventure for me," she said and realized how often she was using that "adventure" line to bolster her anxieties.

The driver welcomed her aboard with a smiling, "Hi, mees."

With one last glance at her luggage, she slid into the seat and held her purse and satchel beneath her feet and the coconut on her lap. Her shoes were muddy and her skirt wrinkled, but suddenly she was filled with a sense of giddy discovery. Raul squeezed partway in beside her, holding the frame as the driver whipped around to return down the narrow road.

Her skirt fluttered in the rush of air. From airplane to taxi to primitive bus to tricycle—it felt as if she'd traveled back in time, or down some primitive social ladder. Next they needed a carriage or donkey ride, she thought with a smile.

The road was damp, and the leaves of ferns and trees at the side of the path were wet from a recent rain. The high whine and gear changes of the tricycle engine cut out all other sounds. The wind pushed back her hair, ruffling the material of her shirt and skirt, cooling the sweat on the back of her neck. Minutes passed as they drove by endless palm trees and a landscape that extended into fields gone wild with brush grown high and occasional piles of empty coconut husks.

"I've arrived," she whispered, wondering how many times her grandfather had traveled this very road.

In flashes through the palms, branches, and bushes, Julia caught glimpses of structures far ahead. As the road curved around, an old majestic arc, a gateway, came into view. Its strong, solid posts were made of orange layered bricks, and its wrought-iron gate was opened for their arrival. Their driver slowed the tricycle to a crawl as they approached.

Beside the gate Julia saw an old man, stocky but frail with age, standing proud and austere. A brightly colored blue bandanna was tied around his head, and he wore a bright red shirt over dark canvas pants. A plume of smoke came from his thin black pipe. And in the crook of his arm rested a large red rooster that he stroked lovingly from head to tail feathers. The rooster appeared as proud as the old man, staring with black beady eyes at the approaching motorcycle.

A boy stood at the old man's side as if the prodigy of something great. And yet, despite the man's arresting bearing, he appeared so shockingly simple and primitive. *A savage nobility of a bygone tribal age,* Julia thought. *Perhaps . . . a witch doctor?*

Raul nodded his head in respect. The old man gave a slight nod in return, then turned his gaze to Julia, his eyes literally sparkling. With a warm smile, he nodded to her as well.

Julia smiled and nodded in return.

"Who was that?" she asked loudly as their tricycle accelerated again.

"He is Amang Tenio. Leader of Barangay Mahinahon. You will meet him another day. I imagine he was standing at the gates to be the first to greet you. Now we proceed to the clan house of your family, which your grandfather and grandmother and their ancestors before them called home."

EMMAN RAN THROUGH THE JUNGLE WITH THE SPEED OF A LEOPARD, his feet so quick he thought perhaps he'd be viewed only as a blur through the leaves. He knew the shortcut to reach the hacienda before the tricycle arrived, but only if he was fast enough.

He'd seen her.

Miss Julia, the granddaughter of Captain Morrison. An American woman on the very road he'd walked a hundred times. And not just any American woman, but one who looked as though she could be from television or a movie.

As he ran, he remembered hearing a field-worker whose cousin lived in the States tell how few American women looked as the movies depicted. He said many were fat and ugly or from mixed-up races and looked nothing like the actresses of TV and movies.

But Miss Julia did. She even had blondish hair. Or close enough to blondish.

His first glimpse at her was like a scene from a movie. Julia's hair fluttered around her heart-shaped face, and one hand held her skirt against such beautiful fair-skinned knees. His heart pounded as it only did when watching a cockfight—or that time he'd been caught sneaking into the cinema and was taken to the police station.

Emman had stood beside Amang Tenio as the tricycle slowed and passed them. Miss Julia's expression was something between curious awe and nervousness; Emman wanted to run up beside the tricycle and tell her not to worry, he would protect her. But his feet wouldn't move until it was too late. Her cheeks were flushed pink. Pink! He wondered how such skin felt to the touch. He supposed the same as his own, but to touch white skin—Emman ran faster to rid such an inappropriate thought. He was sure her eyes were blue as she'd stared at him and Amang Tenio on the roadside. Blue eyes! He wondered if he could sneak up and look right into them, but how did a person sneak up and view another's eyes without her knowing?

A sharp pebble cut his foot as he ran across the road, and he hopped on one foot and yelled, "Owie!" It didn't sound very manly, but there was no one around to hear. He gasped for air to soothe the stinging in his lungs. The high whine of the tricycle was coming from behind—Emman was ahead already, with such leopard feet.

Despite the sting in his foot, he hopped to the softer ground in the jungle and ran again over the barely visible path that would get him to the hacienda house with minutes to spare before Miss Julia's arrival.

He was the first of his friends to see her, and she had seen him too. Their eyes had connected for just a moment. What did she think of him? Would she remember him? Had he looked like a man or just a boy in her eyes?

Emman ran so hard he thought his heart might burst from his chest. He couldn't help the wide grin; he'd never felt such exhilaration in all his twelve years. Now, not only did he hope to impress her by protecting her, Emman wanted . . . well, what did he want? He couldn't quite express it.

All he knew was he'd never been happier in his life.

THE DIRT ROAD SUDDENLY CUT THROUGH THE THICK FOLIAGE AND revealed a clearing in a sloping valley ahead where rice fields and a humble community of whitewashed houses greeted them.

"These were formerly workers' houses," Raul explained, bending toward her ear. "They evolved into family homes that came together into a small village."

The simple wooden homes were built side by side and hugged the stone-paved streets at both sides.

Raul motioned for their driver to pause before the smooth descent. From the corner of her eye, Julia caught the sight of a massive house. It stood separate, starkly dramatic and noble over its faded vine-covered stucco walls. Tall and austere, its weathered stucco columns rose confidently dark brown against a clear cobalt sky as white billowy clouds rolled above its red rooftop.

The driver smiled widely and pointed toward the house. "Clan house of Hacienda Esperanza," he shouted over the engine. "Captain Morrison's home." He increased the motorcycle engine, and Julia hung on to the bar in front of her.

Its enormity took her aback. An impressive mansion, though the age and wear of generations could be seen even from afar. Yet, perhaps even *because of* that, Julia felt the mysterious and digni-fied majesty of the estate. This had been a grand and imposing place at one time. *And it could be once again*, came the wistful thought in her mind.

She leaned forward to gain a better view and caught the proud expression on Raul's face as he took in the setting before them. Built on a large open compound, with secured adobe walls cov-ered waist-high with vines, the clan house's inner grounds were lined by tall palm trees. A garden overflowed with a variety of lush plants and flowers. Bougainvillea or some flowering vine grew wild along its walls, blossoming in pink, white, and yellow.

The house itself was two towering stories tall and had high tri-angular roofs with Spanish red tiles that vaulted up to the sky in various separate angles. It stood separate from its surroundings, a world of its own.

Something came over her, something that had been building around her since her arrival, but now surprised Julia with its encompassing strength. It was like relief or hope, or maybe some-thing of love at first sight. There was a peace about her that had been absent at home. All this she realized as she saw this beautiful and exotic house, dark brown and tall, surrounded by sprouting green palms against the deep blue sky.

"I love this place," she whispered without thinking. *How sur-prising that I love this place I don't even know.*

She felt windswept in a spirited sort of way: her face hot and refreshed, the exhilaration of speeding down the damp road in this bizarre little vehicle, the scent of a tropical forest as evening fell quietly beyond them.

Julia was six thousand miles from anyone who knew her, driving along in a tin box attached to a motorcycle with the driver smiling at her every reaction and a stoic Filipino dangling outside like a captain at the helm of his ship.

The fantastic had become real.

The road turned along a tall stucco wall nearly overrun with flowering vines and then to another set of massive gates opened for their arrival. Julia knew the house, or rather mansion, had been built nearly two hundred and fifty years before, and though certainly worn from the trials of time, it still loomed regal and austere against the deep blue sky.

A considerable crowd was gathered upon the green lawn, some waving handkerchiefs and with smiles as bright as the house behind them. Their enthusiastic welcome made her look behind for other vehicles or the approach of a parade.

"Is that for us?" she yelled up to Raul.

He leaned down and said with the first hint of pride in his tone, "That is for you."

"For me?" she whispered.

The group spread open and moved into loose lines on either side of the walkway, reminding Julia of the palm trees lining the road to the house. The driver stopped at the end of the rock path to the entrance and turned off the engine with a sputter. A light wind fluttered the cotton skirts of a few women and swayed the palms above them. A sweet earthy scent filled the air. Birds chattered like more applause from the trees.

A boy of about ten years came hurrying forward to take her hand before Raul could turn to help her out.

"Thank you," Julia said as she released the boy's hand. He smiled, nodded his head, and disappeared back to the now quiet crowd.

"Who are all these people?" she asked Raul softly before going forward.

"Many are extended family one way or another; some are old hands in the hacienda who still remember your grandfather. All are the men, women, and children of Hacienda Esperanza. They welcome you."

Julia tried to take in their faces, the lines and age, the youth and beauty. Their expressions held expectation and greeting.

Raul surprised her by taking her arm partway up the gray stone pathway; then he spoke loudly. "Miss Julia Bentley, Captain Morrison's granddaughter."

They clapped again with wide smiles; one older woman covered her face in joy. Another elderly woman reached for Julia with both hands, holding her hands tightly as tears fell down her face.

"Dear child, I am your Lola Gloria. Your grandfather was so proud of you when you were born, and he never forgot to mail us your pictures as the years passed by. He loved you so much, and how we loved your grandfather." Tears formed in the edges of her eyes, and she clung tightly to Julia's hands. "Captain Morrison always said he would find a way to come back. And now here you are, his beautiful granddaughter."

"It is good to meet you, Lola Gloria."

"And you, Iha. At long last you have come home."

A young girl tugged at Julia's arm and handed her a blossom, then ran to the lawn where she spun in her thin cotton dress, raising it into an airy hoop as her thick braid circled like a propeller. An older girl scolded her under her breath.

Julia walked toward the mansion, greeting each person, shaking hands, receiving hugs, hearing names she knew she wouldn't remember. One unknown aunt after another, one far-off relative after the next introduced himself or herself to her, along with a few more *lolas* and *lolos*—grandmothers and grandfathers of the hacienda. Such a warm and unexpected welcome!

Julia had left her family behind in the States only to find a long-lost family waiting her arrival in this faraway place. They were strangers who loved her, bound by a history she knew little about, each of them knowing things about her, though Julia had known nothing of them till now. Her grandfather's stories had suddenly come to life; names and faces she hadn't paid much attention to were here before her.

Before long, Raul was at her side, holding her elbow to guide her. "Come now, we usually use the back entrance, but today we open the front doors for you."

Julia looked up at Raul as he spoke; his jaw was firm, and he appeared regal with the love and pride he felt for the plantation. He led Julia up the stone stairway toward the sculptured solid wooden doors with the vintage brass knobs and colored stained glass that were to her open arms drawing her inside.

"The hacienda house has not been lived in for almost twenty years. We use the kitchen and back porch, and I use the study downstairs for business, but the rest of the house has been kept closed up since Captain Morrison was forced to leave. We have opened several areas for your short visit, but of course you may enter any room you wish."

Stepping inside, Julia stopped short at the grand entrance. Polished wooden floors of dark wide planks, a massive winding staircase that reminded her of *Gone with the Wind*. The walls halfway up were covered in a dark aged wood with rich engravings and molded edges. The front windows let in beams of dusty light. The ceiling dwarfed them; Julia guessed it was about twenty feet.

Several older women followed them inside as the rest of her greeters dispersed to unknown places.

"Miss Julia, would you like some iced tea or lemonade?" Lola Gloria asked. She spoke clear English with only a slight accent.

The house had the feel of a museum, antiques that didn't want to be touched, and on the staircase wall, paintings of the hacienda from past eras in large frames. The foyer opened into a parlor with Victorian-styled chairs, a sofa, a lamp.

"It's beautiful." Her voice fell softly into the room.

Raul gave a nod of assent. "We tried maintaining the house as best we could. We have had a hard few decades. But we have retained its grandeur."

"I'm surprised no one broke into the house with such valuable antiques," Julia said, looking at the small piano in the corner, the grandfather clock, the lamps, sideboard, and other furnishings that would bring a large price in the States.

Raul's footsteps stopped hard on the floor as he turned to her. He examined her face and then smiled as if she'd said something humorous. "There was no fear of anyone entering the hacienda house without permission. No one would dare enter, not with the Barangay Mahinahon."

"Barangay Mahinahon?" she asked, surprised that she could repeat the name. A shiver ran through her. Raul had mentioned it earlier, and it seemed she'd heard those words before from her childhood days as well. Had it been childhood ghost stories from her grandfather? "What is that?"

"I will take you there perhaps." He seemed to consider a moment, his look far away. "Or I will at least explain it further at another time. I do apologize that not everyone could be here for your arrival."

"Some were missing?"

"Some of your cousins were not in attendance. They will of course attend the wake and funeral. There have been some difficulties of late. You will meet them all soon enough."

Raul was keeping something from her; Julia detected worry in his face. Dwarfed in the presence of this house and the great unknown around her, she knew there were many secrets hidden within and without.

She'd entered something far beyond expectation, and her short time here meant long repercussions. But exactly what those repercussions might be, and what her role would be, she did not yet understand.

"WHY DON'T YOU GO HOME NOW?" EMMAN COULDN'T KEEP THE annoyance out of his voice.

"Did you see her?" Bok said, climbing the tree at his heels. "Can you believe I touched her hand?"

"I saw her before anyone else." Emman wanted to kick the boy out of the tree and be left alone. She *did* have blue eyes; he knew that for certain now. But he'd been rooted in place while others reached out to take her hand and introduce themselves. The nerve of Bok to rush up before anyone else and help her from the tricycle.

The light went on in her room. Emman took the wooden gun in his hands and touched the knife at his side. He'd protect her, even if she didn't know he was here. One day soon, she'd know. And if any harm approached, Emman would be ready.

He wondered what Miss Julia thought of the hacienda house. From what he'd seen on television, not everything in the United States was grand and imperial. He wondered what her house looked like. Was it like those houses on *Beverly Hills 90210*? Or in the city like the Bronx or south LA—like he'd seen on TV shows and movies? Somehow he couldn't imagine Julia in a run-down house with gangs doing drive-by shootings.

Yet surely the hacienda would impress anyone. Just that day he'd learned more about the inside from his cousin, who had done some woodwork on the staircase. Abner said that the house had ten upstairs bedrooms, a second spacious open-air living room, and a long and large hallway that connected them all. Downstairs were the large primary *sala*, kitchen, dining room, study, parlor, and four more bedrooms. Other than the office and kitchen, the rest of the house had remained unused for over a decade. Sheets covered furniture in many rooms, and the thought of those shrouded objects—would they scare her as she stayed there alone?

Emman would stay the night nearby in case she needed someone strong and brave to save her.

Bok had finally stopped bugging him. The kid had initiative beyond his years, Emman had to admit. And when the younger boy handed him some cigarette butts only half-smoked, Emman decided he could stay.

SIX

He walked down the stairs, leaving Timeteo, Paco, and Frank on their beds in the darkened room. Perhaps they couldn't sleep either. They'd hear his departure as men accustomed to being wary at all times, but none would follow him.

He waved a hand in the air to stop a taxi, and as he told the destination, Manalo wondered when he'd last ridden in a cab and what fare they charged now. Walking the kilometers back to the safe house after the day he'd had did not appeal to him.

The city was still alive with people walking the streets and streaming from the malls. He couldn't believe how many malls had cropped up, and more were being built. When he'd last been in Manila, the economy struggled to such an extent that whole areas of the city were desolate. Now rich developers were being made richer, while the poor remained poor even without Marcos as the unmitigated president.

Rock bands and vendors lined up beneath the palm trees of Manila Bay. Their lights reflected onto the dark water, and far out in the bay ships both large and small could be identified by their pinpoints of light.

As he walked along the baywalk, a powerful longing came over him. He needed more than food or water or rest. He no longer desired success or power or war. What he needed, he could not have. Malaya. All he wished was to crawl into bed with his wife, put his head on her stomach, and feel her hands in his hair. Once there, he'd remain forever and cry a thousand tears.

"Comrade."

"Comrade Pilo." Manalo slapped his back and smiled as if meeting a long-lost friend, in case someone was watching. Their smiles were forced as they asked about each other's families and found a bench before the view of water and night sky.

"What happened tonight?" Comrade Pilo asked him in a lower tone.

"I was hoping you'd know more than I do." Manalo would not accept any form of reprimand after the situation into which they'd been placed. "What is going on?"

"Mistakes were made."

"Yes, that much I know. But why was that boy there in the first place?"

"The granddaughter of Captain Morrison was here today. At the Manila Hotel, in fact." They both looked in that direction and could see the building rising up past the opposite end of the baywalk. "The young man was the driver bringing a Mr. Raul Sarmiento to pick her up. We followed, and the car broke down. Once they approached Manila, I turned the tracking over to our 'friends.'"

"They picked up the boy, which they should not have done.

They thought he had information, but they did not even know the questions to ask him. Our friends do not know about the American woman, Captain Morrison, or the strategic importance of Hacienda Esperanza. And so, you know the rest."

Manalo realized they were sitting on a bench not far from where he and Malaya had sat, oh, how many years ago was that now? Fifteen, eighteen, maybe more. He tried to keep her from his thoughts.

"What is the objective for our going to Hacienda Esperanza?"

"Under no condition can hope for the American woman or Captain Morrison be revitalized. She is the beneficiary to the plantation, but that is not legally possible because she is a foreigner. Unless contracted with a Filipino individual or enterprise, she cannot own the land outright. Their lawyers are working on that, and this is of much concern. We need the land to be sold, divided by investors, or given to the people. But the American must leave. If the hacienda gains some measure of power and her position is associated with that in any way, then the entire region will gain a stronger political stability, and we'll have lost a key region of the country."

"So we encourage dissension."

"Yes. Chaos, fear, retribution. The area must be rife with insurgents, but not necessarily Communists. The Muslims could be contacted, and if they can do our work, then all the better. They care nothing for diplomacy, while diplomacy is our only means of battle at this point."

"The Muslims will kill the woman."

"No, we don't want that. The capitalist sympathizers already have one hero, Captain Morrison. We cannot give them a martyr as well. But the sooner the American woman leaves, the better. I will negotiate with either the Muslims or our 'friends' and see what they will do, and I will try to control their zeal."

"Good luck with that. What about the boy?"

"Let me work on that as well. Your plan was good, to return the body. But I will take that responsibility as well."

Manalo nodded his head in thought. This was what they needed: objectives for their mission, not obscure instructions to go to the area and see what they might see.

Then Comrade Pilo surprised him, saying, "Manalo, you won't go back to the safe house tonight."

"Where am I going?"

"Let us walk awhile, and I will tell you. But you will not join your men for three days' time."

THE SECRET IS IN THE ORCHID.

Julia searched the pages of her grandfather's logbooks, sure she'd read that phrase somewhere. She sat in the massive bed, the books piled next to her. The softly ticking hands of the windup clock pointed to just past four in the morning.

The antique furniture in the room had brought the phrase to her mind. Carved into the thick wood of the headboard, the bed-side table, and the large wardrobe was a design Julia recognized as an orchid blossom and leaves.

The room had a scent of dampness and age, and the house around her creaked and moaned in the darkness beyond the dim glow of her bedside lamp.

Old houses make noises, she reminded herself. Hallways and staircases rarely used now sighed in either annoyance or relief at the movement and life she brought here. An outside breeze further stirred trees against the roof and eaves. Did the house wish to be alone? Or had it longed for living things to move through its empty rooms and hallways like blood returning to deprived veins and cells?

Tiredness had fallen quickly over her after meeting the many people of the hacienda and going on a quick tour. One of the older women had made her a plate of food called *pansit*—some kind of brown noodle mixed in a smorgasbord of meats, vegetables, and seasonings.

She'd eaten at a grand dark-wood *narra* table in what had once been a dining room for entertaining. And as she'd eaten, the three older women had smiled and watched every bite, enthusiastically responding when she enjoyed the meal. Julia learned that they were sisters and distant relatives of hers. They pointed out antiques and told stories through the one sister who spoke perfect English.

"You should eat some more," Lola Gloria had said. "Dinner isn't for several hours."

"Sleep?" another had asked; Lola Sita was her name. They were indeed doting old lolas.

The house was so large Julia thought she could get lost. The rooms were filled with treasures, some from all over the world; Hacienda Esperanza was like a museum with all its collectibles, sculptures, books, and artifacts.

Julia missed dinner; she slept so long and hard. Awakening in the dark of night, she thought of her grandfather here in this very house so many years ago. He and her grandmother had slept in the room across the hallway, Lola Gloria had told her when she asked. Her mother had been born in the same room, a fact she had never shared with Julia. After her grandmother's death, and after Julia's mother was sent to live with family in the States, Grandpa Morrison moved downstairs to the office, never sleeping upstairs again. That floor had been mostly uninhabited for over thirty years.

Julia felt small here. That was the only description she could find. Small in form and small in existence compared to this grand house full of ancient lives, stories, and memories, in a country far from home. Only once before had she felt such a sense of small-ness, as a child in her uncle's boat in the rough Pacific waters beyond the point at Harper's Bay.

She reached for another logbook and carefully turned the pages. There were notes on better farming methods, how to use solar energy for the hacienda house, the best way to restore antiques. Nothing about orchids. Where had she seen those words?

The secret is in the orchid.

Her mother had a painting of an orchid and a wooden hair comb with the same carved emblem. Perhaps this had been her mother's room as a child. Once again Julia wondered why she knew so little about all of this—it was the strangest feeling, like discovering the truth of a parent a child had never known.

She almost missed it. There, in his tight script, written neatly along the bottom of a page. *The secret is in the orchid.*

There was a sketch of the flower beside it, but nothing else. The rest of the page was devoted to a plan for a grain silo.

For the longest time Julia stared at the words, wishing to hear her grandfather's voice explain what he'd written there. Finally she rose from bed and opened the balcony doors, sliding the panels into a hidden slot in the wall.

The second-floor terrace was a refreshing relief compared to the pressing indoors. The air felt crisp and damp, but not too cold. By day the encompassing view included the back courtyards, gardens, the thick foliage along the eastern borders including the overgrown orchid fields, and to the west the vast farm fields ending only in the far-off mountains. Julia leaned over the thick railing with wide carved balusters secured to the balcony. The grandness of old Spain was about this house.

The scent of tropical mountains came on the lightest of breezes to touch her face and push her hair back. Above, the stars shone brightly. There was no light on the horizon in any direction, and in the deep darkness Julia spotted the Big Dipper and then the North Star welcoming her like familiar faces in a foreign land.

There was a rustle in the bushes beyond the back courtyards, then the eerie cry of a night bird. The sound was strangely familiar; Julia felt that she could repeat the birdcall and that she had done so in the past. Her thoughts whirled with both the strangeness and odd familiarity of this land.

The Far East. Southeast Asia. The stretch of Philippine Islands. The Province of Batangas. In her mind, Julia remembered the world map and envisioned coming closer and closer to the pinpoint of space that the hacienda occupied like one faded star in this brilliant night sky.

These days on this side of the earth were foreordained, she felt, to bury her grandfather, assess the lands, and seek a new path for her future.

The night bird called again, a haunting cry. A breeze rustled the fanlike arms of the palm trees.

Julia knew that much lay in store beyond her three goals. And how she wished to know, what was this secret of the orchid?

HE'D BE THERE IN MINUTES NOW.

Manalo stood up in the back of the truck and felt the brisk predawn air slap his face and fill him with the scent of the jungle. He always loved that moment when night made its turn, like the turning tide out on the sea. It was the change of night to a new day, a shift in the atmosphere that could be felt if one sought to perceive it.

The road sign announcing the village ahead sent a rush of adrenaline through him; he felt sixteen again and newly in love.

Only six hours earlier he had been in Manila. Then Comrade Pilo told him he wouldn't be going with his men. Instead of heading to the mountains surrounding Hacienda Esperanza, he was given one day and one night with his family. He'd left at once.

The children surely slept; he would love to see them in their beds. How he'd love to watch Malaya sleep as well. Tonight he would. He would make love to his wife this morning and again in the night, and then he'd watch her sleep and memorize everything about his children and wife to take with him until he saw them again.

And the next morning before he left, Manalo would make love to his beautiful wife one more time and hope in several months he'd hear of another child growing inside her. He worried about her when she was pregnant, especially after his sister's death in childbirth, but she had always wanted six children. He never saw her so happy as when she was pregnant, rubbing her round stomach with joy and glowing with excitement.

He wanted to see this house they'd lived in for six months—a house with running water and a plumbing system. She'd thanked him, knowing he'd pressed the issue after the shanty they'd been in for three months before that. If he had to live apart from them in the jungle, a fugitive from the government, and he couldn't put them in the type of house they deserved, at least they would not live in squalor.

On the phone she'd told him her routine. How he loved just to hear her voice and know of her schedule—it was something he took with him during the days and night of separation.

The baby who was not really a baby now would rise first. The older boys liked to stay out late and would sleep half the day if their mother let them. They resented the moving from place to place, and he'd no doubt hear about it again on this trip. At seventeen and fourteen, they didn't want to change schools again. Aliki was material for a university. Rapahelo would rather flirt with the girls in town and hang out at the arcade or basketball courts. And then there were the twins, his sweet girls of seven years. He wondered if they still liked putting ribbons in their hair and climbing all over his back for horsy rides.

Manalo spotted the welcome sign for the small village and gave the roof of the truck cab a quick pound. He hung on at the rapid deceleration, then tossed out a backpack and hopped out after it himself, giving a one-handed wave to the driver. Never had he returned to the family without gifts. He collected them for months until he saw them—telling stories of the origins and his most recent adventures.

The cocks already crowed as he approached the village. On the porch of a closed-up *sari-sari* store, a dog rose up and stretched, letting out a bark when it saw him. Manalo whistled, and it came cautiously toward him until he patted its head.

"Tell me where Kalye Rondolo is, old mutt. You know the streets here, *hindi*? And what kind of watchdog are you anyway?" He hoped the dog he'd sent the family a year ago did a better job than this one.

The village could hardly be called such, with its few houses and one café grocery. His boys were unhappy with such seclusion and spent as much time as possible at school and in the larger town nearby. At least that's what they'd said on his last phone call.

Manalo turned down a narrow dirt road and dropped into a valley where a morning fog hovered in the air and the scent of wood smoke welcomed him toward home. His pace quickened.

Even after so many years together, Malaya's skin felt glorious; it mystified him how it could be so soft. And the scent at her neck, the depth of her eyes . . .

Then he saw the house down in a thicket of dark trees. He couldn't see wood smoke or any light coming from the windows. Maybe she slept in with the weariness of motherhood upon her.

He jogged now, the pack heavy on his back ready to be unloaded and the gifts distributed. His heart beat hard more from anticipation than exertion.

If his men could see him, the hardened fugitive leader of an insurgent Communist group, running toward his family, nearly giddy with anticipation, he'd never hear an end to their mockery.

Manalo came to the stairway of the porch and stopped suddenly. Instinct bred from years of warfare forewarned him. No roosters crowed the sun to rise; no dog barked. The house didn't breathe life.

He quickly evaluated any danger. His mind flashed to the corpse on the floor—the boy from Barangay Mahinahon. Could it be coincidence they were headed toward that very region? He thought of Comrade Pilo wanting to meet him at Manila Bay, and the sudden and unusual reprieve to see his family. His men were without their leader and traveling to a new region, or perhaps were still in Manila. Manalo remembered how he had once stood inside an empty house as an assigned assassin, with the photo of the man he was to kill. He'd done the job, followed his orders, not allowing himself to question who had been the human behind the glassy, empty eyes. Was someone waiting inside for him in such a way?

Within seconds, Manalo sensed he was alone here. No one waited to put a bullet in his head. He knew before he walked inside that there was no one there at all. He wandered the empty rooms, trying to gather the presence of his family. There was a kitchen, sala, CR, and three bedrooms.

Along a windowsill he found a line of army men lined up. His foot kicked something soft. He picked up a stuffed animal and breathed in the scent of a toy well loved.

They'd left quickly, and recently. The smell of Malaya's cooking lingered in the kitchen. The brick oven was cold, but not as cold as it would be if left empty for more than a day.

The ache of being that close, hours close, overwhelmed him and brought him to his knees. All he knew was the house was empty. And his family was gone.

SEVEN

P rimitive extravagance.

The hacienda house was a mixture of the primitive—Julia thought as she struggled with a small handheld pail as her "shower" in the claw-foot tub, drawing warm water from the deep clay vase at the side—and the extravagant—she looked about at the gold-leaf fixtures and intricately carved wooden doors and baseboards.

In her morning exploration she had also discovered the orchid design throughout the house in the carvings of wood and in many paintings. One of the paintings lining the stairway had a beautiful border of orchids surrounding a couple standing with the hacienda house in the background. Julia stared at the portrait, wondering who these two were in the lineage of the hacienda.

Drifts of lilting conversation with occasional bursts of laughter greeted her as she went outside to an open courtyard at the back of the house. The three sisters sat along one side of a thick wooden table.

"Miss Julia," Lola Gloria called out.

Julia tried out her new acquisition: "*Magandang umaga*," and immediately felt like a fool.

She was rewarded with surprised expressions and applause.

"In case you cannot remember, I am Lola Gloria, and my sisters are Lola Amor and Lola Sita. Aling Rosa is your head cook and our best friend—she is like another sister, though she is a little younger. She is also the wife of Mang Berto, our mechanic and the great lover of your grandfather's car collection. Did you sleep well, and find your breakfast?"

"I slept fine—a little messed up on days and nights. And I did eat. Thank you to whoever brought the breakfast and coffee. It was wonderful."

Julia had found a breakfast tray in her room after her morning "bath." Coffee with rich cream and sugar, French toast with mangoes and powdered sugar, a juice she guessed to be pineapple, fresh-cut papaya and strawberries, and a hibiscus flower in a small blue vase.

"Your breakfast and hot water were taken up by Lola Amor," Lola Gloria said and then spoke in Tagalog to the younger sister across the table.

Lola Amor smiled and nodded. "Yes, Miss Oo-lia," she said. "Welcome you."

"Lola Amor was more interested in cooking and tending the garden than doing her studies. Her English is not too good, *hindi ba ate*? English no good?"

"English no good," Lola Amor repeated as she took a puffy bite-sized pastry from a platter on the table. The cloth-covered table displayed several platters of pastries, coffee cups, bowls, and at one end, a large pile of some sort of green bean.

"My English better, no good too," said Lola Sita. "Aling Rosa very bad English. Mang Berto very good with Captain Morrison. Eat *pandesal*."

She handed Julia a small pastry.

Julia took a bite and announced to the expectant faces, "Yes, this is good. Very good."

"Please join us."

"Coffee? Tea?" Lola Amor asked.

"Oh, I left my cup upstairs. I'll get it."

"No, no, remain here. Aling Rosa will get you another," Lola Gloria said. "And did you find your surprise upstairs on the veranda steps?"

"No, I came down the inner staircase."

"Oh, there was a mango sitting there. I'll get it for you later. I think you might have an admirer." Lola Gloria smiled slyly. "But we are holding hopes for you and Markus. You are not married, no?"

"No, I'm not married," Julia said with a smile. Already the women were trying to set her up with someone. "Is this Mr. Markus Santos you are referring to?"

At his name, the other sisters giggled and whispered to one another like young girls.

"Yes, he is our beloved Mr. Markus Santos—the hacienda lawyer."

"My grandfather spoke highly of him as well. I guess they talked often on the telephone."

"We try finding that man a wonderful wife, but he is not interested in anyone we recommend."

Julia wondered if it were Markus who wasn't interested, or the "recommended" women. But the sisters seemed to think this Markus was quite a catch. They went on describing his attributes through Lola Gloria's translation and own contributions as if selling him on the spot, laughing and smiling.

"He spent many summers here as a boy; his family lived here for a time as well. We taught him how to cook! He wanted to be an astronaut; oh yes, Lola Sita reminded me of the spaceship he built with Mang Berto. Aling Rosa was so angry at them for the mess they made."

The women talked and laughed some more.

"We don't see him so much now. He's busy trying to make our nation a better country—fighting against many of the corruptions we've endured over the years. But I think he needs to slow down now and fall in love. Do you have a boyfriend in the States?" Lola Gloria asked.

Julia hadn't thought of Nathan all morning. "No, I don't," she said, and then realized her answer would only spur their match-making plans.

"A beautiful girl like you? Oh my. When Markus sees you . . ." The sisters chatted together excitedly, and Julia put her hand over her eyes.

Aling Rosa returned with a cup and poured Julia some coffee, moving the cream and sugar across the table to her.

"Do you know where Raul is?" Julia asked to distract the women. "Today I'm meeting him to talk about the financial status of the plantation . . . you know, fun things like cash flow, products, and other assets."

Lola Amor had a blank expression, while Lola Gloria and Lola Sita acted as if they understood fully. Aling Rosa reached into a sack beside the table and pulled out a handful of the beans.

"I have a list to complete during the days I'm here."

Lola Gloria patted her hand softly. "Well, leave some room to breathe, dear girl. You Americans are always so busy, but do you live any longer? Probably you live less, even if the years are longer.

And Raul is in the fields today. He will return after the noon hours."

"What does he do in the fields?"

"Not sure today. I thought they were burning some cane fields, but there is no smoke on the horizon."

"The plantation grows sugarcane?" Julia asked.

"Once sugar was our main industry. No longer, though. There are also rice fields, and you can find pineapples, mangos, bananas, papayas—many of those grow wild at the edges of the fields. None are cultivated as crops, but we use them ourselves."

"What about orchids?" Julia asked. "I've noticed the orchid design throughout the house."

Lola Gloria's expression changed, but to what, Julia wasn't sure. Her sisters noticed.

"The orchid is very important to Hacienda Esperanza."

The sisters had grown very solemn.

"It is interesting that you have noticed so quickly. Even before the time of Don Ramon Miguel, the orchid has held an important role here."

"Who was Don Ramon Miguel?"

"You do not know of him? He was your great-great-great-grandfather. Or maybe not so many greats. Maybe you know him as the One-Armed Spaniard."

Julia shook her head. "Uh, no."

"You do not know of Ramon Miguel Cancho y Guevarra?" Lola Gloria frowned.

Lola Amor chattered to her sister, and the two suddenly burst into laughter again.

Lola Gloria smiled. "My sister says that perhaps when Markus comes it will be like when Don Ramon Miguel met his Julianna. You should know of such stories as the One-Armed Spaniard. This is your very own family."

"Yes, it is my grandmother's family. But growing up in the States, there was little said of the Filipino side of my family. My mother was distant from my grandfather when he finally came home to the States."

"Yes, we remember that. We were so sorry. He loved her very much, but he couldn't leave the plantation. He felt it best for your mother to be raised where it was safer. Then President Marcos forced him out, and he couldn't return. But regardless of those things, you must hear these stories; you are in the lineage of the hacienda."

Julia's eyes moved over the back courtyard with the bubbling fountain and the vast lawn beyond and took a sip of the strong bitter coffee. Her life an extraction of all this? Her life in California mirrored nothing of the primitive *or* the extravagant. In view of all this, it was mediocre at best.

Go find yourself, Nathan had said. Julia knew what he meant. Go find the woman he admired and loved once, and be her forever. And yet Julia suddenly wondered if finding herself might not shock them both in its complexity of depth and history.

She spooned a mound of raw sugar into her coffee, then a dollop of fresh cream. She watched it swirl white into the dark liquid and, like a fortuneteller gazing at tea leaves, wished for a hint of the future to be revealed.

Lola Gloria put her hand over Julia's. "Ramon Miguel Cancho y Guevarra was the architect of this very house."

Lola Amor said something in Tagalog, and she and Lola Sita giggled together.

"My sister says that he was also a most handsome and dashing Spaniard, though in truth, I think he was not so much handsome as he was distinguished, just like our Raul."

As Lola Gloria spoke, the sisters and Aling Rosa began working with unconscious precision. Lola Gloria broke the end of a bean, then pulled the stem along the pod edge before passing the open pod to Lola Sita's reaching hand. Then Lola Sita, hands shaking with age, slid the peas into the bowl and passed the empty pods to Lola Amor, who tore them into two halves for her bowl. Aling Rosa kept Lola Gloria's bowl filled while picking out rotting beans and stones and tossing them into a separate bag. The elderly women were a well-oiled machine.

"May I help?" Julia asked.

"Of course. You can crack those casoy nuts. Get comfortable and listen to the story of your great-great-great-grandfather."

Julia sat on the bench seat across from the sisters and drew the wooden bowl of nuts closer. The small tan nuts required a hard squeeze before the crack that sent several shells flying across the table.

Lola Gloria paused a moment, sending a slow ripple of delay down the line. She had a faraway look in her deep brown eyes, and she smoothed her graying bun though no stray hairs were visible. "Do you believe in love at first sight?"

"Well, I suppose . . . maybe. Well, I don't know."

"Ramon Miguel Cancho y Guevarra would have said no, until that day. A serious man, he was, with intense, sharp eyes and a stance that was ramrod straight. That day he waited impatiently on the dock, feeling the salty breeze off Manila Bay."

"This is a true story?" Julia asked with a sudden smile at the older woman's dramatic style.

The sisters paused midpass; Lola Sita gaped at her. "She ask true? *Oo*, yes, true."

Lola Gloria nodded with vigor. "Oh yes, yes. Except for language translation, the family histories are perfect. They are told from generation to generation. My grandfather told us, and we tell those after us. So now at last you hear one of the stories you should have heard as a *nene*. There are many stories of the One-Armed

Spaniard, but this is the story of the day he met Julianna Barcelona—
the most fateful day in Ramon Miguel's life."

Julia smiled and continued cracking nuts.

"Ramon Miguel Cancho y Guevarra stood on the docks with
the salty breeze coming off Manila Bay, waiting to meet a respected
businessman and landowner who wished to do business with him.
As he waited, Ramon Miguel gazed upon the canvas sails of the
Spanish galleons that billowed out with the wind. The great ships
were docked in the harbor—not just one majestic galleon, or even
two, but six or more in port that day.

"Ramon Miguel had come from España, and surely he thought
often of his homeland, how great she was across the vastness of
the earth. Hundreds of galleons sailed the Spanish flag all across
the world's oceans. They were floating castles and symbols of his
country's vast wealth and power."

Julia was amazed at the old woman's sharp descriptions and
details.

"The year was 1750," Lola Gloria said, shifting in her seat as if
getting comfortable for the journey ahead. She leaned forward as
she worked and talked, drawing Julia into a past that was linked
with her own.

"He was a Castilian Spaniard—proud and solemn. Though he
enjoyed the view of ships from his beloved homeland, Ramon
Miguel was also impatient. He didn't like tardiness, though it was
as Spanish a tradition as the siestas and festivals. Ramon Miguel
was a military man and could never fully relax.

"He carried himself with an air of solid competence—stubborn,
oh, what a stubborn man, to a fault. He kept his black hair a
sleek shoulder-length style and maintained a well-trimmed mus-
tache and goatee—that goatee his only affectation. His signature
clothing was black military pants, high black leather boots, and
a thin white shirt that danced in the humid wind. His right

hand—his only hand—firmly grasped the silver hilt of his well-used sword.

"Ramon Miguel had been a soldier, an heir of the legacy of the conquistadors before him. Through the centuries they secured by their blood an empire overseas. A soldier since he was young, he had traveled wherever España commanded. His brave leadership in battle was legendary.

"But now the One-Armed Spaniard was a merchant of the Spanish Empire, a venture forced upon him after a battle in Morocco against his enemies the Moors. It was the battle that took his left arm. And yet, despite having to leave the military service too young, the years had not been bad to him. Having retired his military commission, Ramon Miguel focused on an overseas trading enterprise with the same relentless zeal he had exhibited as a soldier. The effort was not wasted. With partners in Spain, he had built a fortune for a man of his years—no longer young, nor yet very old—through the lucrative galleon trade that spanned the Pacific up to the Americas for silver and spices. Two of the galleons he gazed upon were his very own."

Lola Sita was muttering under her breath from time to time. Lola Gloria sighed and spoke to her with annoyance in her tone. "*Matuto ka ngang mag Ingles.*"

Then she turned back to Julia. "My sister wants to tell the story, it seems, reminding me of parts that I've already said. I told her she should have learned English . . .

"Someone called from behind him. He turned to see Don Carlos Barcelona with two women in white parasols coming behind him. Don Carlos was a man years older than himself, but he saw Ramon Miguel as an equal, if not his superior, for the success and legend of the One-Armed Spaniard's heroism upon the seas."

Lola Sita interrupted the tale with a gentle pat on her sister's arm and said something softly in Tagalog.

Lola Gloria nodded. "Lola Sita wants to be sure you understand—if a man was called *don,* it meant a man of means, a
landowner, someone of wealth. Such were Don Carlos and Don
Ramon Miguel." She resumed her storytelling voice.

"Don Carlos apologized for their lateness and explained they
had been at Mass. He introduced his wife and was pleased by the
respect Ramon Miguel showed her. And then the don introduced
his daughter.

"The Spaniard turned to a young woman near twenty years of
age, partially hidden beneath a white cotton parasol. Revealing her
face, she said, '*Señor*' in a soft voice that struck him powerfully.
Her clear brown eyes were wide and looked at him playfully.

"Ramon Miguel was stunned by her angelic features—a perfect
combination of European and Asian: heart-shaped face and a light
brown complexion with angles softened by Eastern curves. She was
a woman in full bloom, with touches of girlish innocence remaining. She was dressed for Mass, wearing a white blouse and a pink
skirt with layers at her ankles that swayed in the breeze. Ramon
Miguel couldn't take his eyes from her. At her curving hips a white
satin bandanna was tied at a triangular angle, and when Ramon
Miguel realized he was staring at her hips, even he blushed.

"Ramon Miguel felt the oddest sensation that he was falling
down deep within himself. Julianna's eyes held his with an understanding he'd only encountered in a few of his closest friends and
his long dead brother. Surely it was pure imagination, he thought
in discomfort. The young woman finally shifted her eyes to the
ground.

"Don Carlos was pleased by what he saw. He was a good man
and wished a good marriage for his beloved daughter. The Spaniard
had a reputation for being too serious and disciplined, but Don
Carlos could see immediately that his Julianna would soften
such edges and that a marriage would bring her the security he

wished—and from what he saw between them, she might even have love as well.

"Don Carlos invited the One-Armed Spaniard to eat *merienda*— a snack after lunch—and to enjoy the fiesta in honor of San Pedro with his family. Business would not be discussed that day or even the next, and when it was, it was a different kind of joint venture than either would have expected.

"As they walked along the bay heading toward the city walls of Intramuros, Ramon Miguel felt a shift in the wind, a sudden knowing that the course of his life was about to change. On this day Ramon Miguel Cancho y Guevarra, soldier of Spain, the famous One-Armed Spaniard, was finally conquered, not by war, but by his sudden love for a woman. And never in defeat had a soldier been happier."

Lola Gloria had stopped the assembly line partway through the story, though Julia hadn't noticed much beyond the vision the old woman created with her words.

"After that day, the One-Armed Spaniard became a domesticated man, at least as much as an old soldier of the Eastern seas could be. He married Julianna the next fiesta after searching the southern Batangas to find land for his hacienda. Before he would bring his bride to Hacienda Esperanza, he built the house, the first courtyard, and gardens.

"Their first child was born in Manila while the hacienda was being prepared. If not a labor of love for his wife, Ramon Miguel might have never left her side—so conquered he was by Julianna's gentle softness. He first wished to name the hacienda after his wife, but at her insistence they chose instead the name of their first child, a girl who died only months after her birth. *Esperanza* means hope."

The old woman reached over and patted Julia's hand. "Julianna and Ramon Miguel raised four other children to adulthood and lived many happy years here. The hacienda was developed, and three of the cousin lands were purchased and adopted into the grounds. It was a good time for Hacienda Esperanza—the birth and childhood of a grand estate."

Julia gazed up at the towering house where they sat in the growing afternoon shadow. "How did Ramon Miguel build such a house?"

"Ah, that is a story for another day," Lola Gloria said with a gleam in her eyes.

The palms knocked softly in the breeze, a gentle applause for the story of a man these same trees may have known. Perhaps Don Ramon Miguel Cancho y Guevarra had planted their ancient relatives and tended their growth.

There was silence among them at the end of the story as the women's hands resumed their work. The creak of Spanish galleons against their lines and the whip of the wind in their sails sounded in their ears. The love of a Spanish soldier and a young mestizo girl was now a story told by old sisters . . . yet their love was here also in the pathways behind the courtyards, the design of palms along the driveway, the corridors of the hacienda house.

"Let us make some lunch for our *doña*," Lola Gloria said.

Julia held back her smile at the idea of herself as the doña of Hacienda Esperanza.

Raul had rounded the edge of the pathway and now walked up the back courtyard steps. "You are getting a history lesson, I see."

"Yes, I've heard the story of the One-Armed Spaniard." Julia thought of Ramon Miguel with his quiet and confident air and thought he'd be a man much like Raul. Raul wore no wedding ring, so apparently he'd not yet found a woman to conquer him. Julia smiled at the thought. She'd have to ask Lola Gloria more about this man with the solemn exterior when time allowed it.

"*Maraming salamat*," he said, leaning down to kiss Lola Amor on the head as she handed him a pastry and giggled.

Lola Sita said something in Tagalog, and Lola Gloria said to Julia, "I hope it is not rude when we speak our language. Lola Sita and Lola Amor always frustrated Captain Morrison for not learning English. Especially when many of the workers in the fields spoke it better than they."

Raul had been staring distractedly into space; now he focused, as though he'd suddenly become aware of those around him. "You are comfortable here, Miss Julia?"

"Yes, thank you. Are we still meeting to talk today?"

"Yes," he said with a sigh. "I apologize for my delay. We are having some trouble near the sugarcane fields."

"Trouble?" Lola Gloria asked in alarm.

He reassured the old women and turned back to Julia. "Miss Julia, let us discuss business in the study." He walked into the house, holding the door for her to follow, then down a hallway to the study, which had been her grandfather's long ago. The room was filled with dark wood and the smell of cigar smoke. On the wall were framed maps that looked decades old—one of the Philippines and another of Hacienda Esperanza.

"I do not discuss business with the *Tres Lolas*. Until I know more of the future, I find it unnecessary to cause them worry. You saw what effect the mere mention of trouble has upon them."

"What happened?" Julia asked.

Instead of answering, Raul sat at his desk and pinched his eyebrows in thought. "Julia, this is a delicate business, as you say. For many years Captain Morrison hoped to return to the hacienda. There is much at stake, more than I can easily explain. It is more than this house or your family or even the entire hacienda. There is trouble from beyond our borders . . . political struggles and dangers that we are tangled in."

Raul sighed as the weight of many words and thoughts burdened him. "We had a worker injured in the fields this morning, and I must check on his condition at the hospital. Could we delay the tour of the hacienda until tomorrow?"

"Yes, of course." Julia realized how much the lives of people she had seen upon arriving depended upon the hacienda. It was more than their jobs; it was their entire world, even their heritage and future. Raul might be the only one who realized how unsettled the future was for all of them. Julia sensed that there was even more at stake than the people and the land knew.

And how much of the outcome would depend upon her—a girl from California who some called the doña of Hacienda Esperanza?

AMANG TENIO WANTED TO SEE HIM.

Emman was given the word by his cousin Abner, who kicked at him in his hammock and said only babies slept this late into the day. Emman didn't tell him that he'd only just come in an hour ago from the plantation. This was his siesta, while Abner still poured his morning coffee.

Why did Amang Tenio want to see him?

The revered leader of Barangay Mahinahon had never requested such a thing before. All the people called him "*amang*" or "great father" out of respect more than relationship. Emman couldn't recall one being individually summoned before.

He dressed quickly, then tossed his shirt into the corner of the dirt floor and went looking for something clean. Dangling from a hook in his closet was the shirt he'd worn to his mother's funeral. The sleeves were three inches too short, but he buttoned it up anyway.

The noonday sun warmed the mountain chill and promised a day of sticky humidity. Emman paced the dirt street instead of turning up the road that would lead outside the village and directly up the hill to Amang Tenio's house. He'd been on the grounds many times with the other children, doing training exercises, gathering on the porch above the vast view to hear stories or receive occasional treats.

Now his feet threatened to take him the opposite direction. He hadn't done anything wrong . . . well, not lately, or at least nothing out of the ordinary. Finally curiosity and obedience stopped his procrastination, and Emman headed up the hill.

One of Emman's third cousins worked as part of the house staff and directed him to the back porch, an expression of disapproval on her face. What had he done? Unless this was delayed punishment for his short trip to the police station after he got caught sneaking into the cinema. Emman should have guessed that nothing could escape the knowledge of Amang Tenio.

Beneath the nipa covering, the warlord smoked a pipe in his chair, his gaze turned toward the vast open view of the rolling hills and the wide blue crater of Lake Taal.

Emman shifted by the doorway, and his feet made a creak in the wooden floorboards.

"Come closer, *nonoy*. Come, come." Amang Tenio didn't look his way, only beckoned with one hand. "Is it not a magnificent sight? I never tire of it."

Dark clouds came from the western mountains beyond and over the small peak in the center of the lake. Called the smallest volcano in the world, Taal was actually a small peak within the larger crater. Scientists and villagers alike watched it lately, wondering if it would wake from its slumber as Mount Pinatubo was doing north of Manila.

"Yes." He'd never been actually afraid of Amang Tenio until this moment. He noticed his famous rooster sitting in a chair on the leader's other side, as if the two had been conversing as they took in the view.

"Sit down here. Let us talk. Would you like a Coca-Cola?"

"*Hindi po*," Emman said, shaking his head, though his dry mouth longed for what he'd just declined.

Amang Tenio waved two fingers in the air, and a housemaid quickly appeared with two Coca-Colas. "I can drink them both myself. You must say what you want in this life, or you get very little and miss out on much."

Emman smiled. "I would like one, *maraming salamat*."

"Very good. Now, Emman, you have been training beyond the regular disciplines."

"Yes." The cool liquid slid down his throat. He didn't get his own can of cola often. He and the other children bought narrow plastic bags of Coke or Kool-Aid with long straws. Emman would slurp it up faster than he liked, sometimes sucking up part of the bag and clogging the enjoyment. But his own aluminum can . . . this was a treat.

"Emman, I must discuss something important. It is with regret that you cannot be a child as children should be. None in the Barangay Mahinahon can. As a young man, this did not bother me. As an old man, it is one of my greatest regrets. We are many good things here in our village, but sadly, we are a village of lost childhoods."

Emman wanted to say that he didn't care about lost childhoods; he wanted to be a man. But Amang Tenio continued talking.

"One of our young men is missing."

"One of the men of the Barangay?" Emman tried to think of anyone he hadn't seen lately.

"Artur Tenio."

Artur was the boyfriend of Bok's sister. "I just saw him a few days ago."

"Yes. He was to drive Raul to Manila to pick up the American woman. But the car had trouble, and Raul went ahead while Artur stayed behind to fix it. No one has seen him since then. The car was found, but not Artur."

"What could have happened?"

"We are trying to find this out. And we will." The old man paused then, staring out at the view as if collecting wisdom and guidance from the sky. "There are things you do not understand yet."

"I know that." Emman shifted in his seat. "Like what?"

Amang Tenio grinned, and Emman saw his yellowed teeth and a sparkle in his dark eyes. "I might envy such youth if not for the struggle of life that all men have in their days upon this earth. That struggle for me is mostly over now."

Emman had no response to that, so he took a drink of his cola.

"I need you to watch the American woman. There are many dangers for her. I know that already you have taken this role to protect her."

Emman didn't know whether to stand proud or be embarrassed. "Yes, Amang. I felt she might need to be guarded."

"Very wise of you. Please select some others to help you in the task. I will be kept informed, and the hacienda as a whole will be under constant surveillance. But I'm giving you the direct protection of the American woman. It is children who can best do such things in these strange times."

Emman winced.

"I meant children as the *others* whom you choose, Emman. I wouldn't put you to such a responsibility if I considered you a child. You are twelve years old, nearly thirteen. Shake my hand. You are a man now, Emman."

Emman squeezed as hard as he could to prove that he was worthy.

"There is something more."

"What is it, Tito?"

"Don't ever sneak into a cinema again. Ask me if you want to see a movie that badly. Perhaps I will go with you." There was a slight smile in the stern expression.

Emman didn't smile until Amang Tenio gazed back at the view. "Yes, Tito."

"WHERE ARE THEY?" MANALO STOOD AT THE DOOR.

"Come inside, my brother." Comrade Pilo opened the door wider, glancing out onto the dark and empty street.

Manalo remained just as he had when the housekeeper had urged him in before she went to find her master. "You are not my brother. My brother is dead for this great cause. I held his head and felt his brains through my fingers." The words seethed through his teeth, and he shook from anger and fear.

"Calm down, Ka Manalo," Comrade Pilo said, putting a hand of warning in the air. "Do not forget your place. Come inside."

Manalo hesitated, then entered the house. The floor was of expensive tile, and a chandelier lit the entryway. He followed the older man into a small study with furnishings of the finest woods. Manalo and his men were nomads of the jungle so that the privileged Communists could live like this? Comrade Pilo didn't understand how little he cared for place and position right now. "Where is my family?" he asked again.

Ever the politician, Comrade Pilo motioned him to sit and ordered the housekeeper to make some iced tea.

Manalo struggled to restrain himself.

"I greatly apologize, brother. It was unavoidable. During the hours of your journey we had reason to believe your family's location had been compromised. They were moved in the night. We feared someone would hear the message if we radioed your transport, so nothing could be done. You were gone before we could get someone out there."

"No one came," Manalo said.

For over twenty years he had trusted men like Comrade Pilo

without question. But everything was changing. Within the Communists, new groups were going off on their own. The Red Bolos had pulled off from the larger Communist Party of the Philippines, and for a time Manalo had thought that the best route. But lack of organization and miscommunications were becoming alarmingly common. It was hard to know whom to trust.

"My report said they brought a truck in for you at 0900 hours. But you weren't at the house, nor at the closest safe house."

"The closest safe house I knew about took me two days to reach." He stood up in anger. "I watched for a day at the house. No one came."

The housekeeper walked in with a tray of snacks and iced tea. Comrade Pilo took his time preparing his tea with scoops of raw sugar while Manalo stared at him.

"I don't like discussing business with someone staring down at me. Now sit down, and enjoy a drink and something to eat."

Manalo chose to obey, suppressing the urge to shove the tea glass into Comrade Pilo's face. Comrade Pilo was a politician, not a soldier. And certainly not a guerrilla fighter.

"Manalo, we are a proud lot. Close men who are bonded by our beliefs like a brotherhood. You see the inner working here in the Philippines. But much is beyond here, on an international basis. There are Communists in Korea, in China, in Russia, and in Eastern Europe. It is not the same there as here. And we have seen great disorder in the various factions. Sometimes I think we hold such little semblance to each other that we should not all be called Communists at all. But at the core, most of us want one thing— our people to work together for the common good."

Manalo slammed down his hand, spilling tea from his own untouched glass. "I don't care about these things."

The expression on Comrade Pilo's face shifted from calm teacher to angry dictator. And still Manalo didn't care.

"Where is my family?"

"Do you want me to tell you?"

The reminder that Comrade Pilo held their well being firmly in his hand shook him back down, though he did all to keep from showing it.

"If you want to know, then you must also care about these things. Your life and the lives of Malaya and your children are not your own. We all belong to something greater than ourselves. Our individual lives matter little. Do not forget that."

EIGHT

From his place in the tree Emman dropped the yo-yo, let it "sleep," then flicked his wrist to bring it back. He had a long string, and it zinged far down through the branches without touching. Even in the tree he could do Loop the Loop, Hop the Fence (or rather Hop the Branch), Over the Shoulder, Walk the Dog, and Around the World. Reverse Loop the Loop he was still unable to master—which annoyed him to no end.

His mother had started his hobby, or maybe it was his father, or maybe it was just because he was Filipino. Some said the pastime came from the Chinese, others the Greeks. Others told of primitive Filipinos who sat in trees as he did and used a heavy rock on a string that "rolled up" as a weapon against enemies and as a hunting tool for food. Emman liked to think of that while yo-yoing in his tree.

His mother said his father had used his yo-yo to entertain his friends and impress the girls of the Barangay. His father died before Emman's birth, when he was hired as a bodyguard to some diplomat from China. His box of yo-yos was saved for the son who came a month later.

Ever the soldier in training, Emman had devised a tactical signaling system he called "yo-yo code." When he and his friends were younger, it had been great fun to use it in their games. Although Emman thought military communication by "yo-yo code" was rather ingenious, he knew the men would either laugh or scold at such antics. Now that he was a soldier, with a real gun given to him by Amang Tenio, Emman would try weaning himself from yo-yoing as his mother had once tried to stop smoking.

But not tonight. He'd be alone till after dawn and could practice his yo-yo and smoke cigarette butts to keep him awake. Then he'd get to see Miss Julia on her morning walk before he went home to sleep till noon.

Emman had seen a light in her window for some time now. He wondered what she was doing. Did she brush her hair in long, slow strokes? Was there a television in the house, and if so, what did she like to watch? What kinds of things had she brought from America?

He grew uncomfortable and restless in the tree. He dropped the yo-yo again and again, practicing his tricks until a calm returned to him. Then, as if a breeze that wasn't there had shifted directions, Emman knew he was no longer alone. He eyed his rifle held on other branches within a swift and practiced reach.

A man came through the forest with little stealth; he was not trying to hide himself. His steps were confident, perhaps annoyed. Emman would've thought him a boy except for a harsh curse spoken beneath the man's breath before he actually came within view. He was following a path that would bring him near to Emman's tree.

The man drew closer, then stood at the jungle edge staring for a long while—a very long while, so long that Emman thought that an hour had surely passed, and still he remained.

Emman kept his gun within his peripheral vision, his sight ever on the stranger staring toward where Miss Julia slept, and his yo-yo in his hand. After a time, the man simply walked away in the same way that he came, leaving Emman with the greater knowledge that Miss Julia needed his protection. He must guard her well.

LIGHT AND COLOR.

Footsteps up the wrought-iron steps of the veranda interrupted the vast peace of the morning, filled with light and color. Julia sat drying her hair in the sunshine and gazing across the immeasurable hues and variants of the hacienda grounds.

"Well, you look lovely this morning," Lola Gloria said as she reached the top.

The morning was lazy and calm in a way Julia hadn't experienced since childhood at Harper's Bay or during the few days she and Nathan had spent at the lakeside Gasthof Simony in the Austrian Alps.

When sleep had again evaded her in the night, Julia had made a list of her most pressing concerns, writing her notes and ideas in the last of Grandpa Morrison's logbooks.

Hacienda Concerns:
—Meet with Mr. Santos about Hacienda legal matters. Do I actually decide the future of the Hacienda? Could the land be sold to the people who live here?
—What happened in the fields yesterday? Ask Raul.
—What preparations are needed for Grandpa Morrison's wake and funeral?

—What is the "secret of the orchid"? Grandfather's musings or something real?

But sitting on the second-story veranda after her "shower" with the pail in the bathtub, the questions and concerns encompassing the night simply fell away. The hacienda had such enchanting powers.

Lola Gloria bent down by the stairway. "Look, once again, a gift from your admirer. A mango." Lola Gloria picked up the fruit and brought it toward her.

A teenaged Filipina girl who helped in the kitchen followed the older woman with a wide tray. She set it on the glass-and-iron table, smiled at Julia, and disappeared soundlessly down the stairs.

"That's a mango?" Julia asked, taking the soft yellow fruit from Lola Gloria. "The ones at home are usually green and reddish and much rounder." Around the mango was a crocheted yarn necklace with beads woven within it. "Are you sure this is for me?"

The old woman chuckled. "Of course it is for you."

Julia gazed out across the long stretching lawn, looking for a gift giver to appear. The hacienda gleamed in brighter hues than the night before. Vibrant reflections of colors—greens from the lawns and encircling jungle; reds, pinks, and yellows from the flowers; blues from the sky.

"You like our humble home?" Lola Gloria said with a proud smile.

"It is . . . breathtaking."

Julia put the necklace over her head.

"There were two ways to eat a mango," Lola Gloria said. The constant twinkle in her eye spoke of a mischievous spirit. "The civilized way and the messy way."

"It feels like an uncivilized morning to me."

"Let me show you then."

Lola Gloria selected a mango from the tray and set it on her plate. "Civilized" required peeling with a paring knife and cutting the mango into long connected cuts until it reminded Julia of a blooming yellow flower.

"And now, the fun way. Just put your fingers through the peeling at the top and start pulling it away." Lola Gloria gestured for her to use the mango gift.

Julia peeled off the skin, and juice immediately dripped over her fingers.

"Peel it away and just eat it."

At the first bite, Julia's chin was dripping; she and Lola Gloria laughed as Julia leaned forward and drips fell over the tile floor. The sweet flavor languished in Julia's mouth and filled her senses. Soon her hands, mouth, and face were covered with the sweet juice as she scraped the long white seed with her teeth.

"It's delicious," Julia said, embarrassed, and yet not embarrassed enough to stop. She found a linen napkin and shared it with the older woman, who was eating a mango of her own the "uncivilized way."

Across the lawn, a curious sight caught Julia's eye. Five small boys were sitting in the arms of a huge tamarind tree. They were laughing and pointing at Julia and Lola Gloria.

"Ah, the boys are pleased that, at least in eating a mango, we are as barbaric as they are," Lola Gloria said, dabbing her fingers with a napkin.

Julia noticed that on their shoulders the children carried what appeared to be oversized rifles—she hoped they were sculpted from wood. They dwarfed the small bodies that bore them. The vision was such an oddity that it was almost comical. She went to the veranda railing for a better look.

"Those aren't real guns, right?" The rifles looked very real, resembling stocky World War II rifles from old war movies.

Lola Gloria poured some water over their hands and found several more linen napkins for them to clean up. "No, they are wooden. The boys of the Barangay Mahinahon train with wooden guns until their coming of age. Then they get a real gun and begin their service."

"What service is that?"

"Oh, all that will be better explained by Raul."

One of the boys, a round, healthy-looking one wearing a red shirt, waved at her. They all stood in the branches or clung at odd angles on the tree.

"Hi, good morning!" shouted a boy in a striped shirt.

Julia waved back and shouted, "Good morning," after which the children just stared at her, smiling expectantly, making her uncomfortably embarrassed.

I can't very well carry on a shouting conversation from way up here, she thought. She excused herself by calling down, "'Bye."

The boys waved with their guns on their shoulders and shouted, "Good-bye!"

The rest of her breakfast consisted of eggs sunny-side up, bacon, and rice. Julia was surprised by how much she enjoyed the white rice with the eggs, and was nearly finished when the sound of a vehicle approached the hacienda.

"That will be Markus." Lola Gloria clapped her hands and smiled widely. "I can't wait for him to meet you."

"He's this early?" Julia hadn't expected the lawyer to arrive for several more hours. "What happened to Filipino time?"

"Markus is unfortunately a little too like you Americans. That boy is always on time or early, and he does not relax half of what he should. Come downstairs and let's greet him."

As she rose to follow Lola Gloria back to the railing, Julia noticed drips of mango on her yellow-and-white sundress.

They leaned over the balcony and saw the top of Markus's shiny black hair. He'd stopped on the pathway, and several of the boys came running across the lawn with giant smiles at the sight of him.

An older boy whom Julia had seen earlier stepped out of the jungle and stared in their direction. He wasn't much older than the others, but his demeanor made him seem more mature. Ah, she remembered that one. He'd been with the strange old man with the rooster when she'd first arrived.

Julia's attention returned to Markus, who was handing something to the kids. He then called a greeting to the older boy. The younger boys ran with their hands cupping what appeared to be candy. Once they reached the older boy, they all turned and disappeared into the jungle.

"We're up here," Lola Gloria called down to Markus.

His quick footsteps up the veranda stairs brought a surprising tremor through Julia's fingers and the coffee cup she held. And then he was there, smiling and exuding a carefree strength she hadn't expected from the hacienda lawyer—a relaxed sort of confidence.

"*Magandang umaga,*" he said, kissing Lola Gloria on the cheek. Then he raised his head and paused long, apparently assessing her. A quizzical expression came over his face.

He was certainly good-looking—she'd give Lola Gloria that—with his smooth brown skin and deep brown eyes.

"What?" she finally asked, when he continued to stare.

"I apologize. Standing there, you appear very much at home for a woman in a foreign land. I did not expect this."

Julia felt both uncomfortable and pleased by his encompassing gaze. "What makes it surprising—because I'm an American or a woman or both?"

"Certainly both." A smile played over his lips as he spoke. "An American woman at the hacienda is most unusual—you might be the first, in fact. For a second there, I was sure you were the true doña of Hacienda Esperanza."

Seeing Lola Gloria watch them with such obvious delight, Julia grew more serious. She stretched out a hand and said, "I'm Julia Bentley. I assume you are the hacienda attorney, Markus Santos."

He opened his hands and glanced down at his khaki slacks and black polo shirt. "So even though I dressed casually, I have *lawyer* written all over me?"

"Well, you don't fit the look of anyone else at the hacienda. And Lola Gloria did say, 'That will be Markus.'"

"Lola Gloria, you are always giving me away."

The older woman laughed.

"Yes, I am Markus. At your service, Julianna. Or is it Julia?" He bowed, disregarding the proper "Miss Julia" that most everyone used with her. Yet it wasn't arrogance that Julia sensed in him; rather, a strange and even comfortable familiarity.

"Julia is fine," she said, though she liked the way he'd said Julianna.

"Would you like something to drink?" Lola Gloria offered.

"Does Lola Sita still make *buko-pandan*?"

"Of course, though you just missed my sisters. They have gone to the village."

"Mahjong?" he said.

"Yes, my sisters are addicted. But I will go down and get you buko-pandan—I am not so inept in the kitchen as that." Lola Gloria smiled at Julia as she descended the stairs and left them alone.

Markus walked to the railing of the veranda. "It has been a while since I've been to Esperanza. The beauty never fails to surprise me. I live in a world of concrete and exhaust pipes most of the time." His eyes swept the yard toward the western orchid fields and remained there a few moments.

Julia came up beside him. "The orchid fields could be beautiful again," she said.

"Yes. With some attention, they would flourish quickly. But the hacienda requires so much work already that Raul is unable to attend to them as well."

Julia wanted to say more about the orchids, but the way Markus watched her as she gazed over the lands distracted her.

"Do you always stare so much, Mr. Markus Santos?" she said with humor to alleviate her growing discomfort. He had the kind of eyes that appeared to read everything about her.

"I apologize, and will apologize in advance for future staring. But no, I don't always stare so much. I'm not accustomed to beautiful women with fair skin, light hair, and blue eyes. It is very rare to see eyes of blue in the Philippines. Anyway," he said, suddenly looking uncomfortable himself. "Yes, I do apologize—I'm a professional . . . usually. We will discuss the legalities of the hacienda soon. First, I have one bit of unexpected news, I am sorry to inform you."

"What is it?"

He paused, and she detected that playful smile even as he spoke solemnly. "Unfortunately, your grandfather's body took a little detour in returning to the hacienda."

"What does that mean?"

"They shipped him to Thailand by mistake." Markus chuckled. "I do hope he isn't late for his wake and funeral."

Julia's mouth dropped. "Uh, you are taking this rather lightly, especially for my lawyer."

"Yes, I know. But I have heard stories of your grandfather my entire life, and these past years he and I have spoken on the phone many times. So to hear that even now the great Captain Morrison causes a stir, coming late for his own funeral . . . I must admit, I find it funny."

Julia couldn't help but laugh with him; then she shook her head. "You're right. Grandpa Morrison was always late. Guess nothing has changed."

"Don't be too concerned. We will work hard to get him here. His wake and funeral will be quite an event."

"You know, I think the hacienda is more a part of you than me."

Markus thought for a moment. "I disagree. We don't always realize what is ours until finally we find it." Then he smiled again and quickly added, "Those wise words won't cost you my usual lawyer fee."

"I appreciate that," Julia said, as they turned again to lean on the railing and gaze out over the hacienda. Through the trees, they could see miles and miles of farmland stretching out toward the distant slope of hills and a sharply protruding mountain.

"You know, this land holds a long and complex history."

"I'm discovering that." Julia turned slightly as Markus spoke.

"After World War II, under your grandparents' direction, the hacienda was rebuilt from its near destruction by the Japanese occupation. Sugarcane, milling, and coconut farming alone brought wealth and political influence to the hacienda, not counting the diverse aquatic and agricultural endeavors the families were involved in." He paused. "Did you know the hacienda clan was united under Don Miguel and Captain Morrison?"

"The One-Armed Spaniard? I thought he lived in the eighteenth century!"

"Oh, you've heard that story already. But no, not that Don Miguel. Your grandmother's brother was also Don Miguel. After the war, your grandfather remained here to rebuild a nearly destroyed country. I think your grandmother was part of the reason as well."

"I know very little of that time in my grandfather's life," she said.

"Julia, he was a great man, and that became a golden time. The annual fiesta here was a provincial event. The workers were happy and well fed, and their children were going to school. The plunder of the Japanese was a nightmare of the past as the workers and their families thrived and grew happy and content."

Julia pictured this very house and the courtyard as it must have been. The stucco sides of the house and walled courtyards clean and vibrant instead of faded and in disrepair. The overgrown gardens neatly trimmed; the tables laden with expensive china and silver utensils. The fiestas full of celebration and food. Dancing and laughter, lives not just soothed but restored. It all came to life in her imagination.

"Julia, the people of Hacienda Esperanza are some of the best in the world. For four years, my family lived in one of the staff houses when it was dangerous for my father to live in Manila. You will find every kind of drama played out here, some of them quite comical at times. Have you met everyone?"

"Well, if the welcoming committee is everyone, then sort of."

"I will enjoy giving insight into the backgrounds of your relatives. One of the aunties is always trying to lose weight and says a blood disease will not let her. Mang Berto will keep you trapped in his garage for an entire day showing you his vehicles. And Amang Tenio, the leader of Barangay Mahinahon . . . well, we will introduce you as slowly as possible, so as not to overwhelm."

He turned, and the brush of his arm sent a shiver throughout her. Why did she feel such an attraction to this man? It was his knowledge of the hacienda and its people, Julia assured herself, that she found so captivating. She determined to keep up her guard, keep this friendly and professional, and then say good-bye with no regrets after her grandfather's funeral. After all, what would be the point of an attraction to a man who lived nearly around the world?

"Are you okay, Julia?" Markus asked with concern.

"Why?"

"You appear at war in your mind."

"Just thinking about all of this."

"Yes, this land is enchanting. But hard to comprehend as well."

Surely it was the exotic locale. Although Markus did have a certain charisma. People were probably always drawn to him, and she could only imagine his presence in a courtroom. But not to be married at his age—about thirty-five, was her guess—he was probably a man with many issues.

Julia noticed movement in the jungle and pointed to a few more children coming shyly toward the house. They pushed one another onward to be in front. "Is that a girl with them?"

"Yes, and I think she's found a mentor in you. Most girls from the Barangay Mahinahon would never wear a ponytail unless they were more of the girly sort. She's with the boys, which means she's one tough little lady. So I wager she's acting more like a girl for you to notice her."

The little girl had used a twig or some part of a plant as the rubber band—it was hard to tell from that distance. It kept falling out and she'd stop to tie it again.

"Do these children live on the hacienda?"

"Not exactly. They are the children of Barangay Mahinahon— *Barangay* means village. It's located some kilometers from here, but very much part of Hacienda Esperanza. There is much to explain to you, Julia."

Julia felt impatient. Why did everyone keep saying that? She wanted to say, "So tell me!," but Markus excused himself, saying, "I'll be right back."

He hurried down the stairs and greeted the children partway across the lawn. Once again the younger children surrounded him and tugged at his arm. He slipped something into their hands, and they smiled and ran off again.

The older, more serious boy had come as well and talked with Markus a little longer. Then he turned toward the jungle too. The gun on his shoulder appeared alarmingly real.

The girl waved up at Julia then, took something from Markus, and raced off.

When Markus returned he was holding an odd-looking drink. "Lola Gloria spotted me downstairs and said she'd make you some if you like it." He took a sip and declared it perfect, then offered a sip to Julia.

"No, thanks."

"Come on, I don't have too many germs."

"I don't know that."

"You must try the native cuisines."

"You're one pushy lawyer, mister," Julia said, taking the glass.

"I'm glad you recognize that early on."

"It is . . . good. I think. Sort of sweet, but sort of not."

"Give it time. Buko-pandan is a concoction of pasteurized coconut juice mixed with milk and pandan leaves. You'll get used to it, and then hooked."

"I would've liked that information before trying it," Julia said, sticking out her tongue. "So okay, what are you giving the children down there?"

"It's a secret."

"Not much of one. At least, all of the children are apparently in on it. So if I tug at your sleeve or follow at your heels, you'll tell me?"

"You are quick for an American woman."

"Excuse me?" Julia crossed her arms in protest.

He held up his hands with a devilish smile. "Kidding, kidding. Actually, children usually don't like me, so I bribe them with candies I get in Manila. Then I also look good to the ladies. What woman can resist a guy who's always surrounded by a flock of adoring children?"

"Oh, and this works for you, does it?"

"I don't know. I guess I should be asking you that."

"What do these other women say?"

"Oh, hmm . . . well, actually, no others have seen me at the hacienda. So, how's it working on you?"

They both laughed, and then grew silent. But to Julia's surprise, the silence was of a most comfortable sort. It even bordered on peaceful.

NINE

"You were like this when Ricky died." Timeteo sat in the chair beside him. The table and chairs stood in the shadow of a tree on the edge of a meadow.

Manalo had his eyes on the map, but he saw nothing. He raised his head slowly on hearing his brother's name. "I was like what?"

"Quiet. Withdrawn."

Manalo nodded. "Yes, I suppose I was. And am."

"You will see them again. I think Comrade Pilo even now arranges it. It would be to cruel to give you leave to see your family and then keep you from them for a long while."

"It's not just that." Manalo's eyes focused on the map of the great island of Luzon. His country was made of many islands and provinces within those islands. Here, on a single map, all he held dear was located. He could point to the place that he was, and the place she was supposed to be. Somewhere within the borders of land and sea, Malaya and his children were thinking, sleeping . . . living a life without him.

"What else troubles you?"

Manalo rubbed his forehead where a pounding had formed. "The incompetence. It will be our downfall. If the factions would gather, if we would follow our leaders, we would rise strong. What is it about our people that makes us so lazy and inept? Don't they see what is best for them? The Communists were once much more unified. But just when I start thinking we are getting it together, another incompetent act occurs."

Timeteo looked at his hands. "They didn't follow the instructions. The body was not returned to the village."

Manalo nodded, but his anger toward Comrade Pilo rose up unbidden. "It is as I should now expect."

"So it seems. The body will never be found. The boy's mother will always hold an ounce of wonder, but those of the Barangay will know."

"The boy deserved to be buried in a proper manner. It is a bad omen." Manalo spoke without thinking and was surprised when Timeteo nodded his head and agreed.

"A very bad omen."

So his old friend couldn't rid himself of his childhood either, eh?

"Timeteo, why are you here?"

He frowned. "They brought us here?"

"No, I mean, why did you first join?"

Timeteo leaned back and pulled out a cigarette, handing one to Manalo. "Your brother did this for glory and adventure. And later because of a hatred he could not rid himself of except in the few moments of battle. You came to this because you believed it and wanted a country that was better than it had ever been. A strong Philippines."

Manalo lit his cigarette and inhaled slowly, remembering the idealistic young man he'd once been. "And yet, no matter the motive, my brother and I have accomplished the same. Nothing."

"I came to this," Timeteo said, ignoring him, "because I could not live without my two best friends. And I did not want to be a poor farmer with a hungry family, like my father before me. I guess we all have fought for a better life. A country where the average man is not in constant peril of becoming a beggar or under the rule of whatever leader rises up. And for more than twenty years now, we have been these men. We lost Ricky and many other good men. What more do you wish me to say about it?"

"The truth."

Timeteo chuckled, and a whiff of smoke blew around him. "I think the truth you want me to say is that we've fought for nothing. That Marcos can be thrown down, but our country is as bad off as ever and our cause nearly as lost as when we first began. And that no wonder some men put guns in their mouths."

Manalo was silent.

"Those are truths. I have many regrets. Some things I *more* than regret . . . I do not know how to forgive myself for them. But there are things to be grateful for as well. To serve with your brother, and even more so with you . . . I have had decades of a strong and loyal brotherhood that few men experience. And that is something to be grateful for."

They finished their cigarettes in silence. Timeteo pulled out a flask from inside his jacket pocket and offered it to Manalo, who took a swig and passed it back.

"Manalo."

The grave tone in Timeteo's voice sent a chill through him. "What?"

His friend was silent for a moment, and then said quickly, "I believe in God."

Manalo stared at Timeteo, who stared back as if waiting for a discipline. Then he laughed until he nearly fell from the chair.

"What? Why are you laughing?" his old friend asked with dismay.

"You believe in God. You?"

"In some ways, I always have. But now more than ever. As in, I *believe*."

The emphasis on *believe* made Manalo laugh harder.

Emil, who had wrung the necks of several chickens and was now plucking them, stopped in his work to smile their direction. Manalo realized they must be careful, even among their ranks, about confessing such a thing.

"They asked me to spy on you," Manalo told him.

Timeteo nodded. "They asked me to spy on you. And Paco told me they asked him to spy on us both."

Manalo chuckled again. "Too many years have passed since Comrade Pilo lived in the field. He forgets what is forged between men."

"Yes. He loves to tell his battle stories, but at times I wonder if he spent more than a year out—have you noticed he tells the same three stories again and again?"

Manalo nodded but grew serious. "It troubles me. Not that we fear spying from within, except perhaps from Emil. But that they do not trust some of the most loyal men in the party. What kind of dissension is beyond our viewing, if it's come to this?"

He sighed and wondered again about his family. "I just want it to be over."

ANXIETY AND WORRY.

Those were the emotions that filled Raul's face, even more than the day before. Julia and Markus had gone to the office to discuss hacienda business and found Raul sitting at the desk with eye-brows squeezed together. Markus greeted him enthusiastically, then drew back at the cool response. "What's wrong?"

Raul opened his mouth to speak, then stopped as his eyes moved to Julia.

"Go ahead and talk, and I'll go do . . . something," she said and quickly retreated. She wasn't out the door before the men had begun speaking in Tagalog, their tones intense.

Julia went outside, into the inner courtyard. She heard the sound of a car engine being revved loudly and followed her ears to a covered garage the size of a small warehouse. The smell of oil and machinery permeated the doorway. Stepping inside, she saw four perfect rows of neatly aligned automobiles—all beautifully restored vintage cars. Their hoods and chromed sections were polished and gleamed in the morning light even as they appeared aged and faded.

Julia walked among them, stunned by the collection, their worth, and the care with which they'd been kept. She finally arrived at the source of all the ruckus: a white convertible. Two feet stuck out from beneath its chassis.

At the sound of her approach, the owner of the feet slid out from beneath the car and jumped up to reach inside the open hood and shut off the engine. His face was smudged with oil, and the old Filipino had quite a look of surprise behind his thick black-rimmed glasses. His dirty white shirt was riddled with holes; he wiped his hands on oil-stained denim pants.

"Hi," Julia said, feeling like a trespasser. "I'm sorry to intrude. I heard the engine and got caught up exploring. Oh. Do you speak English?"

"Yes, yes, indeed. I'm sorry for being caught off guard. It's won-derful pleasure you came. Welcome, Miss Julia." His eyes twinkled with welcome.

Julia recalled having seen this man among the greeters of the first day. He was shorter than Julia, and his hair was brushed back with a thick gel. His quirky smile lit his entire weathered face, and Julia loved him at once.

"I'm Mang Berto." He offered his hand, only to retrieve it instantly and wipe his hands again on his denim pants. "I'm sorry. These are my work clothes."

"How can one be clean working with oil and engines?" She extended her hand and took the old man's semiclean one in greeting.

Mang Berto placed his other hand over hers. There was kindness beneath his rough appearance. He smiled continuously, looked at her deeply as if welcoming home a long-lost daughter.

"You looked hard at work down there. I'm sorry for disturbing you."

He spread his right arm wide, motioning to the whole garage. "This is the house garage, and it's never work for me."

"Whose are all these cars?"

"Well . . . I guess they are yours. They belonged to your grandfather, the Captain. He inherited the first of his collection from Don Miguel, who inherited his first cars from his uncle Don Mateo."

Julia looked at the dozens of cars in stunned silence. One of the few things her grandfather had passed down to her was a knowledge of classic automobiles. And from her initial estimate, this was a stunning and expansive collection.

"The Captain was very proud of his cars," Mang Berto said wistfully. "We traveled all over from the auto shops in Manila to junk shops in the provinces looking for parts to rebuild these old beauties. I had hoped he'd return to see how I've cared for them."

Mang Berto pointed to a Chevy Bel Air. "That one was my pride and joy. I say *was* because this is the car that was supposed to fetch you from Manila. Midway on the road it broke down, and I had to get it hauled back to the hacienda." He paused a moment with a frown on his face, then opened the driver's side door for her.

"This was your grandfather's first car of his own purchase. He bought it secondhand from one of the hacienda's business contacts. Not many of these still exist intact, not to mention run at all. Its parts are rare and very difficult to get here in the Philippines, and very expensive—though I ask Raul to buy them anyway." He chuckled. "Why don't you help me see if this baby is up and running?"

Julia climbed inside. The interior had a few cracks in the vinyl, but it was spotless and obviously well cared for. She turned the key that dangled from the ignition, and the engine rumbled to life.

Mang Berto gave the hood a proud and loving pat; then he wiped away his fingerprints. He leaned through the open passenger window. "If only she'd been this reliable a few days ago, you would have arrived in style. Oh my. Raul was so embarrassed that the granddaughter of Captain Morrison arrived by tricycle!" He bellowed in laughter so hard it made Julia laugh with him.

"It was a great experience," she assured him. "I loved it."

"Oh, but it was such a dishonor to us. I felt terrible myself. But it was so funny how upset Raul was over it, and then you arrive and are so gracious. Come now, let me introduce you to the rest of the family."

Shutting off the engine, Julia followed Mang Berto as he led her from one car to the next, up and down the rows of automobiles, nearly thirty of them in all.

"Captain Morrison bought this one for your grandmother's birthday," Mang Berto explained, pointing to a shiny ruby red car. "It was quite the grand surprise. All the people of the hacienda, including the people from Barangay Mahinahon, were there for the unveiling. I shined that car up nice and sweet for your grandmother. Even though she did not share the Captain's passion, this car she definitely loved. She refused to drive any other."

"It's a 1950 Thunderbird, right?"

"Why, yes." Mang Berto took a step back and gazed at her.

"Don't look so surprised. I am the granddaughter of Captain Morrison."

"You are indeed."

"And this one is a Fleetline?" Julia pointed to the dark green car next to the Thunderbird. It had a roofline that swooped back like a helmet, and its hood was high and rounded. "My grandfather had a small model of this on his desk in the States."

"A Chevrolet Fleetline—it's 1950 as well. This was your grandfather's very favorite. We drove it only on great occasions. The annual fiesta and, ah, I recall for the wedding of Sita and Felix as they left for their honeymoon. The sisters decorated the car, and poor Captain was quite nervous about the paint."

"Lola Sita is married?"

"She was. Her husband is no longer living, many years gone. But it was a grand wedding."

Julia smiled, touching the cloth roof of a convertible roadster. This garage was a museum in itself, and the old mechanic its loving curator. Mang Berto led her from car to car reciting the make and individual history of each one, who rode in it and on what occasion and what were the efforts done to restore it.

"The ones in front are all running, for the most part, though I would not trust them to make the journey to Manila. Those in the back haven't run in many years. And I experiment on the middle three, trying to fashion parts from the scraps outside or inventing something to compensate. It gives an old man great joy."

"This is amazing. Could we take a few out?"

"Of course," he said with great excitement. "You'd love the sound of that 1969 Camaro. Purrs like a tiger—well, if I can get it running. The engine has been giving me headaches, but perhaps with a beautiful girl from home, that old car will surprise us and run without even a carburetor or gasoline."

"That would be a surprise." Julia laughed.

From the back row, she saw Raul and Markus enter the shop, talking in low conspiratorial tones and calling for Mang Berto. She wished to understand their words; the seriousness in their expressions chilled her.

"Hello!" she greeted them. "Were you looking for me or for Mang Berto?"

Their surprise showed in the jerk of their heads.

"Let me guess," Markus said in a cheerful voice. "Mang Berto is boring you with the details of your grandfather's car collection."

"I'm enjoying myself immensely," she said, gaining a huge grin from Mang Berto.

Raul still wore the same grave expression he had had in the office.

"We need to talk to you, Julia," Markus said. "And we need to talk to Mang Berto."

The old man wiped his hands on his pants with a look of concern.

"What's wrong?" Julia asked.

"Usually we would keep such a matter to ourselves," Markus said. "But Raul and I agree that as a visitor to our country and also with your role on the hacienda that you should be kept informed of certain delicate subjects."

"Okay, now quit being a lawyer and just tell me."

He paused and grinned at Raul. "She's one to contend with."

"Just tell her," Raul said.

"One of our drivers is missing. And there is word that Communist rebels are congregating in the mountains around us."

Julia wasn't sure how to respond. "So what can I do?"

Raul appeared surprised. "Nothing. We are concerned about you remaining here."

"So am I in danger?" she asked.

Markus gazed at her. "Julia, that is a possibility."

TEN

Pistols and a classic car.

Mang Berto drove them in an old Thunderbird with sleek fins at the taillights. Raul and Markus sat in the backseat with pistols in their belts.

Raul had explained that due to the current conditions and with news of Captain Morrison's funeral and his granddaughter's arrival, extra precautions were required. Markus had touched Julia's arm and told her not to worry, and strangely, she didn't.

They were touring the grounds of Hacienda Esperanza. But "grounds" didn't begin to describe the lands that the property comprised. Mang Berto drove slowly past the vast rice fields to the sugarcane fields. The windows were down, and the air was rich with the smell of soil and agriculture.

"The rice is processed for use on the hacienda itself—there's no profit in it. We have two other cash crops," Raul said.

"Yes," Julia replied, turning in the seat. "Sugar and coconut. Grandfather wrote extensively about them."

"The Captain was fond of sending us articles," Raul said as he, too, leaned over the seat to view them. "He always updated us on the new trends in the market."

They passed a small concrete shrine to the Virgin Mary on the side of the road, nearly surrounded by tall grass. Long streaks from years of rain fell from the crown of her head to the ground. A lit red candle flickered at her feet.

Markus leaned forward with his arms on the front seat and pointed to another field where workers moved long, sheathlike machetes in a smooth rhythm, cutting down the tall sticks of sugarcane. "There are different harvesting methods. The best for the hacienda is to burn the fields first. The leaves burn from the stalk, and the rows of overgrown weeds are cleared out. The cane is then easily cut and taken directly to the mill."

On one side the cane grew higher than her head. On the other side, the field-workers neatly cut the burned field. A strong scent permeated the air, perhaps of burned sugar and cane leaves.

"The fire doesn't destroy the plants?" Julia asked, covering her nose as she tried to adjust to the powerful fragrance.

"The plants are green and moist, liquid rich," Raul answered. "The method is effective before cutting the stalks. The juice holds the high sugar content in the center of the stalk. After harvest, the field is prepared for a new crop. We take part of the cut sugarcane and replant it."

When they reached the men working in the fields, Raul asked Mang Berto to stop.

"It will please the men to meet you," Raul said as they got out of the car. He adjusted the pistol on his belt as he walked ahead.

The men set down their machetes, wiping their brows with colored handkerchiefs. A few took the chance to put canteens of water to their mouths and brushed off their clothing.

Julia caught the mixed scents of freshly cut cane, rich soil, and human sweat.

One after the other, the field-workers shook Julia's hand, looking at her curiously, nearly all with wide smiles and missing teeth. A few held back, more serious and hesitant, then came and respectfully greeted her.

"Hello," she said to each man. All extended a sense of respect that Julia tried to return with her smile and attention.

As Raul spoke with the workers, a few chuckled and nodded their heads. There was camaraderie between them, but also, Julia noted, admiration and respect for their foreman.

Markus raised a hand in good-bye, walking beside Julia as they returned to the car. "I once played in these fields with some of these men. Most of them and their families have been part of the hacienda for generations. They won't soon forget meeting you today, the American doña in her beautiful yellow sundress. I'm sure you gave many of them something to work for today. I know I'd be swinging my machete faster to impress you."

Julia smiled. "You're incorrigible."

Hacienda Esperanza stretched wider and farther than any ranch she'd been on. There were miles of sugarcane fields with men hard at work, more staff houses, a small shanty village that Raul was clearly annoyed about. If left alone, he declared, squatters would grow their own city on the land.

When they reached their other cash crop, the coconut trees, Julia learned about more innovations her grandfather had established. A forest of coconut trees were planted about ten feet apart from one another. Their tall trunks and wide branches provided an effective shade from the glaring afternoon sun.

From time to time, they saw the workers climbing up the trees barehanded with long bolo knives tucked inside scabbards hanging on their hips.

Markus explained more. "Copra is the sun-dried meat inside the coconut nuts. Your grandfather established the hacienda's own processing plants using a hybrid of the latest technology and some local ingenuity, seriously saving on costs. He cut out the middle-man and sold processed coconut oil instead of just the raw coconut materials, quadrupling the hacienda's profits. Now that the Marcos regime is over, your grandfather and Raul planned to restore the plant, which is located near a local port. That was before his diagnosis, of course."

Hopes and plans for restoration—those were what they all sought on the hacienda.

The car passed three caretakers wearing large straw hats. They smiled at the group and raised several long-necked bottles.

"They have a present for you, Julia," Markus said, smiling as he leaned over the seat.

The car stopped by the farmers, who nodded warmly and handed Julia the bottles through the window.

"Salamat," she said, and they laughed in surprise and delight at her use of a Tagalog word. Once they drove on, Julia asked what the drink was.

"*Lambanog*," Mang Berto said, laughing. "Coconut wine, very strong."

From the backseat Raul said, "We'll go to the fishponds and then return to the hacienda. I have much work to do this afternoon."

The fishponds were divided into numerous neat rectangular plots separated by raised dikes made of soil and stone. The breadth and scope of the ponds were staggering, sweeping far into the distance. Flocks of migratory birds rose and landed on the waters in artistic dances.

At the southern edge of the fishponds, huts made of bamboo and palm were built on tall poles above the water. Footprints of livestock and small bare feet pocked the muddy shoreline with water filling the deeper prints. Julia heard children laughing and in the distance, the sound of birds and women talking.

"These are the hacienda's fishponds," Raul explained as they walked toward it. "At one time, your grandfather and I discussed raising fish for foreign markets, but regular flooding during the rainy seasons always emptied the ponds of the fishes."

The joyous screams and laughter of children grew louder as they walked down a slope. A woman with a child in a sling on her hip carried a bucket of water in her arms.

"Look at the children with that *carabao*." Markus touched her arm and pointed to an oxlike animal standing in the pond. It reminded her of a water buffalo with its sleek black hair and thick gray horns that arched straight from his head.

A group of children circled the creature, laughing and screaming as they washed its slick body. A boy jumped on its back, then helped pull a girl up. The boy then tried to stand on the carabao's back, but slipped in a dramatic fall that made Julia gasp.

He popped up from the muddy water like a smiling acrobat as the carabao continued chewing its cud as if nothing unusual was happening. Two little girls, toddler-aged, splashed and squealed in the water holes where Julia guessed a carabao had wallowed in the mud.

Raul stood with his arms crossed at his chest. "That is Mino-Mino. They believe he is their pet, but he is supposed to be working the field right now."

Raul called to the children, who all jumped and dove under the water as if to hide from him. One by one their wet black-haired heads popped back up.

Markus laughed and shook his head. "Those are hacienda children, aren't they, Raul?"

Raul nodded with his pinched expression as he perused the area, as if assuring himself of their safety.

"Different from the children of the Barangay?" Julia asked, remembering the boys and one girl around the estate house.

"Yes, very different." Markus turned and looked at the jungle. "Two different worlds. Barangay children will be near as well, but we won't see them."

"There were some at the house when we left."

"Yes, I know." Raul and Markus glanced at each other, and Raul shook his head slightly.

The children in the fishpond had spotted Julia. They nudged each other and put their heads close together in the muddy water. Finally they came splashing toward her as if in a race. Once they reached the shore, they all stopped and smiled shyly, waiting for one to be brave enough to go forward. Black eyes and glistening hair, brown wet skin, wide white smiles.

"Good . . . afternoon to Miss Julia," said the young girl who had been on the back of the carabao. Her wet dress clung to her thin frame, and water dripped from her hair to the muddy shore.

"Good afternoon," Julia said, reaching out a hand.

The girl turned to her friends, who all giggled; then she stretched her small hand forward and shook Julia's.

"What is your name?"

"Angelita."

The children came closer, and one touched the skin on Julia's arm as if in awe of the lightness.

"Nice to meet you, Angelita. You are very good at riding on the back of that carabao. It looks like a cow to me, though. Have you seen a cow?"

"They speak little English," Markus said; then he translated her words.

The children nodded their heads and a few chattered quickly in Tagalog.

Markus laughed. "They've seen a cow on *Sesame Street* and other television shows from the States. One saw a cow sing a song once in a movie."

Raul rubbed the top of one child's head. "The hacienda is strict about learning English, another requirement of Captain Morrison. It is good for the children of the provinces to know and practice their English as the children do in Manila. I would guess that these little ruffians are missing assignments today to play in the mud."

A boy with narrow almond eyes tugged at Markus's arm and spoke as if he had a secret.

"Mino-Mino?" Markus said to the boy, who launched into some grand explanation.

"He wants me to tell you that Mino-Mino is an outlaw cow. He did some bad things while vacationing near Taal, the volcano."

The boy grinned widely at Markus.

"Taal is the smallest volcano in the world, and according to Joc, Mino-Mino wanted to see what the smallest volcano looked like. So he went on a tour bus specially made for other carabao. But while there, he drank a bit of the funny water and acted very inappropriately. So now, the children are trying to cover him in mud because they are certain the authorities will arrive very soon."

Julia tried to act worried. "Well, I hope they hide him well, so the police don't put him in jail."

When Markus translated, the children jumped up and down, laughing hysterically at her response.

Markus gave her a smile that took her breath away, as Angelita reached a hand to touch Julia's wheat-colored hair.

"Let us go on now," Raul said. "I need to check on something and will meet you at the car." He marched up the hill.

Julia said good-bye to the children, who scampered back to the fishpond.

"Miss Julia," they called over and over as they jumped and dove into the muddy water. The storytelling boy swam out to Mino-Mino and climbed on his back. He called for her to watch and stood up, making the motions of a surfer. "California! Beach Boys!" he cried, making them laugh as he surfed until he lost his balance and with flailing arms fell into the water.

A hot breeze stirred the dust, but mercifully pushed some dark clouds over the sun. Tropical birds chirped and cawed from the jungle.

Markus motioned to a grove of trees ahead where Julia spotted the girl and one of the boys she'd seen earlier at the hacienda. The children of the Barangay.

"How did they get here? Do they play together?" she asked as the children disappeared into the greenery.

"No, except on rare occasions. The children are very separate, very different. Their minds are molded to see life in completely different ways."

She and Markus walked on, and suddenly a few raindrops fell. Then, almost at once, it was a shower falling in long sudden streams.

"Hurry, under here," Markus said, grabbing her hand and racing beneath a thick grove of mango trees.

Raul was down the road on the front porch of a hut, speaking to an old man.

"I've never seen such rain," Julia said, standing close to Markus beneath the branches. It came down so immediate and hard, settling the dust and cooling the air with a crisp fragrance. A few large drops traversed the wide green leaves and dripped on their heads. Unseen birds still cawed and sang.

In ten minutes the downpour passed, and they hurried toward the car.

Raul approached to say that he needed to deal with some things there. "Markus can escort you to the house," he said.

Wherever they went on the hacienda, Julia saw how the people followed Raul, not in fear or loathe servitude, but with respect. Yet much of the hacienda was in disrepair and seemed to lack organization at the lower levels. Something was missing. Perhaps they needed more manpower or tighter unity. How could she, an outsider and a foreigner, know what was needed? The burden was most certainly too great for her to bear.

WHAT WOULD MCCLAIN DO IN A TIME LIKE THIS? MANALO THOUGHT and chuckled at himself. He was being infected by his men's love for the Bruce Willis character in Die Hard.

The men couldn't identify with a policeman in the United States; they certainly wouldn't want to. But they could understand breaking rules, doing what a man had to do—fighting one's enemies without following protocol, continuing to fight even with a knife stuck in one's shoulder.

Manalo was walking in the night again. He thought of the sambar he'd seen in the meadow, and of his wife and children. If only Malaya could hear him calling to her, telling her that he'd make everything all right.

Hacienda Esperanza was only kilometers from their camp in the jungle. They could come in the night. There had been forcible takeovers of properties in the past, many times. Much of his country was pushed and invaded not only by foreign soldiers but by their own as well. The government wasn't strong. They'd most likely cower at a hostile takeover and leave even such a vast and important piece of property to fend for itself. For if the government sent out the army, those in power knew it might mobilize the other political factions, and the entire country might fall into civil war. It could happen. In other countries in such fragile shape, it had happened.

Manalo walked down the road that eventually led to the hacienda gates. Just today he'd heard that foreign and domestic investors were trespassing on the property of Hacienda Esperanza. The foreman's men had run them off.

There was no doubt, they must act soon. But what action to take? This Manalo must carefully consider.

He thought of some lines from the new *Die Hard* movie, which his men liked to quote.

What are you going to do?

Whatever I can.

It wasn't the best tactical advice when leading men, but Manalo was playing this one by instinct. His superiors could no longer be relied upon. They'd messed with his family now. He couldn't trust anyone outside his own small group.

When the sun came up, his men were surprised to see Manalo cooking them breakfast.

"What's going on?" Timeteo asked.

"That's not the line I'm looking for. Think of McClain," he said with a grin as he cracked another egg into the pan.

"Okay. Manalo, what are we going to do?"

"Whatever we can."

ELEVEN

I s there some reason, some superstition behind it?" Julia tugged at the heavy handle on the double wooden doors.

"Oh, yes, it can be very dangerous to use the front hacienda doors." Markus gave Mang Berto a conspiratorial glance.

"There is a story . . . The story is, that um, this um . . . oh, I can't do it." Mang Berto laughed. "The story is that no one uses them, and now they're hard to open. That's it."

Markus gave an exasperated sigh.

"Sorry, Markus. I am not good at tricking beautiful ladies. See, Miss Julia, when Captain Morrison left, we used the kitchen and back courtyard and not the rest of house. Our staff houses and the garage are past the back courtyards, so we enter from there. The humidity and salt air makes hinges rust."

Julia inspected the corners. "Mang Berto, do you have some WD-40?"

"What, miss?"

"Something to clean off the corrosion."

"Oh, yes, of course, miss. I am master at killing that rust."

"Is that all right, Markus, for us to get these doors in use once again?"

"You're the doña of the hacienda; you can do whatever you wish," Markus said with a slight bow.

"I'm only the doña for a short time, but it's a shame to let such magnificent doors and such a grand entryway go to waste."

Markus watched with an odd expression about his features, then waved them to follow him down the path around the house. "I hope Lola Sita made plenty of tea. I could drink a pitcher myself."

The back courtyards and lawns were filled with activity. Women with aprons covering their dresses or jeans and T-shirts used enormous wooden spoons to stir large copper caldrons that hung over fire pits. Steam billowed from the pots, and the air was sweet and smoky. Children played on the lawn and through the gardens. Makeshift tables covered in tablecloths held bags of sugar, glass jars, strainers, and lids. Beside the table were crates of mangoes, and several women sat there peeling the fruit.

One woman in a cornflower blue dress held a child on her hip and stirred a pot. She lifted her spoon and waved at Julia like they were old friends.

"It is for jam, mango jam," Markus said. "This region isn't actually known for it, but someone, perhaps one of your relatives, started the tradition. The women work together; then each takes her portion. If some is left over, they sell it in the sari-sari stores in town."

Julia walked among the women, greeting them, asking their names again and hearing their jobs in the mango jam assembly line while Mang Berto and Markus went for their drinks.

A woman took one mango at a time and dipped it into boiling water. Within seconds she pulled it back out and put it in cold water, from where the seated women easily picked them up and cut the skin away, then sliced the fruit in half to cut out the seed. The bare fruit was strained, rinsed, and mashed.

Another pot was stirred relentlessly; this was the jam cooking. The third boiling pot held glass jars that were carefully removed with a large clamplike utensil. Then the cooling jars were set out until their lids sealed.

It was an impressive process. Julia marveled at the Tres Lolas; they were timeless women moving among the others, instructing them in the tasks, all of it a well-orchestrated dance. The movements of the women, even with toddlers clinging to the skirts of some, covered the courtyard like the waves of heat distorting the air. Many of the women had leaves and flowers woven into their hair, and they hummed or broke into song as they worked.

A little boy ran up to Julia and rubbed his finger on her skin.

"Hello there," she said, bending down to speak to him. He twirled her hair in one finger; then he took one strand and, with a quick tug, pulled it out.

"Ouch!" she said, as he laughed and skipped off with her light-colored hair held up like a trophy.

"You've sacrificed to a good cause." Markus handed Julia a tall glass of iced tea. "That boy will probably put your hair in his treasure box. These children have never seen light-colored hair except on television."

Lola Gloria walked toward them, wiping her hands on her apron. "Your tour of the hacienda was nice?"

"Yes. And what an operation you have here as well."

Lola Gloria gazed around at the women with a proud look on her face. "You should go inside now and rest, Miss Julia."

"Oh, can't I help you instead?" Julia said. "What can I do?"

"Have you made jam before?"

Julia laughed. "Uh, that would be a *no*."

"Then we will give you a simple job. Let me get you an apron. Markus, would you like to help as well? Or are you off to something more important in the city?"

Markus checked his watch. "With traffic, I'd miss my dinner engagement anyway."

"Oh, do you have a date?"

"Well, yes, I have a date, but I will have to cancel. One of those dinners with black ties and delegates to charm."

Lola Gloria glanced at Julia.

Markus kissed the old woman on the top of the head. "Don't worry, I won't marry without your permission. And by the way, my date's name is George. He's a colleague of mine." Markus rubbed his hands together. "So, Julia, let's make jam. Just don't let Raul see me doing woman's work."

With that, they were swept into the dance. Lola Gloria placed them side by side and set them to work peeling mangoes. Markus was nearly as lame at the job as she was.

"What kind of Filipino can't cut a mango?" Julia teased.

"I have my people do that for me," he said with a dignified air. He rubbed his drenched fingers across her cheek, and she jerked back, startled.

"What?" he said. "You had a little something on your face there."

"You are an evil attorney. I knew it from the moment I saw you," she said, wiping off her face with her apron. She nodded toward one of the women, who was scolding them with a pointed finger. "Get back to work, Mr. Santos. You're going to get us into trouble." Julia reached for another mango.

"Explain something to me," she said. "First of all, I know my grandfather willed the hacienda to me since my mother didn't want it. But legally, he can't grant it to me because Filipino law doesn't allow a foreigner to own land. So what am I doing here, other than burying my grandfather?"

"Well, you're learning to make some great mango jam."

"Yes, there is that."

"The hacienda is rightfully yours in many ways, and yet you are right. The laws could keep you locked up in court for years trying to get it resolved, and during that time, you might lose the land to the province or the federal government—which is not what we're hoping to see happen. Or you could give up the land— like to the hacienda people themselves. Many are hoping for that. But such a land needs a head and a heart. The hacienda would quickly become divided and cut into smaller parcels.

"You could also sell it. Investors call my office daily with offers. But I must say that the legacy of this place, how it was birthed and grew all of these years . . . the times of glory and near destruction, and your grandfather's love for it—I can hardly bear the idea of it no longer being Hacienda Esperanza. But I will do whatever you decide."

Julia nodded her head in thought. The future truly did rest in her hands. And again she wondered, *who am I to make such a decision*?

"Other questions?" Markus asked.

"What about the political climate? I know it's tumultuous, but how fragile is the government?"

"Well, you can't compare it to your country. We have been a democracy since before and after the Japanese invaded during WWII. However, our President Marcos was much more like a dictator than a president. He declared martial law and pretty much did what he wished, killed who he wanted, used the country's money as he liked. The nation is still reeling from his time in power."

Markus picked up another cooling mango from the cold water

and began peeling back the skin. "And now we have our president Corazon Aquino—the first female president in Asia, which is impressive. She's the widow of a popular senator, Ninoy Aquino, who was forced into exile during Marcos's reign. On the day of his return, he was assassinated as he got off the airplane. So you see, the country is divided. A minority still support Marcos's ways and think his wife was the true villain—the famous shoe collection was not Imelda's only extravagance. There is also a very strong Communist Party that wants the nation to follow in the steps of China or Russia or Vietnam, depending upon which group you talk to. There are so many different factions within each one, so these are wide generalizations."

"We have many different beliefs within our two major parties in the States."

"Yes, but those different parties and factions within each party aren't trying to overthrow the government and take control." Markus motioned to the scolding woman, who again was glancing at them in disapproval. "I think our talking is dropping production."

"Okay, back to work then," Julia said. "I just want to know if it's safe here."

"Pretty much, yes," Markus said. "And hey, you've got me, Raul, and the whole hacienda to take care of you."

"Oh no, I'm not worried for me." She gazed around at the women and children. "I just wondered what the future might hold for everyone here."

"If only I could predict the future . . . I hope real change is coming to our country. That's what keeps me working late most nights. But who can say what will happen?"

HOURS LATER, THE SUN FELL LOW, MAKING BLACK SILHOUETTES of the palm trees against the sky. Her back hurt and fingers ached, yet Julia paused with a crate filled with the jars of warm mango jam in her arms to gaze around the stone courtyard. The cooking dance had slowed from a jig to a waltz. Red coals smoldered in the fire pits; the cleanup was nearly complete. Markus pointed to a basket with a young child asleep inside. An older woman patted Julia on the back, then winked and moved down the path.

Julia followed a line of three other women carrying crates of jam through the archway of the back courtyards and through the gardens. The path left the gardens and narrowed through the jungle where fuel canisters lit the way. Julia kept a careful eye on her guide, a middle-aged woman in baggy denim pants and a bright green blouse.

Suddenly they came out of the jungle into a neat little row of buildings surrounding a small square. The houses had stucco fences with decorative iron gates protecting their secluded court-yards. Chickens scratched the ground. Laundry hung on lines out-side doorways. Neat pathways of stone led to the houses, which were hung with small palms and large leafy plants in pots. Bougainvillea dangled orange flowers over the stucco walls.

Julia set her crate down in the stack beside a doorway.

"Thank you, Miss Julia. I walk you back, or come in house for some dinner?"

Julia couldn't remember the woman's name; she had met too many people in the last few days. "Thank you, but Aling Rosa has my dinner ready. I can find my way back."

Julia was curious about this tiny neighborhood of maybe twelve homes. The main access to the houses came from the other end where scooters, bikes, and motorized tricycles with sidecars were parked in a haphazard fashion. Round lights hung from trees and archways.

On the path back to the hacienda house, Julia saw five of the Barangay boys come out of the jungle with their wooden guns.

When they spotted her, they acted nonchalant, as if their presence had nothing to do with her.

Partway down the path near the courtyard, she noticed the boys walking behind her. She paused just around the bend to the back of the hacienda house, her hands on her hips and a smile on her face. When they appeared, she demanded, "Are you following me?"

The tallest boy came forward and set his gun against the concrete wall of the courtyard. "I am Emman." He wore an old green army jacket over a brown printed T-shirt and denim shorts. Around his neck he wore a black rosary tangled with other necklaces. Some were simply pendants made of bronze and what looked like images on hard board paper hanging from ordinary black nylon thread.

"Hello, Emman. I have seen you before."

"Yes," he said with a slight smile.

He introduced the rest of his group one by one. Jepoy was the cute stout boy with the red shirt who had greeted her earlier. Amer was a brown, stocky, somewhat muscular boy. Kiko was the smallest and youngest and had a mop of hair on his head down to his eyebrows, and Bok was the thin kid with a funny smile who had first helped her out of the tricycle upon her arrival.

"We are your bodyguards," the small Kiko announced with enthusiasm. The others nodded, except for Emman.

"Oh, you are, are you?"

"Yes, Miss Julia. We are your bodyguards," Emman confirmed. "We were assigned for your protection by Amang Tenio. I am the leader of them. And we will protect you."

"Amang Tenio?" Julia remembered the shaman-looking man from the first day.

"Yes," Emman replied. "He is the commander."

"Uh-huh." Julia smiled. *How convenient,* she thought, *to entertain children by giving them such a task.* "It is nice to meet you, my bodyguards. I'm going to the house now. Have you had your dinner?"

"We have dinner," Emman said. He struggled for words, obviously not fluent in English. He tapped a small leather pouch tied to his belt loop, and Julia wondered what kind of dinner could be kept in that all day.

"If you want something more to eat, come inside the hacienda house. It's not haunted with ghosts, did you know?"

"Ghosts do not make us afraid." His determined expression matched the tone.

"Okay, good-bye then for now."

Emman walked up to her and reached for her hand, which he then kissed the top of. "Good night, Miss Julia."

She smiled as he quickly raced away with the other boys following close behind.

Darkness had fallen, and the shadows loomed above the few lights in the back courtyard. Strangely, her "bodyguards" did make her feel safer as they followed her at a distance.

"What wonderful work done today," Lola Gloria said as Julia entered the kitchen to the scent of something cooking.

Her stomach growled, and she realized suddenly that she was hungry.

Everyone gravitated to the hacienda kitchen. The formal dining room was used only for special occasions, otherwise the Tres Lolas, Raul, Mang Berto, and Aling Rosa, and now Julia took their meals on the back courtyard or in the kitchen squeezed around the table. One end was often covered with cutting boards and discarded ends of vegetables and fruits, the stains of meats, and dusts of flour.

Markus was already there, muttering and washing his hands in the sink with his head downcast.

"What are you saying?" Julia asked, coming beside him to wash the mango stickiness from her fingers as well.

He took a bar of soap and then her hands, gently lathering her fingers and hands and arms up to her elbows. She wondered if he too felt what she did at such an intimate touch. As he rinsed her hands under the cool water and handed her a towel, the glance he gave her made her suspect that he did.

Lola Gloria handed Julia a glass of tea. "We will eat in just a few minutes."

Above the kitchen table were baskets, copper pots and pans, strings of chilies and garlic. In the corner was a large brick oven with open shelves filled with wood. A long shelf held clay pots of different sizes, cast-iron pots and pans, a jar filled with bamboo implements, a stone grinder, and other kitchen utensils. The few modern appliances, like the matching black blender, food processor, and mixer, shared a shelf with primitive wooden bowls and spoons.

Mang Berto entered from outside at the same time that Raul walked in from down the hallway. When Raul spotted Markus, he smirked and said something in Tagalog.

"Oh yeah?" Markus shot something back that included the name *Mara*, which shut Raul up quickly.

"Did you see the American contribution to our supper?" Lola Gloria asked.

Aling Rosa pulled a large steaming pizza from the oven with a massive wooden spatula and set it in the center of the table.

"Pizza!" Julia exclaimed.

"Yes, cheese pizza, with extra cheese and sauce. Your grandfather used to cook for everyone his famous pizzas. It was a favorite treat for us to have. My sisters went to bed early; they were sad they would miss eating pizza. But it's lucky for us, because we'll have more to eat! Do not tell then I said so, but those two sisters of mine do eat a lot of pizza."

The sauce had a sharp tang of rosemary, and fresh basil had been cut in strips for the top. Julia's arm rested against Aling Rosa's, but neither pulled away. The touch of her arm, the warmth prevalent in the room brought an ease that Julia hadn't felt in a long time. Though she couldn't talk to Aling Rosá, the woman smiled at her often. Her face glowed when Mang Berto would touch her arm or kiss her cheek—which, Julia noted, was quite often.

Raul took a bite, and a long string of cheese hung from his mouth despite his attempts to break the strand; it became more tangled around his fingers. He grunted with a slight grin as they laughed and teased him.

Markus sat back and patted his flat stomach. "Captain Morrison gave much to this land, but nothing better than his pizza recipe."

Mang Berto touched a napkin to his lips and then dabbed his wife's chin affectionately. "There is a saying that food is good for man's soul. It is history of our hacienda to heal through food."

"Hacienda Esperanza should have a cookbook," Julia said.

Lola Gloria looked at her in surprise. "But yes, there is a hacienda cookbook. I must show you. We put it away for safekeeping, and oh, where was that hiding place?"

She rose from the chair, and Julia noticed the older woman's hands shaking with age as she started opening cupboards. "Your grandmother, Doña Julianna, compiled the recipes from all the generations of hacienda cooks. Especially from Elena the Cook. Ah, you do not know that story either, I suppose?"

Raul frowned. "You grandfather did not tell you?"

"My grandfather and I were closest in his final months, but not before that. He mostly told war stories and of getting back to the Philippines."

Raul took another piece of pizza. "The hacienda stories are the history of the land and are part of your heritage. Elena the Cook and Cortinez, I have heard of her since my childhood. It is said that her cooking saved the hacienda from ruin."

"How did she do that?"

"You will have to hear the story."

"Tell me then."

Raul shifted uncomfortably and glanced at Lola Gloria and Markus as if for help.

Markus said smugly, "Go ahead, Raul. Tell us the story of Elena the Cook and Cortinez."

"Me?"

Lola Gloria nodded and continued her search through the cupboards.

"Well, I will begin it, but Lola Gloria will tell it best, or even Markus. It was told to me that Elena the Cook was not even a cook for many years. But first, also, that she was not a beautiful woman in physical appearance, but her heart and personality had such beauty that it surprised those close to her when a visitor commented upon her awkward features."

Raul moved uncomfortably in his chair and touched his greasy fingers to the linen napkin on the table.

"She also discovered the flower, and there was Cortinez, but he was before the flower. And the senator who saved the hacienda."

Julia and Aling Rosa glanced at each other.

"There was something about a sister," Raul said. "Let me think how to start." He leaned back and pinched his brows together. "It is difficult to translate."

Lola Gloria stopped her search. "Would you like me to tell the story?"

"Yes, and I will have a San Mig instead."

Everyone laughed, and Lola Gloria sat back in her chair. She folded her hands together and smiled in thought, the corners of her black eyes wrinkled. "Raul began all wrong."

Markus and Mang Berto laughed at that.

"Do not insult me because I have not the gift of storytelling." Raul went to the fridge for a beer.

Aling Rosa rose and kissed Raul on each side of the face to console him, while Lola Gloria paused and settled back into her seat.

"Elena the Cook was not young when she first came into the kitchen," Lola Gloria began. "When she was a child, her mother refused to let her cook or help with household chores. Such things were for the servants. Elena was the daughter of José y Guevarra."

"Yes, that is how it begins." Raul leaned back in his chair with his bottle of beer and stringy pizza.

"Elena's mother, known for her pride and cold precision of house rule, held within her the insecurity of poor birth and low breeding, which she disguised with an facade of elegance and sophistication. She had a great fear that her lack of education would be detected, so she never wrote letters of correspondence, not even a shopping list, for fear of what her crooked letters and poor grammar might reveal. This was a time when the hacienda was in its youthful elegance."

Raul finished another piece of pizza, then again leaned back and rested his hands on his stomach. Markus watched Julia as Lola Gloria spoke. And Julia felt a sense of the story rising, as if the hacienda itself was being transformed back into a time of elegance and pride.

TWELVE

Schooled by the best tutors in the Philippines, instructed by an etiquette coach, and dressed in the finest linens imported from Paris and Madrid, Elena was raised in sophisticated fashion. Her fiesta to celebrate her coming out was the grandest affair with guests coming from as far away as Manila, and seven of her father's business associates from China. No one had seen such an extravagant party, which was exactly what Elena's mother intended.

"Elena's father kept a stressful watch of the books and crunched the finances to accommodate his wife's profligacy. One year an entire field of sugarcane went to her own clothing expenses, and Elena's father was forced to cut the wages of the field-workers. The wife's expenses and debts were taking their toll, and Elena's father was unsure what else he could cut to save them from ruin.

"A docile child, Elena did not rebel against her mother's rule. An excellent student, a cherished girl of the servants, she had a quiet gentleness that some mistook for lack of intelligence. But she was anything but that. Her features were plain, but held such warmth as to seem beautiful to those who observed her.

"Elena's younger sister, Alexa, was much more beautiful, but a great frustration to their mother. A renegade child—oh, I will tell of that girl's story on another day. Alexa was a child of the wilderness, running with the children of the jungle and visiting the squatters, fishing and hunting with the boys, diving from the rocks and bringing home abalone and sometimes a few oysters with rare pearls, which are very hard to find.

"Elena loved her sister greatly. She, how you say, covered up what their mother would consider grave indiscretions. Alexa enjoyed infuriating their mother and endured punishment, even the harshest beatings, with a smile. Elena would cry, but her sister hid her tears behind laughter that only caused the beatings to increase. So this was the household in which Elena grew up.

"What nobody knew was that since childhood, Elena had a secret." Lola Gloria leaned forward, and the hush in the room amplified the dramatic pause.

Julia glanced at Markus, who by now was as engrossed with the story as she was. His expression asked, *What? What was the secret?*, though Julia knew he must have already heard this story, and more than once.

"This secret," Lola Gloria continued, "was something the young woman could not express, not even to herself. Now, Julia. You may not believe me when I tell you this at first. But it is true. And even if you don't believe now, you will eventually. You have the blood of Elena within you, and you will not doubt any of this."

Lola Gloria's eyes held her intently.

"So what was Elena's secret?" Julia asked.

The older woman nodded as if seeing that Julia was duly prepared. "The secret was actually a gift. As a child, Elena could not have guessed that it was unique only unto herself. Alexa was the one who told her not to tell others about it, that it was rare and unique. Just as Alexa understood the ways of the wild and had her own gifts—that will be told another day.

"Her secret was this: whenever Elena came near another person, she could capture a great sense of them, an understanding that could not be defined."

"A sense of them?" Julia asked.

"It was greater than just knowing if, let's say, a cheerful visitor was inwardly sad. Instead, this knowing came in the form of smells and colors. When young men courted Elena, this instinct of people, though unrefined, would distinguish character in an individual. From the men who came for her family money, she caught scents of bitter herbs, rotting fruit, or even once of a type of fish whose smell curled the hairs of the nose. Those young men who came out of duty, around them Elena could distinguish something missing that she could only equate to drinking tea without enough sugar. Others with major character flaws had a heightened odor that overpowered the good scents, as if the chicken adobo had too much garlic.

"There was one young man who loved her quickly for the peace of her presence. He reminded Elena of wood smoke and honey. But the boy was of low standing, and so her mother refused him outright. After that, Elena rebelled for the first time by disregarding every wealthy suitor that her mother was excited about. As a finely groomed man took her through the gardens, Elena would give her refusal outright, much to her parents' utter frustration.

"The full magic of Elena remained dormant for many years. Its release happened quite by accident. An honored guest had come to the family table—a diplomat from Manila, who had journeyed the day to discuss a business proposition with Elena's father. No one knew of the hacienda's financial difficulties, and her father hoped the senator might help him in a business venture that might save their finances."

Julia noticed Markus watching her with interest as the story unfolded.

"The table was lavished with the best hacienda recipes, but much to the distress of Elena's mother, the poor politician enjoyed very little. Señor Emory had been gravely ill for some months and had not yet recovered. His political position was in jeopardy and demanded that he work harder. He had come to Hacienda Esperanza seeking support and partnership with one of the most powerful families in the lower provinces.

"The long journey had proven a great strain, and more than food or conversation, Señor Emory wished for a thick blanket and warm bed. But manners prevailed, and he struggled to remain focused on business wrangling and polite conversation. Elena's father talked endlessly of a new type of ship that could open new exports to more distant locations while Elena's mother fidgeted endlessly, watching every bite the senator took while deciding how to reprimand the cook without her temper costing the household another member of their staff. Elena sat docile and quiet, observing them all.

"In the midst of the dinner tension between the bone-weary senator and the distraught mother, the house butler entered the formal dining room practically on tiptoe. It was critical, he said, that he speak to the don at once. And yet it was Elena's mother who recognized the urgency upon the butler's face. Perhaps the cook had used spoiled meat or sullied herbs. She excused herself from the table and motioned the butler to meet her outside the room.

"'Alexa,' the butler whispered, and the mother's face drained to a gray pallor.

"The girl had been diving off the rocks above the cove. She'd collected as large a basket of oysters as had ever been seen. In the back courtyard, she and the boys of a jungle village were opening each giant oyster and discovering a treasury of shimmering pearls. The hacienda workers had gathered and cheered each little find. Even the kitchen staff had rushed to the yard to join the spontaneous fiesta.

"While the butler knew Elena's father might find relief in such unexpected fortune, he suspected that the distinguished senator might look unkindly upon a family with such a renegade female.

"At the dining table, Elena had long been aware of the senator's suffering. She'd thought to ask the kitchen staff to bring the gentlemen some coffee or tea, but as yet, none had returned to clear away the dishes or offer after-dinner beverages. Elena herself fidgeted more and more as the scent of overripe fruit grew strong in the room. Finally, she could take the senator's discomfort no longer.

"She interrupted in the middle of her father's description of the fastest ships on the South Pacific. 'Sir, our honored guest, may I get you some coffee as you and my father retire to the study?'

"Elena's father gave her a surprised and disapproving expression, but the senator's relief was quite evident even to him. The older man sighed and relaxed his formal stance as if taking off a heavy pack from his shoulders.

"'Dearest child, some coffee would be quite soothing. I have not been well, I'm afraid. It is with effort that I come here this day, though I am most grateful for the gracious welcome. Please give your mother and your cook my deepest apology. My appetite has long suffered. I sadly recall the days of enjoying such a feast as this.'

"'There is an afghan in a basket beside the sofa couch, if you wish, sir,' Elena said in a manner that would not offend.

"And then for the first time in her life, except to pass through to the back or pass an instruction from her mother to the house staff, Elena entered the kitchen. She stood at the doorway, overwhelmed and awed by what she saw. The baskets, canisters, drying herbs hanging from long hooks beside the pots. There was no one else there, and Elena didn't know how to make coffee or even where the coffee was stored.

"She opened cupboards, clay pots, and gunny sacks. The colors and smells of the different foods, like the earthy smell from a bag of beans, the quickened rush of cane vinegar, the brilliance of ground yellow turmeric, the scent of the sea from the clam shells in buckets on the floor, all delighted her. For several minutes Elena forgot the task that brought her there as she explored the scents and flavors, the answers to what she sensed in people and had rarely distinguished individually. No wonder she was so often drawn to the gardens, smelling and exploring. With the different smells, different people came to mind.

"When she came across a jar of ground cinnamon, Elena remembered the ailing senator. Upon the stove, she found the coffee kettle already percolating and steaming hot, and she knew the kitchen staff had not long been absent.

"As she checked the percolating coffee, that feeling of the older man came over her. Elena dropped in a pinch of the cinnamon, then searched the spices for something else. She touched her fingertip into the dark powder of the red pepper, then stirred her finger into some cream from the ice box.

"'Why would I do such a thing?' she asked herself, but somehow she knew that he would greatly enjoy it. One more pinch of cinnamon, the cream added to the black brew, then a single drop of citrus juice and two dashes from other unknown spices.

"Elena gave the grateful politician his cup and saucer, noticing the blanket over his lap as her father continued his monologue, now on Australian traders. Then the face of her mother appeared in the open window behind the senator's head. She motioned for Elena to have her father come outside.

"Over an hour passed before they thought again of Señor Emory. To their distress, they learned that he had returned to Manila. Elena's mother vowed to lock Alexa up, send her to the convent, or ship her away to a foreign country and marry her off to the first man who saw her arrival.

"The next day, the politician was back at their door with his wife.

"'I awoke with the dawn and felt a youth about me that I haven't felt in years. What kind of coffee did your marvelous daughter serve? I believe it cured my ailment at once. From the first sip to the last drop, I felt a strength and cure come over me. Could your daughter make more of that coffee? My wife has suffered from an ailment of the womb since the stillbirth of our son, and she is in pain quite often.'

"It was a turning point for Elena and for the entire hacienda. The senator's wife also felt improvement after drinking a lemonade with a surprising dash of yellow curry that Elena chose to make instead of coffee. Word spread. Her mother had no choice but to allow Elena into the kitchen. She trained beneath the hacienda chef until the old woman happily turned the kitchen over to the younger woman's able hands.

"Her fame grew until the hacienda staff would drive away people and require appointments. They were paid in chickens, fruits, livestock, and sometimes actual money. Elena's healing powers were not always completely effective, but none left her kitchen without some sense of renewal. The family's debts were soon repaid, and the hacienda gained capital through gifts and payment.

"And then Elena met Amerel."

"Amerel?" Julia asked. "I thought the story was about Elena the Cook and Cortinez."

"So it is. But perhaps this is a tragic tale. . . ."

THEY TEASED HIM AS IF HE WERE ONE OF THEM. AND FOR THE first time in a long, long time—at least two weeks—Emman enjoyed every bit of it.

He was their leader now, and that fact had not yet sunk in—at least not with his friends. Emman was a man, a leader, and he'd kissed the hand of the beautiful Miss Julia.

The joy rushed through him, made his legs want to run so fast or make him laugh or shout. And so their teasing made him laugh as he hadn't done for some time. They were on duty for the night, and a game of hide-and-seek became part of that duty. Emman joined in, happy to run and hide and search out captives.

Miss Julia was safely inside the house, right on the other side of the courtyard and hacienda walls, so they could play in the waning moonlight. He had kissed her hand, and her skin was, well, it was a little sticky, he had to admit. It tasted a little like mango from the work he'd watched her do all evening with the other women. That sissy, city-boy Markus had worked with her, but surely Miss Julia—

"You're supposed to come looking for us!" Grace said, arms crossed at her chest.

"I am, I was giving extra time."

"No, you were thinking about Miss Julia again. Everyone knows you're in love with her." Grace's dirty face was scrunched in disgust and accusation.

"Oh, what does everyone know? I was put in charge of protecting her, that's all." But Emman realized the words were exactly right.

He was in love with Miss Julia.

THIRTEEN

ᗺᗢᕽᗢᕽ

Lola Gloria begged off from the story and passed it to Markus, instructing him to tell it correctly and fully while she went off to bed. "I'm too old to stay up after such a day. But do not lose this story, Markus, you understand? A story must be finished in its time."

Raul excused himself as well, and Markus and Julia sat alone in the very kitchen where Elena the Cook once created her miracles.

"So who is Amerel?" Julia asked, surprised at how alert she felt after the long day.

"This was my favorite hacienda story, except perhaps for the Carabao Named Rio Grande. But we'll save that one for another day. Okay, Amerel . . ." Markus rubbed his eyes and pushed his hair back. "I hope I do get this all right, or I'll be in big trouble.

"Amerel was a man described as beautiful—not that I would usually call any man beautiful."

Julia laughed.

"But this is the story, and I have promised Lola Gloria I will tell it as accurately as possible. Amerel was described as beautiful because his features were of masculine perfection. He was known throughout the province not only for his good looks but because of his incredible charm with the women.

"It was during the Christmas fiesta in the village, and Elena had baked several pastries, candies, and cakes. As Amerel walked the booths, with several girls following in his wake, he stopped for a piece of cake at Elena's booth.

"The first bite stopped him with a shudder from his mouth through his toes. His second taste nearly caused him to burst into tears as he remembered his childhood with vivid recollection and longing. As he thought of his years since, of all he had squandered in extravagance and promiscuity, a guilt rose within him so strong that he considered seeking the village priest. But by the final bite, Amerel experienced the honor of a man who'd come home a war hero, and he suddenly longed to do something of greatness.

"He had to know who had made that cake, and he quickly returned to the food stands, sending the other women away. When Elena had given him the cake, Amerel hadn't even noticed her. Now he found her stand near the courtyard dance floor where she was packing up a tray of *yema*—a Filipino candy—to return to Hacienda Esperanza. Amerel felt a spontaneous urge, much to the shock and devastation of a dozen or more young women, to drop to his knees, and he asked Elena for her hand in marriage.

"'My cake made you do this?' she asked. Elena, like all the other young women of the hacienda, town, and beyond the borders of the province of the Batangas, had dreamed of Amerel at one time or another. But she had never entertained any real illusions. Now, as Amerel waited on his knees before her, the band hushed, and all held their breath to hear her response.

"Elena was in a time of weariness, tired of sleeping her nights alone and longing for someone to share her recipes as well as to love and be loved for who she was. Though the scent of oleander came to her—a flower that is beautiful but poisonous—Elena chose to find the fragrance inviting. 'This is not proper, Amerel. But yes, I will marry you.'"

Markus paused a moment. "Are you tired, Julia?"

"Yes, but I want to hear the rest. Are you too tired?"

He answered by taking her hand and leading her outside. Then he carried two of the chairs to the center of the courtyard, gazing up at the sky from time to time before setting them down.

"We can see the stars best from this spot," he said, holding her chair as she sat. "Now you will hear another side of the story. For you see, Amerel had a younger brother named Cortinez."

"Ah, the younger brother, eh?" Julia looked up into the night sky.

"Yes. Unlike Amerel, Cortinez had loved Elena for several years before she'd become known throughout the province. As a child, he had dreamed of a plain-faced girl who had healing in her hands. He would watch Elena in the market and during Mass. Once he went to the hacienda courtyard and waited in a line of peasants who were there for healing recipes, but he rushed away when his turn approached.

"Cortinez knew of Elena's mother, how important money was to her. He had little to offer, being the second-born son without inheritance or wealth of his own and only a small shop where he carved furniture from nari-nari wood. And so he joined an expedition guiding Chinese traders into the jungles of Northern Luzon. They searched for a rare gold ore that he hoped would give him the financial backing to ask for Elena's hand. He was gone two years.

"During the final month of his expedition, while recuperating at a seaside village, a chance coincidence brought a former school-mate into port on a ship with a broken mast. That was how Cortinez learned that his brother, Amerel, had at long last chosen a woman to become his bride. It was his very Elena."

"How terrible," Julia said with a sigh.

Markus smiled at that, then continued. "Indeed it was, and poor Cortinez took that night to drink away his defeat. But all he could think of was Elena.

"Now the beauty of Amerel was combined with a broken character, which is always a dangerous recipe. Except for those honest moments while eating Elena's recipes, Amerel was arrogant, conceited, and if cornered into insecurity, cruel. When Amerel and Cortinez were children, they had seen a girl beaten to death by her father. Cortinez tried to stop the man, was beaten himself, and was the first to run for help. Amerel, a year older than Cortinez, watched the scene until the girl's blood had carefully soaked into the earth. No one accused him of cowardice, but Cortinez was praised for his bravery even though the girl died. But neither boy would speak of the event after that night.

"Amerel drew women young and old. His rivals were eliminated once he turned his eye upon a conquest. Infuriated men of all ages sought his blood. A father tried to kill him; three brothers arrived at his house to confront him and beat a servant by mistake; the jilted fiancé of one of Amerel's conquests left the area in utter devastation. He would have been killed, except that Amerel never traveled without his hired Samoan guard.

"One night, months into her engagement, after Elena had become accustomed to the notion of a future and dared give her heart and soul to believe its truth, and her dress was half-made for the wedding, she was invited to the rival plantation of Hacienda Morales. She suspected the invitation to be a request for a secret cure.

"Only years later did she learn that the Samoan conspired with her younger sister, Alexa, to expose the man Amerel truly was. Elena's cooking had brought unshed tears to the Samoan's eyes for the mother he'd lost in childhood. And though he protected Amerel daily, the Samoan hated his master for taking the virginity of his youngest sister. Alexa as well knew of the allure of Amerel, nearly to her own heartbreak, and she vowed to save her sister from a future of misery."

Markus paused. "Oh, did I say that Amerel had stopped eating the recipes that Elena prepared?"

"No. Why did he do that?"

"Amerel had a portion of good in him, as all men do. And when that goodness was tapped into, he saw himself and all that he had done. That's what Elena's recipes did to him. Amerel didn't want to feel those things for long."

"Interesting. I've known a few people like that," Julia said with humor. But then she realized how she avoided feeling certain things, ignored certain truths about herself. It was as if the hacienda were her own Elena recipe, spotlighting the way she'd run from seeking her purpose in life, fleeing from anything that didn't look safe.

Markus took up his tale again. "Now Elena had never been to Hacienda Morales. When she arrived, she was asked to meet the mistress of the house in the gardens. While waiting, she saw Amerel walking in the moonlight on the arm of an older woman. Their intimacy was evident even from a distance. As they approached, Amerel was startled to see Elena standing there. The older woman found amusement in Elena's distress."

"Oh no," Julia whispered, surprised to feel the pain she'd known when Nathan ended their relationship.

"Are you okay?" Markus asked.

Julia nodded. "What did Elena do?"

"Elena knew Amerel would make some ridiculous excuse that she was supposed to believe. Perhaps that this woman was his aunt or the mother of his childhood friend. He opened his mouth to deliver what she must accept to remain his future.

"She placed her hands over her ears. 'Do not say it to me.'

"He stood very still. 'What a child,' he said and turned back to the older woman.

"Elena walked the kilometers home as a storm rose upon the islands. At the midnight hour, the hacienda gateman was surprised to see Elena come through the misty darkness, and without greeting him as she always did. She continued forward like a lost soul. The gateman wondered if he'd really seen her until he saw her footprints marked on the wet driveway.

"Elena went to the kitchen and cooked the nightly warm milk with cinnamon, nutmeg, and slivers of chocolate for herself and her father. The kitchen maid retrieved a steaming mug for the don of the house and returned to find Elena gone and her cocoa untouched. Later the maid told of seeing Elena standing in the downpour on the courtyard stones, face up to accept the slap of the rain, arms out in resignation. 'How could You allow this? How could You forget me like this?' The maid was afraid and did not stop Elena's angry words to God."

Julia thought again of the months after she and Nathan broke up. Everyone went through heartache. Everybody had times when they had to start over. Every person alive experienced pain. So why couldn't she rise back up? It had frustrated and taken her into a deeper depression, until her work suffered and she'd had to find a roommate to help pay the bills. Her mother had wanted Julia to move home, and for a time she did. For two years, she'd floundered along.

Markus's deep voice pulled her from her past back to Elena's. "The storm did not quiet by the next morning, and it was discovered that Elena was gone. Word spread quickly of Amerel's betrayal and Elena's disappearance. On the second day, villagers from near and far came to search the hacienda for her. They braved the storm for several days until at last it faded. For one week, the grounds were covered in hordes of people who searched and trampled every section of land. Flickering candles filled the cathedral and prayer vigils were established.

"Upon hearing of his brother's betrayal, Cortinez quickly joined the search, haggard from his travels back from the expedition in Northern Luzon. A few interrogated Amerel as to his whereabouts the night and morning of the storm. But the rich doña gave him an alibi for the entire night.

"Elena's footsteps were difficult to trace, but trackers were confident that they'd found her path from the back porch through the gardens to the farthest section of the hacienda that ended at a cliff above the sea.

"Elena's family was surprised at the level of distress caused by her disappearance. They'd never guessed the far reach of their daughter's healing cuisine. Tears and wails filled the courtyards, and there was the scent of foods cooked on small ovens on the lawns as search parties were sent out through the days and nights.

"While Amerel disappeared to his mother's clan house in Mindanao, no one searched for Elena more than Cortinez. He collapsed each night in his quest for her, several nights not returning at all.

"Then it was discovered that Cortinez had not been seen for three days. The search became twofold, and when his footsteps were also tracked to the cliff above the sea, the searchers became fearful, making the sign of the cross and holding their amulets lest they be driven to the rocks below themselves.

"It was said that a curse had come to the hacienda. The candles were lit again, not as much for the poor soul of Cortinez, but for a plague of ailments that swept those who did not search for them. Most of the candles burned for Elena.

"The priest was kept up for days with confessions. A good-hearted man, he prayed for Elena, the young girl he'd always cherished, not just for the famous Elena the Cook. He reminded his flock with confidence, 'God Almighty can save them still.'

"A month later, early in the morning, Elena's parents woke to noise downstairs. Her father crept downstairs to discover the intruder, and her mother, too afraid to remain upstairs alone, followed behind, feeling terror with every step.

"'What if it is the Devil coming to take us?'

Her father held a gun and mother her rosary as they descended the stairs. They followed the noise until they stopped outside the kitchen, hearing pots and pans clatter inside.

"'My God!' Elena's mother gasped as they opened the door.

"Her father nearly dropped the gun.

"There stood Elena in the midst of cooking. And on a chair sat Cortinez.

"Elena's mother grasped her father's arm. 'Are they ghosts?'

"'I do not know.'

"Elena had the quality of a ghost. Beneath her usual apron, her dress was torn and soiled, her hair wild and tumbling over her shoulders as her father had never seen it before. Her face was pale, and when she looked up, she smiled such an expression of peace that it took both her parents aback. The cooking had put a thin misty smoke throughout the kitchen. Cortinez turned in his chair, where he had been watching Elena. His unshaven face and angelic presence confirmed that they were both dead and now ghouls in the house.

"'Mother, Father,' Elena said with joy as she wiped her hands on her apron and rushed to embrace them. Even after feeling the touch of her, the solidity of her being, her parents still were unsure whether or not she was a specter returned to haunt the house.

"Her father studied her movements as she moved back to stir something on the stove. The table was covered with oysters, prawns, cut vegetables, chicken, a bag of rice, and spices of many colors and fragrances. 'Where have you been?'

"'I do not know,' Elena said. Her features had not changed, but a radiance filled her face that made her beautiful. 'Cortinez found me.'

"Elena's mother threw her hands into the air and burst into tears. 'This makes no sense at all.'

"Elena explained that she didn't know she was gone so long, saying that it was as if she'd died or lived in a dream. Then Cortinez came, and he was in that dream with her. Not until they returned from the cove did they know they were actually alive.

"Her mother paused in her tears to stare at Elena incredulously, then covered her hands and wailed again.

"Then Cortinez cleared his throat and said, 'I searched for days, as did everyone. But I believed that my love would make Elena live. I went again to the cliff where all believed she had fallen and been taken by the sea. I climbed down and found a piece of her dress, but I continued to believe. My words were to God, the only God of truth and love, of creation and miracle, of all things good and of holy beauty. To Him I bravely spoke that I would believe until Elena was found alive. I searched down the cliff and on the rocks below. I searched a small beach of black and white sands that was secluded and deep enough to remain even in high tide. I explored until I could not walk another step, and there fell asleep. When I awoke, Elena was there by the sea, picking flowers from a vine that grew up the cliff side. She hadn't seen me yet.'

"'It was this flower,' Elena said. From the cooking table she lifted a soft pink blossom. It looked like a tiny orchid with darker pink spots and a yellow center.

"'It is from the cove,' she said, holding it tenderly. She then plucked it in half, bringing a gasp to the lips of the others, though none were sure why it seemed such a travesty. Elena smiled and dropped the two halves into a large batter. She took several other blossoms and did the same; each time there was a sharp pain within each of them when Elena tore the delicate blossom in half. They were silent as they watched Elena, who was beautiful in an indefinable way, as she stirred the bowl with a smile on her lips.

"At last her father asked Cortinez. 'And what happened when Elena saw you?'

" 'She came to me as if waiting for me. And we stayed there together. I do not remember sleeping or eating, only walking the beach, swimming in the sea, picking the flowers, gathering oysters, and digging for clams. I speared fish and a squid. It could have been one day or weeks perhaps, but none of our catch grew old. It was always as fresh as the day we caught it. We swam and walked. But, sir, we were innocent of all impropriety. There was no thought of anything else or anyone else or anyplace else. We were like children, and even now I can't understand it. I know how it must sound. But at the times, we thought nothing of it all. It was . . . well, it was all we knew. Then one day Elena remembered the village priest and thought she heard him calling to her. So we climbed the cliff. And suddenly we began to remember as we found the path back to the hacienda house.'

"Her father rubbed his head, closed his eyes, and said, 'I must get the priest.'

"Elena cooked through the day and all the next night. She seemed in a dream, and the many villagers who came to see the truth of her and Cortinez's resurrection were too entranced to interrupt her creation. Cortinez watched, made coffee, and slept, but stayed always in the kitchen near Elena. She would allow no one to help her in the cooking. The priest arrived and prayed over the couple, thanked God for returning them, and gave the only explanation possible, 'God's ways are not our own.'

"That evening a multitude gathered, all drawn there as they had been when Elena disappeared and yet not knowing how to leave. And then Elena was at the doorway, peering into the dusk where dozens and dozens of people sat on benches or around tables, some playing games, others talking with babies in their arms.

"They went to silence as they saw her there, hair still wild and the apron now stained with spices.

"'It is time to eat,' she announced.

"Those who took a plate of Elena's paella were said to have become nearly drunk with a joy none had known before. Some later believed it was simply the relief that the two young people were alive, but most agreed that it was Elena's cooking. The batter into which she had dropped the orchid was made into a huge beautiful cake that was beyond description.

"The drunkenness of joy found in the paella and cake infected them all. They laughed and cried. Several guitarists began playing in the yard, and even the old women danced as they hadn't in decades. Cortinez walked among them, observing and smiling. He would touch the shoulders of those eating on the ground and kneel beside the children, whispering things that brought their laughter.

"Two long-held grudges were resolved that night. One was between a man and woman who had loved each other in their youth. A misunderstanding separated them for forty years. That night they reunited and were married the following week. The other was between a woman and her daughter. The daughter had married against her mother's wishes, severing their bond. When her husband deserted her and her child, the daughter remained resolute in her independence. Mother and daughter would see one another at the market and never speak. The older woman stared at her granddaughter as she grew into a young child. But they had never touched or held one another in all the days of the child's life. Nothing dramatic closed the rift that night. After eating the paella, they simply walked from their separate groups of friends and family members and embraced without words or actions. The granddaughter jumped into her grandmother's arms as if it were the most usual habit in the world.

"That night would be spoken of for years to come. New miracles were discovered and most all could have been expounded upon in the retelling except that the miraculous was so profound, embellishment became ridiculous.

"The paella seemed to never end. The cake, though cut a thousand times, still had the upper layer. Some say it was similar to Jesus's feeding of the five thousand, but others feared heresy at such a comparison. Still others said that by giving God His due glory and prayer, such a miracle was only praise to Him and His power on earth and not of pride to Elena.

"The anniversary of that night became the annual hacienda fiesta, a celebration of those who lived and worked upon the land. And Elena's paella was the main dish, her orchid cake the dessert. And so every year Cortinez and Elena disappeared for several nights and returned with the Elena orchid."

Markus took Julia's hand and turned it over carefully, then slowly made the shape of the orchid in the palm of her hand. "That is how Lola Gloria draws it whenever she tells the story."

"Are the orchids in the field from the Elena orchid?"

"Oh no. Every attempt to transplant the orchid has failed. And it's actually been decades since anyone has brought the flower to the house, from what the Tres Lolas tell me. The Tres Lolas believe that when next the orchid is found, the hacienda will again come alive."

"Is it that difficult to find?"

"Apparently. I don't know."

"And do you think it really exists? It's not some mythical flower?"

"Oh, it certainly exists. My grandmother is from the hacienda, and she and my grandfather fell in love here when he worked as a temporary field hand. Our grandfathers were friends; in fact, Captain Morrison helped finance my grandfather so he could study at the University of the Philippines, which is the most prestigious school in the country. My grandfather became a lawyer—I interned at his firm before he died."

Julia couldn't see Markus's face well in the low lights. "So what happened to Elena? Did she and Cortinez marry?"

Markus smiled, she could see that well enough. "You've become infatuated by the story as well, I see. Yes, yes indeed. They lived here at the hacienda where they raised, I believe, four children—you must ask Lola Gloria to be sure. But I know that Elena the Cook is one of your great-great-grandmothers."

"Are they also buried in the cemetery?"

"Well, no. Apparently their bodies were never found."

"What do you mean?"

"The legend says that the night of a beautiful blue moon, when very old, Elena and Cortinez went walking in the night. The kitchen maid saw them holding hands in the garden. Trackers later found their pathway all the way to the same cliff overlooking the sea. And there the tracks ceased. For a long while, villagers believed they'd return. But those in the hacienda knew that they were truly gone. Their presence had left, and the kitchen felt the absence."

The story over, Julia walked Markus to his car. He insisted that he had no choice but to drive back to Manila, though Julia expressed her worry about his driving so late and after such a long day.

Markus paused a moment. "Do you want to know the fate of Amerel?"

"Yes."

"He remained the most beautiful man wherever he lived. But his interest in charm and desire waned completely after Elena. He desired nothing and yet had continuous propositions. He created offense and anger wherever he went. Some believed he desired men instead of women, but it was simply that he lusted for nothing. And soon enough, wherever he went, word would come about his childhood cowardice and his role in Elena's story. And so a folk story began where Amerel was the beguiling villain like the beautiful Lucifer himself. It is said that he scarred his face with his own knife and lived out his final years in an isolated nipa hut on an island in the Visayas. But I do not know if that is true or not."

Julia smiled in the soft light of the night.

"This is a land of myth and folklore, Julia. And strangely, when I am here, I believe every bit of it as truth. The longer you are here, the more you will feel the same. You will see."

They reached his car, and Markus shook her hand gently.

Julia felt a strange vitality run between them. "Nice to meet you, Mr. Santos," she said, smiling.

"And you, Julia." He opened the car door. The interior light shone on his face, and Julia had a sudden urge to walk forward and kiss him.

She took a step back. Recalling her conversation with Nathan at the coffee shop, she said, "Markus, you wouldn't happen to be a rice farmer, would you?'

He raised an eyebrow and chuckled. "That's an odd question."

"I have my reasons."

"I live in Manila and practice law, but I do own some fields. So yeah, I guess you could say I'm a rice farmer. I hope that's not a bad thing."

Julia covered her eyes with her hands and laughed to herself. *Of course*, she thought.

FOURTEEN

The next days brought a slow succession of activity to the hacienda grounds. Manalo's men reported on the preparations for Captain Morrison's body to arrive within days. They kept a record of the comings and goings. Raul was ever on the move all over the hacienda.

The Barangay had their men at the border and sweeping through the plantation, making it difficult to stay for any amount of time. They were formidable foes, that was certain. Other than the Moros in the southern province of Mindanao, Manalo had not met with such skill and discipline. He worried about his men who'd grown lax and weary of jungle life, that they were not the fighters they had once been.

Paco reported to him after he studied the structure of the house and learned the room location of the American woman. Manalo himself remained miles away in the surrounding mountains as they gathered information and came up with plans.

Trouble was incited in the town. Bar fights, the burning of some abandoned cars, some tourists attacked, a few shops robbed, and an owner terrorized.

Manalo was angry about some of the excess and angrier still to learn that it wasn't the Red Bolos who were responsible—the mercenaries had been invited to town. What was Comrade Pilo thinking? And though Manalo feared what occurred when incompetence and undisciplined mercenaries mixed, some of the created chaos was necessary. For Paco reported that throughout the town, people were talking about the return of Captain Morrison as eagerly as the return of President Marcos Ferdinand's body had been despised. Many viewed the Captain as a symbol of hope, change, and progress. If they only knew what democracy bred—greed, selfish ambition, more poverty, and gaps in the class structure. But belief was hard to crush. It was a delicate matter. Chaos and fear could divide, or they could create alliances.

Everything was culminating at the funeral and wake. The mayor was coming out. Corruption fed and clothed the mayor of San Juan. The people would be gathered there to see their hope returned. And the American woman would of course be there—and must not be drawn into the land, but learn to fear it. And soon enough, the death of the missing boy would be revealed, and hopefully Manalo's plan would work.

If Manalo received the word, they would assassinate the mayor, or anyone who posed a threat. Anyone. The mercenaries might be blamed, but this untrustworthy bunch wouldn't keep the secrets of the Communists, and Manalo saw the critical nature of the coming days as he stared into the night sky and analyzed all these insomniac thoughts.

One thing was essential—the American woman had to leave the Philippines as soon as the funeral was over. Her continued presence was a threat that the higher-ups would not tolerate. In all his years as a rebel fighter, Manalo had never killed a woman. He dreaded such a thought, was unsure if he even could. But others would not hesitate. And with his family in the clutches of Comrade Pilo, he was in no position to argue.

Manalo had hoped all night that Timeteo wouldn't delay his return from speaking with Comrade Pilo, and when he heard the footsteps, he rose quickly to meet him on the perimeter of the camp.

Timeteo's face was hidden in the darkness, but his voice sounded heavy as he talked about the meeting. "I met not only with Comrade Pilo but afterward with one of his bodyguards who owed me—don't ask why, it's a long story."

"Does it involve a monkey?"

"Of course, doesn't it always?" he said lightly.

It was their inside joke, because Timeteo had once paid a debt with a monkey for the debtor's daughter. He had won the monkey in a different gambling game. But the monkey was mean and tried to bite the girl, so Timeteo had to pay the debt in double for the misdeed.

"Okay, give me the bad news."

"There has been major chaos in the leadership in Manila and abroad."

"What has happened?"

"The Old Man is dead, and a viable leader is not easily found to replace him. But also it is the effect of the foreign crisis in the Communist movement."

"Yes, I know it does affect us, even here in our jungle exis-tence," Manalo said wryly, thinking of the Communist countries

that had fallen like dominoes in the recent years since the wall of
Berlin came down.

How did men like himself and Timeteo live in such conditions
and remain subject to decisions and plans made by men in palaces
in Beijing or Moscow?

"What did you see as having the greatest effect on us?"

"Well, no one trusts anyone now. They want assurances of loyalty, and the measures of such have been extreme at times. While
the Leftist students at the University of the Philippines march
around and gather support, or at least respect, the fighters have
the eye of suspicion on us—leaders are digging through both our
pasts and our recent maneuvers." Timeteo was quiet a moment.
"We can talk of all this in the morning, if you want. I have to tell
you something."

"What is it?"

"I know where they are."

Manalo felt a cold chill in his veins. "Does Comrade Pilo know
that you know?"

"He does not. What do you want to do?"

"If I go, then it will be noticed and viewed as disloyalty."

"What if I go?" Timeteo said.

Manalo put his hand on his friend's shoulder. "Yes. Timeteo, go
and see her for me. Let me get the backpack of gifts for her and
the children, and we'll give them some money. And set a time that
I can call her or she me on a public telephone."

Poor Timeteo didn't hesitate to leave after just arriving, and
Manalo didn't even ask him to get some hours of sleep. He wanted
his friend to reach Malaya as quickly as possible. His best friend
knew this without saying.

Manalo still couldn't sleep. And though a part of him didn't
know if he deserved it—what guerrilla fighter did—he was thank-
ful to have the feeling of hope once again.

"I COULD SWEAR YOU'VE BEEN GONE FOR WEEKS." NATHAN CALLED in his night, her early afternoon, surprised to find out she was sixteen hours ahead of him.

"Yeah, I guess for me too," she said. "It's such a different world here."

Julia wanted to tell him how she walked the grounds when the morning dew was still fresh on the earth, and that every morning she found a gift outside her veranda doorway—a trinket or new type of fruit. She wished to tell how she'd explored the old coconut groves with the massive piles of shelled-out hulls. A few times she'd stopped by the garage and handed tools to Mang Berto as he scooted beneath the belly of one of his cars. Or how sometimes she was drawn to the path near the overgrown orchid fields where the flowers grew through a mass overgrowth of vines and foliage. She'd discovered a small spring there in the thicket and wondered if it ended at the fishpond. She planned to find out before she left.

Instead, Nathan told her about the accounts he was getting in his freelance advertising business. A few of his new clients were enough to make his competition green with envy. "We have more work than we know what to do with."

"You aren't doing the business alone?" she asked, already guessing what he hinted at.

"No . . . I am," he said. "And if you want to be part of it, it's yours."

Julia stood at the kitchen wall where the telephone was attached. The Tres Lolas and Aling Rosa were in the kitchen, doing their usual cooking routines. Something simmered gently on the stove and filled the room with a fragrance that made her mouth water.

The past few days had been full of peace and solace with such quiet routines. Raul came and went with the hacienda's business at hand, answering her questions about operations over a cup of barako coffee, or leaning over the map he unrolled on his desk.

And then there was Markus. The Tres Lolas talked conspiratorially and said, "Markus sure comes all the way out here a lot suddenly."

"Julia, I miss you. I want you back in my life."

He wanted her back. *He* missed her. Hadn't it always been about what he wanted? Mostly that was her fault, she knew. Julia didn't voice her wants and desires, and so Nathan didn't see how much of their life together had been ruled by him, his feelings, his wants.

When she didn't respond, Nathan asked, "Did you hear me?"

"Yes."

"And? Don't leave a guy hanging."

"If I answer that right now, then I will have to say no."

He laughed, taking it as a joke. "No? Then perhaps don't answer me until you return."

"Nathan, what has suddenly made you so attached to me?"

"It's not attachment, Jules."

"Then what is it?"

He paused, then said with confidence. "I'm still in love with you. I've always been in love with you. Or at the very least, I'm falling back in love with you."

They were the words she had once longed to hear. Closing her eyes, they wove through her. So he loved her after all, or still, or again. It had been the life she'd desired, the life she knew, the life that made her safe. Julia could have that again, but this time she wanted to do it right. Stand up for her wants, grow and become the woman she was meant to be. But had she been in love with Nathan, or with the life with Nathan? Probably both. And yet that life now appeared a colorless dream.

"Julia, listen. I'm here. We made mistakes in the past. But the time apart and the few days before you left confirmed in me that without a doubt you are the woman for me. We were meant to be together. If you aren't sure, that's okay. Take your time; figure out what you want. But I know it's going to be me. I'll wait for you, but don't make me wait too long. No man can wait forever."

"I can't talk about this right now," Julia said.

The Tres Lolas kept glancing at her as she talked. Lola Sita had answered the phone, and though she couldn't speak a lot of English, she certainly knew that a man from the States had called for her.

"Okay," he responded with an edge of annoyance.

"Did you get the phone number from my mother?"

"Yes. She didn't sound happy that you're over there."

"She's not. I need to call her."

"Are there people around? Is that why you can't talk about us right now?" he persisted. Nathan always persisted until he got what he wanted. It was a gift that helped him to snag clients, to build a business, and to gather friends and associates that he chose.

Julia knew she might regret what she now said. "If you want to know, then I'll tell you. I've waited too long to hear those words. You always want what you can't have, Nathan, and you work until you get it. Being here, it's changed me. Even in this short amount of time. I don't know what the future holds, but I know the past is behind me, and I won't go back to it."

"Wow. You really are finding the Julia I first fell in love with. Listen, I'm not put off by this. You take your time. When you get back, I'm taking you to dinner—on your terms, of course. You choose the place, the time, and whatever you want. When is the funeral?"

"The wake begins tomorrow. But, Nathan—"

"We'll talk when you get back," he said.

After she hung up the telephone, Lola Gloria motioned for Julia to sit at the table as she set a cup of hot tea before her.

"How did you know this was just what I needed?" Julia asked.

"Lolas always know," the older woman said with a gentle pat on Julia's shoulder. "Do you want to talk about it?"

Julia did want to talk about it. Lola Gloria nodded with interest as she told how she and Nathan had met eight years earlier, brought together as friends of friends, and how they slowly fell in love. Then the many years together, mostly smooth and uneventful. Good years, good memories. They were right for each other; it was obvious to everyone. And then their breakup and the two years apart.

Julia found herself reciting the facts without emotion, and it felt more like a story she'd once heard than her own. Strangely, those memories were like a black-and-white world, while life here felt vivid with color. And yet this didn't feel like home to her either.

When she had told these things, Lola Gloria sat for a time, then responded. "Julia, be careful following what *feels* right in a day. Our feelings change with a moment, or a word." She added sugar to her own tea and stirred it slowly. "You must find the answer to such questions in life. Not ignore them or go off the momentary emotion. First, seek God in these things. Ask for His guidance. The heart itself is a fickle organ. Then seek your purpose, and once you find it, be dedicated to those things God instilled within you even through the bad feelings." The older woman smiled gently.

"I pray for everyone and all the situations that I know on the hacienda and for our country. I pray our dear Raul will hurry up and court Mara before another man steals her away. A woman shouldn't have to wait that long. And I will pray for you too, little *hija*, that God would guide you in all these matters of heart and life."

"Thank you, Lola Gloria."

"May I ask you about something other than Nathan?"

Julia nodded, expecting to be queried about her feelings for Markus.

"You mentioned your mother while on the phone. Why haven't you called her since arriving?"

Julia knew her mother would be anxious and irritated that she'd been gone so many days without sending word back home. "Well, I've been busy, and when I think of it and calculate the time, it's always the middle of the night."

Lola Gloria gave her a maternal frown.

"That's the truth. But okay, it's also that I dread talking to her. I know how the conversation will go. She won't want to hear anything about how things are here—kind of like Nathan, actually—and she'll just be anxious—anxious that I'm here, anxious for me to return, anxious about everything."

Lola Gloria took her time and stirred her tea. "Before the Captain died, did they reconcile?"

"My mother spent some time with him before his death. I think whatever they discussed brought a measure of peace to my grandfather. But I think my mother still can't quite forgive him. She blames all her life problems on him. Her divorce, her lack of trust in men. I think she even blamed my failed relationship with Nathan on my grandfather—though I'm not sure why."

Lola Gloria nodded in thought and then said, "Another person to pray for—your mother."

After talking to Lola Gloria, Julia left the house and walked through the hacienda gate and down the main road. She thought she'd buy some treats for the children and had an idea in mind. Tomorrow her grandfather's remains would arrive, and she'd been banished from all housework despite her continued attempts to join in and help. Lola Gloria explained that it was insulting to the hacienda to have a guest, their doña no less, doing the housework. Julia left with some guilt, but soon enjoyed the walk and time to think.

Hacienda Esperanza was discovery, layer upon layer.

And strangely, Julia felt that God was easier to reach in this place than in her busy existence in the States. She envisioned returning once a year to recover this solace and peace that soothed her spirit. She felt strong again—in only days—ready to sow ideas, push hope into faith by resurrecting old dreams and having the courage of pursuit.

At the hacienda gate, three security guards smiled and greeted her cordially while remaining at their posts—one on each side and another inside a covered shelter. Julia noticed the firearms on their belts; and instead of casual clothing, they wore crisp uniforms of black pants, white starched shirts, and black shoulder straps with M-16s and the seal of the hacienda on the front pocket.

She waved a greeting, though the assault rifles sent a shiver of fear through her. She increased her pace, swinging a basket at her side, until soon the men were behind her. Julia recalled the daily transformations around the hacienda. The extra trips to buy food, the renewed cleaning and airing out of rooms, the increase of staff working the gardens and courtyards. Preparations made for the return of the last don of the hacienda.

She turned down the road Lola Gloria had directed her to, where she could catch a jeepney into the larger town of San Pablo. Before long a jeepney approached, and Julia put out a hand to wave it down, acting braver than she felt.

"Is this going to San Pablo?" she asked, leaning through the passenger window.

Three men and two children were squeezed together in the front of the jeep. The passengers simply stared at her.

"San Juan. Yes," said the driver.

She walked to the back, bent low, and climbed inside, squeezing into an opening of passengers on the bench running along the side. The dark eyes stared at her curiously. Julia took some Philippine pesos, unsure of the amount. As she wondered whom to pay and if she should do it now or once arriving in San Juan, one of the passengers reached out to take the coins. At first she thought the old woman in the blue dress was soliciting money, until she gave a respectful nod toward the driver and Julia understood. Her bus fare was passed hand to hand by the passengers until the bus driver reached out and took it. A moment later his hand reappeared, and the change was passed hand to hand back to her.

The jeepney made other stops with passengers squeezing in closer or getting off; each time, the fare passed hand to hand up and the change back.

Two girls in school uniforms giggled from the corner and pulled out a celebrity magazine. One pointed to a picture, and they looked up to Julia and then back to the magazine. She smiled at their interest.

"No, she is family of Captain Morrison."

Julia leaned forward to see the speaker, an attractive man in the front corner.

"Yes, I am. How did you—" Then she realized how foolish her question was. If he knew of her grandfather, it was obvious that a Caucasian in the area would most likely be a relative. "I am his granddaughter."

A few others seemed to have already guessed who she was by their knowing nods and smiles. One young woman leaned toward her. "Our family comes tomorrow to wake of Captain Morrison. We see you tomorrow."

"Good, very nice," Julia said as the jeepney decelerated roughly and made a stop near a busy intersection.

"This is San Pablo," the woman said, picking up a briefcase between her feet.

"Thank you," Julia said and followed her. A plume of black exhaust blew around them as the jeepney took off again.

"Do you need assistance here?" the woman asked.

"No, I'm just buying a few things. Thank you."

"Okay. Here is calling card if you need assistance or a ride back to Hacienda Esperanza or anything at all. If not, my family will see you at the wake." The woman shook Julia's hand before leaving and gave her a business card.

People brushed by her along the roadside market. Julia paused a moment to feel their touch, even when jostled a bit, or the current of air at a passing. Many would stare at her curiously, the only white woman around. She thought of all these human entities, each with an individual design and inner machine working to keep on existing. Their thoughts and memories and plans like energy in the air. Children playing, women looking at fruits or flowers. Men standing together watching a television set on a table. Julia had the strangest impulse, wishing to stretch out her arms and gather them all into her. Of course, she kept walking as if unaware of the miracle of life and community and humanity right in this little piece of earth.

The girl at the roadside sari-sari store had set her tables beneath the covered canvas porch of a wooden shack. She put out breads, candies, and snacks in individual containers. A large blue ice chest was filled with glass bottles of Coca-Cola and a few cans of various colas. Julia bought a drink and picked out goodies for the children of the hacienda and Barangay.

In the wooden shack beside them, a middle-aged man smoked and held a water hose, filling up tanks in a wooden cart. Another man had a wide cart filled with buckets of fish where several women gathered around. A woman in a purple skirt and yellow apron pointed inside a bucket. Two large silver fish were set on a scale. They were discussed; the man took them off and then put them back on to be weighed again. Finally, one fish was chosen and rolled in a brown paper wrapping. Sounds of cocks crowing and the zoom of cars and tricycles coming up and down the street mixed with the hum of air conditioners from the larger buildings and homes.

Julia bought the basketful of surprises for the children and then returned to the jeepney stop, hoping for as easy of a journey home.

Back at the hacienda, Mang Berto was napping on the lawn beside a Model T Ford. He hopped up quickly when Julia approached. He rubbed his eyes and set his hands firmly on his hips. "There you are. I was told you ventured out without me."

"The exercise was invigorating."

"In-vigor-a-ting is not a word I know, but I guess it is a good thing?"

"Yes, very good."

"Miss Julia, you must be careful. Let Mang Berto drive you to town if you must go."

"Why? Was it not safe?"

"Philippines is very safe for visitors. Filipinos most hospitable people of the world—at least I hear this said. I do not know the world so well. But this week especially. Your grandfather's return. You are important person to many. And to some, you might be seen as a danger. If they believe you are a danger, then they might be dangerous to you. Do you understand this?"

"Not fully. But I will trust you. Except I rode in a jeepney, and all by myself."

Mang Berto laughed. "What a big girl you've become."

"I needed to go," she said, "to see if I could do it. I felt like a local."

"Yes, okay, fine. But be careful from now until funeral done. Let me drive you."

The outer grounds of the hacienda had come alive since the evening before. Workers were rearranging furniture, cleaning windows, airing out the house, preparing food. The outer courtyards were covered in folding chairs and tables.

Visitors with offerings of food and flowers arrived to meet Julia or stood talking in circles around the house and yard. Bouquets of tropical flowers—birds-of-paradise, orchids, the tubular rose, and others—mixed aromas with the foods being prepared continually in the kitchen. The sleepy veins of the house and outside grounds pulsed with life.

EMMAN TRIED TYING THE THIN BLACK TIE AROUND HIS NECK for the fifth time. It was so aggravating! It had been one of those days, one of those he heard the men talk about in exaspera-tion. Now he was having them. And woman trouble . . . oh boy, was he.

She was beautiful and nice, the American, but Miss Julia was not the most cooperative person to guard. While Emman slept during the day, the boys and Grace had lost her. They thought she was out for a walk and followed her unseen in the jungle, never expecting her to hop on a jeepney and disappear into town. By they time they got to town, she was missing, and then finally they found her back at the hacienda.

Groan.

Emman could not have such lack of discipline in his ranks. Especially since he probed the boys and Grace until Kiko finally confessed that he had caught a green snake that distracted them all, even though Grace kept telling them to focus.

He chewed them out—except for Grace, who was looking strangely less like a boy lately—and had them do calisthenics as well as clean out Bok's family's chicken coop. Plus they'd be feed-ing the chickens for a week—that was Bok's idea, so that he didn't have to do it. His sister was too upset by her boyfriend's disappear-ance to do much work lately.

Emman's cousins said women were more trouble than their

worth, and all the men agreed. But even Emman knew they didn't mean it. And he didn't mean it toward Miss Julia either.

Emman decided to change the schedule now, so he'd be near Miss Julia during the day, though he'd miss the nights with Bok and the ones alone with his yo-yo. For the wake and funeral, he'd been assigned to inside the house—he'd done that assigning himself. At last, he'd get to see the inside of the hacienda house. He couldn't wait!

Maybe he needed to talk to Miss Julia about her wandering off so carelessly. He'd been told of more fights among the field-workers, brawls in the bars in town, and the rumors that a major insurgent action was building up as sure as Mount Pinatubo kept letting off signals of a catastrophic eruption.

Tying the tie in a basic knot at his neck, he hoped Miss Julia might see it and decide to tie it for him like he'd seen on the movies. She'd come close and he'd smell her perfume, feel the briefest touch of her hand brush his neck. Maybe she'd give him a peck on the forehead or cheek. He closed his eyes and envisioned it.

Abner burst into the room. "Come on, Emman, what are you doing? Get your head out of the clouds, or is it in the gutter? We have to get to the wake—have some respect."

Emman hurried to slip on his shoes, noticing how short his pants were—his lack of socks showed for all to see—and the sleeves of the black jacket he'd worn for his mother's funeral were partway up his wrists. He was a man now, a bodyguard to an American, and he still had to wear such clothing. Talk about no respect.

FIFTEEN

❧

"Where did they all come from?" Julia asked Raul as they walked outside the open front doors dressed in their funeral attire. It appeared that hundreds of people were gathered on the front lawn as more vehicles drove down the road to search for parking along the already packed driveway. Some carried more flowers or prayer books, and many of the women held red or white candles that flickered in the descending light.

"The villages all over Batangas and beyond. As I said, your grandfather was a respected man."

The people lined the road like spectators awaiting a parade. Some elderly sat in lawn chairs and held small American or Philippine flags in their hands. The gathering hushed in a solemn respect, even the children who had been weaving and playing around the adults. The only sound beyond the tropical birds calling in the jungle was the sound of vehicles coming far down the hacienda road.

The chrome-covered jeepney gleamed brightly, catching the low evening light as it came slowly down the drive. Her grandfather had requested such a return instead of a grand hearse that most rich men would be carried in. A painted sign over the windshield read "Praise Be to God." Flowers were draped along the front grill, tucked into side mirrors, and tied along the roof all the way to the back to the bumper. As people stood, more flowers were tossed over the vehicle. Behind the jeepney followed a line of vehicles including expensive luxury cars, horse-drawn carts, and several tricycles that filled the air with their high-pitched whines.

Julia followed Raul down the walkway. She gathered with the others along the edge of the driveway. She recognized many in the lines of faces, some she'd met that day as well as the hacienda workers she'd seen in the fields or gardens and house. The cousins were mixed together with their extended families. Julia saw her cousin Mara, who was close to her age and someone she thought could become a very close friend. Mara stood with an older couple beside two other cousins, Francis and Othaniel.

Julia felt the rustle of the children of the Barangay come behind her, surrounding her, instead of peering from the bushes as usual. They were easy to distinguish from the other children by their tattered clothing and necklaces strung around their necks. A few smaller ones she hadn't met before looked younger than age five, and they touched her dress and gave her worried smiles. The boys' hair was slicked and pressed to their heads, and the girl had brushed her matted mess and pulled it into a ponytail again. Brown eyes looked up at her in proud expectation.

"You all look fine, so very fine," she said to them, knowing few understood her at all.

Raul stepped from the crowd as the jeepney slowed to a stop. He leaned into the window and pointed forward to the driver. The jeepney turned and backed toward the front walkway. A number of men gathered and the back was opened, giving Julia her first glimpse of her grandfather's casket. She now saw that Markus was standing with Francis and Othaniel; she hadn't realized he had arrived already. More people pressed in close, with some still arriving and those who had lined the driveway gathering around the jeepney. The deeper silence of voices amplified the shuffle of footsteps, every car door closing, the tropical birds and some rooster crowing in the distance.

Then the pathway parted like the opening of the Red Sea from the jeepney to the house. Raul motioned for Julia and the Tres Lolas, who came behind her, and they walked to the vehicle as Raul, Markus, Francis, Othaniel, and two others from the hacienda lifted out the black casket draped with an American flag.

Lola Sita took Julia's hand and gave her some flowers. The three women put their hands on the casket, and Julia as well felt compelled to touch the smooth, black wood. Grandpa Morrison was inside, having journeyed across the sea to return to his beloved Hacienda Esperanza.

Together with Lola Amor and Lola Gloria, Julia and Lola Sita walked in front of the casket as it was carried toward the house. Mang Berto stood at the open double doors like a butler receiving them.

Julia turned back at the top step and saw Amang Tenio, dressed in a bright red robe. His red rooster was missing from his arms today; instead he held what appeared to be a long rooster tail with a leather strap wrapped around his wrist. He followed the casket, and his voice rose in a chanting cry. He tapped the rooster tail in the air and took heavy, defined steps with his eyes nearly closed. The children of the Barangay came behind Amang

Tenio, holding their amulets against their chests as they bent their heads as if in prayer.

Their footsteps on the hardwood floor and the low chants of Amang Tenio were the only sounds inside the house as they proceeded between the flowers through the entryway and down into the great room. The men carried the coffin to a long heavy table covered in a lace cloth and surrounded by flowers and dozens of candles. Othaniel adjusted the American flag. Around the room against the wall were benches and chairs set in rows. In the back were tables with cookies and carafes of coffee. Instead of entering the great room, Julia saw Amang Tenio and the children of the Barangay standing close at the open double doors. After a few moments, they disappeared from view.

Julia sat on a chair close to the coffin with the Tres Lolas in a row beside her. She'd been told of the schedule of events for the wake and funeral, but mostly her role was to greet extended family and citizens who had come to pay their respects. She thought of her grandfather again, that here was his body just inches from her inside the polished wooden coffin. A shiver of eeriness passed through her; she couldn't help but wonder what his corpse looked like after traveling across the sea from California. The strangeness of death here beside them, so close and acceptable, was something harder for Americans, she'd been told. There was the sense of a more primitive world in the abundance of ceremony for the dead man inside this very box.

The dramatic entrance of an old Filipino priest, walking with his robe just brushing the wood floor, further amplified her thoughts. He carried a censor on a metal chain, spewing incensed smoke as it swung with his steps. He chanted in Latin, and suddenly the mourners in line behind him began to sing. The voices were like dominoes through the house, and soon the song was heard through the windows from outside as well.

The room was quickly filled with people standing or sitting, swaying in their song, sniffling and crying, serious expressions carved into faces.

Julia was the only one silent.

From her place beside the coffin, she saw the glistening tears on the priest's weathered cheeks as he touched the coffin with something more than reverence, holding his hand on the American flag for the longest time. She'd been told of Father Tomas but had yet to meet him, as Raul had made the arrangements with the priest of San Pablo and the hacienda. Julia wondered what the priest and Amang Tenio thought of one another, and what place each held in such an occasion.

After a prayer and the sign of the cross, the priest touched his eyes and turned to her. He smiled as he knelt before her, taking her hands in his. The tenderness in his expression brought unexpected emotion into her chest, and she realized for all the emotion around her she'd had none until now.

"I am Father Tomas. I grieve with you and your family."

For a moment she could hardly speak. Finally she said simply, "Thank you."

The priest held her hands firmly and nodded in understanding. "Your grandfather was great man. He was highly respected here. For his body to be returned to our land holds great meaning. We are grateful and honored to have his granddaughter here as well. It is as if he sent you to us, and we thank him."

The singing rose to a crescendo, and Julia thought of the spirit of the man inside that coffin—she wondered if he indeed knew he'd come home and that she had come with him.

Home. A plot of land, a place of birth, a house, another human being. Perhaps even a faith or a future. Where was her home? Perhaps somewhere in his charts and plans, her grandfather had tried to make Hacienda Esperanza her home as well.

Father Tomas smiled softly. "Tomorrow we talk more of the funeral Mass, okay?"

Julia nodded, and the priest moved on to greet the Tres Lolas. The song ended, and Julia was greeted by an elderly woman who walked with her arms interlocked with a younger version of herself.

"Nakikiramay po kami."

Julia understood their condolences without need for translation. A line formed, extending through the great room and beyond her view. A hand touched her shoulder, and she looked up to Markus, who then moved a chair beside her and translated the soft words of an old man with scars on his cheeks.

"This man says he fought beside your grandfather."

"He fought in the war with him?"

The man was the size of a tall child, and his nodding smile revealed three missing front teeth.

"Yes, and he says your grandfather was very brave and also a joking man."

Markus listened to the elderly man who kept talking to her and smiling; then Markus laughed.

"What did he say?"

"Your grandfather told him and the younger soldiers a legend of the Old West. He said it was a known fact that if a man wore a green ribbon in his hair that the man's enemy would never be able to take his life. He was so convincing that all the younger men wore their hair pulled back or tied even a small piece of it with a green ribbon, even though it seemed a very feminine thing to do.

"Only several days later, one of the soldiers was caught by the Japanese in the jungles and put into some barracks with a group to be executed for being guerilla fighters. The night before the execution, he walked straight up to the Japanese soldier guarding the prisoners and told him that he wore the green ribbon and would not die in the morning. Just then there was a huge explosion in the tent of ammunition. The Japanese thought they were being attacked and in the confusion this man, whose name is Simon, slipped through a hole in the rock wall and opened the front door, allowing the other prisoners to escape.

"When he found Captain Morrison, he told your grandfather about being saved by the green ribbon. Captain Morrison burst into such great laughter that he cried. He admitted that he'd made a bet with Diego, his second in command and, incidentally, grandfather of Raul, that he could convince those men of anything. Diego hatched the idea of the green ribbon, thinking there was too much pride in the men to wear something so womanly. But your grandfather's elaborate story worked, and after that, the green ribbon became a symbol of the group! To this day, many of the men in town wear green ribbons in their hair or around their necks."

"Yes, yes," the man said, continuing to nod and smile. "Captain Morrison say green ribbon." He turned and pointed to the green ribbon holding his long gray hair.

"He says he has many stories of your grandfather to share with you at a later time."

"Say that I'd love to hear them. He should return and tell me before I go."

A frown flickered across Markus's face before he translated.

Julia turned to greet the next family waiting patiently behind. Night came quickly, and it felt like hours that she stayed there, meeting people and accepting their words of sympathy through Markus. The Tres Lolas weaved among the mourners, talking to them, joining in with prayers. More candles were set around the table until the coffin glowed from the small flames.

Finally there was a break in those coming to meet her, and Markus went to refill her coffee. When he returned, he asked, "So, is this very different from the wakes in the States?"

"We most often have the funeral only. Before this week, I thought only the Irish had wakes."

"Many cultures have wakes, Miss Julia. You need to get out more. And the Irish and Filipinos aren't so different, you know, except that we're brown, we like rice instead of potatoes, and we have *duwendes* instead of leprechauns." He smiled. "We did have many Irish missionaries. And our great national hero, Rizal, married his Irish lover just days before his execution."

"Who knew?" Julia suddenly realized then she was hungry. "How long will this go on?"

"Nine days, didn't they tell you?"

"What?"

Markus smiled. "I'm joking—not very polite during a wake. However, at some wakes, the novena takes place starting on the night of a death."

"Novena?"

"Nine days of prayer. Sometimes there are readings from the Scripture, stories of the deceased. It can be amazing how the family and community are drawn together in their faith and prayers. Boisterous family reunions are often the result of a death."

Markus nodded to a family of five standing before them. Julia blinked her eyes and took their hands. The little girl cried against her mother, and Julia wondered if it was in fear or confusion.

More time passed with hands holding hers, words translated by Markus, the singing, the scent of candles, flowers, and incense, the tears. It was well past midnight when Markus finally told her to get some rest.

"Go sleep for a few hours. I will have one of the lolas or Raul sit watch for a while."

"I need some air first." Her head was spinning, from exhaustion or emotion or the scent of the flowers that covered every spare inch of the great room, parlor, and grand entryway.

"I'll walk with you and then get you to your room."

Outside the lights glowed from the trees. There were tables of men and women playing mahjong and poker, smoking cigarettes, and drinking beer or lemonade.

Julia and Markus walked arm in arm in a comforting silence, passing several men asleep on benches and a family curled together on cardboard on the lawn. She estimated that hundreds of people milled around the hacienda. The palms and trees cut silhouettes into the starry night, and music played on a radio beside one of the tables of gamblers. People nodded at her as she passed, as dice were rolled and money was exchanged to the triumphant from the annoyed. There was a haze in the yard from the candles, cigarettes, and flickering lamps that gave a surreal quality to the scene.

Finally Markus escorted her to her room. He rubbed her head in a brotherly way, then kissed her on the cheek, sending anything but brotherly tingles throughout her body.

"Get some rest," he said again. "I'll take care of your guests until you return."

Julia closed the door and leaned against it for a long while. Finally she slid her back down the door and rested her head on her knees.

THE FIRST WAKE EMMAN HAD ATTENDED—HIS AUNTIE'S—HAD scared him half to death. The open casket in the house for two days, the wilted flowers, and the smell of that embalming fluid. He couldn't eat as the others did. His Tito Cris talked loudly with a plate of food in his hand while standing right beside his auntie. Once he actually set the plate on the edge of her coffin, then picked it up and continued eating.

Captain Morrison's funeral was respectable. He hoped someday to have a funeral even half as nice, but not anytime soon, of course.

Sometimes he pictured Miss Julia crying at his funeral, maybe thinking that she might have loved him, and how grateful she was for his saving her life and giving up his own.

Across the room, standing just outside the doorway with a group of mourners, Emman stared at a man he'd seen once before. Then he remembered, though he couldn't be certain for it had been dark. It was the small man from the jungle, Emman was sure of it. He saw the small man make eye contact with another man—and Emman *knew* who that was without question. The man was dressed to look like someone from Manila or overseas. But Emman had studied the "wanted" posters enough to recognize that face.

Moving closer to the winding stairway that led to where Miss Julia had gone to rest, Emman wondered how to guard her and tell Amang Tenio or Mr. Raul what was happening.

Ka Manalo, the leader of the Red Bolo group, was in their midst.

THEY WOULDN'T KNOW HIM HERE, HE WAS SURE. NO ONE COULD possibly guess Manalo was anything other than another contact of Captain Morrison's come to pay respects.

He hadn't implemented a plan. The hundreds attending the funeral granted an opportunity. Manalo and his men could enter the hacienda house and assess for themselves the mood of the people while also getting full access to the layout of the house. The hacienda was magnificent, he couldn't deny. A strand of jealousy and even of wonder went through him at such a magnificent structure. He wondered, if he'd given his life to something like this instead of . . . He cut the thoughts before they continued.

It was too late anyway. He'd been on the watch list for too long for a peaceful civilian life in such a high-profile place as Hacienda

Esperanza. Unless—there was always an "unless"—unless the Communists really did change the political tide of the nation.

Manalo saw the boy's stare. And it made him wonder.

There was a commotion toward the grand front entrance.

Manalo quickly aborted any kind of action when he saw who was walking through the door. Even the boy gaped in utter shock. Everyone knew him, with the horrific war stories seared into their heads since childhood. And on top of that, he had the gall to wear his uniform.

If anything could bind the Filipino people into unity, it was one thing. Hatred. And hatred had just walked through the front door.

THE KNOCK MADE HER JUMP AWAKE FROM HER SPOT ON THE FLOOR. Her travel clock said three o'clock—she'd slept all of thirty minutes. But Julia couldn't tell Lola Gloria or Lola Sita or whoever knocked that she needed a break when they'd been downstairs working all day and night.

It was Raul on the other side of the door.

"A man arrived here from Japan and wishes to see you."

"From Japan? Who is it?"

"His name is Mr. Saeto Takada."

"So he knew my—" And then the name sunk in. Colonel Takada. Even Julia knew the name of the man who had lived briefly in this house not as a guest but as a victor during WWII. She knew of the horror stories of starvation and brutality, though no one had spoken much about it. At the same moment, Julia recognized the potential impact of this man's presence at the hacienda. "Why is he here?"

"I do not know. He will only speak with you. He is in the office."

Julia descended the stairs into a house of whispers. The tension was nearly palpable.

Colonel Takada had lived here, walked the pathways she now walked, had ruled without mercy, had ordered the executions of some relatives of people in this very house. This was the hacienda's enemy, her grandfather's enemy, and thus, her enemy.

Mr. Takada's back was to the door when Julia entered the office, and he didn't turn from gazing at the map on the wall. That map had obviously been there for years, and Julia wondered if Mr. Takada had studied it during the year he ruled the house. From this room he might have directed his troops, signed execution orders, written back home to his wife.

She stood at the door until a younger man she hadn't seen walked toward her.

"Thank you for meeting us," he said, extending his hand. "I am Yoshuri Takada. I am Saeta-san's grandson."

Julia took the hand he extended first to her and then to Raul. The older man had turned toward them, but did not step forward. He was a small man, rigid and proud, with raised chin, clenched jaw, and a sharp fierceness in his black eyes.

"We are the grandchildren of two men who were enemies," said Yoshuri Takada.

Julia nodded at that, finding it hard to look away from Mr. Takada, and surprised at the grandson's joviality in his poignant words.

Yoshuri was taller and was dressed in a well-tailored suit with a tie. He had an easygoing way about him, friendly and casual. "We have come to pay respects to your grandfather."

"This is certainly a surprise."

Julia noticed Raul and the older man staring at one another like two warriors preparing to fight. She felt unsure what to do next. Several men had gathered in the doorway with a child or two peeking between legs and arms. It came to her that these men might not be safe here, that they'd risked much to attend her grandfather's wake. Revenge after such atrocities was rarely soothed with time.

Markus appeared at the door then.

The relief surely showed on her face, but she tried to retain a confident composure. "Markus, come in and close the door."

The younger man was aware of the strained energy that pulsed through the house, but he remained friendly and warm in contrast to his grandfather.

"We would like to present something to you."

Yoshuri spoke to his grandfather. The old Japanese colonel walked to the desk, where a box rested made of an old wood and carved in intricate designs of battle scenes. Mr. Takada opened the box, and as he unwrapped a scarf of deep red velvet, the blade of a sword shone in the lamplight. Mr. Takada lifted the sword from the velvet, holding it flat as he ceremoniously presented it to Julia.

"It is Samurai," the grandson said with pride and restrained excitement. "It has been in my family for four hundred years."

Even Raul stepped to the desk with an expression of surprise. The older man's features remained hard and cold as he handed the sword to Julia.

"Why?" she asked Mr. Takada, then turned to his grandson beside him. "This is too great a gift. I do not understand."

"My grandfather wishes to give it your family now. To the house and the descendents of Captain Ronald Morrison."

"Yes, but why would he, when they were enemies?"

The old man spoke then, staring sternly at her. His jaw was firm and there was nothing decipherable in his eyes.

"He says, 'We were enemies, but I respected him. We are not enemies any more.' This is my grandfather's way of making peace. Of asking for forgiveness, though he would not say so."

Julia thought of the story of dead Filipinos filling the ditches and roadways of the hacienda. Of the innocent women and children locked in the hacienda prison. The Japanese had been relentless in their destruction of Manila, with the city bombed and nearly completely burned by the end of the war. The Japanese were merciless to the American and Filipino soldiers as well as the Filipino elderly, women, and children.

The facts and stories of that time had felt like a history long dead. There had been much turmoil in the years since, and yet the lost were not forgotten. And now here was her grandfather's great enemy and a household of possible avengers gathering behind the door. Julia knew there could be trouble. Takada surely knew this as well, but he had braved the journey into an enemy land to reach toward reconciliation.

The sword was heavy in her hands. "I thank you from our family, for this rare and enormous gift."

Markus gave her a proud nod that gave her added strength.

"My grandfather would like to pay respects to your grandfather, and then we will leave. Our car waits in the driveway."

She looked to Raul for input and received his nod. "Yes, of course."

Julia opened the door with Mr. Takada and his grandson behind her. Raul and Markus followed.

As she feared, the men in the hallway were of the Barangay. They looked like warriors even in their faded jeans and slacks, amulets dangling at their chests—this time she noticed the green ribbons—many with tattooed arms or backs, the designs creeping up their necks from beneath their T-shirts. They wore fighting expressions, hands on hips or arms crossed as they sought to see Mr. Takada. But Julia stood quietly in the doorway until they backed against the wall to allow her to pass, leading the procession. The old soldier followed, staring straight ahead.

News had spread, and the house vibrated with anger instead of grief. An elderly woman jumped forward and spat in Mr. Takada's face. Julia took the woman's hand gently and stepped in front of Mr. Takada. Julia felt divided in her loyalty to the people here and her desire to accept the overtures of an old enemy who came to ask for peace. The old soldier wiped his face with a handkerchief and continued to stare forward.

"He is a guest at the hacienda," she said, and Markus translated to those who might not understand. She hoped that their own ingrained culture of hospitality might confuse their thoughts enough to soothe the anger.

They moved forward past a myriad of faces staring or leering, then into the great room and up to her grandfather's flag-draped casket. Julia stepped aside, and Mr. Takada walked to the coffin. The room quieted. The candles flickered, and the American flag glowed in their light.

Mr. Takada didn't move for several minutes. Finally he made a deep and slow bow, then turned to leave.

Julia and Raul walked with the man and his grandson to their black Cadillac. The car was running, and the driver quickly opened the doors for the men.

The Japanese colonel bowed to Julia, then to Raul and Markus.

"Good-bye," Mr. Takada said.

"Good-bye. And thank you," Julia said.

Yoshuri shook her hand, then bowed to them. This time Raul returned the respect. The older man stared long and hard at her, then spoke and waited for his grandson to translate.

"I thank you for accepting us and our gift. You are like your grandfather. Honorable."

Such words had never been spoken of her. Julia thanked him, wishing she knew what else to say. "And thank you from my family."

They left quickly, and Julia turned to the crowd that had gathered on the lawn. She feared their reaction. Did they think she had betrayed them, she and Raul and Markus, by offering asylum to the greatest enemy of the hacienda? She could not understand the depth of grief caused by the man now driving away. Lola Gloria and Lola Amor were holding one another and wiping their eyes. She looked for her grandfather's war buddy, the small fighter with the green ribbon, and was relieved not to see him there.

"You did well, Miss Julia." Markus touched her arm firmly.

The car's taillights disappeared down the driveway, and people dispersed from their various stances.

"That was certainly unexpected."

"Yes. Do not be concerned. Now that Mr. Takada has left, the wake will continue as usual."

"Who was the older woman who spat on him?" Julia asked Raul.

"Her parents were murdered under Takada's regime. She herself was brutalized and has never married or had children because of it."

"Should I speak to her?"

"No. Some have too many memories to forgive. Others will find peace in the gesture and gift from their family. The anger will not come to you for accepting Takada. I will be sure of that."

SIXTEEN

Julia meandered through the house, which was still full of mourners, some awake, many asleep, until she found her cousin Mara in the kitchen making coffee.

"The last time I saw you, you were asleep in the parlor," Julia said, rubbing her eyes. Mara looked tired but pretty, with her smooth complexion and her hair pulled into a silky bun.

"I saw you sleeping in a chair, practically straight up," Mara replied with a grin, as she dried a large industrial coffeemaker. "There's some coffee on the stove. I'm making a fresh batch for the parlor."

Julia took a cup from the shelf. Through the kitchen window, she saw people cooking on makeshift stoves in the back courtyard and children already at play on the lawn. "Are the lolas sleeping?"

"Yes, they'll be back in a few hours."

"And Raul and Markus?" Julia poured steaming coffee from the percolator on the stove.

"Raul went for a quick check of the property. I'm not sure about Markus. Perhaps sleeping on the couch in the office?"

Julia wondered if Elena the Cook had ever discovered a spice for coffee that would expose secret love.

Mara scooped coffee into the large filter. "I once saw a movie about a funeral in the United States, and it was so different. Very pious and quiet, and at a funeral parlor. Here, the wake usually occurs at the home, like this, and can last for a week or even two, depending on how long it takes for relatives to arrive."

It sounded barbaric to Julia, the idea of a body in the coffin for a week or more. "What about . . . you know, the decay?"

"By the end it can become evident, though of course the body is embalmed first. But death is not unnatural. It is as natural and normal as birth. None of us escapes it." She laughed softly.

Julia tasted the coffee and decided to sip it black that morning. "Most Americans avoid the subject of death as much as possible. It makes us uncomfortable."

"No one is comfortable. It is frightening, sad, eerie at times. Perhaps we understand it better because our land has known so much death. As you have seen, during the wake the family stays with the body through each night, and visitors come at all hours, around the clock. The body is never left alone. The more who come, the more honor to that person."

Julia thought of the people all over the hacienda house and grounds, those up all night, the gambling, talking, gifts of flowers and foods. "It's remarkable when you think of it. This entire land is remarkable."

Mara smiled. "You may not look as if you have Filipino in your genes, but I believe you are becoming more and more a Filipina. You know, many hope you will stay."

"But . . . how can they even think that?" Julia said. "It's really not an option."

"Life can surprise us," Mara said smugly. "I need to check the biscuits and coffee in the parlor."

That day followed a similar pattern as the evening and night before. Julia slept a few hours, and then returned to be with the mourners. Many had stayed overnight and were now becoming familiar faces. For all her offers to help in other ways, her main job continued to be greeting the visitors, who never ceased to arrive. It seemed every inhabitant of the surrounding region and perhaps a good portion of Manila had come through her door. She smiled, realizing she'd called it *her* door.

Julia's cousins filled the house, helping and greeting as well. Mama Clara—Alice and Mara's mother—took over for an afternoon, giving the lolas a break.

When Markus saw Clara, he spoke to her rapidly in Tagalog. To Julia he said, "Remember the one who always made excuses for being overweight and was always dieting, supposedly? That is Mama Clara. I told her how thin she looks—"

The old woman abruptly hit his arm, and Markus gasped and laughed as she sputtered indignantly.

"She said she gave up dieting years ago and I shouldn't tease an old fat woman." He put his hands up in surrender. "I guess some things do change on the hacienda."

Soon flowers drooped and petals littered the floor around her grandfather's coffin. The shadows in the room changed as the day progressed toward another evening. Markus continued to be her translator whenever needed. Once she saw him talking with Raul in the front entry, concerned expressions on their faces. She was curious, but then Father Tomas arrived to finalize plans for the funeral Mass and burial scheduled for the next day.

In the early morning of the third day, the house and outside grounds were renewed into activity as rooms were straightened and more tables made from sawhorses and wood panels. The Tres Lolas wove among the round and rectangular-shaped tables, giving orders, directing placement of chairs and lights.

By early morning the courtyard looked ready for a wedding party with white tablecloths and strings of white lights draped along the stucco walls. While the children of the hacienda gathered bunches of flowers and helped the women pull back the lower leaves to adorn vases for the tables, the children of the Barangay worked on the fringes of the lawn, carving wood with long, sharp knives. Julia couldn't look their way for fear of seeing a finger instead of wood chips flicker to the ground.

Before noon Julia was dressed in another black dress and waiting on the lawn with the mourners, who after the days and night together felt like family to her. There was the woman Julia had met in the jeepney on the road to San Juan, who came with her entire family. The women she'd made jam with now welcomed her as one of their own, including her in stories of their husbands and boyfriends and teasing her about Markus. She also spoke more with the old soldier with the green ribbon—who said nothing of Takada's visit, but instead continued to tell war stories through Markus's or Mara's translation. The children of the hacienda brought her wreaths of flowers and drawings of a light-haired woman on the plantation.

Her "bodyguards" were ever near. They slept on the veranda outside her bedroom when she slept, and once she peeked out to see their innocent faces at deep rest while Emman smoked on the steps, taking a turn at guard duty. Emman was always on the fringe, at times serious and looking like a younger Amang Tenio, at other times smiling or telling jokes to gain her attention.

Julia invited the lone girl in the group, Grace, into her room and showed her dresses and jewelry. Grace carefully touched necklaces, earrings, and a bottle of perfume. She hugged Julia tightly when Julia gave her a yellow blouse that mostly fit the girl. The boys teased Grace over her scented perfume, but continually came to smell her despite her punches to their arms.

As Julia joined the others on the front lawn, she marveled at how quickly she'd come to know so many people, some who knew no English at all, but still she considered her friends. They'd sung together, slept side by side, shared meals, and reorganized bouquets of flowers. Julia had learned mahjong late in the night with Markus, Mara, her cousins Francis and Othaniel, and some villagers. And of course, she felt a further closeness with Raul, Markus, Mang Berto and Aling Rosa, and the Tres Lolas. She wondered if Raul would begin courting Mara—she loved the way they used the word. Markus told her that dating was less prevalent than in the States; many still abided by the tradition of courting a woman with the intention of marriage.

The same chrome-plated jeepney backed up to the walkway, and the black coffin was carried from the house where her grandfather had lived for twenty-five years. Mang Berto stood beside the black Buick parked in front of the house, awaiting Julia and the three old sisters. The other mourners in their black attire loaded into cars, jeepneys, and tricycles. Those from the Barangay crammed into the back of a farm truck.

Mang Berto followed the jeepney on the long road to the village church. The style was that of many Spanish churches and reminded Julia of the hacienda house as well. The red tiles were faded and a few broken; the white stucco was streaked from years of weather and damaged with pockmarks and chunks broken from the smooth lathed walls.

The Tres Lolas fussed with their dresses and hats as they climbed from the car. Julia walked ahead, up the stone steps, as if drawn inside by some force. Her grandmother had come here to light candles and pray, and her grandmother's mother and the mothers before them. Her grandparents had married within these walls, and Julia's own mother was christened here before being sent to the States. Her own history was within this land and the walls of this church.

The tile floor was worn in the aisles, though clean and polished. The ceiling was ornate, with murals of celestial settings; around the outer walls were depictions of the Stations of the Cross. Light streamed through arched gothic windows, and long wooden and bronze chandeliers hung from the ceiling. Outside, the church bells rang in deep resounding tones.

Julia wandered among the familiar faces already in the church, touching their arms in greeting. There was a great depth of peace in this place, and she knew she'd return here before leaving, just to sit and rest awhile.

Mara came and linked arms with her. "Let us light a candle for your grandfather," her cousin said. "And I will light a candle for you and what you must decide for the future."

"What I must decide?" Julia gazed up at a mural on the wall depicting Jesus weeping tears of blood in a lush garden.

"About your place in this life."

Julia didn't argue this time. The need filled her—a need for guidance from a source beyond herself. There'd been too many years of trying to formulate her own life, reach her own dreams, create her own happiness. None of it worked. She had ended up losing or giving up all she'd tried to gain.

The table was covered in candles, many already flickering down to their wicks. Mara reached into a basket of candles, lit one, and set it into an empty space, then closed her eyes and held the rosary beads in her hands as her lips moved silently. She then lit another and prayed again.

Julia took a candle, lit it, and wondered if God could see them there. As she set it down, she felt an overwhelming sense that He did indeed.

They walked the center aisle toward the intricate gold, porcelain, and ivory altar, in front of which her grandfather's coffin now rested; a bittersweet yet cherished sight. Giant bouquets adorned the edges of the steps, and large wreaths stood on easels along the side aisles. The organ began to play, echoing richly from long brass pipes. The altar above the coffin was intricate with its design of gold, porcelain, and ivory.

Julia sat in the front row, joining the sisters. A few others came to greet her, and then Markus appeared, handsome in his elegant dark suit, his black hair slicked back and smooth brown skin freshly shaven.

"How are you today?" His thick black eyebrows were drawn together in concern.

"Do I look that bad?" she said.

He laughed. "Not at all. You look beautiful always, but indeed tired."

Julia moved over for him to sit beside her as the music from the organ suddenly swelled, and many of the mourners began to sing as they entered the church and found seats. Soon the pews were full; then the sides and back were stuffed with standing mourners. Some even peered through the open windows. Father Tomas came from a side door to a small balcony, where he was viewed by all below. He prayed in Latin and then spoke in a mixture of English and Tagalog.

He spoke of Captain Morrison's valor in war; his love of his wife, Julianna; his wisdom in rebuilding the hacienda; and the sorrow of them all over his exile from their land. Honor, courage, redemption, love.

A man Julia had not known enough of. A man who began something great and was forced to leave it. His American family hadn't listened much to Grandpa Morrison's stories. They didn't know him, know of the honor of such a man in their midst. Julia realized how little could be seen in the very details of a person's own life, especially when she hadn't been looking far beyond herself.

The elements of Christ's body and blood were carried to the front. Julia repeated the Lord's Prayer and listened to the other prayers she didn't know. She knew the solemnity of this ritual that was more than a ritual, a symbol and action of the heart and soul. She asked for a pure heart and longed for Christ to be within her. She did want renewal. She did want the bread and wine as the symbol of Christ's body and blood to join within her body and blood.

The stories of those who'd been here before came to her then. The faces of Elena the Cook and Cortinez, the One-Armed Spaniard, her grandparents. Weddings and wakes, infants christened, redemption sought, the Eucharist celebrated—all here within these walls.

The Mass drew to a close, and Julia felt a great weariness envelope her. She grieved for a man, her own grandfather, whom she'd loved and thought she'd known until she came here. He was a cartoon character compared to the real man he had been. How she longed to hear his stories now, to go through his logbooks with him and discover his thoughts and plans to revive this place. During the final prayer, Julia felt something wet touch her hands. It was her own tears.

Julia cried for the man in the casket. He had drawn her close and sent her here, not fully knowing what he sent her to do. She cried for what he'd loved and all that he'd lost. And she cried for her own life, unworthy of stories. For living for herself and fighting her own selfish causes. For the losses that crushed her, that made life empty. For tears that cleansed and for openness to the Divine.

A horse-drawn carriage waited outside. The afternoon light shone on the black wood of the coffin; countless handprints covered the surface. *Someone should have polished it,* Julia thought, and then realized the poignancy of those handprints going with her grandfather into the earth.

The horses' hooves made the *clickety-clack* sound along the paved road as they quickly left the church and south end of the village and went toward the hacienda entrance. It was a long, silent walk. From farther away came the sounds of highway, an occasional dog or rooster crowing, some whispered conversations.

Julia's feet began to hurt, and a few children complained. She'd worn a black dress without nylons in this heat, but her low-heeled shoes chafed the tops of her toes. A few cars crept behind them, carrying elderly mourners. Some of the walkers began to sing again, and a young child raced up to hold Julia's hand as they marched along.

They walked between the lines of palms and through the iron gate; then the jeepney turned down a nearly overgrown road.

The stories birthed from this very earth walked with the hundreds who followed her grandfather's casket. A one-armed Spaniard bringing his bride to the land, a forlorn cook finding true love in a mythical cove, villagers crying to God through centuries of injustices, and the countless voices who would never be named.

They were all here. The stories were the ghosts. And her grandfather, a man revered and greatly loved, had come home to join them.

MANALO AND PACO FINISHED THEIR SECOND BEERS WHILE SITTING at a table outside the *carinderia*. The scent of grilled meat made Manalo's stomach growl. The funeral procession was coming down the street, the *clippity-clop* of horses' hooves and the footsteps of hundreds walking behind were like a cacophonic rhythm of failure.

Timeteo had yet to return with word of his family.

Times were changing. Manalo knew he might be reprimanded for the lack of action during Captain Morrison's wake and for not striking the old Japanese commander out on the road. It surprised him how the American woman had respectfully dealt with the situation without being insensitive to the people. He couldn't help but see something of value in her even if she was an American. Her eyes had glanced over him as she passed, and as he left, she'd come and shaken his hand, asking again what his name was and saying that she felt very honored that he had come.

The boy had come close to her, and while she bent to adjust his tie, the boy's eyes had stared cold into Manalo's. He'd wanted to smile at the boy's ferocious nature. He wondered if his oldest sons were so protective of their mother and sisters.

The carriage came into view first, followed by the people. The American woman walked quietly with the others. Paco raised his eyebrows and did a low whistle when he saw her, but Manalo didn't respond. He was that most rare of creatures, a one-woman man. Perhaps it was because they were so much apart that Malaya was a near mythical being to him. Of course he had been tempted over the years, but it was always Malaya for him and always would be.

"We need to remind them that this country is not safe," Manalo said wearily. He didn't have the stomach or the drive for this anymore, and yet he had no other option. "The American will cower and hurry home. Let us create some fear and send a death threat to her family in the States. We've given respect to the Captain; now we need to do our jobs."

Paco nodded and pushed back his chair. Manalo motioned for another beer.

Because if we do not, Manalo thought, *our superiors might ask for more than threats.*

And even though he had more deaths to his name than he wished to remember, Manalo wasn't itching to add any more.

EMMAN KEPT HER EVER IN VIEW.

He didn't like not having a gun; his arms felt empty and longed even for his old wooden one. But it wasn't respectful to carry weapons in the midst of a funeral.

After Captain Morrison was laid into his final resting place, Miss Julia chose to walk once again. He'd noticed the bright red blisters on the edges of her black dressy shoes. Markus walked with her, much to Emman's annoyance.

Amang Tenio had sent word to the hacienda, where Emman had remained during the days of the wake. The Communist insurgents were near, and yes, they had been watched at the wake. Trouble brewed, and the men of the Barangay, gambling through the nights of the wake, talked it over.

In Emman's young memory there was always some trouble or another in the provinces, in one of the cities or in Manila itself, among insurgents, politicians, and government officials. This time such things had to do with their hacienda. If the cousins all got together, with their lands, all for one cause, it would make other groups pretty unhappy. Like the group that Ka Manalo guy was part of.

There was the scent of rain in the sweet tropical foliage. Miss Julia paused in her walk, then said something to the lawyer beside her.

Markus watched her as she gazed around the wide, green land with an expression that told Emman that he, too, was falling in love with Miss Julia. Emman couldn't really blame the guy, even if he wanted to punch him in the face.

He came closer, and Markus nodded to him in an acknowledgement of respect—not like most of the men in the Barangay who endlessly ribbed him about his youth. Markus wasn't so bad, not really. In the days and nights of the wake, Emman had come to nearly like the guy. But he was still a soft city boy who was too often in close proximity to Miss Julia.

She was talking to Markus again, and Emman was close enough to hear her now. The sound of her American accent was enough for him to listen to all day.

"I'd like to investigate more of my grandfather's plans," she said. "I want to be involved with things here, even by long distance. Like Emman . . ."

She looked at him then—so, Miss Julia did notice his presence after all.

"I want Emman to have a future without a gun. I want Grace to wear a dress if she wishes, and for them to go to school and read about Tom Sawyer instead of hiding in the bushes following me as my assigned protectors."

Grace wear a dress? Yuck. Him without a gun? Even if he moved to Hawaii or the mainland United States, Emman would need a gun as a bodyguard or private eye. And who was Tom Sawyer? He'd never heard of Tom Sawyer on the television set. Women could be a little clueless.

Emman longed to join the conversation—to tell Miss Julia how much he wanted to protect her and that he'd do so her entire life if she'd let him. But he must stay focused, and his faulty English always made him sound dumb.

And then it came. He'd expected something much more dramatic, and because of the subtlety, he didn't take it seriously at first.

A strange noise from ahead, then a scream, and several men went running past them toward the sound. Women grabbed up their children and formed clusters that blocked the road.

"Julia, wait here," Markus said, and he too sprinted forward.

A popping sound erupted. Machine guns.

Julia ducked down, and Emman pushed her lower, covering her as much as he could with his body. More gunfire, closer now, and a sick sensation froze him with the anticipation of a bullet hitting one of them. He spotted Bok and Kiko crawling toward them—Bok had his small knife held out, ready to protect. A dog barked angrily and children were crying, probably more from being abruptly shoved to the ground than because of fear.

Just as quickly the road ahead went silent. Emman rose up and scanned the people littering the ground. No one appeared hurt. He stood over Miss Julia, still crouched protectively low. Except for a few skinned knees and frightened expressions, all on this section of road were fine.

"Thank you, Emman," Julia said, brushing herself off. Then they both appeared to have the same thought. She shouted, "Come on," and ran forward, weaving in and out of the crowd of people, some who were standing, others still crouched near the ground.

"Wait, Miss Julia," he said, racing after her.

He nearly tripped over a girl who was picking up her crying little brother. Emman realized his team was coming behind them, and soon enough they surrounded Miss Julia, who couldn't run very fast in her dress shoes.

Then he saw Raul and Markus standing together on the side of the road.

"Is everyone okay?" Miss Julia asked, out of breath and afraid.

Markus was angry to see her. "I said to wait back there."

And then Miss Julia did a remarkable thing: she smiled. "How can I wait back there when I'm the doña of the hacienda? I'd look like a coward."

Markus didn't find it humorous, but Emman did, even if he still kept guard and stayed close to her. Her brave smile in the midst of conflict endeared her to him all the more, even if she did think Grace should wear a dress.

"The doña you are now?" Raul said, bending down to pick up an empty bullet cartridge.

"That's what everyone keeps calling me. So what happened?"

A large group of people gathered around them, asking questions, pointing toward the left side of the road where a path could be seen leading into the jungle.

"We had a disturbance, no one injured. Shots fired into the air, not at anyone."

"Who did it? Was it because of Mr. Takada?"

"No, not that. This was Red Bolos. A scare tactic."

Emman knew why. They wanted the region and the country, wanted to save it in their own twisted way, and so they murdered and stole and terrorized.

Markus kept looking around as though Julia could be shot any second. But the Communists would be gone, the men of his village hot on their trail.

"Can we get her to the hacienda house?" Emman asked.

"I'm fine," she protested. "Where are the lolas?"

"No, he's right," Raul said. "Good idea, Emman. And the Tres Lolas are ahead and surely need calming as well."

When they had Miss Julia safely in the house, consoling the Tres Lolas, Emman overheard Markus talking to Raul.

"I think she needs to leave soon. Pinatubo is going to erupt. Manila isn't the safest place either; there's talk about another government coup, and she might be trapped there. I think for her own safety, Julia should return to the States."

SEVENTEEN

M analo, I've been so worried."

He closed his eyes in relief at the sound of her voice. At last, at last. Timeteo had sent a message with a date and a time, and as he waited at the telephones, one of them had rung. And now he was hearing her voice.

"I thought something had happened to you and they didn't want to tell me. No one would tell me anything."

"Everything is fine. I'm sorry you were worried."

He wanted to tell her how he'd run to the house and found it empty. How he'd sobbed in the darkness out of such despair. And if he was with her, he'd whisper it all in her ear, and she'd cry and hold him close. But she'd never beg him to stay, though they both wished she would. They knew he might leave everything for her and the kids if only she asked. And then where would they be? Without the party, none of them had any protection at all. Manalo knew too much, and there would be no quiet retirement until something changed.

"Are you okay, *mahal kong asawa*?"

"They woke us in the night. It really scared the kids. It scared me too. I thought for sure—" Her voice broke then, and he could hear her courage dissolve.

"Baby, it's okay. I'm fine."

"What would I do if something happened to you?"

"You won't be on your own. You'll always be taken care of."

"I don't mean that. What would *I* do if I lost you? Even though we're apart, we are together. You are always with me, and I am always with you."

He leaned his head against the metal of the phone booth. "*Mahal na mahal kita.*"

"Oh, Manoy, I love you too. *Mahal na mahal kita.* This scared me."

"Don't let it."

"We are all tired of this life, Manoy. Your children need a home. And after this last move, Akili and Rapahelo are having nightmares. Akili needs his father. He wants to join you."

"Never."

"Never? He needs a man; he needs you. I don't want him to join the cause, but it's his only way to know you."

His son was seventeen years old and had such potential to do much more with his life. Manalo had been fourteen when he first tasted battle, and from there he'd become a hunted fugitive. It wasn't the life he wished for the boys. Their country was supposed to be a better place by the time his children were adults. And here the years had passed and he'd missed so much of their growing up.

"Manalo. I've never asked you to find a way to be with us. But we can't live like this much longer. And so for the first time, I'm asking."

It shocked and thrilled him. She was desperate for him, as desperate as he felt for her. "I miss you, Malaya. Don't worry, I'm going to work this out."

They couldn't talk long, not this time, so they made another appointment. Manalo hung up the phone and sat down on the curb, staggered under the weight of his sadness. Then he slowly rose back up as something more than his longing and loneliness grew within the memory of her voice. More than at any other time in his life, Manalo knew he must do his duty now.

Before the party, before himself, he had to save his family.

"WHAT DOES THIS MEAN FOR US?" JULIA ASKED RAUL, HOLDING up the newspaper at the table. The photo depicted Mount Pinatubo with a plume of smoke and ash filling the clear blue sky. Seismologists believed it was only the beginning.

For several months there had been volcanic activity around Pinatubo. The U.S. Clark Air Force Base had been evacuated as well as the towns around the mountain. Refugees were forced to live in camps. But that was far to the north, even north of Manila, and they were to the south. The distance looked to be about the same as that from San Francisco to LA.

"It means nothing," Raul said.

And Julia translated his simple answers into what she thought he meant; it was a new amusement of hers. . . . *Well, Julia, it doesn't change much of anything here. And there is enough to worry about.*

"Then do we need to worry about what happened at the funeral?"

"No."

No, Julia, the men of the Barangay Mahinahon have you well pro-

tected, and it will not happen again. Though we do need to discuss your departure.

She sometimes asked meaningless questions just to get his simple responses, until he frowned at her smile and Julia worried that she'd disrespected him.

"Are the Communist rebels still in the jungles?"

"Yes."

I'd rather not tell you these things, you being not only a woman but an American as well, but Captain Morrison would want me to show you respect and so I will.

She smiled. As usual, he frowned. Julia picked up the paper and headed outside. At least she had a few days to decide what to do next.

SOMETHING WAS WRONG.

Bok's sister hadn't eaten for weeks. Malnutrition showed in her already bony arms and legs, and no makeup could hide the dark circles under her eyes. She reminded him of a sickly rat, though he didn't want to be mean. He felt sorry for her, actually. Her boyfriend, Artur, was missing. It was discovered he'd been doing drugs, but not excessively. But some of the gossip said that was his downfall. That maybe he had connected with dealers in Manila while he was fixing the car and was now a junkie on the streets. The rumors abounded, and Bok's sister grew thinner.

But tonight, the wails of Artur's mother were heard throughout the Barangay Mahinahon. And that could mean only one thing.

FRANCIS MADE A TERRIBLE CUP OF COFFEE.

The cousins teased him mercilessly when he volunteered to make another pot as they sat around the outdoor table eating.

"Stick to cooking rice," Othaniel said. "But only if you have a rice cooker."

They had arrived with clay pots of food for an impromptu late breakfast. Rice, eggs cooked sunny-side up, some dish that reminded Julia of corned-beef hash but with a different flavor, and fried plantain bananas were in the array of pots covering the outdoor table. Small serving cups held sauces of different colors. Julia contributed a large yellow jackfruit—her morning gift on the veranda steps.

Julia suspected they had come out of worry after the shootings on the day of the funeral. Heightened security. Furrowed brows. The presence of men with guns, not just children from the Barangay Mahinahon.

A different pulse beat beneath the peace of the gentle days.

But it wasn't only fear that brought them together. Mara said the wake and funeral brought them all from their separate lives toward the closeness they'd known as children.

Now Francis and Othaniel nudged each other with their elbows and smiled widely in her direction.

"What?" Julia asked, suspecting she was the newest target of their teasing.

They solemnly tried to eat their meal as she did, instead of holding a fork in the right hand and spoon in the left.

"Hey, look at the mess you're making on Aling Rosa's tablecloth," Julia said.

Francis gave up and picked up his spoon, laughing loudly.

"I can do it," Othaniel said, scooping up some rice, but it fell onto his lap before it reached his mouth. "This is harder than chopsticks. Why do some people make eating so hard?"

Julia demonstrated her skill. "My father always scolded me about eating with elbows on the table. I had to have my left hand on my lap."

"Child abuse, I say," Mara's teenaged sister, Alice, chimed in, happy to be among the older cousins.

"You know, Alice," Julia said, "I keep hearing about a zoo around here. Maybe you could take me one day soon?"

"Zoo?" asked Mara. She looked sweet and casual in her jeans and blue embroidered blouse, her hair in a silky braid.

"Or wherever it is that the apes live."

"Apes? There aren't apes in the Philippines. And the only zoo I know of is in Manila," said Othaniel.

"Maybe it's a preserve or farm. I always hear about it. Maybe not apes. Monkeys, perhaps?"

"There are monkeys in the jungle. Is that what you mean?" Mara said.

"Someone told me about an annual fiesta in the village that's in part a celebration for the monkeys or apes. Like maybe the year of the monkey or something. That you even had a village built for it. I think Lola Sita was telling me, but I couldn't really understand her English, and Lola Gloria wasn't there to translate. A monkey village. Or was it a gorilla village?"

"Gor-il-la village," said Francis with a strange expression; then he smiled and burst into uproarious laughter.

Mara stared at Julia, then, as if an electric current moved from Francis to her, her eyes widened and she laughed so loudly Julia couldn't believe this was her genteel cousin.

"Gorilla village," Mara sputtered.

Julia, with an awkward smile, looked from one cousin to another. It must be a cultural thing.

The others couldn't stop laughing or saying, "Gorilla village."

Finally Francis put his arm around her and caught his breath. "Julia, it's gue-ril-la village, for the World War II guerilla fighters. It was a village of soldiers that began after the war and continues even now."

With that Julia herself was infected by their mirth and laughed with her cousins until the children of the Barangay peered at them from the jungle in wonder.

"So wait," Julia said, finally putting it together. "Barangay Mahinahon and the gorilla, I mean, guerrilla village are the same thing?"

"Yes, exactly," and they all fell into laughter again.

Soon Raul came from his usual morning rounds and joined their meal, but even with Mara there it was clear that something was bothering him. He did chuckle heartily as the cousins told Julia's story of gorillas and guerrillas.

"What is it?" Mara asked him as their renewed laughter died down.

"There was a death at the Barangay Mahinahon," Raul solemnly announced.

"What?" "A death?" "How?" voices chimed.

Mara put her hand on Raul's arm. "Who is it?"

"One of the drivers, Artur Tenio. He would have turned twenty next week."

Raul glanced at Julia in a way that made her wonder about something from when she first arrived.

"Was he the driver when the car broke down?"

She knew he almost said no, but then he nodded.

"And how did he die?" Francis asked slowly.

"That is being investigated."

"Has the wake begun?" Mara asked.

Julia felt a weariness wash over her at the thought of another wake and funeral; then she immediately felt guilty. He was just a kid and deserved more than that.

"There will be no wake. And no funeral."

"What? Why not?" Francis asked.

"There is no body."

No one asked the questions on all of their minds. The possibilities were too sobering to consider.

Julia thought of Artur's family and said, "We should go and pay our respects."

Manalo groaned at the news. So they knew now about the kid. It was right for them to know, even without a body. But the men of the Barangay Mahinahon believed the Red Bolos should be held responsible, as well they should—even if the idiotic mercenaries were the actual killers.

He wished Timeteo would return soon. Comrade Pilo was the last person he wanted to see.

They needed either to retreat or prepare for war.

The newly conditioned 1937 Packard Victoria Convertible, or "Grampa" as everyone fondly called it, growled like the old masculine car it was as Mang Berto drove it with a grouchy frown. Billows of dust plumed over the silver paint and into the clean interior as they followed with the top down behind two tricycles down the long and dusty road to the guerilla village.

Julia thought it funny how they changed cars day by day, depending on which one was running at that particular moment. Besides Grampa, there'd been Night Rider—the gorgeous black Citroen Traction Avant that they'd joked looked liked a hearse for the rich and famous, the 1938 Bugatti Type 57SC, dubbed "the Bond car," as in James Bond, as well as other cars that Mang Berto proudly brought to the house for each occasion.

It was quite a feat for Mang Berto to keep the cars in running condition, considering that he swapped and made do with unoriginal or secondhand parts to fix them. The irony was that the cars were rarely used on the actual roads of Batangas. Their enormous value and Mang Berto's love kept them ever caged within the hacienda grounds.

As they drove, Francis leaned toward her ear from his spot in the backseat to tell Julia that her presence worked well for him. He'd had a love affair with the antique cars since he was a kid but was never able to touch them, much less drive them, because of Mang Berto's obsessive care.

"If you go anywhere tomorrow, will you let me know?" Francis said, and they both laughed at Mang Berto's frown from the driver's seat.

From time to time Julia worriedly searched the road ahead to check on her "bodyguards" on one of the tricycles, only to see their brown faces smiling back at her. Emman clung to the outside of the motorcycle's open-air sidecar, pointing excitedly for Julia to see one scenic spot after another. She shook her head, thinking how many U.S. regulations they were violating by their joy ride.

Despite her concern, it was a most amusing sight to see these precocious children riding a tricycle, packed like sardines and going over the rough terrain that bounced them into the air at times. But oh, how they loved it, from the looks on their faces.

"Don't worry about the kids," Francis said, leaning forward again. "Raul will drive them well."

"Raul is driving the tricycle?" she exclaimed, then laughed as she realized it was indeed Raul surrounded with children and guiding the motorcycle down the rough road. In the confusion of their departure, she had assumed he was bringing a different car or coming later.

The cousins chatted the whole time, never failing to come up with corny jokes and childhood stories and pranks that kept them all laughing—except for Mang Berto, who kept his hands clenching the steering wheel and his steady gaze on the road. Squeezed tightly beside him in the front seat sat Mara and Julia; in the back-seat were the other cousins, Miguel in the middle with Francis and Othaniel on either side.

As they neared the village, Emman as lookout pointed toward the various wreckage that greeted them on the side of the road: an old and rusted Japanese tank with overgrown vines hugging its carcass; ancient military trucks; rusted guns and artillery. All stood silent, never to fire a shot again. There were even two rem-nants of warplanes, Japanese by the faded orange circle on the tail, probably shot down during the war. They were like war trophies, kills proudly displayed in a gruesome but riveting death pose.

Othaniel had warned Julia about the spectacle of war trophies. During the early years, he said, decapitated Japanese heads and dead bodies used to adorn the road until Captain Morrison with the mayor slowly convinced the villagers to take them down and bury them.

"It took a long debate for the guerillas to bury their enemies," Mara explained. "Bitterness ran deep. The Japanese killed many of the men's wives and children and comrades. It was their only revenge, and the burial the smallest step toward healing what cannot be fully healed. Your grandfather spoke to them about God's commands to forgive, which he compared to an order from a ranking officer. It was a foreign concept to them, as it really is for all of us when we are in pain. Revenge, not forgiveness, is our natural response."

Mara brushed back some loose strands of hair that blew into her face. "My uncle told me that when the American soldiers came to the Philippines, it shocked many Filipino soldiers to see them in church, praying, lighting candles, and going to confession. Most Filipino men considered religious service something for women and children. Then they saw these war-toughened soldiers whom they admired, like your grandfather, kneeling in prayer at church. It had an effect on them."

Miguel pointed forward where Emman also pointed. "Look, Julia. We are here."

They passed through a metal arch surrounded by high canopies of lush green trees supported by gnarled brown branches. The arch read Barangay Mahinahon. "Grampa" passed beneath the archway and between the rows of small houses at the side of the narrow road.

Their arrival attracted immediate attention, drawing men from sitting at tables to a standing position. Their stares were curious but intense, and Julia noticed the guns on their shoulders or in holsters hanging on loose belts at their waists.

The road opened up to a larger area, a plateau on top of the mountain, where more houses were erected in a circular fashion. They drove deeper inside the town until they reached a circular area where a monument was constructed—a gazebo adorned with wooden sculptures in the middle, statues of men with fearsome dispositions wielding rifles and raising their arms in defiance. Mang Berto circled the rotunda twice as Mara and Miguel told Julia that the three leading statues were the sculptures of her grandmother's brother Miguel Guevarra, the primary leader of the guerilla group; Diego, and Julia's own grandfather, Captain Morrison, the guerilla's American attaché.

The group then turned right to a midsized convenience store, a larger sari-sari, where more men were gathered, sitting on wooden benches. On the left side was a large open-air billiard hall, while at its opposite side was a *carinderia*, or diner. Mang Berto parked the car at the side and proceeded to honk the car's horn until some men from the billiard hall came over to greet them.

"*Berto kamusta!*" the curious men greeted Mang Berto and Raul. Raul rose stiffly from the tricycle as the children piled out. The village men came ambling toward the car in their thin white sandals and shirts, many of them even shirtless in the humid air. Conversing in their strong-toned dialect, it sounded like they were shouting at each other, but Julia knew this was normal conversation to them.

"*Nandyan ba si Amang Tenio?! Eto kasama ko si Julia, galing Amerika. Apo ni Kapitan Kano.*"

Mara, who had become Julia's official translator for the day, explained that Mang Berto was telling the men that the granddaughter of Captain Morrison wished to pay a courtesy call upon Amang Tenio.

Hearing this, the village men were even more intrigued and came closer to Julia and Mara sitting in the convertible. They leaned close with smiles that grew larger as Emman and the rest of Julia's young bodyguards surrounded the car and postured protectively, motioning the men back from such a famous lady.

"*Gwapa Kana,*" Julia heard again and again.

"That means 'gorgeous American,'" Mara said under her breath, as they got out of the car.

The cousins were greeted by name and with hearty pats on the back.

"None of us has been up here in years. They're pretty excited to have us, the guys especially. And to have you arrive—well, this will be talked about for years."

The commotion grew as some women appeared, mothers with children pushing in between, curious to see what the fuss was all about. Julia was surprised at the disproportionate amount of men among the few women and children.

"Hello. How are you?" a man bravely greeted Julia, drawing the laughter of the people surrounding him, amused at his attempt to speak in English.

"I saw you at the funeral," another said.

"Are you liking our village so far?"

"Yes," she said, though they'd barely arrived.

The brave among the village men routinely pushed themselves in front to speak to Julia and Mara.

"I am Pedro," or Carlo or Ramon, they introduced themselves, doing their best to speak in Tag-lish—a Tagalog-English hybrid language. Julia surprised them with her own few Filipino words like *magandang hapon po*—"good afternoon"—or *maganda*— "beautiful." These words never failed to give joy and laughter to those who heard them, like parents hearing their child's first spoken words.

While waiting for Amang Tenio, Francis decided to recount Julia's "gorilla village" misunderstanding to the villagers. They all listened attentively at first, with expectant smiles, wanting to hear about the young American's impressions of their home. But as it dawned on them that they were in fact being called gorillas, the smiles slowly crumbled into frowns, leaving a sea of uncomfortable silence and disturbed glances.

Even Emman and the child bodyguards appeared offended by the story. Midsentence, Francis stopped his cheerful retelling as Othaniel, shaking his head, nudged him sharply with an elbow. Francis turned left to right with a frozen smile. Julia could feel her face turning red, but there was no place to escape.

Then, amidst the silence, a lone, uncontrolled laugh exploded. Everyone looked around as the enigmatic old man with a red fighting cock in his arms pushed his way forward. And with that, the others roared in laughter as well.

"Good morning, Iha," said Amang Tenio, as he took her hand and bowed slightly. "Forgive my people—we are not that humorless that such things can offend us. It seems it has become a tradition to tease our visitors. And truth be told, it was funny to watch you blush so red. But then, I don't think your lolo would appreciate our making fun of his dear one."

"They were only teasing?" Julia asked with a confused grin, afraid he was just saying so to make her more comfortable. But when she saw the mischievous looks, especially on Emman's face, her mouth dropped.

Julia looked into the face of Amang Tenio. Years beneath the sun had weathered lines around his eyes. A cigar hand-rolled in black paper was tucked into the corner of his mouth.

Amang Tenio studied her intently as well, as if trying to both learn her history and predict her future as only a shaman could. "Come, come, have you eaten? Are you hungry?" he asked them. "Let's go to my house, and I will serve you merienda."

"*Apo,* we just ate," said Mara. "We came to pay respects to the parents who lost their young son."

"Ah, yes," Amang Tenio said. "I am sorry to say that they are not here. They have gone to the relatives of Artur's mother for a few weeks. It has been a terrible thing."

Julia wondered, as she had when first hearing of the boy's death, how they were certain he was deceased. Raul had simply said that it was known, but had not explained. That Amang Tenio had said it and that a body would not be coming—this was the end of the discussion for the family. But for the men of the Barangay Mahinahon, the killing of their own would always be a call for vengeance. The exterior of Amang Tenio and the men at the village was humorous and inviting. But Julia knew by now that these men were warriors above all else.

Now Amang Tenio's eyes lit up. In a dignified and affectionate voice, he said, "*Mga anak,* children. I will be very happy to take you around the village. Follow me."

EIGHTEEN

~✦~

W alking through the streets with Amang Tenio leading the way, Julia found a village unlike anything she'd ever seen. Its roads were lined by hulking acacia trees with huge dark trunks spreading their branches into an arching canopy of green that shielded the group from the harsh sunlight. Amang Tenio pointed upward where electric lights, a multitude of small ten-inch globes, were woven through the branches. He explained that the globes were made with white translucent *capiz* shells.

"At night they serve as the town's lampposts. During the Christmas season, the women and children line the globes with colored tissue paper to make it more festive."

Having expected fortifications and run-down quarters, Julia was happily surprised to be greeted by a rustic hamlet cut from the mountain jungles itself; a community that had achieved a refreshing balance between man and nature.

The rows of homes beneath the trees were mostly made of wood in a traditional Filipino rural construction with rooftops made of woven dried *nipa* leaves. Tall wooden windows slid open and closed on indented grooves to provide a cool ventilation system. They were designed with a pattern of small square cutouts filled with the same white translucent shells that allowed soft light to pass through. Most of the houses stood on wooden pillars, about four feet above the ground. Each house had a small front yard adorned with a humble garden and protected by a simple bamboo fence.

The farther they walked from the town center, the more undeveloped the town became. The side roads turned into brown compacted soil. From time to time they passed a troupe of chickens pecking and scratching the ground unattended, looking for food. A brown piglet surprised Julia as it suddenly appeared from nowhere—they both squealed in fright, much to everyone else's pleasure.

Two smiling old men shouted a warm and friendly hello from their wooden bench under a lush tamarind tree, where they sat playing checkers. Julia noticed that the wooden board was obviously homemade; the chips they used were ordinary bottle caps. Amang Tenio introduced Julia and the cousins to them.

"Iha . . . you are so . . . *maganda*—you know, beau-ti-ful," one of the men said, gawking. His thick black hair was frozen in place by a flowery-scented pomade. He wore a red Hawaiian shirt and carried himself confidently. "I knew your lolo. He was the last of our commanders, and it is a sad thing that only in death could he come back. Our family visits your Lola Julianna's grave *severy araw ng patay* . . . how to say . . . the Day of the Dead. We keep it clean and with flowers."

"Thank you, from my entire family," Julia said. "I was told how the guerilla villagers have taken care of our ancestral graves in the absence of my grandfather. I know how much he appreciates this even now."

The other man gained Julia's attention and stuck out his chest, saying, "Yes, your lolo gazes at us from heaven. Captain Morrison was good man. He was fierce as soldier and loyal friend to his men. My father fought with him."

"And mine did as well," the first said again, giving her a look of charmed flirtation that made Mara nudge Julia's arm. "We were his bodyguards."

"Ah, like Emman and the others are mine," Julia said. She thought of these two older men as boys following her grandfather. She pictured Emman as an older man retelling stories of his younger years over a game of checkers with one of the other boys.

The second man continued, "And my *kumpare* is right, Iha. You are so *gwapa* and very *matangkad*!"

"Don't bother the woman now, and hey, I am taller than you! So stop dreaming," teased Red Shirt.

"That so, but I'm much more good-looking than you!" countered the other.

The group erupted into laughter at this exchange, including Julia. At home, two older men vying for her attention would have made her uncomfortable, but these two were just funny and lovable.

Francis nudged Julia and pointed to Emman, who appeared to be sulking. He was not at all amused at the flirting older men. But seeing Julia looking at him, he immediately shook his head and smiled, as if to apologize for his two elders.

"Do you like my home?" he asked.

"Yes, Emman. It is like nothing I've ever seen. I like it very much."

Emman smiled proudly. The other children passed out drinks of Coca-Cola in clear rectangular plastic bags with long straws inside. Julia accepted hers from Emman with a smile that made the boy who carried a gun on his shoulder turn a bright blushing red.

As they held the clear plastic bags and sipped from their straws, a muffled noise of people shouting diverted Julia's eyes to the edge of town. She saw a large circular building, apparently made of bamboo, and processions of people going in and out.

Amang Tenio noticed her curiosity. "That is our famous cock-fighting arena. Sometimes people from surrounding provinces come here to watch and bet at the competitions."

Emman added, "Sometimes millions of pesos are bet during tournaments. Berdugo here"—he pointed to Amang Tenio's red rooster—"Berdugo is one of its famous champions."

Amang Tenio smiled proudly, nodding, as he again stroked the noble fowl. "This is actually Berdugo the Twelfth. He is from a long line of champion fighting cocks."

"*Berdugo* means 'executioner'!" added Emman enthusiastically.

Amang Tenio eyed Julia. "Would you like to watch a match, Iha? Many from the village will be attending."

"Umm . . ." Julia hesitated, not wishing to see the creatures maim and slaughter each other, but also not wishing to offend anyone in the village.

"You don't have to, you know," Mara said, seeing Julia's discomfort. "I myself do not go to such events."

"Well, why don't you?" Francis countered. "You might as well, Julia, as you are already here. Chances are you won't have the opportunity again. After all, you are in a country where this is legal. Besides, you can always say that some people forced you into it."

Julia suddenly wondered where Raul had disappeared to, wishing for the advice she usually perceived from his expression in any matter.

"How violent is it?" she asked Mara. "Will you go if I go?"

"I haven't attended since I was a young girl. But I will go. It's definitely a view into the more savage side of my country."

"Well . . . okay, I guess."

Amang Tenio smiled and led the way, leaning on his cane as he walked while he carried his rooster in his other arm. Emman kept looking back at Julia and smiling, barely containing his excitement at showing her his village's main attraction.

Julia followed, dreading and yet curious, not knowing what to expect. One thing she did know was that this village was extremely proud of what she was about to see.

A loud roar greeted the group as they stepped inside the bamboo and wood "coliseum," entering from one of the four side entrances. The air was cooled by a light breeze coming from the huge open windows surrounding the building, and yet it was still thick with tobacco smoke. A clamoring mass of men, and a few women, sat on circular bleachers, level upon level. When Amang Tenio sent word ahead, a row opened to let their group find space close to the front.

Circulating at the lowermost steps were men wearing folded white bandanas around their heads, facing the spectators, shouting, "*Sa pula, sa puti, sa pula, sa puti!!!*" over and over again. In their left hands they held neatly folded cash between their fingers in a fanlike arrangement. Pointing from one spectator to another with their right hands, they confirmed bets by a simple nod and a hand signal. It was organized mayhem once again.

At the coliseum's center, on its lowest level, was dry ground in which was dug a circular fighting pit. In it stood three men, two of whom faced each other from opposite ends. In the crook of each man's arm he held a fighting rooster, which he gently stroked, almost lovingly, from head to wingtip to tail. Both roosters looked proud and muscular, one covered in lustrous and vibrant feathers of black and orange and the other mostly white with streaks of black on its wings.

Francis pointed out one of the roosters and directed Julia to look at its feet. Attached by leather straps to each of the bird's legs was a blade about two and a half inches long that curved wickedly into a sharp point.

"Those are razor-sharp blades," Francis yelled over the shouts for Julia and Mara to hear. "These birds are bred and exist only to fight."

The third man in the center gave a nod to each man, signaling them to lower their fighting roosters to the ground. Upon hitting the dirt, both birds surged forward, straining against their owners' hands, their attention intently focused on each other. The feathers on each bird's outstretched neck stood upward like a cobra about to strike.

The referee gave another signal, and one after the other, each owner squatted on his feet holding his fighting rooster in his hand while the referee held the bird's head outstretched. The other owner then carried his rooster forward over the outstretched neck and allowed his bird to bite the other rooster's neck.

"It's to make them more aggressive," Francis explained.

Both roosters strained again in their handler's hands as they were returned to the ground. Slowly, the two were allowed to draw even closer. Staring, beak to open beak, the fighting cocks were a picture of forceful fury restrained.

The referee stood in the middle with his right hand extended between the two birds. He looked from left to right, nodding to each handler, then brought down his hands suddenly, shouting, "Fight!" Simultaneously, the roosters were released from their owner's grip and each bird rushed forward on the attack.

The black-and-red rooster jumped high above its white foe, its bladed feet brushing its enemy's head lightly as it crouched down on the ground to avoid the other. Rushing forward, the white bird again was beaten back as the black one jumped high above its head, its feet extended. The white bird slipped past the deadly blade, but this time followed up with a jumping charge of its own. Jump and counter charge, each rooster proceeded to attack the other in fury until the two fighters were lost in a hurricane of wrath and violence. And with each jump the audience shouted with enthusiasm.

"*Sa pula! Sa puti!*"

"That means 'for the white, for the red!'"

After a few moments of this exchange, the two birds started to circle each other warily. Inches from each other they came to a full stop, their necks outstretched, eyeball to eyeball, they lowered their heads, staring each other down.

The silent appraisal suddenly erupted as both roosters jumped upward with their wings spread wide and flapping, their clawed, bladed feet extended. And with a shock, just as immediately as the fight began, it ended.

The proud black-and-red rooster suddenly dropped to the ground, lifeless. Its neck was extended as its head lolled insensibly downward in a gruesome death pose. The shouting echoed in Julia's ears as the losers and the winners around her bemoaned or cheered their fate.

Meanwhile the referee grabbed the white rooster with both hands, enclosing its wings, and brought its beak to its fallen enemy's neck, which it quickly bit. A loud applause was heard as people shouted and clapped in recognition of a good fight.

Julia sat, stunned. A sick and fascinated horror filled her as she watched, riveted to her seat. The way the birds fought at first seemed absurd. All the shouting for two chickens jumping around seemed ridiculous. Then the fevered conflict with the attacks, escapes, and counterattacks generated a fascination in the struggle itself. Julia unconsciously even found herself rooting for the underdog. But the suddenness of the end shocked her.

Here were not two boxers in the ring furiously hitting each other with padded gloves for recreation. Those long deadly curved

blades were for killing. One could get lost at first by the two birds'
dueling interplay, like watching Samurai fence in an old Japanese
or Kung Fu movie. But the all-too-real death in the end gave a
rude awakening.

Julia looked a row below at Berdugo, the red rooster Amang
Tenio so lovingly stroked. She wondered if being here made the
bird want to fight. A sudden, deep pain pierced her heart. Francis
had told her how cherished these birds were to their owners. How
could people raise them so affectionately, constantly petting them,
carrying them all around town in their cages, troubling themselves
to find the best foods, then subject them to such a horrible end?

A master's betrayal to his charge.

Mara, whose arm was linked to Julia's own, looked at her sadly
and shook her head.

"Does that offend you?" Amang Tenio asked, turning to watch
Julia intently. She looked at him, not knowing what to say and not
wishing to insult their host.

The old man smiled a sad smile of understanding.

"What do they do with the dead roosters?" Julia asked, unsure
why she was asking.

"*Tinola!*" shouted Francis, referring to the chicken broth soup
Aling Rosa had cooked for Julia at the hacienda.

"Sometimes," said Amang Tenio. "Often the owner cannot bear
to eat his slain rooster, but feeling it unthinkable to waste the
meat, he gives it to friends or relatives to consume."

Julia felt a further shock at these revelations. It seemed like
eating a beloved pet.

"Let us go now, before our female guests lose their appetites
completely."

Leaving the coliseum, Amang Tenio led the procession back
toward the rotunda and down a different road to his home, the
town's clan house, for some merienda.

As they walked, Julia mulled over her mixed emotions. How strange this land was compared to where she had grown up as a child. Strange, and yet she felt such an affinity for it as well, an inner familiarity. It was a land of paradox, and this small beautiful village a microcosm of that paradox. Built in such a homely and peaceful place, and yet its reputation in fighting and savagery could be felt and seen in the details.

Julia struggled with the feelings evoked in the arena, of getting lost in the primal undulating excitement of a fight and then the jarring end, the sudden death. The guilt of having enjoyed a spectacle while feeling it to be wrong.

Mara linked arms with Julia as they walked, and though they didn't speak, Julia sensed her cousin's quiet understanding and support. She knew her days in the Philippines were soon coming to an end, and though she wished to be lost in the moment and in her own thoughts, there was much that rested upon her in the next few days.

Julia thought her heart might break in a way it never had before on the day she left this exotic land. Once you knew things, it changed you, and she wondered how she'd fit back at home again.

Before long, the group stood in front of what could only be the clan house of Barangay Mahinahon. It stood in the center of a very large lawn littered with rows of blooming kalachuchi trees, their fragrant white flowers dangling toward the ground. The house exuded an aura of dignified authority and solid oldness. But unlike the hacienda house, the Barangay clan house had a sparse and humble appearance.

It was half the size of the hacienda house, and its walls were bare and unpainted. It stood on strong but weathered wooden pillars that raised the home about seven feet in the air. A grand terraced staircase made of adobe and gray concrete invited visitors to the entrance upstairs.

"Waaah . . . Lolo," shouted three children as they ran toward Amang Tenio.

The old man automatically extended his right hand, holding the cane, as two boys and one stout girl each in turn held the old patriarch's hand and touched it to their foreheads. One by one, more of the children that peppered the house's lawn followed the ritual. Having finished their greeting or blessing, Julia was unsure which, the children either darted all over the grassy expanse in a game of chase or sat underneath a big kalachuchi tree in one corner of the garden. The humble and warm atmosphere of the home dispelled her expectation of what a warlord's abode should be.

"These are my *inaanaks*," Amang Tenio proudly said. "My godchildren."

Amang Tenio led the group upstairs to an open-air veranda at the back of the house. Her child bodyguards, she realized, had actually stayed behind to play with the other children—except for Emman. He had followed them inside and continued his watch of her even then.

From the veranda, Julia saw that the entire village was built hugging the forest-filled mountainside. The veranda overlooked a tangle of tall trees and overgrown vines that marched down a steep ridge more than a thousand feet deep. Below was the far-off view of a bright blue lake with waves sparking silver from time to time. Its calm waters spanned the horizon, surrounded by the blue green haze of the encircling hills and mountains that enclosed it. At the middle of the lake sat one small island where rose a lone volcano. It was tall and majestic in its isolation, even if small for a volcano peak, cone-shaped with a wide-open crater full of blue water.

Julia could see fishing boats, as small as toys from her vantage point, traversing the waters in a slow glide, encircling the edges of the singular island.

"We call that 'the lake within the lake,'" said Mara. "The mountain in the middle of the lake is Taal volcano, and inside its crater is another lake complete with its own school of fishes. The volcano is active, though it has been more than a century since it erupted and buried a whole town under its ash and rock."

"It's beautiful," said Julia in awe. It was stunning, unexpected to see a large body of water, when mountain and forest had been all she'd seen for the past few hours. She'd had no clue of what waited beyond the tree line.

"You know, Iha, this whole land was given to us by your great-uncle, Don Miguel," Amang Tenio said as he sat beside Julia. "Don Miguel was the brother of your grandmother, Julianna, who was of course the wife of Captain Morrison. Don Miguel, Captain Morrison, and I all served under the Mabagsik guerilla group. The Captain was the official liaison of the American army to the guerilla groups in this region."

A tray of drinks in tall glasses was carried into the room and passed around. The cold tea had a refreshing taste of ginger, and Julia quickly drank the entire glass.

"After the war," Amang Tenio continued, "destruction was everywhere, and many of us had nowhere and nothing left to go back to. Don Miguel and your newly married grandparents willed this land to the surviving guerillas and helped them start over. In doing so, the whole village became as family to the Guevarra clan. And your grandfather and grandmother became the automatic *ninong* and *ninang*, godparents, to every child born in this village."

"I will admit that I'm surprised at how beautiful your village is, when it carries such a fearsome reputation. I was expecting something quite different," Julia said.

"I am sure Raul and perhaps Markus also were hesitant for you to come. For many reasons, they wish to protect you. Not many outsiders are allowed upon the lands of Barangay Mahinahon. We are at heart guerilla fighters with a serious approach to training, much like the training for our cockfights.

"I'm sorry, Iha, that what you saw upset you. The sight of death has a powerful effect in many people, even if only birds do the dying. But to let you leave without seeing something that strongly defines this town would be a crime, perhaps. I felt your tour would not be complete without knowing about the *sabong*—the cockfighting."

Julia nodded, unable to say whether she regretted it or not. Everything about this village, and even this man, confused her. Her first glimpses of Amang Tenio has been like some mythical illusion. And now she sat beside him, unsure if he was more like an ancient wise man or a mafia boss, and sipped tea before this grand view.

The cousins were silent, sitting in chairs close to Amang Tenio and herself. Not even the stern Raul was immune to the cousins' teasing, but to Amang Tenio they showed a deep respect, listening quietly as he continued his discourse on the sabong.

"Many find the sport barbaric, and a movement to ban the pastime rises from time to time. But it has been in our country's culture for far too long to be so easily eliminated. Besides, I find it curious that this strong reaction is found mostly in people who do not themselves kill their own food. They buy it already cut and neatly packaged at groceries.

"In many ways the cockfighting illustrates the old guerillas' predicament," Amang Tenio said. "Each champion rooster descended from a long bloodline of fighting cocks. If cockfighting were banned as a sport in this country, the thousands of gamecocks bred for fighting would have nowhere else to go; they cannot be released back to the flock. The only recourse would be to kill off the entire breed."

Julia understood all that he said, but still it was hard to accept.

"You have heard, of course, how soldiers of war experience post-traumatic stress syndrome, as it is now called. The soldier finds himself so trained and bred into killing or traumatized by what he experienced that he struggles to return to normal societal living."

"Yes, I know of this," Julia said.

Amang Tenio looked from one of his guests to another. "It is hard for you young people to understand how war changes the people who endure it. Hand-to-hand fighting, surviving torture or administering it upon the enemy, holding dying comrades in one's own arms as their life blood seeps through one's hands—such experiences did something to the guerilla fighters and soldiers. After the war, the whole country was broken and ravaged. Every survivor lost family and homes and had nowhere to go."

Stroking the rooster he still held in his arm, Amang Tenio continued. "Like these fighting cocks, we couldn't return to our former way of life. The constant killings, stress, and paranoia of the war years had marked us separate from the general population. Although every citizen suffered, the guerrillas had loosed a savage instinct within themselves to help save the country. They could no longer mix well with the people—especially our renowned Mabagsik guerilla group. We had pushed ourselves more than any other.

"This village became a respite for the old guerilla campaigners, a place to rest after the fighting. We called this village Barangay Mahinahon, the Village of Calmness. Even men who still had family and land to return to often opted to transplant themselves here and live amongst their former comrades—sometimes with their families, sometimes without. For giving us this land, and with the strong bonds of camaraderie forged during the war, your family earned the undying loyalty of the Barangay Mahinahon—not only the remaining fighters, but their descendants as well."

The silence that followed the telling of this tale was only broken when a servant returned with a tray, which she set down on the low table between their chairs. "Have you eaten *halo-halo*?" she asked.

"I haven't tried it," Julia acknowledged, "although I've heard about it."

The cousins expressed mock horror that Julia had not yet eaten the Filipino version of ice cream, consisting of assorted fruits, beans, and jams topped with shaved ice, cream, and evaporated milk.

Othaniel showed Julia how to mix the ice and the fruits together with a spoon before eating. Julia was unsure about eating a dessert that included small beans and something that appeared to be made of gelatin—and amused by how seriously the others seemed to take the stirring-up ritual. But with the first bite she was sold on the combination of tastes and textures—not unlike Barangay Mahinahon itself.

She smiled inwardly. Her desire to see the "gorilla village" had brought her an experience far beyond her wildest imaginings.

NINETEEN

Light showed in a line beneath the kitchen door. Julia pushed it open, and the Tres Lolas and Aling Rosa looked up at her in surprise.

"Iha, so you could not sleep with the *bagyo*?" Lola Gloria asked. The open door brought the scent of baking and spices, a comfort in stark contrast to the tempest outside.

"The storm?" she asked, and nodded her reply.

The bagyo had arrived not on tiptoe but with furious foot-steps across the night sky. The wind came in loud whips and howls, the palms clattered loudly, and rain pounded the roof, causing an abrupt cacophony of fury. The lights had gone out, and Julia was glad she'd been told how to light an oil lamp in case of such an event.

"We were enjoying our cleaning up, and the storm got too ferocious to get ourselves home."

"So you are having a little party?"

Lola Gloria chuckled. "We rested a little in the parlor; then Raul came to make sure we were all right, and that woke us into a cooking mood. He now sleeps in the office, and Mang Berto will soon be heard snoring from the parlor. We are baking—come join us."

Julia set her oil lamp on the counter; the lamps flickered around the room as the wind bellowed hard against the house. Thankfully, it was quieter here than in her room. The lower section of the large stone oven crackled with slow-burning wood. She saw Raul's jacket hanging on a hook on the back door, still dripping water.

"This is quite a bagyo." Julia leaned on a chair beside Lola Sita, who was rolling out dough on a wide cutting board.

"Yes, the storm is bad," Lola Gloria said. "There will be damage. The huts by the fishponds and village do not fare very well. Always some tragedy comes. And so, the old women will cook, tell stories, and drink something to warm the old bones that want to quake in fear."

"That certainly sounds better than hiding up in my room, terrified that the roof will fly off. The kids are not out there, are they?"

"No, Raul sent them to his staff house. That was another reason he came. He promised to keep guard of you in the house. It was the only way he could get Emman to go."

Julia smiled. She worried about the children still; this storm sounded as if it could level a stone castle. How would roofs made of tin or nipa fare in such weather?

"The hacienda endures storm after storm," Lola Gloria said, as though she could hear Julia's thoughts. "It takes a beating over the years, repairs are made, and still it stands strong."

Julia caught the long gaze in the old woman dark eyes. "Yes, I see that it does," she said. "And what are you cooking?"

"We drink chocolate and make *pandesal* for breakfast."

There was a loud howl, and something crashed against the house. All five women jumped and looked at the ceiling.

Once they calmed back down, Julia said, "The four of you could be chefs."

"Your great-grandmother taught us, but it was mostly Aling Rosa and Lola Amor who paid attention. I was more interested in books, while my sisters liked cooking and sewing."

"I wish I had more time to learn some of the recipes before I return home."

Lola Gloria looked up at her. "That is right, you will be going back soon. Let us give you a crash course in Filipino cuisine, then. What else can we do with this wind howling so loud that only the men can sleep through it?"

She translated to the others, who smiled and chattered away as they eagerly accepted the assignment.

First, they reminded Julia of the staple she'd been eating since arriving—rice. It was more common than bread was in the States.

"Without rice at every meal, Mang Berto doesn't feel he has eaten," Lola Gloria translated from Aling Rosa's comment. "It is this way for many of us."

"It's interesting how you eat with a fork in one hand and a spoon in the other. The cousins tease me about how I eat single-handedly."

"Well, we like to scoop up and drizzle one of our sauces into one bite. We are most hearty in our eating and go about it with great enthusiasm."

Julia laughed at that truth she'd witnessed during the many meals she'd shared with them. "Yes, and you are always trying to feed me too, every other hour it seems."

"Well, it is quite surprising how little you eat and how dainty and proper your nibbles." Lola Gloria translated what she'd said, and all the women joined in laughing.

"I've tried to figure out Filipino cuisine, as compared to Chinese, Indian, or Thai. It doesn't seem to be as distinct."

"That's because we're quite a combination—the Spanish influence mixed with the Asian. Our native cuisine is often gentler; then we accentuate everything with strong-flavored condiments."

Lola Gloria named the basics ingredients and spices in Filipino cuisine: mango, tamarind, heart of palm, lemongrass, miso, palm nuts, jicama. Sticky rice. Noodles made from rice, wheat, and mung beans. The heart of the banana, used as a vegetable. The inner portion of the young banana flower, fresh, dried, or canned in brine or water.

Julia was given spices to smell and sometimes sample, and the lolas pointed to cans and jars of other ingredients. Coconut milk, cream, thick milk, thin milk, oil. Coconut gelatin made from fermented coconut juice dyed different colors and sold as strings or cubes.

"I tried cubes like this in the halo-halo at Amang Tenio's house."

"Yes indeed," Lola Gloria confirmed.

Partway through the lesson, the lights flickered on and the women froze in place, surprised by the brightness. When a moment passed, and the lights stayed on, they gave a cheer.

"At least for a bit, you can see better what I am showing you," Lola Gloria said. "They may go out again soon."

"I love all the little sauces," Julia said as they all relaxed again.

"Oh yes. Our *sawsawan*."

Lola Gloria explained the sauces Julia had been tasting for the past two weeks—fish sauce, dark soy sauce, native vinegar, dried shrimp paste. These were mixed into a variety of flavors like garlic, ginger, red chili peppers, peppercorns, onions, cilantro, and limes.

Lola Sita interjected in hesitant English. "She try *bagoong*?"

"I'm not sure," Julia said, unsure what she'd eaten.

"Do we have a green mango?" Lola Gloria asked. She went to the refrigerator and rummaged. "Here we are."

The green mango wasn't a different variety; instead it was unripe and the firm consistency of an apple. Lola Gloria put slices on a plate and poured a strange reddish sauce beside it.

"That is *bagoong*. Only try a tiny speck."

Julia dipped a corner of the mango slice into the sauce. She tasted the tartness of the green mango mixed with a strong tangy flavor of salt and fish that surprised her senses all through her nose.

"What is it?" she asked, and her tart expression made the women laugh.

"It's fermented shrimp."

"Fermented shrimp?" Julia looked closer at the sauce. It was a clearlike liquid with tiny red specks that together made the sauce the red color. She realized the specks were the tiny shrimp. She didn't want to know what the fermenting process was about.

She noticed the cookbooks on a shelf beside canisters and hooks of hanging garlic, peppers, and other dried vegetables. Both English and Tagalog books filled the narrow bookcase. She smiled when she spotted Julia Child and Richard Simmons among the titles.

"Didn't you say the hacienda has a cookbook of its own?" Julia asked.

"Oh, yes indeed, you must see it. It is one of the treasures of the house, only—sometimes I forget where I put it for safekeeping. And then the other day, I found it and meant to show you." She went to the shelves and started searching again. "You know, Iha, sometimes our best treasures are right in front of our very eyes, and yet we nearly miss them altogether."

"Is that it at the end?" Julia asked, pointing to the spine of a book without a title at the end of the long shelf.

"Yes, it is! I guess sometimes we need others to help us see the treasures." She laughed and reached for the book. The cover shifted, loose on the spine. "We know the hacienda recipes by heart. I haven't cooked directly from one of the recipes in here since I was a girl."

She set the fragile book on the table, and the women circled around it, speaking in such excited tones that Julia wished she could understand them.

"Funny how we never look at this treasure, and it's right here with us every day. Go ahead and look inside."

Julia carefully opened the cover, and Lola Gloria translated the inscription inside: *For the family before and the family to come. Eat well and bring the past within you. Made in love.*

On the second page, a drawing of a young woman had been pasted with the name Elena Barcelona and date 1825 below it. Elena the Cook did have plain features as her story told, but there were both kindness and mischief in her gaze. How Julia wished to see her laugh and smile as she worked on some healing culinary concoction.

Next came a family tree. Long names and dates of births, marriages, and deaths. She spotted Ramon Miguel, the One-Armed Spaniard, in the lineage.

Then came a blank page with only the words *Sa Simula*.

"That reads "beginning, in the beginning." These are the earliest recipes here. Many of the ingredients and measurements we would not know now."

As she turned delicate pages, Julia noticed that the cookbook was divided into sections by the eras of the hacienda. She thought of Hacienda Esperanza as its own entity with a birth, childhood, youth, adulthood, middle age . . . perhaps now it had come into old age. Was this the final age of the hacienda? Or could the land truly be renewed to a new life and era, turning back the clock?

Suddenly the lights went off again, and with sighs and light-hearted complaints, they returned to the lamplight as the storm continued. Julia pulled the lamp close as she paged through the book; the lolas resumed chatting and sipping cups of chocolate. They had all become accustomed to the howling storm outside, the rain on the windows, except when an occasional louder blast hit the house. Inside the cookbook Julia found decorative borders and sketches of ideas for presentation. The author had also been a decent artist, but some of the pages were worn so thin the ink had faded beyond deciphering.

"Well, this house is filled with mysteries," Lola Gloria said. "Iha, you have not even explored all the rooms in this house."

Lola Amor was leaning over Julia's shoulder as she paged through the book, and suddenly she pointed and gave a cry of excitement.

Lola Gloria looked. "The Orchid Cake."

The other women covered their mouths in excitement.

"It is the most revered dessert of the hacienda, but it has not been made in decades."

Julia recalled her grandfather's note. *The secret is in the orchid.*

"It's the orchid from the story of Elena the Cook and Cortinez and their secret cove," Julia said. "The cake that they ate at the fiesta and never ran out of it."

"Oh yes, see, you are learning the stories," Lola Gloria said with a proud smile. "There was a man when we were very young, before the war, who knew the cove of Elena and Cortinez. He worked in a position much like Raul's. He would bring the orchid, and we would always have the cake."

Lola Gloria glanced at Lola Sita. "My sister was too young for him at the time, but she was so much in love with him. He was killed by the Japanese."

"Oh." Julia didn't know what to say.

Lola Gloria put a hand on her sister's back. "He was a good man. Very brave. He was one who saved our lives, and he met the young Captain Morrison during the war. It is a story I will tell you one day. But since his death, no one has found the orchid, though a few have searched for it. After the war, the annual fiestas were held for a time. The cake was made, but we used other orchids beside the Elena orchid. Of course, the magic was gone."

The other sisters spoke together in rapid tones.

"We believed Captain Morrison would find it. Or Raul. Or Markus. Or one of Amang Tenio's men. When we were younger, we ventured ourselves to the cove to find it. My sisters believe that if the orchid is found, the hacienda will be redeemed once again. Only God knows if the hacienda's future will include the Elena orchid or not."

Around the recipe someone had drawn borders of leaves, the hacienda house, a river, and a dotted path to where the plant was supposedly located. A picture of a small orchid was also drawn in the lower corner.

Lola Gloria leaned back, and the wooden chair creaked louder than the wind outside. "I suppose you would not know the story of the Orchid Traveler. You see, Elena's orchid was someone else's long before Elena was born, even before it came to the islands of the Philippines."

Julia smiled, realizing that another story was beginning. Aling Rosa poured her a cup of warm chocolate, and she settled back to listen.

"The first man upon the land was a savage traveler, a primitive native from an island people somewhere in northern Indonesia or Malaysia. Some say he was from farther away, perhaps Australia or Japan, or even the tip of the South American coast—but I think that is all exaggeration. But even a primitive man may find himself in love—in this case, with the chieftain's daughter.

"As children they would play among the coral caves, collecting shells and watching the bats pour from their darkened upside-down slumbers as evening turned to night. But ever since her ritual ceremony into womanhood, the chieftain's daughter had avoided the young warrior so determinedly that it only inflamed his love. He would do anything to have her as his beloved wife.

"The chieftain, however, sought a marital treaty with a neighboring tribe, hoping to secure peace after years of skirmishes. When the young warrior sought the chieftain for his daughter's hand, he met with scoffs and insults. 'What can you offer the tribe by such an alliance?'

"The entire tribe mocked him for such initiative. He went to the coral caves for three days. When he returned, he walked through the huts, where all his fellow tribesmen stopped in their work of making stone arrows and spears to watch him and went to the chieftain.

"'I will have your daughter as my own,' he announced. 'If you marry her to any other man, I will kill you and him and take what is mine. I will be gone for a time and a time after that, but I will return and you will give her to me. I will have something to offer the tribe when I return.'

"No one spoke, not even the chieftain. The young warrior's fierce determination impressed them to silence.

"As he walked away, he saw the flap of the girl's hut door stir, and for the briefest moment saw her eyes upon him. It was all he needed to endure what was to come."

Lola Gloria stopped and took a sip from a drink that Lola Sita had placed before them without Julia even realizing it.

"The young warrior set out in a boat of his own making, first scouring the coastlines as he moved from island to island. At times he went inland upon those strange lands and searched for food or fished along the foreign coves. He saw other primitive tribes and once stayed a week with a group of friendly villagers, speaking through drawings and hand motions. At his side he wore a pouch, the contents of which no amount of curiosity or coaxing could persuade him to reveal. And every night without fail, the man dreamed of pink flowers with a touch of yellow climbing up a rock cliff—and also of a door flap and a glimpse of brown eyes upon him.

"During this time, the chieftain's daughter would walk to the coral caves every morning. She would pause on the shore and stare long at the horizon. Sometimes she stayed overnight in the caves, which worried her father at first, but then he ignored it because of more pressing matters at hand. Two warring tribes had formed an alliance.

"The chieftain's greatest foe came asking for his daughter in marriage to form an unshakable treaty. Despite the rationality of such a political move, the chieftain hated the other man. He loathed the idea of marrying his daughter to such a vile man, who treated his other wives with disdain and cruelty. And in his mind he continued to hear the parting words of the young warrior every night before he closed his eyes.

"At long last, after a change of many seasons, the young warrior turned toward home, ready to claim his bride. When he arrived at the island, it looked just as it had when he'd left it. His steps were determined, as they'd been two years earlier. He carried in his hand an orchid blossom to where the chieftain sat in his chair staring out to sea. But the chieftain would not look at the flower or at the man.

"It was then that the young warrior gazed around and saw that the tribe was half what it had been, and none of the warriors remained. The children and women looked starved and haunted. He crouched low to hear the chieftain's hoarse whisper.

"'You would be dead also if you had not left us.'

"'Where is she?' he asked.

" 'She is dead.'

Julia's face fell, and Lola Gloria smiled and patted her arm.

"The warrior stood. 'Where are the ashes of her funeral fire?'

" 'There are none. He took her, and she is dead.'

" 'I will find her yet.' The warrior stood and looked back to the sea. His legs still felt weak on solid ground. 'Why did he not kill you?'

" 'He has. Is this not the worst death of all?'

"The young warrior had not slept in many days in his determination to return to the island. He went back to the beach and turned his canoe over, still dripping wet and swollen from the months of sea. Neither man nor boat would rest that day. As he prepared to heave the boat into the water, a young boy ran down the steps to him.

" 'Where are you going now?'

" 'To find her.'

" 'But they say that she is dead.'

" 'She is not dead. I will find her.'

"The boy looked at him. 'You are right,' he said. 'She is not dead. She lives at the coral caves, though only her mother and I know this. We fear her father will give her to the chieftain if he knows she lives. The warriors of our village did not die in battle—at least, not battle with flesh and blood. They died in a battle against the gods of the storm—the sea, the wind, the sky. A monsoon came while you were gone. The chieftain believed it was a curse sent by you or the other chieftain for his delay in sending his daughter.' "

The house shook suddenly with a torrent of wind and rain as if for emphasis. The other sisters laughed and muttered nervously as Lola Gloria continued.

"The young warrior ran quickly to find her. She was waiting at the cave opening, her long black hair dancing in the breeze off the sea. Above her, pink orchid petals dangled from the vines.

"The warrior took her hands and told her, 'In my dream, I was instructed to take the petals of this very flower and leave them all over the many coastlines. After a time, I would return, and where I found the vine growing and flowers blossoming again, that would be our new land. I have found that place. It is a long journey, but we must go and begin a new life there.'

"The young woman said, 'I, too, have dreamed while in the coral caves. I was told to prepare for your return, and you would take me to a foreign land to begin a new life. I am ready.'

"From the village, they brought the boy, the girl's mother, and a few others. The chieftain refused to leave and died alone on the cliff top gazing toward the horizon. And as you have guessed, the land of the hacienda was first inhabited by these young lovers. One of their descendents married a child of the One-Armed Spaniard.

"They arrived at the hidden cove that Elena and Cortinez discovered later. They came to this land with nothing. Do you know what it is like to have nothing?"

"No, I suppose I do not."

Lola Gloria smiled then. "They did not either. Because in fact, though they came with few earthly possessions, they truly had everything."

The other women, though unable to understand the English telling of the tale, had been lulled into a comfortable silence while Lola Gloria spoke. Lola Amor dozed in her chair as Aling Rosa and Lola Sita set dough to rise near the warm brick and adobe oven.

"Darling Iha," Lola Gloria said, putting her hand over Julia's. The old woman's hands, covered in age spots, felt soft and sure. "All these stories are a part of you, because you are part of the hacienda. We are the generations, the hands and feet, the heart and the soul, the blood flowing through a land that has been on a long journey and all of us with it. The heart has been missing for a long time. A new heart has come to bring life once again. You, my child."

Julia didn't respond. How could she explain that she couldn't stay?

Suddenly she became aware of a pounding sound from without. It had been going on for a while, she now realized, but with the howling and crashing of the storm, they hadn't recognized it for what it was: someone was knocking steadily on the front doors.

Aling Rosa caught on at the same moment and put out her hand and shushed them sternly.

As a group they jumped up and crept from the kitchen, oil lamps in their hands.

Julia held the lantern high to see the visitor standing outside as Aling Rosa opened the large wooden doors. The young man's hair and face were drenched in rain, his clothes muddy and sticking to his body. The Tres Lolas hung back, huddled together, while Aling Rosa demanded to know what he was doing there.

Julia felt she should probably take over, but she had a language barrier, and Aling Rosa seemed to be doing just fine, handling the situation like a courageous mother bear protecting her own.

"He insists on speaking to Raul," Lola Gloria translated for Julia. "He says he won't leave until Raul comes."

"Does he need a towel? Should we let him come in?"

"Let us first see Raul's reaction."

The man wiped his dripping hair from his forehead, self-conscious beneath the stares of the five women. Julia recognized him, perhaps from the fields. Then she recalled, he was the handsome man from the jeepney who had known who she was. He had attended her grandfather's wake, but she didn't remember him at the funeral.

Raul came to the door, rubbing his eyes. When he saw the young man shivering in the doorway, a look of surprise moved over his face, and he quickly ushered the stranger inside. He peered into the darkness before helping Julia push closed the heavy doors.

Lola Sita had disappeared and returned with towels.

"Go back to your cooking or sleeping," Raul said to the women. "I will take him to the study, and we will discuss this in the morning." He looked at Julia. "Let me talk with him."

Julia nodded her head. The man gave her a steady gaze and then followed Raul to the study, leaving a trail of mud and water in his path.

ON THE SAME DAY, BOTH TYPHOON YUNYA AND MOUNT PINATUBO wreaked havoc onto the northern provinces of Luzon, Philippines. As the mountain shot its colossal ash cloud into the air, the cyclonic winds of the typhoon blew in, greatly exacerbating the damage. Roofs collapsed under the water-laden ash—some areas were practically raining mud.

This was the news coming in, and Manalo, his men, and some villagers surrounded the radio in the *carinderia*, listening to the reports. They'd spent the night in the basement of the sympathetic owner, not knowing their country was suffering from more than a simple storm.

Manalo wondered about Malaya's extended family. She'd certainly be frantic, wondering if they'd been evacuated. How he wished to be there for her, to comfort and reassure her.

In the morning Manalo went outside to a wet world. The sky was clear with some remaining clouds from the storm, but according to news reports it would soon be covered with ash. In the north, the day was like night. Manalo stretched his arms and watched villagers picking up pieces of roof and cleaning up debris that covered the muddy streets.

The country was in turmoil. The work of his life had amounted to little. Things weren't any better; in fact, they were worse! And now God Himself—if he too believed in God like Timeteo—was raining down His wrath. It didn't escape anyone's notice that the one of many volcanoes in their country to erupt was right in the path of the U.S. Air Force base—and even more so in the prostitution capital of Angeles. Even God wanted the American soldiers and the vile professions out of the Philippines! Manalo was thinking like a regular Catholic, he thought with amusement.

Then he saw them coming down the street. They were covered with mud and walking with the weariest of steps, but Manalo recognized them at once. His best friend and his oldest son.

Manalo stepped into the street, stunned. They stopped before him. "What are you doing here?" he said to Aliki.

Timeteo sighed heavily. "I couldn't stop him. He followed me, and then we met the storm."

"I've come to join the fight, Father," Aliki said with pride.

And as Manalo held his boy-turned-man in his arms, he knew the world had most certainly gone mad.

TWENTY

J ulia awoke late in the day to a silent world outside. There
was a unique quiet after the storm, even with the birds
singing happily of their survival. Everything was drying out in
the wane sunlight. Branches and coconuts, palm fronds and broken tiles littered the courtyard and lawns around the hacienda
house.

She was finishing her breakfast and looking again into her
grandfather's logbooks when Lola Gloria came to speak to her.

"Miss Julia. There is a dispute between two women. They ask
you to help them, to mediate the problem, and to give decision to
stop their disagreement."

"Me? Why me?"

"You are the doña of the house. This is usually my role, or that of the head of the family. But with you here, they wish for you to mediate."

Julia closed her grandfather's book with a thud. She'd been reading about energy options like hydroelectricity by water pressure, solar panels, and a modernized windmill.

"But I'm no mediator." Julia wanted to laugh, except that Lola Gloria appeared to be completely serious.

"They had an argument over a pig. Whatever you decide will be respected."

Julia sank her head into her hands. "I can't decide such a thing."

"Please, Iha, do consider it. Such things unresolved can cause friction for years to come, and these two have been friends since babies. They are young women, they made jam with you, and of course they attended the Captain's wake and funeral. Your decision will not be questioned."

Julia found Raul working on a ladder against the house, supervising some workers as they cut down a broken tamarind branch that dangled precariously against the roof. Broken tiles littered the ground around the ladder.

"The phone lines are down," he said. "The storm and volcano erupting in the north caused a lot of damage. It always happens in storms such as these. But at least the electricity is back."

"More eruptions, eh?"

"It was *the* eruption," Raul said.

"How long for the phones?" Julia asked. She couldn't keep putting off her departure—and her family would undoubtedly be worried when they heard about the eruption.

"It could be today, or it could be a week."

"Great," she said under her breath. "Raul, I don't want to interrupt, but I guess some women are here. They had a dispute and are asking for help in resolving it. Is that something you have done in the past?"

"At times. But with a woman in the house, they would wish the matter solved by you."

"That's what Gloria said. But I can't do that."

Raul leaned an arm on the terrace roof and held the side of ladder, looking down at her. "I told them you might not like it."

"You knew about this?"

Raul smiled at her rising anxiety. "Go and hear what they have to say. I will come with you."

"No, this isn't something I want to start. I'm leaving soon."

He came down the ladder and gave final instruction to the workers. Julia recognized one as the man who had arrived the night before in the storm. When she'd asked Raul earlier in the morning about the mysterious nighttime visitor, the foreman had simply said that he was a confused young man and had come to ask forgiveness. For what, Raul apparently wasn't ready to admit to her.

"Yes, you are leaving soon," he said. "But until then, why not help as much as you can?"

"You're enjoying this, aren't you?" she accused.

There was an actual smirk on Raul's face.

"Why would I enjoy?" he said solemnly as he reached the ground, but again she caught his amusement.

The two women arguing in the back courtyard stopped immediately when they saw Julia and Raul step around the corner. Each held a child on her hip and greeted Julia enthusiastically. One had a beautiful smile; the other woman was plain, but spoke a few words of greeting in English. They wore faded but clean dresses with aprons and flip-flops. Their hair was pulled into neat ponytails.

Raul spoke to them, and they immediately began talking again. Julia sensed the quick anger that grew between them. Raul held up a hand, and their speaking ceased.

"This woman," he said, pointing to the one with the beautiful smile, "says that several years ago they made an agreement to buy a young sow together. They purchased it with money earned from selling vegetables at the market. The plan was to breed the sow and sell some of the piglets and grow others to be butchered.

"The other woman says they had agreed that the first litter of piglets would be hers and the next litter would be the other woman's to sell or keep, whatever she chose. The sow birthed a large number of piglets, and she believes her friend is afraid the next litter will not be as large. That is the disagreement. They've been arguing about it for a week, and their families are being divided."

Both women stared at her; then they began to speak again, waving their arms and moving close to her. The children in their arms began to cry, so the women only increased their volume to be heard. Julia felt their breath on her face, and her neck tingled as they moved in even closer. They expected far too much.

Raul did nothing.

"Wait, wait," she pleaded with arms up. "Raul. I can't do this."

They were waiting for her response.

"No, really. I cannot decide on something like this."

Raul looked disappointed.

Julia turned and walked quickly away, moving through the courtyards and gardens down the pathway through the staff housing. She could smell a mesquite fire and fresh laundry flapping in the breeze. Some boys looked up from playing marbles in the dirt and said hello as she passed.

What did they expect of her? She was only a guest, there for a few days longer. Her grandfather was buried, her job nearly done. What kind of place was this, where she couldn't do her own laundry, but she was expected to make a life decision for two women she knew nothing about? If she made a mistake, there could be animosity between childhood friends for life.

Julia walked by a small section of land given to the staff to farm for their own use. She hadn't explored this area on her daily walks.

She continued down a pathway to the rice fields where grass-covered divisions cut the fields, into squares with milky water filling the insides. A few workers with wide triangular-shaped hats were bent over, walking slowly through the water.

Looking behind her, Julia hoped she had ditched her ever-present shadows this time. She needed a measure of solitude, some time to think. It wasn't just these two women with their disagreement; it was all the expectations. The respect, the smiles, the hope. That was it.

She had become their hope.

At the end of the rice fields, Julia looked back. Her young bodyguards were nowhere in sight. Her shoes were caked with mud. The pathway turned from the rice fields, and Julia guessed that if she could see the hacienda house maybe a mile back, she'd be walking parallel to it. She reached the back of the overgrown orchid fields and the trickle of a stream. Twice she stopped, waiting to see if she were followed. She didn't want to return, not yet. No one came. At last, she was truly alone.

She pushed through the brush, though her arms were scratched by branches, and kept going until she reached a giant bamboo forest. The bright green stalks were wide and tall, over twenty feet high, turning the light an ethereal jade. The confining foliage and warmth of late afternoon were like a sauna, bringing beads of sweat to her brow and making her shirt stick to her back. A wind came through the tops of the towering bamboo, fluttering the tall leaves but bringing little relief to her on the ground. Onward she went, until suddenly the trees opened and it was all sky.

The high cliff was sharp, and she could see far below a cove of black rocks with a dark sandy beach. The aqua waters of the sea stretched out to meet the gray-blue sky. Julia hadn't expected the sea this close to the hacienda; then she realized she'd been walking for at least an hour, maybe more.

At the very edge of the cliff she pushed off a few pebbles with her shoe as she leaned forward as far as she could. She'd been told the sea formed the easternmost border of the hacienda, but her walks had never taken her this far. A crisp breeze of salt air mixed with a tropical sweetness cooled her face and neck.

Far below, the waves rolled softly over the rocks and beach. Julia searched the ledge and finally saw stone steps going downward, worn down and barely visible. They'd been cut into the rock ages ago and softened in shape by the weather and erosion of time. She took one and sought the next as she wound down the cliff.

With a jump off the last few steps, Julia reached the bottom.

The small beach was a strange mix of black sand and then, closer to her, a creamy white. Julia sat on a rough volcanic rock and pulled off her shoes. The air off the waves cooled her face and toes. Looking across the water, she saw other islands jutting from the sea. Her arms stung and itched from the branches; red lines swelled in places. She moved around the rock and let her toes sink into the pale sand as a wave slid over her feet. As she cooled off with her feet in the water, Julia took in her surroundings.

The small rocky beach was secluded by massive rocks, and the thick green foliage was a canvas enclosing every space between. Unless viewed by a boat coming in close or from the cliff directly above, this place was completely hidden. It must be the cove from the story of Elena the Cook.

Julia left her shoes on the rock and hurried to the rock cliff, down along the wall, examining any flower and even the smallest plants. It didn't take long to reach the other side of the cove. But none of the flowers she saw even closely resembled an orchid, let alone the sketch she'd seen in the recipe book.

But at least I've found the cove, Julia told herself. Maybe the orchid bloomed at another time of year. Or perhaps it had all been a myth.

Now hot again, Julia rolled up her muddy jeans and waded a

few steps into the translucent water on the darker sand side of the cove. She stripped off her shirt and jeans, tossing them toward shore, then dove into the water. Instantly she was transformed. Julia wished to laugh beneath the water—laugh and breathe while diving deeper and deeper. She'd always been jealous of mermaids, but never as much as at this moment.

Her face went from water to air, and she took a deep breath, filling her lungs. The salt stung her eyes, and Julia had to keep them closed and blink for some moments before she could see again. The thought of sharks came to her, but she cast it out. Paradise found could hold no such dangers. She thought that surely Elena and Cortinez had swum here as well, and perhaps the young native warrior and his beloved new bride.

Her legs kicked gently, easily staying up with the buoyancy that only equatorial waters offered. A variety of tropical fish swam with her; the water became more colorful as she moved over a coral reef and the fish became more numerous. Julia wished for a mask and snorkel and thought how rare a place this hidden cove was, a tropical paradise seen by very few.

She swam farther out, then turned back and stared up at the massive wall of the cliff. She spotted something at the end of the cove where the rocks jutted outward and down into the water— an ancient landslide had once fallen there. On the other side of the rocks was another small portion of the black sand beach.

There was more beach, she saw, as she swam around the black rocks. The rockslide had cut off the end portion of the beach from the rest. And there, climbing up the sheer cliff, was a flowering plant with delicate pink blossoms.

THOMAS MAGNUM, PRIVATE INVESTIGATOR, HAD TIPS FOR HOW TO follow someone.

Once Magnum was following a beautiful white woman, the wife of a client, through an airport. Emman had never been to an airport, though he'd once ridden a motorcycle down a dirt runway, but it appeared to be an exciting place. For a while, Emman had thought of becoming a pilot.

Magnum said first of all, when tailing a suspect, always blend in with the crowd. Emman didn't have a crowd while trying to find where Miss Julia had disappeared to, but he did have a jungle. And who knew what waited within it? He tried blending in.

Tip number two: a good private investigator had to be constantly on guard for the unexpected.

That Miss Julia's muddy footprints were going so far from the hacienda house was unexpected, and so he tried to be ready for anything.

Tip number three: act perfectly natural if spotted.

He still hadn't spotted Julia, so that wasn't a problem yet. And it had become pretty natural to follow her.

Tip number four: if spotted, look as if you just happened to be there.

Yeah, right.

Magnum had a secret name for the wife of his client. Code name: "Legs."

Emman didn't feel a name like that would be appropriate for Miss Julia. Though she did have very nice legs, he'd noticed. It was his job to notice everything, right?

Why didn't Miss Julia understand the danger? Did she think it had disappeared? She was like one of those movie stars running off from their bodyguards. This was what his cousins meant when they said in exasperation, "Women!"

Emman nearly stepped off the cliff, so deep was his frustration and so thick was the brush at that vantage point. A light disturbance in the earth showed her path to the same point, and he suddenly worried that she had fallen. He couldn't see down through the wall of green foliage, but further inspection didn't indicate a fall—though he shivered at the vision of her lithe body swallowed by thin branches and air.

Then Emman's feet froze as he recognized where he was.

"She found it," he said aloud in amazement. Very few ever came to the Cove of Cortinez. Emman saw an outcropping and moved downward with sprightly movements. At a turn in the rocks, he could see the cove.

One of the funniest parts of the *Magnum, P. I.* opening song was when Thomas is standing in the ocean helping a woman learn to swim. He glances down right at the view of the woman's . . . back end. Seeing Miss Julia swim in the ocean, Emman thought he must surely have the same funny grin on his own face.

He decided he'd better head back to the top and wait for her to return.

Emman tip number five: if, after assessing a situation and finding it safe, always give a client her privacy . . . even if you didn't really want to.

JULIA ROSE FROM THE WATER AND STOOD DRIPPING WET BEFORE the sheer, vine-covered cliff. The pink flowers were delicate and small, nothing really impressive compared to some of the large orchid blossoms in the fields. And yet, upon closer inspection, she was surprised at their intricate and delicate beauty.

Julia thought of Lola Sita and Lola Amor. How excited they'd be, and yet . . . if she was uncomfortable with their hopes and expectations now, she could hardly imagine the response were she to return to the hacienda with the first true Elena orchid blossom in over fifty years.

Part of her didn't wish to disturb even one of the perfect blossoms, but after long consideration, Julia pulled a flower from the vine. She sat on the sand and held it in her open palm. It had only a very light scent. Julia touched her tongue to the edge of a petal, unsure why she felt compelled to do so.

She fell asleep in the soft sunlight with the orchid in her hand. Later she woke to the shadows that had stretched like a blanket to shade her. The thin gray clouds reminded her of a world outside the cove.

As she rose from the sand, she spoke aloud with such surprise that she laughed as well. "I'm in love with a rice farmer," she said.

TIMETEO STOOD BESIDE HIM, ARMS CROSSED AT HIS CHEST. THEY watched as Akili sparred against Paco along a grassy knoll. The boy had practiced since a child, but Manalo hadn't thought he'd be this good. If the boy were someone else, Manalo would take him at once, as an asset to his band of men.

But he wasn't someone else. He wasn't some unknown man's son. Aliki was his son.

There could be no changing the boy's mind, despite all Manalo and Timeteo had said to the boy in the past hours. He was determined and stubborn, as stubborn as Ricky and more intelligent than either of them. But for all his studies, disciplines, and innate talents, Akili had longed for his father—Manalo could see it all through him. And that created a weakness in him, making him overly zealous, wanting his father's approval.

How, Manalo wondered, had life become so difficult? He'd gone down a path and made choices that seemed right. And here he was. Perhaps a man could not just journey down life trying to make the immediate correct decision, when a larger life plan for himself and his family was needed.

And now his son, who could be anything he wanted, was choosing a life in the jungle as a Communist insurgent. Aliki knew nothing of what he asked.

Manalo sought a way to change the path that stretched forth before him. He needed to end it, and soon.

His family would only be safe under certain conditions: if they all left the country (something he could not do unless he went, God forbid, to a country like America), if he continued until his status as enemy of the state was changed, or if he was dead.

"My friend," Manalo said. "My brother, I need to ask you about something."

"What is it?" Timeteo asked.

"I need to ask you about God."

They both instinctively glanced around casually to see who was in earshot.

"Yes?"

"Does this belief of yours go all the way to, say, Christianity, or something as bad?"

Timeteo did not respond for so long, Manalo thought he must not have heard.

His oldest friend finally turned toward him and shook his head in humor. "I would not have expected to say such a thing. But yeah, I guess it has come to that."

"How does that work with what we do . . . and who we are?"

"It is becoming more and more my dilemma."

Manalo nodded gravely. "We need to talk then. For I think I have a plan."

Julia found the Tres Lolas gathered as usual for their late afternoon merienda in the back courtyard. They jumped up when they saw her, worried at her disheveled appearance.

"What happened? Raul said you were upstairs resting today and not to disturb you."

"No, I was on a walk."

For a moment she paused, unsure if she was prepared for the reaction and consequences of what she couldn't stop herself from doing.

She placed the orchid blossoms on the table.

There was a moment of inaction, then sudden recognition. Lola Sita gasped and covered her mouth, then spoke in rapid Tagalog as sudden tears fell down her cheeks. Then she hurried into the kitchen with one of the orchid blossoms cupped in her hand.

"She said she'd forgotten what the flower looked like," Lola Gloria said, picking up another. "It was in her nineteenth year that Lola Sita last made the Orchid Cake with the Elena orchid ground inside the batter. Fifty years ago. No one has brought an orchid from the cove since that time."

No one spoke, but Julia saw that Lola Amor stared at the flowers and tears also crept down her face. Even Lola Gloria struggled with emotion.

"You have brought us an incredible gift, Iha." Lola Gloria held her hands tightly clenched, and her voice shook. "You've returned to us our past, and our stories are made alive again with such an offering. And perhaps this symbol will be a sign of blessing for our future. We thank you."

Julia excused herself to shower. She was so dirty that she first sprayed off her clothes and salt-sticky hair in an outdoor shower in the back courtyard, and then she went upstairs for her bucket and tub bath.

When Julia came out of the bathroom with her hair wrapped in a towel, Lola Amor was waiting in the hallway; her eyes red and swollen. She hugged Julia tightly and spoke long with words Julia didn't know, but whose meaning she could perceive. Then Lola Amor kissed both her cheeks and left her.

Julia returned downstairs awhile later to the fading light. At the back courtyard, the old women sat talking in placid tones. They motioned her over, just as Raul walked from the house with a clipboard in hand.

"There you are," he said upon seeing her. "Julia, I must ask that you not go out alone again. It was very difficult to keep track of you."

"I was followed?" Julia said, and thought of how she'd swum half-nude in the cove.

"Emman lost you for some time; then he found you at the cove, though he didn't go down."

"You know where the cove is?"

"Of course, but I haven't been there in decades. It's overgrown and miles from the work. But even with your bodyguards, it is not wise right now to disappear into the jungle."

"What's going on, Raul?"

They heard a car roar up the driveway, and a moment later Markus rounded the corner from the side walkway. "You found her!" His hair was sticking up on one side, and his shirt was only halfway tucked into his jeans. "Julia, where have you been?"

Raul, Lola Gloria, Lola Amor, and Julia looked at one another and laughed.

"What?"

Markus had such a confused expression—he looked to Julia like an adorable little boy trying to make sense of an adult situation.

"What's going on?"

"For a big-shot Manila lawyer, you sure look funny," Raul said. "Julia is safe and sound."

"There wasn't traffic, and I drove like a madman. I got here in two stress-filled hours."

I love him, Julia thought with amazement. *I love that sheepish look on his face, the way he runs his hand through his hair. I want years to know everything about him.*

Markus's confused expression only deepened at the way she stared at him.

"I think you need coffee—or a stiff drink," Lola Gloria said, rising from the table.

"It's been intense in Manila as well. The storm did a lot of damage, and tensions are high in the political realm." Markus kept glancing back at Julia as he spoke. "Someone in the Barangay radioed me that Julia couldn't be found, your phones were still out, and they said a member of the Red Bolo group was spying on the hacienda and showed up here in the night."

Lola Gloria exclaimed and then translated for her sister, who covered her mouth in fear.

All this was happening as Julia swam and napped in the cove— it struck her as funny somehow. Raul gave her an annoyed look when she chuckled, and Markus continued to appear confused.

Julia tried to be serious. "The whole Barangay thought I was lost? And, Raul, did you know that guy was part of the Red Bolos?"

"It's okay," Raul said to the sisters, ever trying to protect them. He appeared annoyed at Markus for worrying them.

"Sorry," Markus said with that same sheepish expression.

MARKUS TOOK SOME PAPERS FROM THE COMPUTER PRINTER. "SO we are all agreed on this. The two of you will be joint owners of Hacienda Esperanza. That way, Julia retains being heir to her grandfather's plantation, and it is legal because a Philippine citizen owns it with her. We will divide responsibilities and establish a system of checks and balances. Once a year everything will be assessed and audited. We will approach the cousins about creating an even larger cooperation with their lands with a governing board of directors. Julia must get final approval from her family, and then she can do her duties from the United States, if she wishes."

Raul and Julia nodded in agreement, and Markus handed over the papers for their signatures.

When Markus went to his car for something, Julia finally had the chance to ask Raul about the two women. "Did you resolve the conflict about the pig?"

"No. They are to do nothing for a few days."

"Why didn't you take care of it?"

"It would be better received from you. I mediate disputes with the men."

Julia sighed. "But if I create such a thing, what will happen when I'm gone?"

Raul turned a page in the open logbook on the desk. "We return to the old system. But you have come up with an idea to resolve the problem, haven't you?"

"Why would you think that?"

Raul's eyes flickered to her, then back to the book. "Tell me what it is."

"Okay. The women could divide this litter and every one following. They each can decide whether to sell or raise the piglets under their care. If an odd number of piglets is born, the extra one can be given to one of the squatter families so it helps someone else and there's no further argument. The sow must be kept and cared for by both of them, unless they agree to do something with it."

"I will tell them tonight when I return to the staff houses."

"But wait . . . do you think it's a good solution?"

"Julia. You know that it is. You do not need my approval. There are some things you must simply be confident about. If you do not know, seek the answer. But when you have the answer, do not second-guess yourself."

"It's a lot of pressure. It's dealing with people's lives."

"It is very important. And judging is to be done with great thought. It is right to find the burden heavy. But if you have the answer, then give it and move on. There are many things to think of on the hacienda. Give weight to what is heavy, and carry it when it is yours."

"I'll be leaving soon."

"Yes, so you keep saying."

Markus returned to the room, and the phone immediately rang. "I guess that means they're working again." He answered it and frowned. "Julia, it's for you. Would you like us to leave, or take it in the kitchen?"

Julia guessed it was either her mother or Nathan. "I'll go in the kitchen." It surprised her how much she dreaded saying hello to whoever was calling from home.

"Julia, where have you been?" Nathan sounded angry. She heard a click as Markus set his line down. Strangely, she wished he'd stayed on.

"I've been—why, what happened?" A cold fear spread through her.

"What happened? We've been trying to call you all yesterday and today."

"We?"

"Me, your mother, Lisa, your stepdad. We've called every number we have. We even tried that lawyer guy. I already contacted the U.S. embassy."

"Nathan, calm down. There was a storm and a volcano erupted and the lines were down. Why are you so upset?"

"Yes, we heard about the typhoon—that's the same as a hurricane, in case you didn't know—and the volcano was the worst eruption in modern history. It's all over the news."

"Oh," she said. "I haven't watched the news since I got here."

"Julia, I can't believe you're just calmly sitting around as if nothing is happening. We've been frantic. Your mother received a death threat about you!"

"What?"

"She was warned that if you didn't leave the country, you would be targeted to be killed."

Julia leaned her forehead against the wall and closed her eyes. The scent of a stew or something good made her dry mouth suddenly water. She nearly laughed, finding it strangely humorous that anyone found her dangerous enough to threaten, but laughing would infuriate Nathan.

"We're getting you the next flight out of there."

How strange to imagine that in just days, she might be driving from the airport through the city northbound. How she loved San Francisco—the skyscrapers and triangular-shaped Transamerica building—the ancient looking Coit Tower, Alcatraz on its island with sailboats and cargo ships passing by in the bay waters. From San Francisco, she'd cross the grand Golden Gate with the orange beams and arches contrasted against a flawless blue sky or a gray foggy morning.

Hacienda Esperanza would quickly feel like the past, or like a long dream she'd just awoken from. Right now the hacienda was real and home was memory, but she'd be so changed, there was no going back to the person she had been. Julia knew this as she stared out the kitchen windows at the view of the old Spanish courtyards and the green rolling fields extending to the far-off mountains.

At home she'd be comparing everything to here. Friends and family would quickly grow tired of her words . . . "at the hacienda . . . did I tell you about . . . the best mangoes I've ever tasted are from the Philippines."

She'd meet with her old girlfriends and hear how Bradley and

Natasha finally settled on a china pattern for their bridal registry, and thank goodness with the wedding only seven months away. Mindy would retell tales from her most recent shoe-buying binge. Shanna and Mark would have returned from a trip to Europe and say how the French were exactly the stereotype of rudeness. Shanna would say how brave Julia had been to go on her trip to the Philippines, since France seemed nearly too foreign to her.

Julia wouldn't fit there anymore. She'd long for this, for the people, the land. And for Markus.

"Are you there, Julia? Hello?" Nathan sounded more annoyed than concerned.

"I'm here. Calm down, Nathan."

"Are you seriously telling me to calm down?"

They'd researched the people behind her death threat, he told her. They were a Communist offshoot, but the Communists in the Philippines were ruthless killers—they'd assassinated a U.S. captain in Manila only four years earlier.

"And then a volcano erupts there as well!" His voice was shrill with anger as if it were all her fault, even Mount Pinatubo.

"Was it a death threat or just a warning?" she asked, noticing that Raul stood in the doorway of the kitchen with a look of concern on his face. "Why don't you read me exactly what it says?"

The line was silent for a long moment; then Nathan spoke. "Listen, Julia. You will get on the next possible flight from Manila. If not, we'll get the U.S. government to make sure that you do."

TWENTY-ONE

❧

The scents were irresistible as usual. Julia would greatly miss that.

"Ah, Julia. Try this." Lola Gloria leaned over the pot that Lola Amor was stirring and took a spoonful.

"It's delicious. What is it?" She hoped it wasn't tinola after the mention of the dead rooster being turned into the chicken dish, though she knew this recipe would not include losers from the sabong.

Lola Gloria shook her head. "There is a story to this recipe."

"Well, of course there is. There is a story for everything and everybody here. I bet there is a story for that plastic spoon."

"Oh no," said Lola Gloria. "I ordered that spoon at a Tupperware party. Well, I guess there is a story behind it, 'cause it's the first time I bought something like that, and Aling Rosa hates it. She refuses to use it."

"Ah, you see? A story even for the spoon."

"It is true. This hacienda cultivates more stories than crops. Much to our undoing. But let me tell you of our dinner tonight."

Julia peered into the steaming pot on the stove as Lola Gloria gave it another slow stir.

"Tonight Aling Rosa and the Tres Lolas will present paella. It was first served for the wedding of the One-Armed Spaniard to his young bride, the first Julianna in our lineage. The One-Armed Spaniard requested the meal often. It is a dish that takes all day to cook."

"Wasn't paella part of the story of Elena the Cook?"

"Yes, indeed. The same recipe, though Elena improved upon it greatly. So now please take a long nap if you wish, then wash for our early dinner. Aling Rosa will bring some water in a few hours. We will have some guests tonight."

The weight of the days fell heavy upon Julia: the wake, the funeral, the journey to Barangay Mahinahon, the expectation and responsibility. She slept the afternoon away.

The sound of voices could be heard through the house when she descended the wide staircase later beneath the gazes of the ancestors of Hacienda Esperanza. She wished for a long, hot shower, not a bath that required someone to haul up a tub full of water or a shower awkwardly given from the clay pot. She missed the hard water pressure on her back in her modern tile shower at home. If she weren't leaving, an upstairs shower and bath would be the first thing she would have installed.

As Julia walked into the kitchen, she noticed the table was missing from the center.

"Perfect timing," Lola Gloria said, turning from the counter and handing her a pot of rice.

"Good evening, Miss Julia," Aling Rosa said in slow English as she took a dish from the oven and motioned for Julia to follow her outside.

Familiar faces already surrounded the two tables pushed into one: Mang Berto, Raul, Mara, Francis, and young Alice. Julia was disappointed not to see Markus's face among them.

"We were wondering if you'd wake in time," Mara said, as she walked around the table placing silverware. "Francis thought perhaps the Barangay scared you into sneaking away in the night, but I said no way."

Francis laughed and nearly tipped backward in his chair. "You don't have to tell her everything."

He rose to greet her, and Julia feigned nonchalance.

"What's to fear from a guerrilla village, my dear cousin?" she said. "It's just a place of jungle warriors, cockfighting, and a hillside that once was covered in decapitated heads."

Francis kissed her on the cheek. "I guess the savageness of our country is something we grow accustomed to. Whether that's a good thing or not, I could not say."

She smiled. "There's never a dull moment, that's for sure."

The tables were covered in linen tablecloths and napkins. Small candles sat beside each plate with fresh white flowers woven around the table settings. The small lights hung for the funeral were like stars in the trees and along the courtyard wall, granting enough light to the deepening dusk to see the food on the table and provide a peaceful ambiance.

Gloria brought out the pot of rice and set it in an open space.

"Where is Markus?" Julia asked, afraid she might actually blush just by saying his name. Was it written all over her face?

Othaniel rounded the corner from the side walkway. "Here I am!"

"And late as usual," Mara said, as they all greeted him.

"And yet I always have a grand excuse. This time, I was

searching the shops of San Pablo, and look what I found. In honor of Julia: two bottles of California wine." He held up a chardonnay and a cabernet sauvignon, and the others clapped in excitement.

Othaniel came up the short courtyard steps and kissed Julia's cheek, then proudly turned the bottles to show the labels.

Recognizing the winery, Julia smiled broadly. "I know this place. I attended a wedding there once."

"Wonderful. Tonight we have California and Philippines in its own merger of food and drink and family. However, the native Californian must open the bottles, since I do not have such a talent. I hope the extensive hacienda kitchen has a corkscrew."

She laughed and took the bottles. "I hope so too."

Aling Rosa brought the corkscrew out and everyone watched as Julia opened the bottles. Few there had tried wine in a country too tropical for vineyards to produce well, and they eagerly set out glasses.

Lola Gloria and Aling Rosa together carried a huge iron pot through the back door. "Presenting Paella of the Hacienda Esperanza!" They set the pot at end of the table; Aling Rosa lifted the glass lid, and the steam billowed upward, sending an intoxicating aroma through the air. Julia peered inside at the mixture of rice, shellfish, vegetables, sausage, and many spices.

Mara waved Julia over to the empty chair beside her. "The sisters know how to bring a meal to life," she said gently.

Then Raul rose from his chair, and everyone quieted. "Let us say a prayer of gratitude to our God the Father," he said.

The pot of paella was too large to send round the table, so plates were passed and served. There was much laughter, stories, and helping after helping of food around the table.

Julia tried dishes she hadn't seen before. "What is this?"

"It is like a leafy vegetable cooked in coconut milk."

"And this?" She took up a fork in one hand and spoon in the

other and tried eating doublehanded. She'd reach for a bit of sauce with her left-handed spoon, then with the fork, mix the sauce with a bite of meat or paella.

Alice started talking to Julia in Tagalog, till her sister reminded her: "English, use your English."

"What is it like in California?" Alice asked from across the table. "Do you eat foods like this and gather with family?"

"The food, well, it's nothing like this. At least not where I live."

"Is it mostly hamburgers and french fries?" Alice asked, and the others laughed.

"Our food is very different. Sometimes hamburgers, steak, and mashed potatoes. Usually a single vegetable, not mixed often in a sauce like this. There are ethnic restaurants—Mexican food is practically Californian food now. America is such a diverse mix of cultures that I'm sure in some families they do have meals like this. Just not mine."

Francis asked seriously, "So are Hollywood movies accurate as to what America is like?"

Julia laughed this time, as they all looked at her questioningly. "I wouldn't go that far. Maybe some of them, somewhat. Is dinner together like this a normal thing here?"

"During holidays and fiestas. But not every night, not always," Mara said.

"I usually eat alone. Well, now I do," she said, then felt awkward. How suddenly far away that life felt again, as if not lived by her at all but by someone she'd once known.

This dinner, with these people, the breeze just touching the tallest palms, the air warm and filled with the sweet scent of the tropics and the smell of shellfish, roasted meat, rice, fruits, and the myriad of foods on the table—all this was more real than anything she'd known. Rich and alive and vibrant. The thought of her life in the past few years was like a faded painting, drained of nearly all the color.

Julia gazed at their faces, lit by the candles. Smiles and laughter, jesting in English but also in words she didn't know but didn't need to. Even Raul relaxed in the setting—though Julia noticed how often he glanced at Mara or chuckled at her stories. Aling Rosa had pushed back in her chair and leaned her head on Mang Berto's shoulder. Othaniel and Francis were tag-telling a story about getting caught driving one of Captain Morrison's cars to Manila for an international fireworks competition.

"When we got back, we pushed the car down the driveway so no one would hear the engine. And there was Mang Berto standing in the middle of the road with his hands on his hips." Othaniel started laughing so hard at the memory he couldn't continue.

Mang Berto shook his head, a wide smile on his face, as Francis finished. "We thought he wouldn't notice one car missing—we picked out a car from the back of the garage. We were in so much trouble."

Julia felt a deep sadness that this was her last meal with them, perhaps forever. She promised herself to come back soon, to be involved with the hacienda from afar as her grandfather had, but she wondered if it would really happen once she returned home.

One thing she knew for certain: her life didn't hold a future with Nathan. It would hurt him, and she regretted that. But there were some things a person couldn't go back from. And Julia knew there would be no going back from the changes wrought in her by this place—Hacienda Esperanza, the plantation of hope.

SHE FOUND HIM IN THE OFFICE, WHERE HE HAD WORKED ALL through the dinner with her cousins. "I didn't even know you were here until Raul told me as we were eating dessert," she said. "I missed you."

"I didn't want to be there for it," Markus said.

By the look on his face, Julia knew what he meant. Once the cousins found out that the dinner wasn't just a meal together, but a farewell, it had turned into a time of very emotional good-byes.

Francis used every manipulation to try to keep her, finally saying, "This isn't over. I'm asking God to intervene."

Julia fetched Markus a plate of paella and a glass of wine, which he savored slowly.

"You have brought life back to the hacienda, Julia. Just by your presence, and then with the orchid. It's rather amazing," he said. "I wish I had been there with you at the cove."

"Yes, I wish that too," she said, at nearly a whisper.

He stood up abruptly. "Come with me." He reached for her hand and led her through the house to the tall front doors and then outside. "There are no stars," he said, looking up into the night as they stood side by side.

Without a word, they started walking hand in hand, a force of tingling between their entwined fingers. At the hacienda gates, Markus stopped and turned toward her. The small lights along the post and down the driveway reminded her of fireflies.

"What are we going to do?" Julia asked.

Markus touched the strands of hair that fell near her eye, brushing her cheek with the back of his hand. "I don't know."

He stepped closer to her, and she caught his cologne or soap or perhaps it was just his presence, a surprising combination of warmth and strength and desire and intrigue. Her longing for his lips upon hers grew overpowering.

A smile replaced the same longing in his expression as he looked at her. "I want to kiss you. But it's hard when I know there are young eyes peering at us from the jungle."

Their heads turned together, and some bushes moved slightly about fifty feet behind them.

Markus frowned. "I hope it wasn't Emman."

"Why not?"

"He's in love with you too."

She laughed a little. "He is?"

"Oh yes, he is. And we wouldn't want to hurt the kid, ruin him for life and for all other women." Markus was joking, but not entirely. "Can you tell that sort of happened to me around his age?"

"Oh, really?"

"Yes. A girl broke my heart when I was twelve, and I've never recovered. Until now."

"Uh-huh," Julia said wryly.

"Hey, did you even notice what I said . . . that Emman is in love with you *too*?"

Julia nodded. "I noticed."

"And you just ignored it?"

"I figured you'd say it if you really meant it."

"Oh, I really mean it. Come here." He pulled her around the outside wall that bordered the hacienda's main grounds and kissed her then, with a length and width like histories behind and a future before.

"I love you, Julia," he whispered close to her ear. "How do I live without you now that I've found you?"

"I'm not supposed to go," she said, and knew it was true. Grandfather Morrison had known it as well. "I will stay."

He sighed and shook his head. "No, you have to go back. It isn't safe right now. But know this, Julia. I have fallen in love with you in a way that I've never known before."

She felt it too, encompassed by this love that rose so surprising and true. When had it happened exactly? she wondered. It seemed to have started the moment they met, but only in retrospect did they see it. As if their souls had found each other, but their minds didn't realize until it was slowly revealed.

"I am in love with you too, Mr. Santos, my attorney-at-law."

"As your attorney, I must advise you against falling in love with a Filipino man. Especially this particular one, who has fallen so deeply he will never want to let you go."

"Then don't. Don't send me back."

Markus groaned. "It doesn't make sense for this to happen now. If you stayed and something happened to you . . . Your family received a death threat! Those are not jokes here. You must go back to the States."

So quickly, her happiness soured within her. How could she leave when she'd found this? "Then how do we give us a chance? Long-distance relationships are hard enough."

"I will wait for you, find a way for us. But what about Nathan? It doesn't sound over between the two of you. You might change your mind when you get back."

"It has been over with Nathan for a long time. Just lately, when it became a possibility, I was unsure. But being here, I know for certain that he and I are finished."

Julia couldn't imagine being back in California now, away from the hacienda. "I don't want to go. And you know, if we are apart, you could be the one to change your mind."

"No. If I commit to you, then I'm committed, Julia. It's just how I am. And I want to be the man . . . well, it's crazy to say all these things so quickly, and with you going in the morning."

She came close to him and lifted her eyes to his. "Say them. Your words may be our chance to make it while apart. Let's say everything, and have those words to keep us strong until we're together again."

HE HEARD ABOUT IT WHEN HE WOKE. TONIGHT HE HAD PLANNED to take night duty, but instead the news kept him in his hammock with his face turned toward the wall.

Emman couldn't believe Miss Julia was really leaving.

She was leaving without him.

MARKUS LEFT WHEN THEY RETURNED FROM THEIR NIGHT WALK, saying it wasn't good-bye yet. He'd take her to her flight, but he needed to get all the final documents ready for her to sign first. She would have dual power over the hacienda, even though she'd be in the States. But until she left, they needed to keep that information private.

Mang Berto waited outside the car, shining the paint or windows from time to time as the engine idled smoothly. It was about six in the morning, but there was no dawn on the horizon and still no stars in the sky. Some of Julia's baggage had already been tucked inside the car's trunk.

Julia walked through the courtyard and then onto the lawn. There was no movement in the dense foliage. At least three children should be there, guarding their doña with the seriousness of secret service agents. But no one came out, even to say good-bye.

"Salamat, Emman," she called toward the jungle. Still no movement at all.

The Tres Lolas had packed more things for her to take home to the States than Julia knew what to do with. As Raul carried the boxes to the car, Julia saw Emman come from the trees and jog toward the house, then down the side pathway to the back. He carried the rifle on his shoulder as naturally as any army soldier. He didn't look her way or wave his usual greeting, or grant a farewell.

Raul closed the trunk of the car. "Are you ready, Mang Berto?"

"Yes, we are ready," he said, patting the door with his rag before opening the door for Julia.

The Tres Lolas and Aling Rosa hugged her with streams of tears falling down their faces. They hadn't spread the word far about her departure. It would cause too much attention and might compromise her safety further.

"We never made the Orchid Cake," Lola Gloria said sadly.

"Make it for the cousins and for Markus. And we'll have it again when I return," Julia said weakly, knowing none of them had much faith in that happening any time soon.

The car's engine came smoothly to life, and Emman suddenly appeared in the front yard. Julia looked for a way to roll down the window to say good-bye, but he turned away without smiling. She wondered if it was too dark or if the windows were too tinted to see in. Emman ran determinedly down the road and disappeared into the jungle.

Julia found the handle and rolled down the window, calling him too late. "What's Emman doing?"

"He took his job of protecting you very seriously," Mang Berto answered simply.

Raul, sitting beside her, had no comment.

"Yes, I know. And he did his job well. So why won't he say good-bye?"

Mang Berto shrugged his shoulders. "Perhaps it is too painful."

The car moved slowly down the driveway and through the gates to the hacienda house, then drove down the road. They approached the main iron gate to Hacienda Esperanza. Emman stood opposite the side of the security guard with a stern and worried expression.

"Mang Berto, please stop for a moment."

Mang Berto pulled the car up beside the boy, and Julia stepped out.

"Good-bye, Emman."

"Good-bye, Miss Julia."

"I hope to be back soon. Is there anything from Manila or the States that I can send back to you?"

There came no response, no wide smile or acknowledgement of her. "Come now, Emman, don't be that way."

Emman ran ahead again, his gun on his shoulder and out of sight.

"Well, should we proceed?" Mang Berto asked.

"In a moment." Julia couldn't hide the disappointment in her voice.

Raul watched from the car. "He's from the Barangay. His life is here. It's an adventure when he goes to San Pablo."

"I should have taken him to Manila. Maybe you or Markus could show him the city."

The men didn't respond, and Julia returned to her seat in the vehicle. "Those kids should play and dream and, I don't know . . . be children, I guess."

It was Mang Berto who replied. "There are no easy answers. I am sure for an American it is shocking. Even for most Filipinos it would be quite savage. But for us at the Hacienda Esperanza, it is different. Man was perhaps created equally, but he is not born equally. And each man must find his own place in his own station and take pride and honor in the life he has. Are your American children better humans or adults for living the American lifestyle?"

Julia thought of the stereotypes that were often sweepingly true: spoiled rich kids, undisciplined children, the allure of drugs in every rung of the social ladder. How were those lives better because instead of growing up with a wooden gun on their shoulders and learning respect and honor, those children played video games and soccer?

"I still can't get myself to like or accept it."

Raul nodded. "It is understandable. Be careful with them, Miss Julia. Be careful with Emman and the others."

How, exactly, was she to do that?

Julia recalled Emman standing solemnly in his cut-off pants and faded T-shirt by the hacienda gate. She tried to envision him in trendy jeans and a rock band T-shirt with a skateboard in his hand. She wondered even more what Emman would think of the skyscrapers of Manila, of an art exhibit by Picasso or Degas. The image was nearly impossible to conjure, yet it thrilled her despite her reservations.

"I guess we should go," she said. As they drove away she looked back and saw Emman standing in the center of the road. He began running after them, and then they turned a corner and left the boy behind.

Just then the car halted again. Another driver coming toward them motioned them over. Markus.

His car was a strange gray color, and he left it running as he came to Julia's window. "I was afraid I would miss you."

"What are you doing here?"

"You can't go to Manila. The volcano has caused catastrophic damage. The city is a mess, flights are being cancelled, and there are rumors of another coup attempt."

Julia jumped from the car and into Markus's arms. "I guess you can't get rid of me so fast."

"As if I wanted to."

Julia saw someone approaching from the corner of her eye. "Emman!" she called. "Your work is not done. I'm staying."

"Well, until the next flight," Markus said with regret in his tone. "But we'll take every day we have."

"Oh no, I'm staying. This was the answer I was looking for."

Markus and Raul glanced at each other.

"Unless my presence causes a problem or danger for anyone else?"

"No, it will not." It was Emman who spoke, standing proudly and biting his lip to keep from smiling. The morning was coming though it was such a strange reddish gray world; the tiny flakes started so subtly that they nearly didn't notice.

"Look, Emman. It's snowing." Julia put out her hand.

"It's ash from the volcano," Markus explained. "It's covering most of the Philippines and is expected to go across the South China Sea to Cambodia and Vietnam."

"First time that I see snow." Emman copied her with his hand palm up; then he inspected his hand. "We cannot make a snow-man. Maybe an ash-man?"

Julia laughed. "It's Philippine snow. And the miracle of it is also the miracle of my new life at Hacienda Esperanza."

SHE WASN'T LEAVING. IT COMPLICATED MATTERS. AND YET HE WAS also strangely proud of her. The American did have Filipina blood in her after all.

It was not what his superiors wanted. There would immediately come orders that Manalo would not follow, and yet someone else might. He had to tread carefully, and there was only the slightest chance for full success.

But regardless of the outcome, in a few days, his family would be free to live as they deserved. And for that, Manalo would know his life had not been in vain.

THEY EITHER HAD FORGOTTEN HE WAS IN THERE, OR THEY THOUGHT he was asleep. Emman heard them right outside his window. Only a mosquito netting covered the opening, so he heard every word.

"What are they going to do about it?"

"What are *they*? We shouldn't wait for anyone. *We* should take care of it, since he was our friend."

It sounded like his cousins and their friends.

"Tell Rigo what you told me."

"It was the Red Bolo group. Ka Manalo is the leader. They think Artur was probably tortured before they killed him."

Emman sat up. His hammock rocked, and he put out his hand to stop it from hitting the window ledge.

"You don't think we should wait for orders?"

"Why should we? Would they have waited at our age?"

"Then let's figure out what we're going to do."

TWENTY-TWO

"You almost left without saying good-bye," Amang Tenio said, walking into the room where Julia had been staring at the telephone and rehearsing how she'd tell her mother and then Nathan that she wasn't coming home.

"Hello," she greeted him. "Come in—or should we go outside?"

He nodded solemnly. "Outside sounds good."

As they walked through the house, she said, "I am sorry for that, for the abrupt departure that so quickly became a return."

They settled at the outside table, and he immediately pulled out a large pipe with deep carvings covering the dark wood.

"I am told that you plan to remain here."

She paused a moment, wondering if he approved. "Yes. I would like very much to do that."

"Good. I was just discussing it with my friend Father Tomas, praying for ideas to make it so."

Julia found the combination intriguing. "You and Father Tomas are friends?"

"We have been great friends for many years. We debate theology and the subject of peace and war. You might be surprised to discover that we hold many same beliefs. I light candles upon entering the church and ask for redemption through the Son of God. Father Tomas would like to make me a full-fledged respectable Catholic without my 'warlock robes' as he calls them, most lovingly of course. And I would like to get the Father a bit out of his stiff collars and onto the veranda to smoke pipes and marry him off to one of my sisters. We do disagree about some things."

"Where is Berdugo?" Julia asked, finding it strange to see Amang Tenio without his beloved rooster resting in his left arm. He seemed oddly thinner or missing something.

"I think that bird of mine believes himself the king of the Barangay Mahinahon. Today he remained in his cage and gave me a look of great disdain when I told him I'd be coming to town. I didn't mind too much, for his royal highness gets pretty heavy for an old crippled man to carry." From around the handle of his cane, he unhooked a silver chain.

"Julia, I have something for you," he said. "Even though you may be staying now, I want you to have this to remember Barangay Mahinahon, the village of apes, monkeys, and most certainly guerrillas." He handed her a small silver pendant in the shape of a square.

"Thank you very much." Julia felt Amang Tenio's pleased smile all through her. She latched the hook around her neck, then held the cool silver in her hand.

"Raul told me that Captain Morrison mentioned in his letters how sharp you are in business, how successful you were in your company."

Julia thought how meaningless it sounded now, compared to the heritage of this place. She'd risen up the corporate ladder until she no longer cared and fell right back down. "Yes, I was successful . . . for a while."

Amang Tenio reached a moment to stroke the rooster that was absent in his arms. He looked down in surprise, chuckled to himself, and gazed a long while over the green fields.

"You also found Elena's orchid."

"Yes."

Amang Tenio pointed out to the land. "Iha, you have seen how the Barangay renews itself through our young, the old fighters passing their skills to their children. It was the same for the leadership of the hacienda as a whole. The times ahead belong to the new generation, to the children of its former leaders. I have talked to your cousins as much since they were children with the hope that every new generation learns from the mistakes of its predecessors. Children are always the new hope.

"We needed the Captain; the land needed him to heal. But he did not come as we wanted. But you came, Julia," Amang Tenio said meaningfully, looking at her sideways.

"But—" She wanted to argue about such a grand role, but he put up his hand to keep her silent.

"You should have known these things before. You see, the time of your elders has passed. Many have hung their hopes on you. Hoping you would take a stand. They look to you to be the person your grandfather was, or someone of similar quality. Hoping that there is enough blood of the Captain in you to make you care about the hacienda as he did. I know it's an unfair expectation."

Amang Tenio's nearly black eyes stared deeply into hers. "This is why Raul seems to have mixed emotions concerning you. One part of him wanted to believe you were the long-awaited hope, while another part felt he was only fooling himself and irritated that people were hanging their hopes on an American with no real connection to the land. And yet deep inside, he also hoped you could do something—though he doesn't even know what." Amang Tenio paused, deep in thought. He squinted his eyes, making more wrinkles down his cheeks.

Julia felt the weight of his words, of a responsibility greater than she thought she could handle. Before she'd come, Julia would have cast it off outright. Now she considered it, half-wishing she could rise up for such a role even as she felt completely ill prepared.

"Do you like your necklace, Iha?"

Julia held it in her hand. "Yes, it's beautiful."

"Father Tomas blessed it today. That was another purpose for my visit to the church. There is something written on the back of it."

Julia took the pendant and tried turning it around, seeing only very small writing in a unfamiliar script. "Is that Latin?"

"Yes. From the Scripture verse of 2:10 of Pilo's letter to the Ephesians. The translation is, 'We are what God has made us . . .'"

He reached for her hands and spoke with each word and sentence defined. "We are what God has made us. Created in Christ Jesus for good works. Which God prepared beforehand. To be our way of life.

"That will be for you, as it has been for me. Each person was made for a specific purpose. The men in the village were made to be fighters. And fighters we were. But we need to fight *for* something. Our purpose is not for ourselves, but for others around us and for the greater purpose of God's mysterious plans. Wherever the journey of life takes you, do not forget these things. Do not forget that verse that you now carry with you."

They rose and walked through the late afternoon sunlight, shining through the palms and high wide leaves of the tamarind and banyan trees.

Amang Tenio had spoken his words to her, offering wisdom for her to hold near her heart. It felt orchestrated, this time in her life, from the emptiness at her grandfather's death to the weeks at the hacienda. Orchestrated by a plan much greater than them both.

MANALO THANKED TON AND SENT HIM TO BACK TO WHERE THE other men were eating around the outdoor kitchen they'd set up. They were moving frequently, knowing any one spot would eventually be unsafe.

"Well, that was unexpected," Timeteo said.

"Yeah, but what does it mean?"

Amang Tenio wanted to meet. The message came from one of the men of the Barangay Mahinahon to Ton and Leo at the carinderia in town.

The strangest part about it was that Manalo had been plotting a meeting with similar means of communication. It was easy to identify one of Amang Tenio's men by their distinct clothing—but how did they know the twin brothers were his men?

Manalo hadn't planned to involve anyone except Timeteo. Now all his men would know, which meant that unless he instructed them directly not to speak of it—which would incite more curiosity and at some date in the future might endanger them—he had to carry on this plan knowing that Comrade Pilo might hear of it.

"I trust Lon," Manalo mused aloud.

"Yes. But it shows the harshness of these times that we must even consider the loyalty of our own men. We would have not questioned it before."

Manalo nodded. "We will do this meeting, but I don't trust this situation."

"We'll take extra precautions."

"We always do," Manalo said with a wry grin.

"We'll take *extra*, extra precautions."

"Yeah, you better start praying to that God of yours."

Manalo had actually seen a Bible among Timeteo's belongings since they'd begun sharing a tent. It was worn and had lines marked throughout. He'd been going to bed before the others for maybe a year or so. Now Manalo knew why.

Timeteo gave him a strangely sheepish look. "Who would've thought you'd be saying that to me?"

"What changed you?" Manalo asked.

"My *wife*."

Manalo raised an eyebrow. "Excuse me. How does a whore lead you to Jesus?"

Anger flashed over Timeteo's face.

"I'm sorry," Manalo said, putting up a hand. But the woman was a prostitute. What did Timeteo expect?

"She was forced into it by her father as a girl. The life was destroying her. I went to her for more than sex. After a while, I went only to talk. We both were seeking answers beyond what our lives consisted of. I gave her some money, and a Christian group helped her train as a seamstress."

Manalo stared at his oldest friend for a long time. All the jokes and references about his "wife" had been to cover up that his heart had softened beyond that of even a normal man, let alone a rebel fighter. He shook his head. "Just when I thought I'd seen and heard it all . . ."

MANG BERTO SLEPT UNDER A TREE WITH THE LARGE CARABAO, Mino-Mino, sniffing at his stomach. Emman approached the old man with gentle footsteps across the grass, hoping he wouldn't spook the massive animal and cause it to trample the dozing figure.

Mino-Mino suddenly bit on to Mang Berto's hat and flung it up and down in her teeth, sending the old man into fits of laughter.

He jumped up and began a tug-of-war with the carabao. His hat escaped the jaws of the cow, but not without deep indentations and wet slobber.

"I thought you were asleep," Emman said as he reached him.

Mino-Mino lumbered off with a nonplused look in his droopy eyes.

"I was faking it," Mang Berto said with a laugh, leaning his hand against the trunk of the tree. "Seeing how close that old girl would come. Curiosity isn't only for cats and people, you know. Did you ever hear about the old carabao Rio Grande who lived near the fishponds?"

"Rio Grande, like the river between the United States and Mexico?" Emman knew that name from some Westerns he'd watched.

"That very one, yes indeed. He was an old relative of Mino-Mino, perhaps her grandfather. In a village about ten kilometers from here, there lived a boy, eight years of age or so. He lived with his deaf uncle who took him in after his parents died. Oh, that's a tragic story in itself."

Mang Berto dabbed his forehead with his handkerchief and leaned close. "Now a deaf uncle might sound good when you have no one else, but this was a mean old man. He loved to drink and sometimes disappeared for days, only to return in a terrible state. The boy made a few friends and created a lot of trouble in the village—oh, he could be a bad kid, that one.

"His teacher started walking him to school every day to make sure he went. She said he was brilliant, which he liked very much to hear, especially because she was pretty, and smelled good to boot.

"The boy loved stories and reading. His dead parents had left two books, and both were in English: *Heart of Darkness* by Joseph Conrad and *Kidnapped* by Robert Lewis Stevenson. He read those books again and again until the sentences were not such a struggle to decipher. And so for a year, the boy stayed with his uncle. Until the day he met Rio Grande.

"His uncle was sleeping after being carried home that morning by his friends, and the boy was reading a new book, a gift from the teacher. The book was about gunfighters in the Old West of Arizona. Suddenly an old carabao put his whole long face up to his horns through the window of the boy's room."

Mang Berto cleared his throat and tried using a young boy's voice. "'Well, hello there. I'm going to name you Rio Grande. What can I do for you?'"

Emman couldn't help but smile.

"Old Rio Grande couldn't speak, of course, but he stared at him so long, the boy knew what he wanted. That old carabao wanted to take him for a ride."

Mang Berto smiled widely.

"And so just like that, the boy gathered his things and wrote a note for his teacher. Then he tucked the book into his knapsack, put a flat-brimmed straw hat on his head, and climbed onto the broad smooth back of Rio Grande.

"The boy rode on that carabao all through town and beyond. Many came to see the sight of a traveling carabao with a boy on its back. The sun beat down upon the boy, who had forgotten to bring a canteen or anything to eat."

Emman thought of the many times he'd been in the jungle without his canteen. It was a terrible feeling.

"At long last, Rio Grande came to a long fishpond. The boy stayed on the carabao's back, though he dropped his knapsack on the shore. When the brown muddy water reached Rio's stomach, the boy stood up and dove right in. The boy swam and even drank that muddy water, he was so thirsty. After swimming awhile, he crawled out upon the warm grass and went to sleep.

"A voice woke him. 'Can I help you?' He thought it was his mother at first. But this wasn't a weathered woman of the sea; this was a refined Filipina in a crisp dress and parasol blocking the sun from her smooth skin. She was not a beautiful woman, but her perfume smelled so pleasant—he did so love a nice-smelling woman—and her gloved fingers gave her such a delicate and proper air that he was intrigued to no end.

"The boy jumped up and wiped the grass from his back. He gave his name and introduced Rio Grande. The woman stared at him and then at Rio Grande. The boy stared back. He'd never seen a woman so sophisticated and wearing such beautiful clothing. He noticed her horse-drawn buggy, how white it was. Even her horse was white.

"As the boy and woman stood silently observing each other, a loud noise filled the air. A strange contraption came zipping down the dirt road with a plume of smoke rising behind. It was a motorcycle, but the boy had never seen a motorcycle before. He stood in awe and fear at the speed and appearance, deciding it must be some kind of mechanical horse. The motorcycle suddenly stopped, skidding to the side. The woman's horse jumped and reared and didn't calm until the engine was turned off.

"'You might come in a little slower next time,' the woman said with a calm smile on her face.

"The couple met in an embrace that shut out all things around them. Then the young man noticed the boy. 'Who are you?'

"'He is my new friend,' the young woman said.

"'Greetings, new friend. What do you think of my new toy?'

"'The boy could not speak; he was still in such awe of the metal horse.

"'You like it that much? Very good, very good indeed. I will give you a ride home if you like. Where do you live?'

"The woman interrupted with an invitation to their picnic. She then said to her husband, 'You will thank me many times for this in the future. This boy is here for us.'

"From a basket she pulled clay pots of savory rice and foods he'd never tasted before. The boy watched and, though his stomach groaned with hunger, copied their polite manners instead of shoving fistfuls of food into his mouth as he wished.

"'Have you ever worked as a house boy?' the woman asked. 'Or in a mechanics garage?'

"The boy shook his head, but smoothed down his hair and stood up all the taller.

"'Would you like to live here and work for us?'

"'What about Rio Grande?' the boy asked.

"'I think he'll like living here just fine,' she said, pointing to the pond.

The old carabao looked so happy the boy thought he saw him grin.

Mang Berto slapped his leg dramatically. "And that is how Rio Grande found his place, and the boy as well. It didn't stop the hard times, the struggles, and the challenges. The boy later fought in a war and barely survived. But what was important was that the boy knew where he belonged after that. He even found a wonderful woman to love him, and sort of tricked her into marrying him."

Emman looked at Mang Berto suspiciously. "Is that boy an old man now?"

"Well, funny you should say that . . . yes, he is."

Mang Berto was the funniest old guy Emman had ever met. "He doesn't happen to love old cars, does he?"

Mang Berto put his half-chomped hat back on his head. "Well, I'd have to ask, but I'm assuming that he does. Now were you just passing by, or did you come to find me?"

Emman had nearly forgotten why he'd come searching for Mang Berto in the first place.

"Yes, I was searching for you. I need to see Amang this afternoon. He is in the woods collecting some herbs for Father Tomas. Could I borrow one of the tricycles?"

"Hello, Mang Berto and Emman." Julia walked up the pathway, followed by five "soldiers." They weren't being discreet, but they were certainly keeping Julia in sight. "What are you two up to?"

"Oh, telling stories when I should be working. Emman is heading off in one of the tricycles to see Amang Tenio."

Emman hoped Julia wouldn't think he was shirking his duty. "I will be gone a short time. I am leaving the others with you."

"I actually hoped to talk to Amang Tenio again," Julia said. "I could drive you in one of the cars—if that's okay with you and if Mang Berto allows it?"

"Who am I to stop you?" Mang Berto said in his jovial manner.

But Emman remembered how Amang Tenio had told him not to let Julia leave the hacienda grounds. He'd said that for at least the next week, more guards were to be posted. And already someone had gotten past him; Emman hadn't been present during the storm when that betrayer had come to the house. The foolish women had even opened the door before Raul came—Miss Julia could have been killed!

Raul and Amang Tenio had ordered that nothing happen to the man, the spy, who lived in the village. He owned a carinderia in town and admitted helping Ka Manalo and his men for weeks, even giving them shelter during the storm. He said it was because they had threatened to destroy his little café. But upon hearing of the many atrocities done by the Red Bolos, he'd come to the hacienda house to tell what he knew and seek refuge. Emman didn't think that was any reason to forgive him for having helped their enemies, even if he had switched sides now.

All this meant he and his soldiers should be on further alert. Well . . . he wondered what Magnum, P. I. would do.

"Emman?" Miss Julia said.

He made his decision. "Okay."

Bok gave Emman a look of concern.

"We'd better bring the others along with us," Emman said, which made Bok's eyes widen all the more. Emman didn't know whether that was from fear of getting in trouble or excitement that he'd get to ride in a car with Miss Julia. Probably it was a mixture of both.

"Okay," Julia said as they walked toward the garage. "We'll be back in a few hours."

"Be careful," Mang Berto yelled after them. "And Emman . . ." He switched to Tagalog. "Perhaps before you leave here, Mino-Mino will stick his head through your window and take you where you are supposed to go."

Emman looked in the direction that Mino-Mino had disappeared. He didn't need a carabao to give him guidance. He could take care of Julia, and someday he'd be able to do it all by himself.

TWENTY-THREE

The "soldiers" climbed with their guns inside the car. They all had rifles now, except for little Kiko. Julia wanted to put the rifles in the trunk—she'd never feel comfortable seeing children with guns. But they insisted that as soldiers, it was required.

Six kids and Julia squeezed into the car, some sitting on laps or dangling out the windows.

"Where is Grace?" Julia asked, missing the lone girl in the bunch.

Young Amer said, "Oh, she's becoming a regular girl. It's gross."

Ever since the Red Bolo group had invaded the hacienda on the day of the funeral, the children had replaced their wooden guns with real firearms. They were armed bodyguards. They were *her* bodyguards. The hacienda's future army forces already trained in warfare instead of playing baseball or chess or video games. Their lives were cockfights, amulets, guns, and fighting. And protecting their doña.

She looked across little Kiko to Emman and asked, "Where to?"

"Go toward town, and then I will tell you where to turn."

For all their excitement, the troupe drove in silence. The children in back were simply excited to be along for the ride and settled back, enjoying the luxurious car. The ones lucky enough to be by the windows extended their arms out the sides, letting the wind rush and lift their small hands like birds in the air current.

Emman was the only one who kept his serious demeanor, sometimes glancing to see if she noticed. Julia wished she could give him a ferocious hug and tell him to have more fun.

She turned on the radio and found a station playing a mix of Filipino songs and American oldies. When "Lollipop, Lollipop" came on, the children started singing along softly. Julia joined in, and soon they were singing loudly and laughing as they yelled, "Pop! Ba-ba-bum-bum." Even Emman sang along, with his head turned out toward the landscape and a grin that he tried to cover.

Bok leaned forward from the backseat to ask her loudly, "Miss Julia, what does *o-kay-do-kay-artay-cho-kay* mean?"

"Say it again?" Julia asked.

He repeated it faster, and Julia said, "Okie dokie artichokey?"

"Yes, yes, that's it! What does that mean?"

"It's just a funny way of saying 'okay.'"

Bok laughed and repeated it a few times, with the others in the backseat chiming in. "Miss Julia," he called up again. "Is *hap-py-go-luck-y* a funny way to say 'happy'?"

Julia glanced back at the humor gleaming in the boy's expression. "Yes, I guess it is."

"I saw on TV this guy call his son *happy-go-lucky*, but when I called Emman that, he punched me in the arm."

They all laughed at that.

A slow Nat King Cole song came on next, and the kids all sang gently.

I'm happy, Julia thought. *I'm so completely happy in this moment.*

Life held the most unexpected surprises. Some filled with pain, and others filled with such enormous wonder she could cry for the beauty of their discovery. It seemed that her old life had never existed, and yet how wonderful that it did. Her past was as much hers as the hacienda's past. It was all just part of the journey to today and into tomorrow. Julia had to go through the pain—face it, feel it, look at it, and then somehow she was able to accept what it had brought to her and heal. But the healing didn't bring her to where she'd been; it took her someplace new.

Emman directed Julia outside of town and along a curving road into the wooded mountains not far from the rough road of Barangay Mahinahon. This road, paved years ago, was pocked with potholes and washed-out edges. Julia drove carefully, mindful of the lack of seat belts. She also didn't want Mang Berto to have a heart attack over one of his damaged babies.

The boy pointed to a smooth pull-off area, and Julia turned, seeing a small road cut into the jungle. They drove down the secluded road for some time until it ended in a small clearing. Emman was sitting on the window frame watching for Amang Tenio when a surprised expression came over his face.

Around the corner they encountered a half-ruined house and a group of men with weapons in their hands.

"Turn around, Miss Julia," Emman said under his breath. "Boys, get your weapons."

The children sprang into action.

Before Julia could turn the wheel, she saw two armed men step into the narrow road fifty yards behind them.

"Wait a minute," Emman said.

And then she saw Amang Tenio.

He put his cane in the air. "What are you doing here?" he said angrily, first to Julia and then to Emman.

"You said you were gathering herbs."

"You had instructions. They were not to be questioned. Emman, you've brought Julia into the exact danger we're trying to avoid."

Emman held his gun protectively at his chest and stood up further in the car as if to protect her.

Julia realized this was some kind of summit between warring leaders. She saw a man standing where Amang Tenio had been, his guerrilla fighters a dozen feet behind him. An equal number of Barangay Mahinahon men faced them. But the two men on the road were not their allies; she knew this in a moment.

Even as she saw young Bok jump from the car with his rifle in hand, Julia didn't fully register danger.

"Boys, stay around the car," Amang Tenio said in a firm tone. The old man moved steadily back to the meeting of men.

WHAT KIND OF A PLOY WAS THIS? MANALO WONDERED. IT MADE no sense for Amang Tenio to request this gathering and then bring the American woman straight into the midst of negotiations. The old sage was regarded with respect and honor, but Manalo had seen enough corruption in men of integrity to know not to trust anyone. The American woman and a carload of armed children arriving just when the old man had said he wanted to negotiate a peaceful solution for her to remain at the hacienda.

Manalo wanted Comrade Pilo to be taken down, and the Barangay Mahinahon could do this. So why the woman, here, now?

Manalo's thoughts ran the gamut of possibilities. Perhaps Amang Tenio wanted to blame the Red Bolos—but why, when they actually had orders to eliminate her if no other solution could be found? What if this was some kind of test from higher up—did they really distrust him that much? Or had they been lied to and brought to this meeting to be ambushed? The code between guerrilla fighters had been broken before, though he could hardly believe it of the famous fighters of the Barangay Mahinahon.

Manalo motioned for Timeteo, and his old friend came forward. Manalo glanced beyond the American's car to where Paco and his son blocked her vehicle. This could be bad. And for now, no one was leaving.

But something was definitely not right.

And the sky looked like blood.

EMMAN STARED WITH THE FIERCEST GAZE HE COULD MUSTER AT THE leader of the Red Bolos. His hands wouldn't stop shaking, and his ears were ringing or pounding like a heartbeat or both; he wasn't sure.

He'd put them all in danger. He should have listened; it was the most basic rule of a soldier—follow your superior's order. But he'd thought Miss Julia was safer with them, especially going to where Amang Tenio would be.

Then Emman remembered his cousins talking about Ka Manalo. He was the man responsible for Artur's death. They wished to avenge him, and now Emman was here. Perhaps this was his great opportunity to show his worth.

Little Kiko was climbing out of the truck. Emman put his hand out to stop him, but the boy got off balance with his wooden gun in hand. Kiko grabbed at the gun and Bok tried to grab him, while from the corner of his eye Emman saw the guerrillas react, both theirs and the Red Bolos.

He lifted his rifle and pointed it directly toward the chest of Ka Manalo.

JULIA SAW AMANG TENIO, AND THE FOUR CHILDREN REMAINED
planted in front of the white Packard. Then Kiko started to slide off
the side of the car. She tried to grab him as the others responded.

The old man's face was contorted in alarm as he hurriedly tried
to gesture the children to lower their guns. The bandits were fast
and well trained. The moment they saw the children aim their
guns, they immediately drew their own firearms.

Julia sank lower in her seat as Amang Tenio shouted for her to
get down. The gunfire began. Strangely, a gun sounded like the
pop from *Pop! Ba-ba-bum-bum* in the song they'd just been singing.
Her heart felt cold with fear. She could see Kiko standing with a
stunned expression; she wanted to move, but she couldn't make
herself get to him.

Then she was moving, just more slowly than her brain wanted
to go. Grabbing the back of his shirt, Julia pulled the little boy
over the side of the car and into the front seat, where she pushed
him down into the floorboard.

Suddenly the driver's side door opened, opposite the side
where the gunfire had started and abruptly stopped. Bok peered in
and said, "Miss Julia, come on."

She hesitated, and he motioned again. "Emman said to get
you."

Julia no longer saw the men down the road; not seeing them
was more terrifying than seeing them. As she left the car and followed Bok into the thicket, she was afraid they'd reappear at any
second.

"Where are Kiko and the other boys?" she asked. "I thought
they'd follow."

"I'll go see," Bok said, but Julia grabbed his arm.

"Not without me."

"Just for a minute, Miss Julia. Two are louder than one."

More gunfire dropped them to the ground, and Julia crawled

beneath the fans of a large stand of ferns. Bok had disappeared. Birds were flying in the air and cawing in anger at the disturbance, and if not for their reaction she might have wondered if it had all actually occurred. The jungle settled into an eerie silence.

Everything had happened so quickly. She waited, feeling the impact of their sudden peril. The cool earth brought a shiver through her perspiring body as she huddled beside a hollow tree trunk. Julia listened intently, but the loudest sound she heard was her own heartbeat. Then a bird chirped, the familiar call she'd heard often from the hacienda porch. As the sound drew closer, she suddenly heard a very low whisper, so close she jumped and nearly screamed.

"Miss Julia?"

A small hand reached through the bright green leaves, and she took it.

"Come on," Bok said in a hushed but fearful voice. They moved rapidly through the brush. Julia had no idea which way they were headed, back toward the car or deeper into the jungle, but then Bok stopped and lifted back a makeshift lid. Together they slid into an old underground bunker, virtually invisible in the jungle. They crouched inside and closed the hatch above. Light filtered through the bamboo slats and foliage growing over the top. Bok wiped his face, and then she saw blood.

"You're injured," Julia exclaimed, leaning close to examine him.

He shook his head and turned to show he was okay. He sat very still as Julia stared at him in concern until suddenly round tears came spilling from his eyes. His lips shook and he sniffed.

Julia took his small body in her arms, setting his gun awkwardly away from them. He shook silently against her shoulder for a long time with his fingers rubbing one of the shells of her necklace between his thumb and fingers. When he finally pulled back, his cheeks and the shoulder of her blouse were smeared with dirt, tears, and blood. Bok looked embarrassed, but Julia took him into another embrace.

"It's okay," she said over and over again.

Finally his empty sobs fell still, and he remained against her until Julia thought he'd fallen asleep.

"People were shot," Bok finally whispered, his shoulders shaking anew.

"Who?" She pulled the boy away from her, trying to see his face in the low light.

"The leader of the other group and some others. Emman got shot in the leg, but I think he's okay. And—"

"Emman!" Julia wanted to rush out of there and help, not cower in a hole in the ground. "Who else?"

"My godfather," he said, and large tears once again fell from the boy's eyes, and he buried his face against her shoulder.

"Amang Tenio? Are you sure?"

The boy nodded his head. "They killed him."

IT CAME TO HIM AS HE STARED UP AT GREEN LEAVES THAT MOVED in the breeze. The sky was an odd color. And then a knowledge came over him that he was made of earth and becoming earth again.

Manalo didn't wish to die. He longed for mountain roads and to be an old man with a pipe telling stories to his grandchildren, going fishing with his oldest friend. And yet now, as his life bled into the earth around him and he heard the gunfire and shouts of Timeteo and others he didn't know, he knew it was right, that he must die. His family was not free with him alive. And though Malaya would long for him always as he would her if she'd left him first, his wife would understand that it was their joint sacrifice for their children to be free.

There was something he and Timeteo planned. Ah yes, not

quite this, but the same effect. His friend would take care of his family. With him dead, the chain would break now—his son would not seek revenge, for Timeteo would give him the letter. His son would not follow in footsteps that dripped in blood.

What have you done with these years that I've given to you?

Someone was talking to him. And he saw who it was. And he remembered, knowing who spoke as he knew no one else in all the world.

"I'm not going to live."

"What, what did you say?"

Take care of them. You must be the one to tell her. Tell my sons the stories, but tell them I want them to be fishermen or farmers. Tell them to have many children. Let them love. . . .

Manalo thought he was speaking, but he realized his lips would not form those words. Timeteo stared into his eyes and gathered it from him, this he believed.

"When did he get here?" Manalo asked, gazing beyond Timeteo.

"Who?" Timeteo said. Ah, so his friend heard that time. The gunfire had stopped. A car sped away.

"You must go," he told Timeteo.

"No. I will not."

He wanted to say that if he didn't go he would be arrested, or the men of the Barangay Mahinahon would take revenge and who would tell Malaya and they may not be assured of her safety or that she'd be taken care of.

The only word that came out was "Go." Manalo then asked, "Where are we going?"

Timeteo thought he was speaking to him.

I've failed at everything and always while trying to choose what was right. And so it ends. Manalo thought or heard it said that it wasn't the end, but only a beginning; in spite of his failures, there was still time to redeem, though much had been lost.

What did it mean? Manalo could not tell. But he would go there, he knew, and find out.

And as he went away, to walk awhile, he whispered good-bye to a girl with the silkiest black hair—and he couldn't for the life of him remember if it was his wife or one of his daughters. And in the end, it didn't matter. He loved them both and someday would find them again.

TWENTY-FOUR

Nightfall came, and from a great distance Julia and Bok heard more gunfire, the sound of automatic rifles in a barrage that lasted only a few minutes. Then some scattered shots and again, silence. Julia prayed silently, hidden in a dirt hole with a young boy in a country far from all she'd ever known. She thought of her mother, and of Nathan, and of the concerns she'd filled her life with while living in the States. And then she thought of the people here she'd come to love so quickly.

Bok made the birdcall a few times with his head outside the hatch. Finally there came an answer. The next moment Emman appeared and, once he'd joined them in the underground bunker, turned on a flashlight. He took Julia's hand and helped her outside.

"What happened, Emman?"

"It is over now, Miss Julia. I am sorry I was so rough with you."
He brushed off dirt from her shoulders.

She couldn't see his face. "Is Amang Tenio dead?" she asked.

Emman didn't answer. He turned the flashlight off again. "Take
my hand and come quickly. Markus has a car at the road."

They shuffled through the jungle to a road that wasn't far from
the hatch. Emman signaled with his light, and a truck rumbled
to life.

As they approached the truck, Julia saw Markus standing at the
open passenger door. He ran to them and took her into his arms.

"Are you okay?" he gasped, pulling her tighter. "If anything
happened to you . . . oh, Julia, I've been searching for you everywhere—"

"I'm fine. Especially now," she whispered close to his ear. The
strength and warmth of his body made her wish she could disappear
inside of him. In the dim light, she saw that Emman was limping
heavily, struggling even to walk. "Markus, Emman is hurt!"

Raul was already grabbing Emman and helping him to the
back of the truck. Bok jumped in behind him.

"We'll get him help," Markus said, helping her into the truck
and then getting in beside her. Raul climbed in on the driver's side.
"Emman insisted upon getting you and Bok out of the woods.
We'll take him and the others to the hospital now. Then I'll take
you to the hacienda."

"The others? More are wounded? What happened, Markus?"

"We must go quickly," Raul said gruffly. His voice softened as
he put the truck in gear and they moved forward. "I am very glad
you are okay."

"Thank you. But shouldn't we have Emman up here with us?"
She turned to search for the boy through the back window.

Raul shook his head. "He'll want to be with the other men."

"One of you must tell me—is Amang Tenio dead?"

Both men were silent for a moment, which answered her question. Dread and grief flooded through her. Closing her eyes, Julia leaned back in the seat. Then she looked quickly again through the back window. "What about the other boys?"

Markus took her hand and held it firmly. "There were a few injuries, but Amang Tenio was the only one of ours who was killed. One of Ka Manalo's men shot him. The boys couldn't save him."

Raul told her what had transpired after that. The rest of the Red Bolo group retreated in the wrong direction and went straight to the advance of the younger men of the Barangay Mahinahon, who were on their own mission of revenge. Very few of the Red Bolos escaped.

"The local police and national army are already investigating. You will be asked some questions."

But Julia heard very little more. She leaned into Markus. How she longed to rest within his arms for hours or days or even a lifetime.

She let the tears come. Amang Tenio, the wise man she had drunk tea with, who had given her the necklace she wore . . . that man was now dead.

EMMAN'S LEG ACHED. HE'D BARELY BEEN SHOT; UNDER DIFFERENT circumstances, he might have been proud of his first battle wound.

They would have forced him to the hospital, but Emman knew it was time for him to disappear. He'd jumped from the truck when it slowed for a turn, and hurried into the foliage in case Bok or one of the other men had seen him. The pain in his leg was nothing. A deeper pain engulfed him, and he was lost within its throbbing truths.

In the deepest part of the night he'd gone to his tree. What a struggle it was to reach his usual branches. There he found a full pack of Marlboro Reds, still sealed, in the crook of the tree where

Bok always sat. It was the boy's offering to him, just as Bok had nightly sneaked up to leave a token for Miss Julia. Emman had been jealous that Bok thought of doing that for her. He knew she thought it was probably him instead. But it was always Bok, the kindhearted kid who so often thought of others. And to make Emman feel better, he'd left Emman his first full pack of cigarettes.

But nothing could make him feel better. Ever.

They'd find him at the tree eventually, he knew. And he could never return to the Barangay Mahinahon, not even to get his belongings. His yo-yo was tucked inside his jacket pocket, and he felt guilty even for that and the cigarettes. Why should he have anything good now?

He knew a better hiding place, one he'd found when he was a small boy and his mother died. He often went there to feel safe, and after a time, he was able to go back to the others as if unscathed by it all. Awkwardly he climbed back down and headed for Mang Berto's garage.

Morning came too quickly. He rested against the soft vinyl and wrapped his leg so no blood got on the carpet, even though he had chosen the oldest and least-restored car in the back of the large building. He was both hungry and thirsty, but he couldn't leave this hiding place in the daylight.

Then he heard her voice right outside the car. "Emman?"

He wanted to run.

Instead he cried. He cried and cried, and she held him like a baby. Magnum, P. I. would be ashamed. No private investigator, let alone a warrior or a leader of a guerrilla group, would act this way, and yet he couldn't stop.

"Amang," he whispered.

Miss Julia was silent a few moments, and he looked up slightly to see the expression on her face.

"Yes, Emman. It is a terrible thing."

"I failed in my assignment." He tried to explain in Tagalog, then remembered that she couldn't understand. His choppy English could never express what he wished to say.

"Listen, Emman. You aren't just a man, you are also a boy. And all men and boys make mistakes. Your mistake wasn't the reason for Amang's death. Don't you think God holds all life in His hands? He knows when and where life will begin and end."

Emman leaned into her arms again, hanging on tightly. How good it felt to be held like that.

"Things are changing at the hacienda, Emman. And it's time you were able to be a boy again, just for a while. Then you can go back to being a man."

He felt weary, so weary of the weight. "Okay," was all he could muster the strength to say. And Miss Julia helped him stand up and walk into the light of day.

EPILOGUE

A life and a homeland.

And on a violet evening, a grand fiesta brought hundreds to the lawns, rooms, and courtyards of Hacienda Esperanza.

On the front stairway, the singing of schoolchildren ended to grand applause. Father Tomas gave the opening prayer, and the fiesta began.

Julia found her mother on the upstairs terrace.

"It is exquisite," she said, leaning on the railing.

The evening light filled her mother's face with a soft glow—Julia had never seen her looking so winsome. Below them, children and adults alike laughed loudly as they played *patentero* on the lawn. The guitarists played a Spanish tune. The yards could barely be seen for the decorations and people. Unlike the day of her grandfather's funeral, when it was all white flowers and table-cloths, this evening was filled with color. The arches, eaves, and gates were covered in colorful paper flowers made by the hacienda children. Soft yellow lights wove through trees and wound like candy cane stripes up the palm trunks. The tables closest to the house were already laden with food.

"I was so angry that you didn't come home," Julia's mother said softly.

"I didn't want to hurt you, Mom. I'm sorry that it did."

"It wasn't just about you, really, though of course I've missed you. And I deeply regret not coming for the wedding. I've spent a large portion of my life bitter about this faraway hacienda and my father's love for it. And then it stole my daughter as well—with the help of a handsome Filipino attorney. But it was the best thing that could have happened. For all of us. I'm just sorry that it took me so long to realize it."

Julia put a hand on her mother's shoulder. She and Markus had agonized over the decision to marry without her mother's presence, though she had reluctantly given her blessing. They'd had a small, intimate Filipino wedding . . . meaning everyone from the hacienda, Barangay Mahinahon, and Markus's large family attended. Emman even rose to the occasion and stood beside Raul in the wedding party. Julia's roommate and best friend, Lisa, came from the States, and while it was bittersweet not having the rest of her family there, time was softening the hurt. And now her mother was here, standing beside her. Once again Hacienda Esperanza was a land of hope.

The plantation stretched out before them. The sugarcane fields had been burned as another harvest ended. Mountains and farm-lands, nipa huts and fishponds, the road to Barangay Mahinahon, pathways ever battling an encroaching jungle, orchid fields in neat rows, a cove with magical flowers, and all the people of the hacienda and Barangay Mahinahon—all these were brought together into a cohesive whole. The slow restoration had begun.

"It hasn't been an easy year. The volcano and typhoon certainly wreaked havoc on the country. But we've come through it."

Julia pointed out the coconut man performing below them. He came by occasionally to visit with Mang Berto and for gatherings where he could prove his talent. "I'll get you some fresh coconut milk when we go down."

She identified some of the people around the hacienda grounds, like Mang Berto and his new assistant, her cousin Francis. They had worked for months to prepare the cars for this event, and the shining beauties were parked at angles on the side lawn of the hacienda, ready to give rides to many who had never been inside a car of any kind before.

"Are you ready to go down and meet some more people?"

"Almost," Julia's mother said. "I love this view from above."

Piñatas hung from the trees, and children gathered beneath, eager to collect the candy and toys that would soon spill forth. The sun was setting above the voices and laughter, a violet sky fading into pinks and yellows over an endless green landscape.

"There is Emman," Julia said with pride in her tone.

She watched him walk with a slight limp that he proudly tried to overcome. He was growing tall and turning into a strong and handsome boy—he had certainly caught the eye of his old jungle buddy Grace.

Emman had a defined inner strength for one so young, even while his struggles over that day in the jungle continued. He was a child turning to a man, and his life had different possibilities now.

"Markus and I have taken him to Manila a few times. He saw his first art exhibit in Makati. And we've had fun going through the treasures of the house."

The heritage of the Barangay Mahinahon was in the boy's blood.

But now, as he went to the fields with Raul every morning and worked with a tutor several evenings a week, Emman mulled over the good of both Hacienda Esperanza and Barangay Mahinahon in his thoughtful mind. He was a young Amang Tenio, she thought.

Thinking of Amang Tenio, Julia felt a fresh stab of longing for his wise words and demeanor that provoked such respect and intrigue in those who had known him.

"Grace and Alice are over there," Julia said. "Alice is another cousin—Mara's sister. And Grace was once a guerilla fighter, but look at her now."

The girls worked side by side, setting out food and utensils. They had a strange and sometimes awkward friendship. Grace took Alice into the jungle to explore and get dirty; Alice shared her fashion magazines. At times Grace had to be reminded that she was a lady and not a guerrilla fighter, but she had made amazing academic progress in the past semester of school.

Some villagers and hacienda workers wore traditional dresses and shirts. Julia herself wore a white dress that hugged her figure and had ruffled sleeves, reminiscent of a bygone Spanish era.

"I have so many people to introduce you to and so many things to show you," Julia said, taking her mother's hand. A rush of joy filled her—the meeting of her old life with the new, the fiesta's return after so many years, the thankfulness she felt to be part of something so grand and filled with spirit and joy. And most of all, the great depth of love between her and Markus.

"Okay, then. I'm ready."

As her mother stepped away from the railing, Julia took another look at her. In her white puffy-sleeved blouse, flowing skirt, and dangling turquoise earrings, she looked carefree and spirited. "Mother, you look beautiful."

Her mother's face glowed with pleasure. "Thank you. The island air does wonders."

As they reached the lawn at the bottom of the stairs, her mother jumped. "A cow!" she exclaimed.

The carabao stretched its long neck to sniff at her mother.

"Mino-Mino came to the celebration," Julia said with a laugh.

Bok pulled the carabao, whose back was covered with laughing children from both the Barangay and the hacienda.

Aling Rosa carried a large cast-iron pan of paella to the buffet line, bringing cheers and applause from those nearby. Hundreds more would arrive all through the night. They had come for the Fiesta of Hacienda Esperanza. A fiesta to celebrate those who worked the land and those who loved the hacienda, friend and neighbor, visitor and stranger alike.

The music continued: acoustic guitar, violin, saxophone, drums. Later there would be a cultural dance telling the history of the hacienda, and later still, karaoke and more games. But the grand event would be the eating of the long anticipated Orchid Cake. Julia and Markus had gone to the cove several nights earlier to swim in the water around the rocks and collect the blossoms for the cake.

Julia wondered if the Orchid Cake would have its claimed effect—would new loves be found, alliances made, broken hearts healed, and love finally requited? In any case, she hoped Raul would finally make a definitive step toward Mara. She'd done her best to give him advice, and while he acted annoyed by her "interference," she'd seen that he usually followed her suggestions.

As the hours passed, Julia lost track of her mother. Eventually she found her sitting with Lola Gloria on the upper veranda. Julia had never seen such peace in her mother's face.

"Hello, dear," she said. "I was about to hear a story." She took a scoop from her tall glass of halo-halo.

Markus called up to Julia just then, motioning for her to join him on the courtyard where couples danced to the strains of guitar.

She smiled. She would put aside her duties as doña of the hacienda and dance within her husband's protective arms, or perhaps walk beyond the hacienda gates with him. Markus said he wished to walk the grounds soon, and ask for God's continued blessings and protection upon Hacienda Esperanza. Perhaps, he'd suggested, they should leave orchid blossoms as a token of remembrance.

"I'll be right down," Julia called to him with a wide smile. She then said to her mother, "You may be there awhile; Lola Gloria has a never-ending supply of stories."

"This one sounds very intriguing," her mother said. "It's about Doña Julia, the Red Bolos, and the bravery of the young fighter Emman."

Julia stopped a moment, shaking her head at the older woman. "I don't think my mother wants to hear that story. It might make her worry."

"I want to hear all the hacienda stories. And this will be the perfect one to start with."

As Julia walked down the stairway to where Markus waited at the bottom step, she heard Lola Gloria speak in her storyteller voice.

"Doña Julia came from a country far away, a wealthy nation full of power and prestige. She made the long journey across the great ocean on the back of a giant bird until she reached Hacienda Esperanza to bury her grandfather, as was his request. It is important to know that she did not plan to stay. But no one knows the great changes that come when a person walks bravely into her destiny."

The night was filled with music, food, and laughter. And as she joined the fiesta again, Julia thought of all the stories, people, and deeds that had created Hacienda Esperanza. They were the past, and now she walked with them as well.

ACKNOWLEDGMENTS

When this story began several years ago, I was in a state similar to Hacienda Esperanza. The hardships were evident even as God was always there with hope and grace to lead me forward. And through these years, the dark season has turned again to renewal. And so, I wish to thank some people and more than those here.

My parents, Richard and Gail McCormick, from broken sinks to broken hearts, your support and advice for me and the kids is more than I can write. Thank you both. Cody Martinusen—for admirable strength, a warrior soul, but tender heart and a humor that always make me laugh. Madelyn Martinusen–you're always my sparkly girl. I admire how you care, laugh, and seek to express the beauty within you. Weston Martinusen—what an abundance of love and depth of thought exists in your young/old soul. And by the way, I love you infinity times infinity (top that).

I could write much in expressing my gratitude to the following. Know my words within the writing of your name: my sister Jennifer Harman, Shawn Harman, Alanna Ramsey, Jenna Benton, Amanda Darrah, Tom Carlson, the Carlson/Namihas Family, One Heart prayer group, Michelle Ower, Laura Jensen Walker, Katie Martinusen, Tricia Goyer, Quills of Faith Writers Group, which would not be without my partners and dear friends: Maxine Cambra and Cathy Elliott.

To my editors at Thomas Nelson: Ami McConnell and Natalie Hanemann, whose belief, support, and guidance in writing push me to greater heights. You both are amazing! To LB Norton—you put more than a polish on this book, and it was such fun working with you. And to Allen Arnold—for guidance, incredible support, and enduring wisdom.

Thanks to my mentors/friends/kindred writer souls: Robin Jones Gunn, Paul McCusker, Travis Thrasher, Kimberly Carlson, Anne de Graaf. The journey would be much lonelier, and I'd make more mistakes or have given up, without the five of you. Janet Kobobel Grant—you are more than my agent, you are mentor and friend.

To the Coloma family—for a warm and wonderful Filipino welcome. And Pratibha Manaen, my Nepalese friend. Someday we will see each other again.

To the Filipino hero in my own story, Nieldon Coloma. You displayed God's love in my darkest hour. Who could guess we'd travel a long and difficult road that would not end but take us to the start of a new journey from individuals, to best friends to one life together. I am so grateful to be your wife.

And I give unending gratitude and devotion to my God whose love and redemption saves me again and again.

READING GROUP GUIDE

1. Redemption is a steady thread throughout the story of *Orchid House*. How do you see each of the main characters seeking some form of redemption? In what ways do you see Hacienda Esperanza experiencing stages of redemption?

2. What does Emman want most in his young life—both on the surface and subconsciously?

3. Manalo becomes jaded in the cause that he leads and longs only for his family. Have you ever experienced belief dissolving and disillusionment? What helped you through such a time?

4. Julia has spent her years trying to satisfy herself and create a comfortable existence. How do small steps of faith beyond herself change Julia's life into the one God planned for her?

5. What cultural discoveries did you make about the Philippines in *Orchid House*? Have you experienced a culture that has been shaped by the dominance of foreign rule or a dictatorship? Discuss the impact of such a society, and in what ways freedom in a nation can have both good and bad outcomes.

6. *Orchid House* is filled with unique characters from the past and present. Name some of your favorites and what traits drew you to them?

7. Who or what are the antagonists in *Orchid House*?

8. The near-mythical family stories are the foundation of Hacienda Esperanza. How can our family or cultural histories shape our modern lives?

9. The Hacienda Esperanza can be considered a character itself. What life stages do you see it going through?

10. In the opening of *Orchid House*, the elderly couple prays, asking God to bless and continually redeem the land and their descendents. Do you believe God hears the prayers for future generations? If so, does that change anything in your own prayer life?

11. Did you experience any moments of revelation or a cultural discovery that gave you new insight, or perhaps will shape your life journey or purpose?